11/19

P9-DWO-458

Hope's Cadillac

Hope's
Cadillac

Patricia Page

W. W. Norton & Company
New York   London

Copyright © 1996 by Patricia Page

All rights reserved
Printed in the United States of America
First Edition

For information about permission to reproduce selections from this book, write
to Permissions, W. W. Norton & Company, Inc., 500 Fifth Avenue,
New York, NY 10110.

The text of this book is composed in Janson with the display set in Janson
Composition by Crane Typesetting Service, Inc.
Manufacturing by Quebecor Printing, Fairfield, Inc.
Book design by Chris Welch

Library of Congress Cataloging-in-Publication Data
Page, Patricia.
Hope's Cadillac / by Patricia Page.
p.   cm.
ISBN 0-393-03974-9
1. Divorced mothers—Texas—Houston—Fiction. 2. Divorced women—
Texas—Houston—Fiction. 3. Houston (Tex.)—Fiction. I. Title.
PS3566.A3347H67   1996
813'.54—dc20   95-47593

W. W. Norton & Company, Inc., 500 Fifth Avenue, New York, N.Y. 10110
http://web.wwnorton.com
W. W. Norton & Company Ltd., 10 Coptic Street, London WC1A 1PU

1 2 3 4 5 6 7 8 9 0

The author wishes to thank the Corporation of Yaddo and the
Centrum Foundation for their support.

Hope's Cadillac

1

Hope loved Houston. This was heresy among the people she admired, liberals and Unitarians mostly, who complained of freeways and refineries, the vulgarity of the Astrodome and the pollution of the ship channel, the absence of zoning and the highest per capita murder rate in the country. "Where else in the world have the buffalo been imagined to speed?" she would ask, referring to Buffalo Speedway, which ran straight north past her house. She liked to remind people that Billy Graham had called Houston a more sinful city than Hollywood. Lately, she'd been asking, "What's the first word ever spoken from the moon?"

Someone would usually quote Neil Armstrong. "One small step for a man . . ."

"No, no, no! Houston! As in '*Houston*, Tranquility Base here'!"

"Hope's from Indiana," her friend Calhoun would explain.

Her husband, Clay, was from Indiana, too, but Clay was immune to the influence of place. He had spent four years at Indiana University without once catching basketball fever or succumbing to the madness of the Little 500. He could travel the globe (which he did periodically as a pilot in the Air Force Reserve) and return without souvenirs. Clay Fairman was a man of firm ego boundaries, which anyone could see as he nosed the family's new '69 Cadillac—purchased on time and the euphoric strength of a recent promotion at Houston

9

Power and Light—up the entrance ramp of Houston's Southwest Freeway.

Hope had opposed the Cadillac. It would embarrass her, she said. That was her only argument.

Clay had emphasized its engineering, its solidity. "If there were a Chevy with the weight, the power, and the reliability, I'd buy another Chevy," he told her. "This has nothing to do with pretension, Hope. It has nothing to do with flamboyance." He didn't mention expense, despite his zealous frugality. (Clay would drive miles out of his way to find a Shamrock gas station, which sold gas for twenty-five, rather than twenty-nine, cents a gallon.) "You couldn't buy a safer car," he added cannily. "When you're behind the wheel of a Cadillac, you're on the safe side of an accident."

To see him at the wheel was to believe him, as he slipped into the stream of traffic, not too heavy on this Sunday morning. He drove with one tan arm draped from the window; it was not yet hot enough for the air conditioner, and the air was still dilute and fine. In the backseat, their nine-year-old daughter, Amber, was hunched over a book. An outlaw reader, Amber appalled her friend Rachel by skipping the middles of books. Amber read for the gist of things.

Her brother, Patrick, who was three, sat in the opposite corner studying himself in a hand mirror. He had just discovered eyebrows. He raised and lowered them, squeezed them together, and patted them with small fingers. Now and then he broke off his investigation to whisper to a five-foot stuffed alligator, its long tail curled on the floorboard, its plaid body draped across his knees.

At the Montrose exit, Clay cut from the outside lane across the paths of an old finny Chevrolet and a new Dodge Dart station wagon, provoking angry honks. Hope frowned. The Cadillac had infected Clay with hubris, in her opinion. Yet she admired the way he negotiated the traffic circle of the Mecom Fountain. Here the old, diagonal Main Street built by Houston's founders met the strictly right-angled Montrose Boulevard laid out by the city's nineteenth-century expansionists. This disorderly arrangement had cars entering the traffic circle from unexpected directions, darting from lane to lane, honking deliriously.

Typical Houston! Hope liked to say, going on, with no encouragement whatsoever, to propose the Mecom Fountain as Houston's spiritual center, a stance that invariably inspired Clay to point out that, *in reality*, it was the cooling system for the Warwick Hotel.

"Sally Kellerman bathed nude in this fountain yesterday," said Hope.

"Who's Sally Kellerman?"

"The star of that movie Calhoun's an extra in. As we could have been, had you been a little more adventurous." Calhoun had tried to talk Hope and Clay into joining him as extras. "You'd make a great policeman," he'd told Clay. "The script calls for lots of policemen."

"It wasn't a question of adventurousness," said Clay. "I just wasn't interested in spending my day off with a bunch of weirdos."

Amber set her book aside and edged forward to better hear what her parents were saying, slinging her arms with boneless abandon over the front seat, spaghetti string-arms, according to her nastier classmates. Amber worried about her skinniness and today wore two T-shirts and flaring bell-bottoms to give herself heft, a strategy that would later have her sweating and flushed as the July day gained heat. "Was Calhoun a carrot?" she asked.

For his wedding last year, Calhoun had dressed as a carrot, a fact recorded in home movies he'd shown them. Clay was not in sympathy with this gesture. It was Clay's opinion that to wear a carrot costume to one's wedding was not only ludicrous but ominous, and since the marriage had failed after only six months, he felt his view validated.

"No, Calhoun was just a man in a crowd, honey, that's mostly what extras are," Hope explained.

"Which is why your father declined the opportunity," added Clay. He punched the cigarette lighter and reached for the package of Kools on the dashboard. He shook them out of the package, one by one. All had been broken in half. He glanced in the rearview mirror, but Amber's head was bent low over her book. Her campaign to persuade him to stop smoking had entered a guerrilla phase. Clay frowned and turned on the radio.

When they reached the church, he backed into a tight parking space—tight for a Cadillac—with just two fingers on the wheel. Hope never looked so at ease as this. She tended to forget where the various buttons were—for the windows, the air conditioner—and was always groping for something when she drove.

The Unitarian church Hope and Clay belonged to was not the long-established First Church on Fannin but a new congregation in the Montrose. It had been a small fellowship until last year, when a majority of the members decided to hire its first minister, Alex Sanford.

"Where else?" Clay had remarked when Hope first told him that the church she was thinking of joining—and which was fast gaining a reputation for unorthodoxy—was located in the Montrose. He may have been simply according the Montrose its due—most deviations from the norm were apt to be carried out beneath its venerable live oaks—or he may have been registering disapproval. It was hard to tell. Clay left their social life—a category of experience he felt included churchgoing—to Hope. Most of their friends were her friends; Clay was ill at ease in social situations. "Hell is other people," he liked to quote. He lived real life at the office. He was sensitive to appearances, though, and usually went along with Hope's plans without complaint.

The Montrose was a turn-of-the-century neighborhood just east of downtown, with white, wealthy River Oaks to the west, the black Fourth Ward to the north, and Rice University to the south. It encompassed azalea-studded parks and sleazy strips of commerce, sylvan esplanades and trashy back alleys, stately residences and low-slung apartment houses, one of which was famous for its bidets. A person could take a Transactional Analysis class in this part of town, join the Esoteric Philosophy Center, have a drink at a gay bar, or get tattooed at the Black Dragon. Insomniacs could do their shopping at Houston's only twenty-four-hour food market. Empanadas were sold on the street, and a bowl of Cuban black beans could be had at a small grocery that also offered plantains and lengths of sugarcane from its produce bins. The Montrose was Hope's favorite neighborhood.

The church had formerly belonged to the Church of Christ. A few years ago, the congregation had decided to build outside the 610 Loop, where most of their members had moved, rather than cope with changes in the neighborhood. A dome marked the nave, and two arcades extended from it in opposite directions. In one were classrooms, and in the other were the minister's study, a kitchen, and a community hall.

After checking to make sure Amber and Patrick (alligator in tow) had reached their respective classrooms, Hope and Clay joined the stragglers making their way down the dingy hall to the sanctuary. Except for recently refurbished classrooms, the building was in considerable disre-

pair. Outside it needed paint badly; inside were chronic plumbing difficulties, a ceiling that snowed plaster, a carpet patched with silver duct
tape. Various committees had been formed to solve these problems, and
attempts were made now and then. But the down-at-the-heels atmosphere seemed to please the moderately prosperous congregation. They
wore the building in something of the same spirit that middle-class
college students wore patched jeans and threadbare shirts. They often
jokingly called themselves misfits. Vanity may have played a part in this,
but they did represent an outpost of genuine naysayers, and if their
resistance failed to express itself in much outward nonconformity, it still
gave a measure of intention and definition to their lives. They knew
who their friends were. TO QUESTION IS THE ANSWER was pasted to the
bumpers of their cars.

Hope stopped to greet a white couple with their newly adopted black
daughter, then hurried on to catch up with a Germanic-looking woman
in a gold-and-scarlet sari who had just returned from India. Although
she and Clay had joined the church only this year, Hope felt she had
finally—after five years in Houston—found some kindred spirits. "I
wouldn't say 'kindred,'" Clay had remarked. "'Kinky' is more like it."

Walking slightly behind Hope, Clay wore a smile which a detractor
might describe as a smirk, but Hope saw as an effort to shore himself
up in the face of the unpredictable. Hope found this expression touching,
much as she found his haircut touching: sides clipped very close up to
the crown, where a thatch of straight brown hair showed the teeth marks
of careful side-to-side combing. It was the sort of haircut seen on small
boys, slicked down for school pictures, or astronauts, a haircut impervious
to breezes.

The congregants took seats in the folding chairs (the Church of Christ
people having taken their pews with them) that circled a carved table
holding the collection plates and a clear glass vase of gladioli with
bubbled stems. A few minutes later, Alex Sanford strode down the aisle,
and the service began.

No one doubted whom to credit with the increased vitality and new
nimble spirit of the church. In Alex's first year as minister, membership
had doubled, even though this was his first church, his first Unitarian
church, that is: he'd been a tent preacher in what he called his past life.
He'd come to the Montrose fellowship after divinity school and a year's

residence at Esalen in Big Sur, which gave him a certain cachet among those of the congregation who looked toward Esalen as the mecca of the human potential movement. (These were few. Most of the congregation had never heard of Esalen.) Alex had met Alan Watts and Fritz Perls there; he had been rolfed. He found that the psychotherapists at Esalen were not so much interested in helping their clients devise strategies of life adjustment as in leading them to higher forms of consciousness. This was how he saw his own task.

Over his dense, thickset trunk atop a wiry substructure, Alex wore a yellow sports coat in contrast to dark green slacks. Black eyes with the sheen of charred wood dominated a face otherwise obscured by a thick beard, and dark hair fell to his shoulders from a receding hairline. Alex was more arresting than handsome, the quality of his attraction more in the nature of certain smells, acute but hard to specify.

The sermon this morning was "Conscience: Bondage to the Past." Hope leaned forward expectantly.

Alex always delivered his sermons extemporaneously, which impressed everyone, even Clay. Unbuttoning his sports coat and slipping his hands into his pockets, Alex began by calling up an image of conscience as the angel who sits on our shoulders, "clucking and mewing whenever we have a desire, the conscience that makes cowards of us all. Freud called it the superego, Perls the parental tapes, but by whatever name, what perches on our shoulders in the guise of conscience is simply the agent who had power over us in the past. When we listen to our conscience we listen to the ghostly voices of our parents, our parent's parents, our parents' parents' parents—the collective voice of the past." As he spoke, Alex kept his eyes on his audience, fixing first one, then another in his gaze. "Our moral personalities are little more than hand-me-downs."

Hope listened, her body angled forward as if into a wind. Alex's words had something of that force for her: she felt light and aloft on them, high above ordinary life.

"Conscience has power . . . but no life," he told them. "Lacking roots in our senses, it is a lifeless force. Conscience separates us from our bodies and the here-and-now. It turns the living, pulsing present into the dead past." He lowered his voice. "The dead past."

He paused, eyes directed inward. When he looked up again, he spoke in a modest, intimate tone. "Some years ago, I had an affair. An affair of the heart."

Alex often referred to his own experiences in his sermons. He understood the value of an emotionally frank confession—for the listeners as well as the confessor. The congregation lauded his candor and tried to assume a posture of decorous incuriosity. But this morning most faces showed an unabashed avidity.

He had left the Baptist Church, he explained, and was employed as a social worker, "an arid period of my life, a time in the wilderness." Alex began to pace, the rhythm of his speech accelerating as he described falling in love. The electric readiness of the senses! The realignment of the world around a radiant point! Sometimes he strode to and fro; sometimes he planted his feet and threw his arms wide in expansive gestures. The mystery of it! The cell-by-cell alteration of corporeal being!

Yes! Hope was thinking, elated. It must be so!

His affair had marked the beginning of his emotional participation in life, Alex told them, his plunge into life-giving waters. "But! You may be saying, some of you may be saying, But! Wasn't this an illicit affair? Wasn't I a married man? Wasn't she a married woman? Yes! yes! and yes!" His arms shot skyward, jabbing at each repetition. "Where was my conscience? you might ask. Where was my sense of right and wrong?" He smiled and tapped his chest. "Right here." He tapped his shoulder. "Not here." He tapped his chest again. "Right here. Because I do not say we shouldn't live by our consciences. No. And I do not say there is no such thing as right and wrong. No. What I say is that we need a new kind of conscience. Not some secondhand set of moral strictures . . . not some garbled playback of the parental tapes . . . but a conscience based on feeling. Yes," he added, softly, almost whispering again, "feeling. For isn't feeling the essence of virtue?" He dropped his hands to his sides. "And aren't those acts from the heart the authentic good deeds?"

Hope nodded with each gesture: one, two, three. It was remarkable how something she had never thought of before now seemed so obvious, so shapely. It was as if Alex had reached into the dark cubbyholes of her mind, where she'd squirreled away bits and pieces of thoughts, to assemble a coherent and desirable whole that had been there, fundamentally, all along.

He closed by reminding them of Eve. He described the sentient reality of an apple—the mingled oppositions of sweet and tart, the juiciness, the satisfying spherical shape, the bold color—and he suggested to them that perhaps Eve was not the sinner they'd always been taught she was. "Perhaps Eve," he said, "was much more simply . . . much more importantly . . . the first person to think for herself!"

His eyes swept the congregation, and his expression eased, seeing that his message had been received. Bringing his hands together in front of his chest, he asked for a moment of meditation. Heads bowed, and the softly muted sounds of faraway traffic and the whir of the air-conditioning system filled the space where his voice had been.

The offering was next, and the ushers came forward.

Hope, who had been very much stirred by the sermon, now relaxed, her senses curling inward. She leaned back in her chair, ran hands down her thighs, and looked over at Clay, who was busy scribbling with the barest stub of a pencil on the back of his program. Formulas and diagrams filled the margins, and now he was writing over the print itself. Hope recognized the minus signs that indicated electrons. Clay had watched the Apollo spacecraft land on the moon last month with a slightly different, certainly less awed, perspective than most. What had captured his imagination was the power supply on the Apollo—an array of photovoltaic cells. Clay was one of the few people just then who understood what "nonrenewable" meant. He saw this as a personal opportunity and felt himself about to play a role in the world of energy. Might not photovoltaics be a viable technology for electricity right here on earth?

Hope tapped his wrist. He looked up, and she held out to him the wooden collection plate. Taking it from her, he passed it on to the woman sitting next to him.

"You didn't put anything in!" Hope protested.

He shrugged and resumed his scribbling. Only with the announcement of the closing hymn did he fold up his program and put it in his back pocket. He rose, hymn book in hand, to silently mouth the words; Clay was tone-deaf.

After the closing hymn, the congregation gathered in the community hall for the coffee hour, a chaotic affair with children running about and people calling to one another across the room against the rising volume. Groups formed and re-formed. An eavesdropper passing from one to another might hear apocalyptic pessimism one moment and millennial euphoria the next. The world was conflagrant in violence and war, its very elements under attack by polluters. Or: the world was experiencing the dawn of a new age, where individuals would be free to develop the unused ninety-nine percent of their capabilities, an expansion of potential that would eventually exhibit itself in nations and result in universal harmony and cooperation. The world was doomed, the world was perfectible—both beliefs were espoused here, often by one and the same person, and they all talked urgently, trying to pack everything they'd been thinking all week into this one hour of conversation with like souls.

"... an almost inexhaustible raw material," Clay was explaining to a small group near the coffee urn. A few granules of sugar from his half-eaten doughnut dotted his lower lip, and a borrowed cigarette burned at his hip, where he rested one hand. "Silicon is the second most abundant element on earth. It's expensive to make a cell with the necessary efficiencies, sure, but once you cut out the waste in the manufacturing process ..." He bowed his body forward and lifted the hand holding his cigarette, as Amber brushed behind him, grabbing the cigarette as she ran by and headed for the ladies' room.

Over near the door, Hope was meanwhile talking to Alex, with Patrick astride his alligator at her feet. "I'd never thought of conscience as maintaining the status quo before. I'd never thought of sex as overthrowing the social order."

Alex smiled. He reached out and gently removed a flake of dried mascara that had lodged on her cheekbone. "Did I say that?"

2

CLAY DID NOT WANT TO GO TO THE PARENTS' PARTY. "I HAVE nothing to wear," he said. "I'm out of Che Guevara T-shirts."

The party was to celebrate the opening of the Blossom Street Free School. Hope and her friend Chloe Whitney had been prime movers in establishing the school. Chloe had wanted a school where her daughter, Rachel, could be educated as a freethinker, not a Texas belle, and she had convinced Hope of the worthiness of this goal. By the end of a summer spent planning and organizing, Hope was the school's most enthusiastic parent, but Clay still had reservations. He questioned whether or not kids would learn anything in a school without regular classes and report cards. He questioned the competence and character of Calhoun, the school's teacher and director. And as he had pointed out more than once, the "free" in "free school" did not mean free of charge. In fact, he said, tuition was rather high, at one hundred dollars a month, and could someone please tell him what their children were getting that public school could not provide?

"Liberty. Equality. Brotherhood," said Calhoun, infuriating Clay, who told Hope that he would give the school six months.

The free school was largely an outgrowth of Calhoun's fourth-grade Sunday school class. As the children emerged from his classroom with homemade sundials and zithers, stethoscopes and fruit leather, eager to explain about the earth's rotation or the definition of sound as vibration, the amazing lub-dub of human heart valves or the preservative effect of removing moisture from food, the parents had come to feel that their children were learning more on Sunday mornings than on all the weekdays put together. For his part, Calhoun said Sundays were a lot more rewarding than the weekdays he spent teaching sixth grade in Spring Branch. Someone—no one could remember who, maybe Calhoun himself—suggested the idea of starting a school of their own, a free school modeled on the new education experiments taking shape around the country. The classroom wing of the church was empty during the week. Why not put it to good use?

Working nights and weekends on the classrooms, the parents replaced carpet and old plumbing fixtures, sprayed for roaches, scraped and painted. They felt that beneath their hammers and brushes and sponges, something new and hopeful and defiant was emerging. They spoke of The Child. The Child did not need to be taught. The Child had a natural proclivity to learn that was snuffed out early by conventional education. In a free school, The Child's mind could develop unconstrained and unconfined. A free school was a place where The Child's curiosity and intelligence and imagination would be at liberty.

The school attracted attention in the neighborhood, mostly from young hippies, who dropped by now and then during the reclamation work. Everyone was courteous. The hippies did not comment out loud about lacquered hair or tiny alligators on polo shirts, and the parents did not remark on unpatched rents in dirty jeans that revealed an absence of underwear. When the school opened in September, with nineteen students, three of them were from "the ranks of the literally unwashed," as Clay put it. Their proximity to Amber was a concern to him. One of the children was named Paisley, and he cited this as an example of the irresponsible parenting one could expect from this "element."

Hope was a little intimidated by the hippies. She saw superiority in their defiance of convention. Her friend Chloe, on the other hand, was unimpressed, pointing out that they had nothing to lose, after all.

"The unwashed probably won't be at the party," Hope told Clay now. "There's a big concert at Liberty Hall. Shiva's Headband or something."

"Can we leave early?"

"If you want."

"Promise?"

"I guess."

THE HIPPIE CONTINGENT did attend, however. Hope attributed this to a sense of parental responsibility and Clay to an inability to afford tickets to Shiva's Headband, but both were surprised to see one of the couples—Fern and Hermes, parents of a nine-year-old named Adam—in the kitchen with Alex, Chloe and Fletcher Whitney, Calhoun, and Ocie Ballard, the school's sole black parent. Alex was explaining Trust, a game he was using in his new Open Relationships class. "All you have to do is fall back into someone's arms. . . ."

Hearing this, Clay faded toward the door and headed for the hors d'oeuvres, ignoring an anxious look from Hope. She watched him disappear, decided against following him, and, pouring sangria into a Styrofoam cup, returned her attention to the group.

"I take it Trust is not a game," said Chloe.

"It is a game. Games are serious business. Watch any child." Alex went on to discourse on the subject of play.

"Where are the trustbusters when we need them?" Chloe whispered to Hope.

To see Chloe and Hope together was to think of the city mouse and the country mouse. Hope's lightly freckled face, her pale eyelashes and brows, the wisps of sandy hair escaping their arrangement on top of her head—all gave her the look of a plainswoman, although there was none of that erasure of spontaneity and expectation one sees in old photographs of women standing by sod houses or covered wagons. Still, one could imagine her in gingham or calico, the streamers of a poke bonnet fluttering in the breeze, her sole claim to beauty a set of very white, even teeth, resplendent when she smiled.

Chloe, on the other hand, possessed a blond Scandinavian glamour—translucent, illumined skin, lemony hair, gray, heavily lashed eyes—gifts she seemed to disclaim, however, by dressing haphazardly, shunning makeup, and pulling her hair back in a careless ponytail. When men admired her looks, she managed to imply they had a problem. Yet Chloe did not evince coolness so much as a conciseness of character. She considered Hope's eager friendliness a flaw. "Your tail's wagging," she would comment *sotto voce* when Hope beamed a little too brightly or gushed appreciatively.

"Who will go first?" asked Alex, looking around.

"Not me," said Hermes. "I don't need to play a game to learn that I don't trust anybody. I already know that." Hermes was so thin it was hard not to think of him as a boy. His elbows showed white through his skin, and his jeans hung on him as they would on a clothesline. His T-shirt clung to a chest the width of a cereal box. "Trust: the opiate of the masses," he said. "I don't even trust my own father."

"Wise. Very wise," murmured Calhoun, tugging on the battered felt hat he wore to protect against air-conditioning. Light sparkled from the stubble on his chin; he was growing a beard. "No one trusts his father."

Hope gave him a severe look. "I do."

"That's because of your unfortunate name."

Calhoun maintained that Hope's parents had doomed her to a life of pathetic optimism in naming her. He said she heard the coo of a dove in the rasp of a raven, making her easy to con. To Hope's rebuttal that she was named after her father's sister, he replied that inherited hope was even more lamentable.

"It's not my father, it's my mother I don't trust," Hope was saying.

"Classic," said Alex, putting an arm around her and giving her a squeeze. "So. Who wants to be first?"

Chloe's husband, Fletcher, cleared his throat. Tall and hunched, with a beaked nose, very red lips, and noticeably large feet, he looked especially out of place tonight in an Oxford shirt and tie. Hope had never fathomed Chloe's attraction to him. (She didn't say this, of course, partly because she sensed that Chloe saw little point in a person's being married to Clay.) To Hope, Fletcher fit the stereotype of the English professor he was: prudent, abstracted, sexless.

"I'm not at all convinced," he said, in his low, considered tone, "that this is an appropriate parlor game."

"This is the kitchen, not the parlor," said Fern, who was as thin and unkindled-looking as Hermes. "I'll go first. Hope? You can catch me."

Hope was surprised that Fern had chosen her instead of Hermes— she and Fern didn't know each other very well—but she took a position behind her, as Fern flipped a hank of long brown hair over one shoulder and shook out the folds of her long skirt. Carefully cupping one hand

inside the other, she positioned them just below her small breasts and
closed her eyes. Her breathing took on a rhythm that suggested she was
counting. In spite of these preparations, she fell back twisting to one
side, and if Hope hadn't caught her, she might have landed awkwardly
enough to break an arm.

Ocie Ballard surprised everyone by volunteering to be next. A heavyset
black woman, a community activist fairly well known around Houston,
she had heard about the school from Chloe, whom she'd met at a legal
aid workshop at the University of Houston, where Chloe was finishing
her law degree. Flexing her arms as if preparing for a boxing match,
she called on Calhoun to catch her.

Calhoun tugged on his hat. "Me?"

A scythelike smile sliced forth from Ocie's chestnut face. "Now don't
he jus' look like a rabbit at a dawg convention?" Everyone laughed, a
little uneasily. This was Ocie's get-down voice. One often suspected a
joke in the making without quite getting it. "If this dude drops me, call
the NAACP."

Ocie fussed with the hem of her blouse, adjusted her beads, clapped
her hands to her sides . . . and froze. Seconds ticked by. In the silence,
a joke drifted in from the adjacent community hall. "So AJ asks the
hippie: 'What do you think of the Indianapolis 500?' and the hippie
says: 'Hey man, they're all innocent.'" Hermes frowned, and Hope
pretended not to recognize Clay's voice.

Finally, Ocie let herself go. Calhoun gasped as he caught her. "All
right!" he grunted, setting her upright again, like a doll.

The scythelike smile flashed forth. "You should see my boogaloo."

When it came Hope's turn, she asked Alex to catch her.

"My pleasure," he declared, stepping forward.

He had scarcely spoken when Hope fell back into his arms, so easily
that everyone insisted she choose another partner. Selecting Chloe, she
fell just as precipitately into Chloe's arms. She tried Calhoun next, then
Fletcher, then Fern, and finally Hermes. Each time she dropped back
as if she were nothing more than a sack of sand.

"Now that's *trust*," said Fern.

"Maybe Hope's hang-up is she's *too* trusting," said Chloe.

"Maybe Hope doesn't have a hang-up," said Calhoun.

"Oh, I'm sure I do," Hope said eagerly.

* * *

IN THE SCIENCE room, various groups had clustered around the aquarium, the rock collection, and the insect zoo, and Hope tried not to notice whether or not anyone was looking at her photographs of the school's first weeks, displayed on a bulletin board along one wall. She'd taken them for a photography class. Some of them were a little out of focus or under- or overexposed, and she wondered if something was wrong with the camera, an old twin reflex she had picked up at a garage sale. That may have been, but it was also true that she became easily frustrated with f-stops and shutter speeds and light-meter readings, and she often just snapped. So it was not surprising that the results were amateurish. They often startled her, too, as if she hadn't quite seen what she was looking at. In a photo of one of the early parents' meetings, which she recalled as heady and boisterous, the parents looked surprisingly frail, with a taut expectancy in the expressions, as if they were anticipating arrest, as if, in the next moment, there would be a knock on the door.

The photography class was another of Hope's attempts to fight drift. She and Chloe used to talk a lot about drift, the sense they'd had of floating on their lives rather than living them. But then Chloe decided to go to law school, leaving Hope to drift on her own. Now she was always taking one class or another—yoga, ceramics, Chinese cooking—substantiating Chloe's premise that housewives were the last of the world's dilettantes.

A few people had gathered around her photos, and Hope felt mild alarm at the prospect of their judgment, but on eavesdropping, she realized they were discussing bosom makeup, not her photography. "Not only can you get a 'cleavage delineator,'" a woman was saying, "but a tip blusher for that glistening, rosy hue."

Hope spotted Clay in a corner, where he was talking to Mindy Eck. Sitting in what were probably the only two adult-sized chairs in the school, they looked like chaperons.

"... the superhighways of the utility industry," Clay was saying as Hope approached. "Overhead transmission lines can carry more electricity a lot more efficiently. Plus, you don't take up as much land. So the public benefits all around. High-voltage lines keep rates low, and—" He looked up at Hope. "Is it time to go yet?"

"Aren't you having fun?"

"No."

"We've been talking about some of the weirdos here tonight," said Mindy, rolling large brown eyes behind tortoiseshell glasses. The school's only single mother, she was the source of a good deal of speculation, partly because of a body that left no doubt as to its purpose here on earth, and partly because some people thought her a good match for Calhoun. (Chloe was not among them, saying that she couldn't imagine Calhoun in bed with a bouffant hairdo.)

"Actually, I was explaining about high-voltage lines," corrected Clay. "You two know each other, don't you?"

Hope nodded. "Mindy and I took the kids to the Museum of Natural Science last week."

"We measured lung capacities." Mindy playfully expanded her convincing chest, then blushed and drew in her shoulders. "In liters."

"Now there's something the school should be teaching," said Clay. "The metric system. This country should have adopted the metric system long ago."

"Oh, I don't know," said Hope, a sangria-inspired resistance rising in her. "I like our system."

"No one else does," Clay advised her. "The rest of the world thinks we're nincompoops for not having standardized measurements."

"Why does standardization have to be the point?" Hope asked. "A foot is such a nice, human measurement. Anyway, it's part of the way we think now. You would never centimeter your way across the desert, for example." Clay and Mindy looked blank. "As opposed to inch," she explained.

"Uniform standards of length and mass are fundamental to a rational society," said Clay.

"What's more fundamental than the human foot?" asked Hope.

"It's not legal."

"The human foot is illegal?"

"The foot is not a legal measurement in the United States," Clay explained patiently. "It's customary, it's sanctioned, but it's not, strictly speaking, legal."

"I didn't know that," said Mindy.

"Few people do, but Congress has never actually passed a law fixing the standard of weights and measures," he told her.

"Oh." Mindy looked down and rearranged the horseshoe-shaped white collar of her navy-blue dress.

Hope felt suddenly inappropriate. Her made-in-India maroon halter, embroidered in gold and decorated with tiny mirrors, had seemed festive when she put it on. Now it felt whorish, her flowing harem pants gaudy. "Well . . . I was just . . . passing through, really," she stammered. "I just wanted to say hello."

"Hello," said Mindy. Hope felt dismissed.

The group that had been discussing bosom makeup had passed on to the news of Ho Chi Minh's death, and as Hope walked by, a hand shot out to grab her wrist. "Never mind," Alex whispered in her ear, as he took her elbow and guided her out of the room toward the side exit.

"Never mind what?"

"Your husband." He opened the exit door, and they stepped outside. The warm night was thick with the odor of the petroleum flower, as people referred to Houston's distinctive fragrance, and overhead the sky was milky with reflected light. A quarter moon was visible, however, above the downtown skyline. "He's still at the cliché level."

"The cliché level?"

"The first level of neurosis. Whereas you, I'd say, are approaching impasse." Hope fidgeted with the tassels of her sash, as Alex went on to explain that living at the cliché level meant to be out of touch with your own feelings, limited to the fatigued approximations of conventional expressions. The second level, role-playing, was an expanded version of the cliché level and could include bits of original expression, so long as it did not noticeably disturb the lineaments of the chosen societal role. "Impasse," he said, taking her hand, "occurs when the supports of the first two levels have become obsolete, before authentic self-support has been established. A person in impasse experiences nothingness, a debilitating passivity having more to do with self-annihilation than contemplation."

Nothingness. Was that like drift?

". . . grief! anger! orgasm! joy!" Alex was saying. "The thing is to come out of yourself and participate in life!"

"Oh, yes, I totally agree."

"Do you?"

"Oh, yes."

He looked at her for some seconds before speaking. "You're a very agreeable person, aren't you." She sensed that agreeable was not the thing to be, but before she had a chance to respond, the door clanked open, and Fern and Hermes emerged.

"Join us?" invited Fern, taking a small pouch and a packet of ZigZags from a pocket in the voluminous folds of her skirt.

Hope shook her head no, but Alex, dropping her hand, said he didn't mind if he did. For the second time that evening, Hope felt dismissed.

"I CAN SEE the headline now," said Calhoun in response to Hope's report. "Free school goes to pot." Calhoun had not moved from the kitchen. His strategy at parties was to stay in one place and let chance determine the evening. He maintained that chance and our response to it comprised the meaning of life.

"But what if the party gets noisy?" Hope pressed. "What if those old people on the corner call the police? Lee Otis Johnson got thirty years for handing out a single marijuana cigarette," she reminded him, referring to a case much in the papers just then.

"Joint."

"Joint," she repeated obediently.

"Lee Otis Johnson is the wrong color and has a bad case of flap jaw."

"Well, you're the wrong color to make jokes about it!" said Chloe, joining them.

Calhoun raised both hands in a gesture of surrender. "Hey! I'm just stating the facts. I contributed to his defense fund. What more can Mr. Charley do?"

Chloe had several suggestions. He could join the citizens' group working for Johnson's release. He could write to the governor. He could purchase—from her, she had a ready supply—a bumper sticker reading FREE LEE OTIS NOW.

"What would I do with a bumper sticker?" Calhoun refused to own a car and was perhaps the only grown man in all of Houston who rode a bicycle.

Chloe ignored this. "A man's life has been completely ruined. Only in Houston! Can you imagine this happening in New York or San Francisco? Duluth even?"

"We all know that what holds this city together is racial tension," Calhoun said cheerfully.

"Cynic," Chloe accused.

"Comes from an excess of self-control."

It was hard to tell just how much of a cynic Calhoun really was, because he enjoyed the role so much. He liked to annoy the parents by saying that granola was bad for the gums or that Coke toughened up the digestive system. He insisted to cat lovers that cats had no curiosity at all beyond the what's-in-it-for-me variety and claimed his sole educational tenet was: everything you know might be wrong. In the presence of children, however, something bright and tender and original came to the fore; he was a born teacher, which was what the parents relied on.

"That reminds me," said Hope. "Any luck recruiting students from the Fourth Ward?" She tried to sound offhand, not wanting to betray any anxiety that the Fourth Ward, the black neighborhood only a few blocks from the school, might harbor dangerous and hostile neighbors. Voicing this anxiety would be akin to a racial slur. At the last parents' meeting, everyone had decided that the school needed some black and Chicano students. "We don't want this to be a lily-white school," Chloe had reminded them. "That's what we're against. One of the things."

"No luck so far," said Calhoun. "Unless you count Frederick."

Hope and Chloe exchanged an uneasy look. Frederick showed up at the school now and then, his ebony face lightly dusted, the sleeves of his T-shirt ripped out, his cotton pants torn along the pocket seams and at the knees, exposing mosquito-bitten skin. He lived on the street, as near as anyone could determine; he was known to cadge meals at the Happy Buddha and sleep under porches. *Under* porches, Hope had thought to herself when she heard this. *Under* porches. She couldn't shake the image.

The children were afraid of him, in spite of the fact that he was shorter than Amber and weighed even less. But he extorted their quarters and stole their lunches with such an air of pragmatic menace they were intimidated. A couple of families had offered him the merit of their own homes, but the results had been distressing. He had introduced his young hosts to a wide vocabulary of obscenities and had stolen money, matches, and one Sunbeam hand mixer.

"He was here yesterday," said Calhoun. "On yet another new bicycle."

"Stolen?" asked Hope.

"I wouldn't say stolen. I'd say recirculated."

"PERVERT ALERT," WARNED Clay, as the Cadillac approached the Strip. They had left the party around eleven-thirty, which had seemed early to Hope, who feared that the party had just been getting started, but late to Clay, who accused her of breaking her promise.

She looked out the window. People liked to prowl this section of Westheimer in disguise: drag queens, James Dean impersonators, platoons of booted women in hot pants. The midnight pulse of the area throbbed—music blared forth from the bars and clubs, revelers wobbled beneath the flashing lights, cars honked at friends or prostitutes. Clay's reference was specific, however. By perverts he meant the gay men on promenade, arms entwined about one another's waists.

The crowd thinned as they drove south of Westheimer, and the streets were empty by the time they reached the freeway.

"Did you have a chance to talk to Fletcher?" she asked. *Did you have a chance*, a mildly flattering way of asking, as if Clay were in such demand he could barely squeeze in a conversation with a lesser light, as if his mind were so occupied he might understandably neglect one.

"Briefly."

"What did he have to say?"

"He's writing a book about the music in Shakespeare's plays." Clay's tone indicated both respect and lack of interest. "He proofreads by reading backwards."

"He's a strange man, isn't he?"

"Not particularly, no. Now Leaf, or whatever her name is—"

"Fern."

"Fern I'd call strange." Clay accelerated to pass a dilapidated pickup on the right. "Hey buddy! Park it behind the Pine Curtain, willya?" he called through the closed window as they sped by, a suggestion he always made to slow drivers, all of whom, he insisted, came from the piney woods of East Texas. Hope silently cursed the Cadillac.

Exiting the freeway, they coasted into their neighborhood. The symmetrical rows of brick homes, surrounded by magnolias and oaks, looked reassuring even in the darkness. Reaching their street, Clay pulled into the drive and said he'd wait there while she paid the baby-sitter.

As she entered the house, Hope recalled something her younger brother, William, had said on his only visit here, before he had disappeared into what he called the underground resistance and Clay called the poltroon platoon. "Nothing can ever happen in this house, Hope." She knew William's remark was intended to provoke, but tonight she felt comforted by it anyway. She went to check on the children. Amber stirred but didn't wake as the pencil of light from the opening door elongated and spread to envelop her. In sleep, Amber looked more childlike, her vehement posture at rest. She slept on her side, arms crossed in front of her chest, hands grasping her shoulders.

In the next room, Patrick, located in the middle of a mound of stuffed animals that included his five-foot alligator, didn't move. Hope gave in to an old impulse to check his breathing and crossed the room to bend over him, studying his back until she caught its barely perceptible rise and fall. Content, she retreated and pulled the door soundlessly shut. Nothing made her feel safer than the sight of her sleeping children.

When Clay returned, Hope was already in bed. Her grandmother's mantel clock chimed once. Clay slipped in beside her with the resolution and stealth she knew meant sex, and was even prepared for, having inserted her diaphragm earlier, just in case. He put a hand on her hip, and she turned.

If Clay's body lacked the sinful splendor of their adolescence for Hope, it retained a measure of its strangeness, and she gave serious attention to the hard pads of his pectoral muscles, the trough of his back, the taut pouch of testicles. And Clay responded in kind, tracing her hipbone and the inside of her thighs, spreading the folds of her intimate flesh, kissing her ribs. As Clay ladled her breasts into his hands, she felt the slow rise of heat gain urgency, and when he rolled onto her, she had no complaints. She welcomed his weight—ballast.

3

THE BLOSSOM STREET FREE SCHOOL OCCUPIED NEARLY ALL OF
Hope's attention that Fall. She and the other parents hovered
on the periphery of their children's domain, impassioned and apprehensive, as fearful as they were hopeful of the school's success. The only
requirement for accreditation was fifteen minutes of Citizenship (which
meant the pledge of allegiance to the state of Texas and self-government
to Calhoun), and Citizenship was the only compulsory class. Whether
or not the children would attend the others was the question. So the
parents were ecstatic when the "AfterMath" class, taught by a Tenneco
accountant with a good grasp of gambling schemes, proved popular, and
the conversational French class taught by one of the mothers, a vivacious
native speaker, became loyally, if sparsely, attended. On Wednesdays,the
Rice String Quartet, whose violinist had two children in the school,
played to a respectable young audience, and a large contingent of students
always gathered around the Vista volunteer who dropped by every now
and then with a dead animal to dissect.

Chloe commented that it would have been hard for the school to fail
at that point. So much interest and attention were being lavished on
the children, they were bound to learn. The problems would come later,
she predicted, when everyone's enthusiasm had waned.

Nevertheless, these were contented days, with the school off to a
good start and the children happy. Chloe and Hope were sharing chauf-

feur duties. Chloe delivered on her way to classes at the University of Houston, and Hope fetched. Most afternoons, Hope tried to arrive at the school a little early in order to capture the splatter of shade beneath the live oak. The Cadillac did not quite fit within the silhouette, but Hope parked so that the seats, at least, were in shadow. Then she would sit on the school steps to wait for Amber and Rachel, as Patrick investigated sprinkler heads, pebbles, and such.

She was sitting there one day, alert to an odor of incense from inside the building and wondering what was going on, when Patrick, in pursuit of a black-and-white cat that had been hanging about the school, veered suddenly toward the street. A van painted with a celestial scene of stars and planets was speeding toward them.

"Patrick!" Hope screamed, halting him just short of the curb, as the cat disappeared into the shrubbery. The van pulled in behind Hope's Cadillac and shuddered into quiescence. For a minute, Hope didn't recognize the driver, who looked to be about twelve years old in jeans, a checked shirt, and a straw hat. It was Fern.

"Hoo-boy, I'm beat," she said, coming up to sit down next to Hope on the steps. She closed her eyes and began to massage her eyeballs with the tips of her fingers. "This earnin'-a-livin' shit's draggin' me down." Fern explained that she had taken a new job to pay for Adam's tuition. "They call it market research, but what you're really doing is pushing sausage. You even have to provide your own TV tables!"

Hope allowed that passing out sausage samples at supermarkets might be dispiriting work. Twisting the tie of her wraparound skirt, she wondered if Fern saw her as just a housewife, a sort of parasite who wouldn't know the first thing about earning a living.

"I miss *Space City!*" said Fern. "But hawking that rag just wasn't cutting it. I thought it would be more profitable. You buy the paper for a dime and sell it for twenty cents—double your money, right?—but for one thing, the paper only comes out twice a month, and for another, it's hard to get nonfreaks to buy it. Some do, though. Usually, they give you a quarter, and you just sort of pretend to forget to give them their change. They don't notice, you know, because they're in their cars, the light changes, they gotta get goin'. A few call you on it. Then you smile and look cute and give them their fuckin' nickel back."

Hope might have lost a few nickels this way herself. She occasionally

bought an issue of *Space City!* from one of the vendors who hung out
on the corner of Montrose and Westheimer. In its pages she'd learned
how to make long-distance calls without paying for them and that Blond
Lebanese was selling for five dollars a gram, Mex bricks for ninety. She
hadn't cared for the poetry and thought the names of the rock groups
advertising there—Spooky Tooth, Atomic Rooster, Bubble Puppy—
were more creative. She could not feature what was so funny about the
Fabulous Furry Freak Brothers. But she read things there she didn't see
anywhere else, things about Vietnam, police brutality, corruption. One
item recently had caught her attention. A two-year-old had been bitten
by a copperhead snake in the uncut grass surrounding his apartment
house in the Fourth Ward, sparking a rent strike. Ocie was involved in
that one.

An outbreak of squeals and shouts erupted behind them, as a rush
of children emerged from the classroom entrance. "Look out! I'm a
molecule!" shouted one, bumping into his schoolmates and careening
off onto the lawn. In the next moment, Rachel was at Hope's side.
Rachel's blond perfection might have doomed her to embalmment as
the incarnation of innocence, but she was saved by her voice, which
seemed to come from a throat scarred by an excess of life and cigarettes,
the husky voice of an over-the-hill cabaret singer. She showed Hope a
map she had made of the wind currents in the science room, which
they'd tracked by observing trails of smoking incense. Hope praised the
neatness of Rachel's arrows and asked where Amber was.

"I don't know. Reading, maybe," Rachel answered, her compromised
timbre full of doubt.

Inside Hope checked the likely places, including the reading nooks—
beanbag chairs stuffed into corners—but Amber was in none of them.
Running into Calhoun and Mindy Eck in the hallway, she asked them
if they'd seen Amber. Mindy's doe eyes slipped sideways, alarming Hope
for a moment before Calhoun said he'd seen her less than an hour ago
in the kitchen, making her map of the wind currents.

"I checked the kitchen," Hope told him.

"What about the belongings room?"

"That's an idea." Hope set off in that direction, wondering if anything
was happening yet between Mindy and Calhoun.

The belongings room was a separate space off the kitchen, where the children kept their jackets, lunch boxes, and other paraphernalia. Hope didn't register what was happening at first. She stood on the threshold and stared, unable to attach meaning to the two figures at the far end. She recognized Amber, though, with her back to Hope, and Frederick, facing her, one arm raised and in his hand a drawing compass.

"I'm gone poke out them jelly-ball eyes, baby."

Amber, her spine rigid, did not turn, as Frederick lifted obsidian eyes to Hope. Hope stared into them, helplessly afloat on sounds that seemed very far away: the click of checkers on a board in the next room, water running in the kitchen, a chant from the backyard: *The worms crawl in, the worms crawl out/The worms play pinochle on your snout.*

Hope brought all her being to bear on the word *Don't*, trying to straitjacket him with her gaze. *Don't.*

He didn't. Hope would never know what weighed in his decision, but he considered for a moment, then closed the compass and put it in his back pocket, a simple, straightforward movement—recapitulation was not in it, nor was triumph. It was a gesture like drawing a glass of water, unadorned of value. But as Amber ran to bury her face in Hope's stomach, he raised his eyes to Hope's again and she read there: *You owe me.*

STILL SHAKEN, HOPE shepherded Amber and Rachel and Patrick down the school steps and toward the Cadillac. She decided to take them to Rosamunda's for snow cones. That would give everyone a chance to calm down before returning home.

After settling them in the car and stowing the wind-current maps and lunch boxes, Hope found herself pulling out after Fern's van. As Fern outdistanced her, Hope noticed something odd about the KEEP ON TRUCKIN' sticker on the van's bumper. The T and the R had been printed very close together and in such a way that from a distance, it read KEEP ON FUCKIN'.

Startled, she glanced at Amber in the front seat. *Fuck* was a word Hope had never once in her life uttered. She wasn't against it, exactly. She just didn't want Amber to see it.

"Hey!" Amber said, as Fern's van turned the corner. "Did you see that, Mom? 'Keep on fucking!' Did you see that?" Hope admitted that she had.

Ten minutes later they were at Rosamunda's, a rickety enterprise on Alabama made possible by Houston's lack of zoning laws. RASPAS, POP-CORN, SODA WATER was spray-painted on the plywood facade. Sword-points of light darted from Rosamunda's gold-plated earrings as she peered boldly at them from the building's sole window. "*Buenas tardes, mis muchachos.*" She looked at Amber. "How's your love life, *chula*? How's that blondie boy?"

Rosamunda was referring to Fern's son, Adam, who occasionally accompanied them here. Amber made a convincing show of mock retching, and Rosamunda shifted her attention to Patrick.

"The light of my life!" she announced with fond drama, resting one hand against a generous span of brown breast erupting from a red-and-white-striped jersey. Hope thought Rosamunda one of the most beautiful women she had ever seen. She had photographed her and was quite pleased with the result. So was Rosamunda. She had sent a copy to her son in Vietnam.

"What'll it be, handsome?" she asked Patrick. He ordered a medley.

"*Perfecto!*" cried Rosamunda, scooping up a cone of shaved ice, which she then drizzled with lime, raspberry, and cola syrups. Amber and Rachel squinched their noses and ordered plain raspberry. Rosamunda shook her head, disappointed in their paucity of culinary daring.

SOME OF THE parents held with Calhoun that Frederick wasn't so much hostile as lacking in the concepts of friendship and cooperation. These were blanks in his worldview, they said. Others agreed with Mindy Eck, who said Frederick should be reported to the authorities, the sooner the better.

Hope might have agreed with Mindy right after the drawing-compass incident, but since then, she'd had reason to reconsider. She'd been unable to resist the idea that she did owe him somehow, and when he insisted she sit next to him during the Wednesday concerts or share her sandwich with him, she obeyed. He liked to have her read to him, mostly magazine advertisements. He sat spellbound, his gamy odor wafting up to her, while she read to him the advantages of Kraft cheese or Cutty Sark Scotch.

He wasn't interested in books, but one day he broke through the circle of younger children surrounding her as she read them *Lyle, Lyle Crocodile*, insinuating himself beside her in the beanbag chair, an intent look on his face. The book was a favorite; the kids rejoiced every time Lyle, the most ardently cordial reptile in the city, flummoxed the grown-ups with his artless, sharp-toothed grin. But when Hope got to the part where the manager of the department store haughtily declares, "Madam, we do not allow crocodiles in our store," tears began to travel down Frederick's cheeks. The giggles of the other children tapered off, and they grew solemn. Hope stopped reading for a moment, then, slipping an arm around Frederick's thin shoulders, continued. Later, she asked him why he'd been crying.

"I weren't," he said, returning her gaze with such straightforward composure, Hope realized that he'd been unaware of his own tears.

He loved the Cadillac. She never knew when he would slip from behind the pittosporum bush as she pulled up to the curb and sidle over to slide a finger along the car's hood, making a wavy track in the dust Hope never quite found time to wash off.

One day she gave him a ride in it. She had taken Amber and Rachel to school, helping them carry inside a large and fragile cardboard representation of the known universe, and when she came out, Frederick was sitting on her fender.

"I need a ride," he said.

"You do? Where to?"

"Noplace. Just a ride."

He got into the front seat and had the radio on and tuned to KYOK the moment Hope turned on the ignition. So his cultural deprivation was not *total*, she thought. "Which way?" she asked, and he pointed straight ahead.

They drove north of the city, nearly to the rice fields, before turning back. They didn't talk much, although Hope tried.

"Do you have any brothers or sisters?" she asked.

Frederick, busy trying to make his automatic window accelerate, didn't answer.

"Where does your mother live?"

Now he fiddled with the cigarette lighter.

He asked a question or two of his own. He wanted to know if what Calhoun said was true, that an ocean was water as far as you could see. Was it really salty? Could they go there?

"Someday," Hope promised.

Back at the school, he turned to her before getting out. "I'se born for this car," he advised her.

4

HOPE AND CLAY WENT HOME TO INDIANA FOR THE HOLIDAYS. They always spent Christmas in Bloomington with her family and New Year's in Indianapolis with his. Clay liked to drive straight through, and they traveled at night so that the children could sleep through most of the long trip. The Cadillac had a shelf in the back between the rear window and the seat, roomy enough for Patrick to use as a bed, while Amber had space for her churning limbs on the seat below. Clay and Hope took turns driving, listening to late-night radio as they hurtled through the dark.

It was just getting light when they reached the rolling countryside around Bloomington. Clay was at the wheel, and Hope gazed out at the plump, furred bellies of earth, searching for the dirt road leading to Lost Lake. Clay had taken her there on their first date. He'd had a car and a major, two particulars that distinguished him from the freshmen boys she had dated and gave his two years seniority an aura of maturity and direction. His eyes were the color of blue hollows in snow.

To get to Lost Lake they'd had to ford a creek and climb a hill, where the lake seemed to suddenly rise up out of the earth. From that moment on, Clay became identified in Hope's mind with the familiar yet occasionally astonishing landscape of southern Indiana, which may have had something to do with her willingness to lie down with him a month later on an old army blanket beneath the fiery maples of Brown County, although it was also true that she was intemperate with curiosity and freedom. She still thought of orgasm as a spiraling leaf. She'd tumbled into love with Clay in just that way, curling and twisting in delicious descent. They were lucky for six months.

He had been willing to marry her, for which she had been grateful; she could never have faced her mother with the news. They eloped to Illinois, where girls only had to be eighteen to buy liquor, although boys had to be twenty-one, which meant that Clay had to wait for her in the car, the motor running, while she went into the liquor store to buy rum for their Cokes, a scene that made her feel a little sleazy somehow. Clay had gotten drunk on their wedding night, if *wedding* was the right word for their city-hall ceremony, the only time she was ever to see him in that condition. When the elevator man in the worn hotel where they were staying made a lewd remark, Clay had threatened to fracture his jaw, and Hope had had to throw her body onto his to prevent him, just like in the movies.

Clay's mother had collapsed when they told her they were married. *You're too young!* she railed at them from her hospital bed, a judgment Hope still disputed. Adulthood was not a matter of chronological age. *You're ruining your life!* Events had not borne out this judgment either, in Hope's view.

Her own parents had not objected very strenuously. They, too, cited tender age, but they willingly contributed a space heater and Hope's grandmother's quilt when Hope and Clay rented an unheated cottage off-campus. They never discussed Hope's premature pregnancy. She was seven months along before they even acknowledged it.

Hope didn't think of these things much anymore, only when they returned to Indiana. Clay might have forgotten the details entirely. They lived in Space City now; they were an old married couple.

A MURDEROUS GENTILITY leaked from the white front porches and steep roofs of the neighborhood where Hope had grown up; the shadows had depth. At least, that was how Hope saw it. "Shootings are unlikely there, but poisonings are not out of the question," she liked to comment to friends.

Clay turned onto the two parallel strips of concrete that made up a driveway better suited to the width of a Chevrolet coupe circa 1940 than a 1969 Cadillac and had scarcely turned off the engine when the front door to the house flew open and Hope's father emerged—short, dapper, balding—gesticulating in a babel of sign languages and followed by Princess, an aging cocker spaniel.

"What's this? Vertical takeoff?" muttered Clay.

"He's just welcoming us," Hope said. "He's just excited."

"Will you get a load of this jalopy!" Wally enthused, drawing close, giving off the fragrance of Vaseline hair tonic, which he continued to use despite his scalp's depleted resources. "Pretty snazzy-roo. How much it set you back, Clay? Hey . . . are these the same kiddos I saw in June? Holy schmoly, what are you feeding them?" He bent to hug Amber and Patrick, as a bounding Princess circled them, first clockwise, then counterclockwise. "Come on in! Come on in!" he urged, with all the heartiness, all the fervent hospitality of the disappointed.

Inside, pinecones were heaped in a basket on the drop-leaf table where Hope used to perform magic shows for William. He had believed in every trick, even those clumsily executed, and claimed he still did.

William would not be home for Christmas. After graduating from Ball State a year ago, he had shunned the shelter of graduate school and disappeared. Hope received phone calls from him now and then against the background of traffic noise. "Where are you now?" she would ask, and he would reply, as if she were eight instead of twenty-eight, "That's for me to know and you to find out." He said little about himself, with the result that he existed for her as she had last seen him, his tall frame barely containing his unrest, his thin face dark with adolescent mullings, hair to his shoulders. He had gotten over his crush on Julie London.

Hope glanced around the room. Electric candles stood in triangular formation at the lace-curtained windows, and a carol book was open on the upright piano. The blue flames of a gas heater flickered behind a white ceramic grill. One of Hope's earliest memories was leaping from the skimpy mantel above that heater into her father's outstretched arms. The moment lasts much longer in memory than it possibly could have in life, a moment so outside the ordinary that she recalls floating up, not down.

"Where is she?" Hope asked.

Wally twitched his head toward the ceiling. "Upstairs."

"Migraine?"

He nodded.

At a small landing about halfway up, the staircase angled sharply to the left before rising to the dim upstairs hallway. Here Hope had done a good deal of eavesdropping as a child. In the hallway, her feet rang against the metal heat register, another good eavesdropping site, but telltale, leaving a reddened grid on her cheek.

She stopped at the open bedroom door. "Mother?"

Maureen lay in the darkened room, a narrow strip of felled flesh beneath the bedclothes, a damp tea towel over her eyes, her short auburn hair matted close to the scalp. A pale, freckled arm rose from the shadows. "Don't come too close. You might jar me." Maureen's voice was vivid in her stricken condition, like the hectic cheeks of a tubercular.

Hope, who considered her mother's migraines hypochondriac imaginings, took a light tone. "What's this? The luck of the Irish?"

Maureen ignored her. One did not mock the luck of the Irish in this house. "How was your trip?"

"Long."

"At least you don't get carsick." Motion sickness was another of Maureen's afflictions.

"Patrick gets carsick," Hope reminded her, failing to resist the familiar desire to thwart, "but he and Amber slept through most of the trip. There's enough room in the Cadillac for them to bed down on long trips." To her dismay, she began to boast. "It's a very roomy car; we love it. It rides beautifully. It has cruise control. Clay says—"

"Don't talk. It hurts my head."

Hope drew up a cane-seated, straight-backed chair, letting it scrape across the floor. Beside her, pushed up against the wall, was the glass display case from her grandparents' old candy store, its strap licorice, horehound drops, and rock candy now replaced by her mother's needlework projects, old *House Beautiful* magazines, medicine bottles, a cut-glass creamer holding streetcar tokens. Hope recalled her mother's long, narrow hand fishing out a token on the frequent occasions when a small Hope threatened to run away from home. Whether Maureen had meant the tokens to be a means of leaving or returning was not clear, but Hope would keep one in her pocket, fingering it as she wandered the town until nightfall, which, in spite of her resolve, inevitably found her rounding the corner toward home, humbled by hunger and the dark.

A little older, she would chant nastily while Maureen braided her hair.

Oh dear, bread and beer,
If I were married, I wouldn't be here.

"Just you wait," Maureen would say, yanking on a skein of hair. "Just you wait."

Maureen occasionally threw things at Hope during Hope's sulky adolescence, odd bits that wouldn't break—a spoon, a red box of May-belline mascara, a tin of tooth powder—perhaps to compensate for her loosening grip. These days, however, since Hope's marriage and the births of her children, their relationship had progressed or deteriorated, Hope wasn't sure which, from war to mere skirmishes, from the full-fledged battles of the past to the cautious parrying of the wounded.

"Can I get you anything?" Hope asked after a while.

Maureen's sigh was a wind on the moors. "No, I don't suppose you can."

"I guess I'll go back downstairs then."

"I guess you will."

WALLY HAD RECENTLY moved his workshop from the cellar to the garage, managing somehow to preserve its disorder intact. The workbench extended along all three walls and was littered with tools and wrinkled diagrams and rusty-lidded baby-food jars from which spilled screws and nuts and other findings. What drew the eye, however, were the half-dozen or so machines Wally had cobbled together in pursuit of perpetual motion. Some were in various stages of cannibalization, missing an armature or a spring or a wheel. Others, like the two cake tins mounted on a horizontal rod, appeared incomplete by design.

Wally and Clay stood in front of one of them, clouds of condensed breath forming and disintegrating between them as they argued, while Amber and Patrick, bundled in jackets and scarves, fiddled with the tools.

"You're just in time," Wally said, catching sight of Hope, who skirted a glowing electric heater to join them. "I was just about to explain. You see these spokes here? Hollow! Inside each one there's this little steel ball that rolls back and forth. It's the shifting weight that makes the wheel go around." He nudged one of the spokes, and it began to move, the steel balls clicking back and forth.

"I'm almost there," he said to Clay, his voice dropping into the register of masculine exchange. His hands, large for such a small man, hovered protectively as his brainchild rotated, balls clicking in a regular rhythm. "I need to work out a few bugs is all. I think my problem is in the shape of the cam."

"Your problem is friction and always has been."

"Well, it's to get rid of that last little bit of friction that I plan to change the shape of the cam."

Clay passed a hand over his bristly burr haircut. "You're up against the first law of thermodynamics here, Wally." He glanced at Hope, and she smiled, proud of all the things Clay knew. "You're taking on the universe," he continued. "Energy can be neither created nor destroyed. That's why you have to give your contraption a push to start it."

"It was a very little push."

"It's not a matter of *degree*."

"Laws are meant to be broken."

"Not scientific laws!"

"Well, now, it's my impression—and correct me if I'm wrong, Clay, you're the fella with the credentials—but it's my impression that it's not so much the first *law* of thermodynamics as the first *theory* of thermodynamics."

"A theory that has withstood enough tests over time to make it a *virtual* law."

"Virtual, not *actual*." Wally folded his arms across his chest, resting his case.

"When, Grandpa?" Patrick hooked a finger on one of his grandfather's belt lugs and tugged. "Now?"

"I promised him I'd turn on the turret lathe," Wally explained.

Numerous gears spun into motion as he flipped the switch, setting up a grinding howl. "The gripping jaw!" he yelled over the noise, pointing to it as Patrick's shoulders shuddered up toward his ears in a thrill of horror and bliss.

"As a member of the utility industry, Clay can't be expected to appreciate my work," Wally pointed out later to Hope. "It could ruin their business, you know."

MAUREEN COULD BE inexhaustible. In the throes of a migraine, she naturally failed to project this potential, but released from pain and faced with the challenge of Christmas, she had a demonic energy that propelled her tidy, compact body into furious preparations. "We still have wreaths to make!" she cried in the midst of baking cookies, plunging her hands into a bowl of flour and sending up a chalky cloud. "We haven't decorated the banister yet!" There were other grievances, too: cards to be addressed and mailed, a tree bought and trimmed, gifts wrapped.

Wally and Hope tried, sometimes successfully, to help, but Clay would have no part of it, retiring to a corner of the living room with back issues of the *Reader's Digest* to make his point, ostentatiously opening to "Laughter Is the Best Medicine." Hope didn't feel she could argue. She knew his tolerance had seriously eroded, though, when she came on him one afternoon whispering into the phone in the hallway. "My mother," he explained, placing a hand over the receiver. His mother? Why? They would be seeing her in three days.

"Do I need to talk to her?" Hope asked.

"No. That's okay."

Hope was relieved. Between Hope and her mother-in-law lay a profound lack of conviviality. Most recently, at Clay's father's funeral, Hope had overheard Lydia, who must have known Hope was nearby, remark to a relative that Hope lacked taste. This was true but had been unknown to Hope until then, and the judgment made itself instantly at home, ready to surface during confidence crises despite Clay's impatient declaration that he had *married* her for her lack of taste, for crissakes.

CHRISTMAS MORNING PROVED that preparations had been out of proportion to the event, as usual. Hope and Maureen managed to mystify each other with their gifts again. Hope stared at the plastic contraption in her lap, at a total loss.

"An egg peeler," Maureen informed her. "You put the egg in here, and it comes out there, peeled."

"Oh."

Maureen opened the tiny box Hope handed her and held its contents in her palm for a moment before making the toneless observation that it appeared to be a rabbit.

"An ivory netsuke. It fastens onto a kimono sash."

"I don't have a kimono sash."

"Well, I know, but . . ."

Later, in the kitchen, Hope and Maureen might not have been pleased to know how similar were their gestures. They both used dish towels for pot holders, tasted with an index finger, and ran their hands over their hips before trying anything ticklish, like unmolding a salad. Neither was a clean-as-you-go cook, but they moved assuredly through the stacked pots and pans and scattered utensils, somehow clearing a space to chop celery and slice onions, somehow locating a clean bowl for fruit cup, all the while deftly avoiding Patrick, who sat on the floor, patiently spoon-feeding Princess eggnog.

When the doorbell rang, Wally answered it, calling to Maureen and Hope, "It's the Hooligans!"

Maureen looked up from basting the turkey with an aggrieved frown that had not changed much over the thirty years Wally had been saying "Hooligan" for "Hoolihan." With a wave of the baster, spraying drops of fat all around, she hissed, "Keep them busy for ten more minutes," as if she were engaged in a conspiracy and the arrival of her brother Art and his wife, Dolly, had introduced an element of high risk.

Art, short and beefy, neither of which interfered with his view of himself as a charmer, stood in the doorway for a moment on entering, allowing Hope to bask in the odor of motor oil as the cold air eddied about them. He had no doubt spent this day, like any other, bent over an engine. A familiar presence on the stock car circuit, Art had enjoyed emeritus status since retiring from driving, regularly consulted by the local racing fraternity on the trickier challenges of making a car go fast. He loved the world of speed with a loyalty as tender as it was absolute, attending races in sickness and in health, never failing to visit the injured. He was patient with neophytes. Hope considered these his sole assets.

His wife had not been named in vain. The regularity of Dolly's small, upturned nose, bowed mouth, and properly spaced eyes, together with a slightly precious style of dress, gave her an air of replica. Wally said he prayed for the day when she would get a joke, but Hope defended her, saying she was not dumb but beaten.

"Well, well, well, it's Hope," said Art, stepping back from the embrace. He acknowledged Clay's presence with a cautious handshake.

"It's Hope," agreed Dolly, smiling.

"More or less intact," Hope said. "Where's Eric?"

Art looked down to supervise the unzipping of his brown poplin jacket. "He'll be along."

According to Maureen, relations between Art and his son were at a new low. Eric had dropped out of high school and was devoting most of his waking hours (which were evidently few) to his garage band, thus living dangerously below expectations. There had been talk, Maureen said, of "giving him the boot."

"Wally can fix drinks if anyone's interested!" called Maureen from the kitchen.

"Is the pope Catholic?" said Art, winking at Wally, who headed back toward the kitchen, inquiring over his shoulder, "Seven and Seven?"

"Just a little ginger ale for me, Wally," said Dolly.

Art asked Hope if she had heard from William.

Hope's morale, always a spindly construction in the context of family, collapsed. The last phone call she'd received from William had been over two months ago. He was embarking on a new career, he'd said, bringing to Hope's mind explosives, splintering ROTC buildings, and laboratories collapsing onto experiments funded by the Defense Department. But it turned out he had embarked on a career of guerrilla theater. "Surprise theatrics conducted behind enemy lines. Harassment of the status quo." He was learning the art of mime, he said. Everyone thought he was a natural.

Hope could believe it, recalling his numerous garage performances— William as Huck, William as the Youth in *The Red Badge of Courage*, William as Davy Crockett. Neighborhood kids had to pay a nickel;

Hope got in free. He'd kept everyone mesmerized by force of excessive energy as he charged about his imagined stage in constant heroic motion.

"I haven't heard from him in a while now," she told Art. She glanced at her father, who was staring into the blue flames of the gas grill. William did not communicate with their parents; Hope was the go-between. This was pretty much as it had always been. "I'm worried about him."

"Oh, I wouldn't be, if I were you," said Art. "He's probably having himself a good old time up there in the wilds of Canada. Snug as a bug in a rug." Art stretched his throat to elevate a satisfied chin. His son might be a disappointment, but at least he was not a draft dodger.

THE TABLE WAS lavish, as it always was at holiday time, in spite of fallen family fortunes. Maureen insisted on living up to the heirlooms. A swath of crimson-berried holly wound around cut-glass bowls filled with butternut squash, creamed onions, parsleyed mashed potatoes, and three different salads, as well as small dishes bright with homemade pickles and cranberry sauce and peaches spiked with cloves. A glistening turkey reigned from the head of the white damasked table, and each place was set with Grandmother Hoolihan's bone china and silver worn so thin the forks had the delicate weight of chopsticks. Amber's favorite touch, miniature silver spoons with bowls the size of teardrops, lay half buried beneath white crystals filling tiny individual saltcellars shaped like shells.

"Sit wherever you want," Maureen urged. The tips of her hair were wet with perspiration, and she was slightly out of breath, having made great efforts to single-handedly have all the food on the table while the steam was still rising from it. The last to sit down, she delivered the blessing.

"Bless us, oh Lord, and these thy gifts which through thy bounty we are about to receive through Christ our Lord and Him alone with no help whatsoever from Benedict the Fifteenth or any pontiff since, amen."

"Aunt Wynne's spinning in her grave, sis," said Art, as heads unbowed and Wally began scooping the dressing from the turkey, releasing aromas of sage and celery.

"I hope so."

"Now what was it she called Mother, sis?" he prompted.

"The devil's huzzy!"

Clay and Hope exchanged a look. How many times did they have to listen to this story?

"The Church of the Immaculate Heart of Mary, wasn't it, sis?" Art's question was barely audible through its sieve of mashed potato, but Maureen heard it clearly enough.

"Yes, and nine-o'clock mass, no later, on account of Sunday dinner, and we all had to be there, all four of us, in our Sunday best, of course, and me in this little fur coat I hated, and you, Art, scarcely out of your christening gown, and Da wouldn't go, being the sort to leave bead-banging to the women, as he put it, and myself only five, some help but not enough to get us there on time, not on the dot anyway. Dressed her down the minute we walked in, the priest did, from the pulpit! you'd've thought he was waiting for her, waiting his chance, but did she miss a beat? No, she did not. "I've got four under five, father, and I'd like to see *you* have them ready for nine-o'clock mass every Sunday!' And walked out, us kids trailing after her, bows to her string. Walked out forever. That's when Aunt Wynne called her the devil's huzzy." Maureen paused. "And died a year later."

"This turkey is just perfect, Maureen," said Dolly.

"I think it may be a little dry," said Maureen modestly, picking up her fork.

"It's perfect," insisted Dolly. "Don't you think so, Art?"

Art nodded, his attention now fully focused on the food.

THEY TALKED FOR a while about other relatives, about the variable quality of the steaks at a downtown hotel restaurant, about the possibility of a shopping mall outside of town. Maureen, who imagined she had a weight problem although she tipped the scales at barely one hundred pounds, bitterly questioned the wisdom of a government that would take cyclamates off the market. Art commented that with the death of Eisenhower, the country had lost its one and only military mind. Clay and Hope exchanged a look. Next topic: Vietnam. (On this subject Clay and Hope were strictly neutral, as required, Clay said, by the Hatch Act, which forbade government employees—and in Clay's interpretation, their spouses—to participate in politics.) But before any discussion of Vietnam could get underway, Dolly intervened. "Judy Garland, too." Everyone looked at her. "Judy Garland died this year, too," she insisted, barely audible.

By the time second helpings were passed around, the conversation had shifted to the student body election at Indiana University. Ordinarily, this would not have been of much interest to anyone at the table, but that year a black law student was running, and it was much in the news. Maureen wondered.

Wondered what? Hope ignored Clay's look.

Maureen wondered if they were ready.

Ready for what?

Well, to lead. Certain qualities were required, after all.

And did she doubt that these so-called certain qualities were lacking in certain races?

Yes, in fact, now that Hope asked, Maureen did. And she wasn't the only one either. Science, for example, told you.

Science!

Take your sickle-cell anemia.

"Amber! Patrick! Close your ears," Hope ordered. "I don't want you to hear this."

Patrick clapped his hands over his ears, but Amber resisted, giving Hope one of those pitiless, watchful looks that seem to be a specialty of nine-year-old girls.

"It's true," put in Art. "And I can tell you something else. I can tell you from my own experience . . . *they cannot drive.*" He leaned back to see if the enormity of his charge had sunk in.

"Isn't this fascinating?" Hope said to Clay. "A gene that determines driving ability."

"Maureen, are there chestnuts in the dressing?" Dolly asked anxiously. "I keep thinking I'm tasting chestnuts. They're wonderful, if there are any."

"Art's right," said Maureen. "I've seen them drive straight through stop signs."

"Well, sure," he said. "Road signs are nothing to them. What do you expect? There weren't any road signs in the jungle, right?"

Hope's fork clattered to her plate. "That has to be the stupidest thing I've ever heard in my life!"

"Hope!" Maureen clutched her knife.

"I've got a baker's dozen of 'em in my mechanics class," Art went on, unperturbed. "And I can tell you this: they have no affinity whatsoever for the combustion engine. Tools might as well come from Mars, as far as they're concerned. You give 'em a wrench, and you try your damnedest to show 'em how to use it, but it's no go! They can't even *hold* a wrench correctly. Wally, you know what I'm talking about, how you kind of heft it in your palm a second before you go to work with it? These are things your dad and I don't even think about," he explained to Hope. "That we just do automatically. Right, Wally?"

"Well, I think we're getting into some stormy waters here, and maybe, seeing as it's Christmas Day—"

"They'll never improve their image," interrupted Maureen. "Individuals are another thing, I've always liked Pearl Bailey, I've always *loved* Pearl Bailey, but as a race they're connivers and will do anything to avoid doing what they're told. I had a cleaning girl once—"

"Woman!" Hope wailed.

"—who never rinsed the counters after she scrubbed them, no matter how many times I told her. She always left a film, and I cannot abide films."

"And I'll tell you something else," Art put in. "You can always tell when you're in a colored neighborhood. Half the cars will be parked going the wrong way—"

"Okay! I quit!" Hope stood up, her napkin falling to the floor. "I resign. Count me *out* of this family, as of now!"

"—and the other half will be up on blocks!"

CLAY CAUGHT UP with Hope on the landing of the stairway, where it angled sharply to the left. He put his arms around her, and she leaned against him, her head on his chest, bulwark against inherited insanity.

"Why do we come here every year?" he asked.

"It's the last time. It's absolutely, positively the last time."

Clay returned to the dining room, and Hope stood for a moment on the landing, listening to him announce their departure, delivered with the satisfying superiority she would never have been able to muster, and then went upstairs to pack. Amber followed. Hope explained that they would be going to Grandma Lydia's a day early, and wouldn't it be fun to play with her antique music boxes?

"She doesn't like us to touch them," Amber said, with a look implying that if Hope didn't know this, what did she know? She turned and left the room.

Hope started throwing clothes into suitcases, mixing up hers and Clay's and the children's, not bothering to fold anything. She had nearly finished when Wally came in.

"Hopie, Hopie, what's this? What are you doing?"

"Leaving home. It's about time, don't you think?"

"No, of course not, this will always be your home."

"No, it's not." And it's not yours either, she wanted to say. It's hers.

"Hopie, Hopie, calm down," Wally pleaded. "Think of what you're doing. How many colored girls would leave their families, reject their own flesh and blood, because of some bad remarks about white people?"

Hope threw a skirt into her suitcase. "It's not the same thing."

"It isn't? Then explain to me. Let's talk this over. Let's calm down here. Let's straighten things out."

"I can't hear you, Daddy. Something has happened to my ears." Hope slammed down the suitcase lid and snapped shut the clasps.

"Is there *anything* I can say?"

"No."

There was, of course. He could say: Your mother is wrong, and you are right. She waited for a minute, giving him a chance. He stood there in mute appeal. She picked up her suitcase and shouldered her purse.

As he descended the stairs in front of her, she paused until he disappeared where the staircase angled sharply. Then, skirting the heat register, she entered Maureen's bedroom, clean now of the accouterments of illness. The bed was made, the bedside table empty of water tumblers and medicine bottles. The sliding door of her grandparents' glass display case rattled softly as she slid it to one side and dipped her fingers into the cut-glass creamer.

The token was no larger than her thumbnail—was everything smaller long ago?—and very thin. Her grandmother had died on a streetcar, a heart attack, a satisfying valedictory, if she could only have savored it, her feud with the trolley company being second only to her feud with the Catholic Church. She slipped the token into her purse.

Downstairs, Maureen and Art and Dolly still sat at the table. Maureen and Art, masters of the immutable grudge, did not look Hope's way, but Dolly surreptitiously wiggled a few brave fingers. Wally, wordless with misery, saw Hope and Clay and the children out to the Cadillac. Don't look back, Hope told herself, as they pulled away, but of course she did, with the result that she would be haunted for a long time by the sight of her father standing on the front lawn, backlit by the porch light, one hand shuttling back and forth, back and forth, looking for all the world like one of his perpetual-motion machines.

5

It was a bright, warm winter in Houston that year, the wrong weather, Hope told Chloe, for misery. Looking back, she would search those balmy days for clues. Perhaps Clay had been more withdrawn than usual. More critical. Edgier. It was a fact he had taken more Air Force Reserve trips—to Bermuda, the Azores, the South Pacific, once even touching down in Vietnam for half an hour with an emergency delivery. He'd received a campaign ribbon for that one. Patrick sometimes wore it pinned to his T-shirt, clomping around the house in Clay's flight boots, an old set of dog tags clinking against his small chest.

Perhaps she had been too busy at the school—helping out with art projects, chaperoning field trips—in spite of (because of?) Clay's increasing disapproval. He often made disparaging remarks about the hippies and continued to complain about the tuition. He questioned Calhoun's character, saying he smelled a rat. Hope steered conversations away from the school when she could. She had not told him about Frederick, for example. She didn't want Frederick to end up on the debit side of Clay's ledger. And perhaps this sort of reticence, added to the mass of the unspoken that had gathered over the years, muffled her awareness. Or perhaps one doesn't see until one is ready to see, although Hope wouldn't have said she was ready on the February morning she called Clay at work.

A faint humming resonated along her nerve fibers when a new receptionist, who did not recognize Hope's voice, informed her, "I'm sorry, but Mr. Fairman is not in the office today. Can I take a message?"

Hope mentally flipped through scenes from their morning routine: Clay eating an egg, Clay checking the contents of his briefcase, Clay walking out the door carrying a second cup of coffee. "No, I'll call back," she heard herself say, as if she were someone else, as if she had business.

She stood for several moments, fingertips on the receiver, stomach constricting, trying to remember what her plans for the day had been. A vast sponge in her head seemed to have absorbed them.

Housecleaning, it occurred to her, improbably. Perhaps she should clean the house.

Hope's inadequate housekeeping was a sore point between herself and Clay, who considered unpolished furniture and unwashed floors a sign of maladjustment, marking one as an outsider. "Disorder without, order within," Hope said in her defense, but this was not true. She contained an abundance of disorder within; it was the effort of trying to arrange this disorder into something coherent that left so little time for housecleaning.

She had found an ally in Chloe, who, on her very first visit to Hope's house, had breezily undermined Clay's viewpoint. "Housework bowdlerizes life, don't you think?" Chloe had said, stepping nonchalantly over a box of spilled crackers and a squashed paper cup, skirting an overturned tricycle, and removing a pile of unsorted laundry from a sofa to the coffee table in order to sit down.

Hope had subsequently used that phrase to counter Clay's remonstrances. But how inadequate it seemed now as she looked around at the unwashed dishes on the counter, the gray splotches on the unwashed floor, the grease streaking the appliances, and the dirt-darkened wood behind the handles of the cabinet doors.

Hope used the crevice attachment to the vacuum cleaner for the first time that day, sending it down between couch cushions, behind bookcases, underneath the refrigerator. With old socks on her hands, she removed dust from each slat of the venetian blinds. She took a toothbrush to the tile grout in the shower. As she scrubbed and scoured and polished, she saw herself industrious and occupied, perky and clear-browed in the way of women in television commercials.

"What's wrong?" asked Chloe that afternoon when Hope dropped off Rachel from school.

"What makes you think something's wrong?"

"You've shrunk. You shrink when you're upset," Chloe said.

HOPE WATCHED *MR. ROGER'S Neighborhood* as she waited for Clay to come home from work that evening. She sat in the wing chair in the family room, legs draped over an arm. Mr. Rogers was assuring his audience they could not be flushed down a toilet. He held up a piece of pipe, pointing out its small size.

The quiet and cleanliness of the house, the fragrance of floor wax in the air, wasn't lost on Clay as he walked in the door. Cautiously, he removed his suit coat, folding it neatly over the back of an Early American rocker. "The house . . . the house looks great," he said, a little awestruck. "Where are the kids?"

Hope turned to him a freakish face glistening with a pearly foundation that gave her an alarming pallor. Smears of green paste had congealed on her eyelids beneath the penciled chevrons of her eyebrows, and pink stains spread downward from her cheekbones toward a mouth coated with an iridescent lipstick the color of fish scales. Even without the lunar light of the television set, her face had the bizarre exaggeration of a Kabuki actor or a female impersonator. To herself, however, Hope had not appeared particularly outlandish. She'd spent considerable effort with her brushes and tubes.

"They're renovating the bomb shelter," she said. "Yesterday it was a submarine. Today it's a hospital."

The bomb shelter had come with the house. Hope always pointed this out to people, not wanting to be associated with the paranoia she felt it represented.

Clay reached into his shirt pocket for cigarettes. "The house looks great," he repeated. His tone, tamped down and fenced, set her body humming again, but she answered with equal temperance.

"Tomorrow I plan to do closets." After giving him a gaudy smile, she returned her attention to Mr. Rogers, who was now singing a song about flushing.

Clay lit his cigarette and sat down in a chair, loosening his tie. He picked up a copy of *Newsweek* from the lamp table. The cover pictured dead Asian bodies strewn like laundry over cratered terrain. He fanned the pages and set it down again. "Do I have time to take a shower before dinner?"

"I called your office this morning." A simple statement. She didn't ask where he'd been. Boundaries of individual privacy had to be respected. Even in marriage. Especially in marriage. She wouldn't pry. She was offering her bit of the truth and was prepared to accept whatever he offered in return.

Clay got up and crossed the room to reach behind the television set, retrieving the jar lid he kept hidden there, Amber having donated all his ashtrays to a neighbor's garage sale. He stared at the screen as Mr. Rogers finished his song. "That guy is truly repulsive."

"He calms me. But feel free to change the channel."

Clay clicked the dial forward until the head and shoulders of Walter Cronkite filled the screen. Clay watched for a moment as images of starving Biafrans replaced Cronkite's propitiatory expression. Then he turned to face Hope, not looking at her directly, however, but at her left shoulder.

"I took the day off," he said, "and drove to Galveston."

"How wonderful!" Hope's voice was devoid of irony. Galveston *was* wonderful; the radiant sand, warm waters, and cheesy beach shops made the notion of endless summer a true possibility in this southerly latitude. "It's not like you, though," she said, struggling to bring to mind a new Clay, a spontaneous Clay who had gone to Galveston to celebrate the extraordinary winter weather.

"No," he admitted. "It's not."

Hope glanced back at the television. "Bad news is just not his bag," she said, gesturing toward Walter Cronkite. "See how apologetic he is? How deeply he regrets having to tell us people are starving in Biafra? He's better on space coverage." She swung her legs to the floor and sat up straight. "So. You were saying."

Clay's expression became absorbed and deliberative. He returned to his chair, rested his elbows on his thighs, and leaned forward, his loosened tie hanging straight down, away from his body. "I was saying . . . we were *both* saying, I think . . . that I am not myself."

"It happens! We all have *days*. You know how I get every fall. It's nothing to worry about. You probably just needed a day off. You're probably just tired. Don't you think?"

Clay looked at her, and for a moment something passed between them too compressed and dense for expression.

"I think we should wait until later to talk about this," he said. Hope sat for a moment, pinching up the fleshless skin from the back of her hand. "You should wash that stuff off your face," he added gently, and she saw herself then, as surely as if he'd held up a mirror.

AT DINNER, PATRICK refused the spaghetti, splaying his small hands across his plate. He didn't like tomatoes and had learned to recognize them in cooked form. "Eat, Patrick," ordered Clay. Patrick's chin crinkled as his lower lip protruded.

Hope begged silently for peace. Were the tiniest wedge of patience to detach from her composure just then, the whole contrivance of herself might crumble into dust and rubble.

"I may have overdone the garlic," she said. "Kids taste things more acutely than we do. They have more taste buds."

Patrick began to blow bubbles in his milk, which he always drank with a straw.

"Stop that, Patrick," Clay ordered.

Patrick exhaled into the straw with just enough force to ripple the surface without making bubbles.

"Patrick, I'm warning you—"

"*La plume de ma tante est sur la table!*" broke in Amber. Her eyes darted from Hope to Clay to Patrick. Clay smiled at her. Amber's French class constituted one of the free school's few saving graces, in his view.

"*Je m'appelle Amber!*" Amber pointed to Patrick. "*Voici mon frére!* Now you. Say: *Je m'appelle Patrick.*"

"Shem pell Patrick."

"He did it! He's speaking French! You're speaking French, Patrick! He's speaking French, just like me!" She chattered on. She was writing a report on Edouard Manet. Did they know what a mistress was? What a mistress *really* was? She did.

Hope glanced at Clay, but he wasn't listening.

At the end of the meal, Clay pointed to Patrick's uneaten spaghetti. "I don't think you've qualified for ice cream, Patrick."

"Maybe he'd like a banana," suggested Hope, jumping up and hurrying to the fruit bowl on the counter. "A banana is not really dessert." She put one on his plate.

"It's rotten," Patrick complained.

Clay set down his water glass. "It is not rotten, Patrick."

"It has spots."

"The spots mean the banana is ripe, not rotten."

"I hate spots." Patrick stared stubbornly at his spoon, his forehead bunched in curved furrows resembling a pair of longhorns. Ordinarily, Amber would have commented on this. Patrick's longhorns were familiar; they even appeared in his baby photos, proving, Amber said, that he had been born bullheaded. Tonight, though, she made no comment.

"The spots are on the outside," said Clay. "You don't have to eat them. Look." Clay peeled the banana and set it on Patrick's plate, where it looked pale and excremental against the blue plate.

"Actually, a banana this ripe has lost a good deal of its potassium," ventured Hope.

"Hope! For crissakes!"

She fell silent, overwhelmed by an obscure shame.

Routine carried her through the next two hours, as she cleared the table, put away the food, did the dishes, and wiped down the counters. After supervising Patrick's bath and reading him a story, she turned out his light with a sense that she had just cleared a series of hurdles.

"In bed already?" she asked, entering Amber's room and sitting down on the edge of the bed.

"Uh-huh." Amber was propped up against her pillows, reading. She wore a polka-dotted nightgown she'd outgrown long ago but refused to relinquish. Its hem, which had once reached the floor, now came just below her knees, and the puffed sleeves looked like small, measled balloons balanced on her shoulders. A glass of water sat on her night table, as well as a notebook, a pen, and a stack of books. She looked prepared for the onslaught of a debilitating disease.

"Planning to read in bed for a while?"

"Uh-huh."

"Well, have the light off by nine, okay?"

As Hope leaned over to give her a kiss, Amber flung her thin arms around Hope's neck with such force Hope was pulled off-balance. "Don't go, Mom. Please."

Hope lost starch then; whatever had been keeping her spine straight drained out. She lay down on the bed to take Amber in her arms, feeling Amber's distress trafficking busily beneath her skin, and stroked Amber's breadcrust-colored hair, so fine it barely covered the slight irregularities of her skull. Taking Amber's hand in her own, she slowly massaged each finger until Amber's breathing slowed and deepened, and Hope knew she slept.

IN THE LIVING room, which had emerged sleek and symmetrical from beneath its usual jumble after Hope's cleaning, Clay had set an open bottle of wine and two glasses on the coffee table beside a bouquet of magenta cosmos Hope had picked earlier. The table, a circle of glass set on a pine frame, had been a wedding gift from William, who had built it in his high school shop class. It was an anomaly in this room furnished from Ethan Allen.

"Where did you get the wine?" Hope asked. They never drank wine unless there were dinner guests.

"At the liquor store."

"I guess I meant why."

Clay was sitting on one of the two matching love seats on either side of the coffee table. He tapped ash from his cigarette into a soap dish. Hope hesitated, then sat down next to him. He handed her a glass, and she took a sip. His own was half empty; he ran a finger around its rim.

"Clay, if you have something to tell me, please . . . "

He nodded judiciously, as if she had scored a point, and he was determined to be a good sport about it. "I don't expect you to understand this," he said.

"Oh, but I will! I can!"

"I need to retool."

"Retool?"

He nodded.

Hope thought at first he meant to change jobs. So many people were doing it just then. Chloe had a friend who had resigned from a job as an economic adviser at the United Nations to become a color therapist. A woman from the church, a bookkeeper, had moved to New Mexico recently to study pottery.

"I need a place of my own," Clay said, pouring more wine. "An apartment, something cheap. To think." He'd been depressed lately, he went on. He'd been to see Fred Quine.

Fred was the flight doctor at Ellington Air Force Base. Hope knew him slightly. He liked to tease the wives about the Reserve trips their husbands took. "Wings up, rings off," he'd joke.

Fred had diagnosed stress and assigned him some relaxation exercises. Clay spoke haltingly and didn't notice the cigarette burning perilously close to his fingers. Hope watched, fascinated.

"Did Fred prescribe an apartment?" she asked, not taking her eyes from the burning tip as it closed in on Clay's flesh. "Is this some sort of *Playboy* cure?"

An aggrieved expression passed over Clay's features, and he turned from her, showing a severe profile. "This is no time for sarcasm, Hope."

"I'm sorry. Really. I'm sorry." A weight pressed against her chest so palpable that she could imagine its form: a leaden block flattening her breasts, pushing into her lungs, forcing her to take quick, shallow breaths. She tried to escape it by sitting up straighter, but the weight only gained force.

"Your cigarette," she said in a nipped voice, pointing.

He started, saw that the cigarette had burned nearly to its filter, and stubbed it out.

"What you're saying doesn't make any sense to me," she said.

"I *knew* you wouldn't understand."

Rebuked, she fell silent, and gradually the absence of words between them unrolled and spread into a vast plain. *The rain in Spain falls mostly on the plain*, Rex Harrison sang softly in her ear, as she began to cry, not in sadness—the loss of love was not yet a reality—but in bewilderment and fright.

Clay took her wineglass from her hand, set it on the table alongside his own, and began to unbutton her blouse. Making love to Hope was his way of comforting her. It sometimes worked. Tonight, however, she felt acutely estranged from her body, and it was with a dim sense of self-betrayal that she allowed him to draw her to the floor to lie awkwardly half beneath the coffee table. She looked up through the glass into the yellow eyes of the cosmos, their heads bowed over, her mind tenaciously rooting among certain questions. What would living in an apartment be like? Neither she nor Clay had ever lived in one. They had always lived in houses, however ramshackle. Would Clay have to buy a new bed? What about other furniture, pots and pans? How did one go about retooling?

Clay pulled her toward him, maneuvering her on top. Raising up on her arms, she felt the stir of his breath on her skin as he cupped her breasts in his hands and closed his eyes. "Hope."

THEY DIDN'T TELL the children right away. Separation was not a coherent enough concept, not yet a story to be told. Clay left for work every morning and came home every evening. Hope picked up Amber and Rachel from school, applied Band-Aids to wounds when necessary, fixed meals. Clay went to his monthly Reserve meeting, and Hope went to her Wednesday-night photography class. Clay's announcement had briefly broken the surface of their life only to sink out of sight again. Hope had even begun to think Clay might have changed his mind, when he announced that he had found an apartment.

"It's not much," he told her. "A little one-bedroom off Memorial."

"When?" she gasped. "How?" Meaning, when had he found the time to look for an apartment? How had he summoned the resources?

"IT WILL BE like I'm gone on a Reserve trip," Clay told Amber and Patrick, digging at the skin around his thumbnails, where he had chewed bloody craters. He would be seeing them often, he said. Very often. Very, very often.

The four of them sat in the living room on the opposing love seats, the glass table with the magenta cosmos between them. Amber, so pale her eyes looked like raisins in raw dough, sat very upright, very close to Clay on one love seat, hands in her lap. Patrick, whose legs didn't reach the floor, sat beside Hope on the other and twisted the felt tooth of his stuffed alligator, which lay across his knees.

"I need a time-out." Clay made a T with his hands. "Sometimes people need a time-out." As if on cue, the mantel clock sitting on the bookshelf chimed the half hour. "To think."

"Is this a divorce?" Amber asked.

Clay went very still; he stopped worrying his thumbs. Hope had the fleeting sense that if she asked him to stay just then, if she told him she loved and needed him, that the children loved and needed him, he would change his mind. But she remained silent, whether through pride, inertia, or an unacknowledged impulse to be free herself was hard to say.

The moment was soon lost, in any case, for in contradiction to everything they knew about him, Clay suddenly burst into tears. His jaw slackened, his mouth went loose and rubbery, his eyes pinched shut, and he began to cry and scrabble at his thighs, making a raspy sound on the polished fabric of his khakis.

Hope sat with knees pressed together, fists clenched. He had no right!

Amber flung herself on him, grasping the wings of his collar. "Don't cry, Daddy! *Please*! Don't cry."

For a moment, Patrick simply looked rapt, as if enchanted by the sight of his sister and his father weeping and clinging to each other, but then without warning, his head fell back, and a cry of sheer animal distress escaped his throat, signal of something pierced or torn, a wounded paw, a ripped ear.

Unable to bear it, Hope, too, broke down, gathering Patrick in her arms, alligator and all, so that the four of them sat there weeping, loyalties confused in the face of unspecified peril, the locus of comfort lost.

A CURIOUS LACK of friction characterized the days before Clay left. In his spare time, he trimmed the shrubbery, fixed the running toilet, and paid bills. Hope felt skewed and off-balance alongside his self-command. But when she inquired about the location of the fuse box or how to change the filter of the air conditioner, she carefully fit her words to the matter at hand and sounded as reasonable as he.

In the evenings, after the children were in bed, Clay filled cardboard boxes with his belongings.

"I feel like killing myself," Hope told him.

"Don't be silly."

She took to driving the 610 Loop to avoid the sight of him packing. The thrum of tires against the pavement rounded up those parts of herself that had come loose, and the dashboard panel of the Cadillac glowed reassuringly with accounts of oil pressure, temperature, gas volume, and speed.

Amber continued to ask vigilant, resistant questions. Did Clay intend to smoke in his new apartment? Would he have a telephone? Could she call him whenever she wanted to? What about their allowances? Would they still get them on Fridays?

"What if I get sick at school like Daphne did, and her father came to get her, and he took her to the doctor's, and the doctor made them go to the hospital because he thought it might be leukemia?"

"It wasn't leukemia," said Hope.

"I know, but I'm just asking, what if I need tests or something?"

Clay gave her a long look. "I'll *be* there, Amber."

Patrick, on the other hand, seemed to have forgotten Clay was leaving. He would turn four in a week, and the prospect of a pirate party and a pedal fire engine engaged him when he was not studying the delicate bones of blown dandelions or the soundlessness of clouds.

CLAY LEFT ON a Monday morning. Hope had to admit that he had been right, it was a lot like a Reserve trip, the departure, at any rate. He appeared in the kitchen—too late for breakfast, his ride to work about to arrive—with his flight bag and an extra suit over his shoulder. Hope and the children sat at the table, Amber waiting for Chloe to pick her up for school, Hope buttering toast for Patrick, and Patrick blowing bubbles in his orange juice, while Hudson and Harrigan made buddy jokes on the radio.

Clay set down his gear to give Patrick a hug. "See you, pardner." He hugged Amber, too, who submitted stiffly, arms at her sides. A horn honked, and Hope hurried over to kiss him, the slice of toast balanced on the palm of her hand. She missed his lips, landing a little to the right on a cheek still moist from shaving cream. "I'm gone," he said, as he did every morning.

So it was a goodbye like many others—hasty and habitual—yet freighted enough with the unspoken to cause Hope pain.

She turned to Patrick. "Who do you love?"

"Mommy!"

Cheap trick, but she felt better.

6

HOPE SHRANK FROM CALLING HER PARENTS. SHE HAD NOT SPO-
ken to them since Christmas. She hadn't expected to hear from
her mother—Maureen had refused to speak to her aunt Wynne on her
deathbed—but she thought her father might call, on the sly maybe,
some night when Maureen was in bed. This would have been unlikely,
though. Her parents reserved long-distance phone calls for deaths and
births, believing that a postage stamp was sufficient to bear what happened in between. Where a separation fell on this spectrum wasn't clear.
Marriages did not dissolve in her family; they devolved, into wrestling
matches, where the important thing was to come out on top.

On the other hand, her parents might want to know that the father
of their grandchildren had just left them to retool. Or they might not.
Maureen and Wally, preoccupied with their own drama, were not enthusiastic grandparents. They would disapprove of Clay's dereliction of
duty, but that might be the extent of their response. They had never
liked Clay, in any case. He made no secret of his contempt for Maureen's
ailments or his exasperated scorn for Wally's perpetual-motion
machines, and these attitudes did not endear him to them. Yet their
lack of affection for Clay was unlikely to translate into sympathy for
herself. She imagined there might even be some gloating on Maureen's
part. Wally would pretend not to understand. *What's that? What's that
you're saying? Just a second. Let me get your mother.* As she reflected on

all this, Hope fingered the streetcar token she'd taken with her after the Christmas visit, wearing it thinner and thinner, or so she imagined. Finally, she called.

Wally answered. "Hopie! It's lucky you called just now! Guess what? I think I've solved the problem. I've changed the number of spokes from six to seven, and I think it's going to work! The odd number unbalances the wheel just enough to keep it moving. I know what Clay means about friction, but I really think I've got it licked this time." He spoke as if last Christmas hadn't happened, as if he hadn't stood on the lawn, backlit by the porch light, one hand moving back and forth, back and forth.

"I can't," Hope whispered. Her chin trembled, and she began to pull the pins from her hair with spasmodic, snatchy movements.

There was a pause. "You can't what?"

"I can't tell Clay."

"Why not?"

"He's gone."

After another pause, Wally asked, "What do you mean, gone?"

Hope told him that Clay had left and was living in his own apartment. "It's temporary," she said. "It will be like a Reserve trip."

"Just a minute," said Wally. "Let me get your mother." He called Maureen, and they talked for a few moments, but Hope couldn't make out what they were saying. She waited a long time before Maureen came on the line.

"Hope, listen, is it another woman?"

"Oh, Mother. Clay?" With her hair down, Hope could look quite girlish.

HER MIND KEPT snagging on the suspicion. She might be sorting dirty clothes or struggling with the lid to the dill pickle jar or reaching into the meat bin at Weingarten's when she would pause, lift her head, and lose herself in the possibilities. One possibility was the receptionist who had quit without notice several months ago. What was her name? Jennifer? Yes, Jennifer, that was it. Or Polly, the widow who lived down the street and often called upon Clay to help her move furniture or advise her on lawn care. And, of course, there was Jan, the flirtatious wife of Clay's commanding officer in the Reserve. The possibilities proliferated as Hope stood arrested in the midst of some routine, head tilted, eyes unfocused, until someone bumped into her, or one of the children demanded her attention, or the phone rang.

One night she tilted her head in just that way, as she was about to put a record on the turntable. This time, however, not a name but an image rose from the void: two people, a man and a woman, perched on the only two adult-sized chairs in the building.

Leaving the turntable silently spinning, she went into the hallway to take the phone book from its niche. Sinking to the floor, she propped herself up against the wall and turned its tissue pages. As a child, she'd had a recurring dream of book pages so thin they evaporated from her fingers, and she half expected this to happen, but, no, they remained palpable, whispering maliciously, until she reached the Es. Backtracking a page, she ran a finger down the left-hand column and found the number she was looking for. A sudden lapse in substance made the effort to stand, or at least rise to her knees, altogether beyond her. She reached up to grasp the cord, pulled, and the phone crashed to the floor in a medley of bells. She set it upright again and dialed Mindy Eck's number.

"Hello?" The voice immediately evoked the doe eyes behind the tortoiseshell glasses. A hand reached in to squeeze the breath out of Hope's lungs, and she had difficulty speaking. "Is . . . is . . . is . . . Clay there?"

"I'm sorry, but you have the wrong number."

"This is an emergency."

There was a pause before the receiver clanked down on a table or a countertop, some hard surface. Hope heard a murmur of voices, footsteps. Or was she inventing all this?

"Hello . . . Hello? . . . Hello! . . . For crissakes, who the hell is this, anyway? Hello!"

Hope set the receiver back into its cradle without a sound. She sat motionless, suspended on the hum of her body, her hand still resting on the phone, as if what she had just heard was irrelevant, and when the phone rang a moment later, she heard its jangle and felt the vibration travel up her arm, but she failed to connect these sensations to the notion of communication. The phone rang eight, twelve, fifteen times, and she did not stir.

"Mom?" Amber had come out from her bedroom blinking into the light and advanced down the hall, as the phone continued to ring. But when she reached for it, Hope stayed her hand. "I'm afraid it's for me, honey."

"Hope? Hope? That was you, wasn't it? I know it was. An emergency! What a lousy trick. There is no emergency, is there? *Is there?*" The line fizzled faintly. "I didn't think so. It was just a lousy trick. Jesus, you scared me. I thought something had happened to the kids. I was *going* to tell you. If you had only *waited*."

Amber crouched beside her, and Hope spoke slowly, as she looked into Amber's frightened face. "It's all right . . . everything's all right."

" 'Everything's all right!' " repeated Clay. " 'Everything's all right!' I could have predicted that line."

Catching up the bottom ruffle of her polka-dotted nightgown, Amber wiped Hope's cheeks, as Clay imitated Hope's voice, making a sour whine of it. " 'Everything's all right.' You know what you remind me of, Hope? One of those inflatable clowns you punch, that bounce back up with the same stupid smile. 'Everything's all right.' "

THE NEXT MORNING, after seeing Amber off to school and arranging with a neighbor to watch Patrick, Hope walked out into the backyard, her grandmother's quilt under one arm, the dew turning her buff-colored huaraches a deep brown and darkening the hem of her pink chenille bathrobe. It was another mild day, the sky an enchanted landscape of Houston's famous cumulus clouds, signs of unstable air masses, Clay had explained to her once, countering her enraptured response with scientific fact.

Stopping in the middle of the yard, she lifted the metal ring of a trapdoor, barely visible in the grass, as in a fairy tale, to the bomb shelter. She descended the metal stairway to a narrow galley. Four cots dropped from the wall on heavy chains, and at one end of the shelter, behind a white curtain on a stainless-steel armature, were the shadowy shapes of a sink and toilet. Shelves intended for food supplies now held their husks—emptied boxes and cans the children used to play "house" and "store"—and a few board games—Clue, Mousetrap, Candyland.

Wrapping herself in the quilt, Hope lay down. Her body felt spartan to her, reduced. She had the sense of being not under the earth but in it, the earth a hollow ball, hurtling through the universe, herself its lone passenger.

She had in mind to sleep. She'd lain awake all night, a corrosive verdict of undesirability settling on her like mildew, exuding the musty odor of disuse. Her mind had teemed with images of coupling bodies: Clay's buttocks pumping between Mindy's thighs; Mindy triumphantly riding Clay; the two of them entwined side by side, chewing on one another's bodies. Here, away from the marital bed, in a space with dimensions narrow enough to suit the discarded, perhaps sleep would come.

Adultery. The first time she'd come upon that word, she'd thought it meant the state of being an adult.

She recalled the last time she and Clay had made love, only a few weeks ago. Perhaps he had made love to Mindy the night before. "This body, this body," he had whispered, eyes closed. "How I love this body." Whose body?

Wrapped in the quilt, her moist skin grayish, Hope looked larval as she lay there alternating between the two miseries of abandonment and betrayal, her cot an island, she its Ariadne—used, forsaken, duped. Clay had lied to her. When? How often?

Being lied to made you a little crazy. What you thought was, wasn't. Certain memories would have to be rearranged. Certain memories would need to have a thick black line drawn through them. That could take the rest of her life.

Her mind leafed back through memory to rest on two teenage lovers fumbling beneath the fall foliage of Brown County State Park, a rough, olive-colored army blanket beneath them. She could not recall this without the soft focus of romance. What had she really felt aside from hope? Attraction, she decided. Appetite. Curiosity. The unexpected arousal of the soles of her feet had surprised her, the sharp sensation in her nose, so improbably like the gathering of tears.

An immense urge to be another person rose up in her, to be let loose, to unfasten herself from what held her. She would have liked to disappear, like William, without a trace. Without a strand of hair, a chip of bone, a drop of blood.

William. Come misery, he had always been available, if taciturn. He was always waiting for her when she returned from running away. He sat with her on the wooden swing in the backyard when she went there to escape Maureen's flying missiles. Later, when she got her driving license, she would take him with her on long, silent rides at perilous speeds.

Hours passed. It was surprising how quickly.

When she heard the trapdoor open, releasing a sudden shaft of sunlight and a freshet of mimosa-scented air, she turned her head to watch feet descend the ladder. As the ventilation fan switched on, two figures came into view.

"Hope, for crissakes, what do you think you're—"

Hope flew from the cot, trailing the quilt, which fell away as she reached Clay and began to thresh his body with her fists. He turned his back, hunching over slightly, his breath escaping in short grunts. An eerie descant hovered above the savage breathing: Chloe's moan.

CHLOE SAID SHE would always regret calling Clay. "I panicked when Calhoun phoned to say you hadn't picked up the girls," she told Hope later. "It was so unlike you. I called and called, but there was no answer, so I drove to your house to check. Everything was so *quiet*. I knocked and no answer. I circled the house, looked in all the windows. No sign of you. All the doors were locked. The car was in the garage, so I figured you hadn't gone anywhere. I got scared. . . . "

Hope, twisting the phone cord into a mass of knotted shapes, only half listened. Chloe had already told her this. She'd been afraid Hope had committed suicide. Suicide! She couldn't possibly have managed it, couldn't possibly have figured out a lethal dosage or negotiated the purchase of a weapon.

"I went by her house last night," Hope interrupted.

"What?"

"I hired a baby-sitter and went by her house last night."

"Whose?"

"She uses hair spray. AquaNet. Isn't that bad for your lungs? Her lung capacity is not as great as mine. I happen to know that."

"Oh, Hope."

Prowling the periphery of the house, carefully avoiding fragile plants and keeping as much as possible on the grass so as not to leave footprints,

Hope had passed from window to window. One of them looked in on Mindy's bedroom, where Hope had spied the can of hair spray on the bureau alongside a familiar bottle of AquaVelva. AquaNet, AquaVelva. Cute.

A few minutes later, wedged between two boxwood hedges, she had looked through another window. Clay and Mindy were watching television, sitting on a couch, holding hands, looking so young, so like college kids, Hope felt robbed of her own youth. Their faces wore the semiblank look television induces, yet Hope saw there a normality in judicious contrast to her own aberrant conduct out there in the boxwood.

"Hope, I'm worried about you. I think you need to see someone."

"What kind of someone?"

"I think professional help is in order."

"You mean a psychiatrist?"

"Well, some kind of therapist. Maybe Alex could recommend—"

"Okay, but let me ask you just one thing. If you were having an affair, would you watch *television*?"

"Oh, Hope, this is what I mean. You're going round and round. If you could talk to a professional, someone detached—" Chloe broke off. "Did you hear that? Did you hear that click?"

Chloe was convinced that her phone was being tapped. Reports from the Houston police on Fletcher's antiwar activities, accompanied by eight-by-ten glossies of crowds with Fletcher's head circled, had been arriving with some regularity on the desk of Fletcher's department chairman. Hope couldn't believe the FBI or the police were interested enough in Fletcher to tap his phone. She wondered if Chloe's fears weren't a way to exaggerate his importance.

Nevertheless, just now she saw in her mind's eye a short, fat policeman wearing earphones in some basement, drinking coffee from a Styrofoam cup and listening to her story. He is bored with her misery, bored with her melodrama. He clicks off the listening device, gets up, stretches. He goes out for a breath of fresh air.

ALEX'S OFFICE WAS in what had been the administrative wing of the church when the Church of Christ congregation had occupied it. The Unitarians having little to administer, three of the offices were now used as storerooms for chairs, sound equipment, carpet samples, and so on, while the fourth belonged to Alex. It, too, looked like a storeroom. Books, pamphlets, and newspapers had migrated from the jumbled shelves to his desk, a couple of side tables, an old gray sofa leaking its stuffing, and even the floor. Drawers of a file cabinet stood ajar.

Alex dragged a scarred oak swivel chair from behind his desk, dropped into it, and threw one leg over the arm. The fringe along the top of his knee-high moccasins shimmied for a moment, then stilled. "I'm not surprised," he said. "But I thought it would be you."

Hope had cleared a space for herself on the gray sofa, where she sat, knees pressed together, hands folded in her lap. "Me? I would never have an affair."

"Oh, I think you would."

Hope didn't know whether to be offended or flattered. "Chloe's afraid I'm going off the deep end."

"That woman needs uncorking."

Alex and Chloe did not enjoy mutual respect. Chloe considered Alex an opportunist, and Alex thought Chloe repressed. At bottom they had fundamentally different approaches to life. Alex believed in change. Chloe believed in remedy.

Alex raised his arms and, lacing his fingers behind his head, leaned back. "Anyway, what's wrong with the deep end?"

His question confounded her, as his questions usually did, and she said nothing, pocketing this one for later examination.

"It's time to move beyond the shallows, Hope."

She looked out the window, where Amber and Rachel were among a group playing a game involving a noxious touch. "Chloe thought it would help if I talked to someone detached."

"Someone detached would be someone dead."

"Well, I think what she meant was—"

"I know what she meant. But there's no such thing as a detached observer. Do you *want* to talk?"

"I guess that's what I'm here for."

"Well then?"

Alex turned out to be a good listener, relaxed and thoughtful. At Esalen, he had been considered a natural therapist, and with dedication and training, he might have become a great one. Many people had thought that. He had a rare empathy, and when he chose to surrender himself to it, he shed his whole personality. Gone were the strident gestures of the evangel, the assumed mantle of the guru, in their place a compassionately reflective surface.

It was no small talent. He said little, almost nothing, as Hope talked, yet she felt Alex saw through the tangle of her life to recognize a woman more valuable than circumstances might indicate, more competent, more resourceful, more attractive. She talked for over half an hour. Hope had never spoken uninterruptedly before; she was not used to monologue. But as she talked, she felt recognized and understood. And if to be understood is, in a sense, to be loved, it was perhaps not surprising that even as she talked of Clay's betrayal, of her own jealousy and inertia, her gestures became more animated and smoothly joined, her voice steady. When she finished, she settled back into the damaged upholstery of the couch feeling at ease.

"What is it you want, Hope?" Alex asked softly.

"I don't know."

"We are what we want."

She wished he hadn't said that. She didn't want to be embarrassed by the paltriness of her desires. "If we want nothing, does that mean we *are* nothing?" she asked.

"Everyone wants. From the very first breath. Desire is our first impulse." After a long silence, he added, "The second is fear." The irises of his eyes were so dark as to be indistinguishable from his pupils, so that each eye was like a camera's open aperture. Hope felt exposed. At last.

"Do you want Clay back?" he asked.

"No." The word sprang up, a grinning, long-nosed jack-in-the-box. "No," she repeated, testing the word for truthfulness. Windows in her head opened up, and a breeze swept through. "No."

7

Ty's Steak House served aged beef, baked potatoes or french fries, and salad with a choice of dressing. Big, heavy chairs with leather seats and padded arms sat at right angles to equally weighty tables of dark wood. The red carpet was thick and spongy. Ty's wouldn't have been Hope's first choice, but she was here on Clay's invitation. He had said he wanted to talk to her. She supposed he wanted a divorce.

She had never been to Ty's before, so she was surprised when the two waitresses at the condiment table waved and called Clay by name. A faint nausea wafted up from her stomach to collect in her throat. It occurred to her that he might be accustomed to bringing Mindy here.

"I guess you've been here before," she said.

"Squadron dinners," he explained, adding, "Not that many."

Their menus, which were a good two feet tall, listed a half-dozen different cuts of beef. Hope decided on the Ladies' Filet (nine ounces instead of twelve), medium rare, and Clay ordered a sirloin, well done.

"I don't know whether it would be better to talk about this before or after dinner," Clay said, as the waitress left, menus tucked under her arm.

"Is it about a divorce?" asked Hope, proud of herself for being the first to say the word.

Her response cheered Clay. "Yes, as a matter of fact, it is. I think we need to file. The whole business takes a while. We need to work out a settlement, and then there's the six-month waiting period. My lawyer thinks it might be best . . . he thinks maybe you would like to be the one to file. You could cite irreconcilable differences."

Hope was taken off-guard. "Your lawyer? When did you see a lawyer?"

"A while ago."

The waitress brought their salads, and Hope waited until she had left to ask, "How long ago?"

"Does it matter when?"

"Yes. Yes, I think it does."

"Why?"

"I might need to revise." Hope's ears were full of a strange sound, like a hammering under water. She swallowed, but the sound persisted.

"What do you mean?"

"Well, like say last December 12th, just to pick a date, say it's December 12th, and you come home from work looking . . . dimmed, and I ask you: Bad day at the office? And you say yes, and I'm thinking: Poor guy, bad day at the office. But maybe that was the day you'd been to see the lawyer. That's just one example of what might need to be revised. In the light of more recent information." Clay didn't say anything, and Hope shook out her napkin and spread it neatly across her thighs. "So by Christmas you were already considering a divorce, unknown to me."

"I didn't say that."

"I was on trial, so to speak, although I didn't know it."

"I wouldn't put it that way. Look. Can I tell you what I came here to say? What the lawyer and I talked about?"

But Hope wasn't listening. Her heart was beating fast, and there was something she had to know. "Remember Christmas Day? Remember how just before dinner you were on the phone in the hall, and you said you were talking to your mother? You were really talking to Mindy, weren't you?" She watched as Clay's expression laced up. She had the sensation of sinking, sinking down through the floor to the basement, and down through the basement to the earth, and down through the earth to its hot center. "You lied," she whispered.

"I didn't—"

"You did."

"I didn't want to spoil your Christmas."

"You lied."

"It's not a lie when you're trying to protect someone's feelings," Clay said.

"It isn't?" Her voice began to wobble. "The thing is, I wouldn't have made love with you that night if I'd known you'd been talking to Mindy, if I'd known you'd already seen a lawyer."

"Hope, I didn't say—"

"There are lots of things I wouldn't have done, if I'd *known*. I wouldn't have toasted the New Year, for example, the brave, new decade." She began to pick at the napkin in her lap, plucking it up to make tiny, starched peaks here and there.

"Look! I'm giving you everything!" he blurted out, half standing up, rattling the silver. Hope drew back, frightened. She was always expecting him to throw something at her, although he never had. He sat down again. "That's what I came here to tell you," he said more quietly. "I didn't come here for all this . . . this hairsplitting. I'm giving you *everything*—the house, the furniture, the . . . the Cadillac . . ." He chopped the palm of one hand with the stiff fingers of the other as he enumerated his concessions. "Everything. Everything I've ever *worked* for. Everything I *dreamed* of having. I just want out, Hope. I just want a chance to start over."

Neither of them spoke as the waitress arrived with their steaks. Noting the tension, she set the plates down soundlessly, pushing Hope's untouched salad to one side and taking Clay's empty plate. She floated away, unacknowledged.

"Do we have to eat these?" Hope asked, staring at her filet.

"We have to pay for them."

"I know we have to pay for them. But do we have to eat them? I don't think I can eat mine."

"Well, if you don't mind, I'm going to eat mine." He picked up his fork and steak knife, and she watched as he made a neat incision into his sirloin and transferred a well-done chunk to his mouth. "Maybe we should have talked about this *after* dinner," he said when he had chewed and swallowed.

"It's better this way. This way I don't have anything to throw up."

"Hope, please, I'm eating."

She picked up her fork and speared a French fry, trundling it about her plate for a moment before setting down her fork again. "A divorce! I still can't believe it. I don't know what do to!"

"Get a lawyer. That's the first thing." He reached across the table and cut himself a piece of her steak. He ate it, then signaled the waitress, who hurried over.

"My wife's steak is too well-done," he told her. "She ordered medium-rare."

"Oh! I'm sorry, sir. I'll bring another—"

"Don't bother," he said. "Just bring the check."

When the waitress was out of earshot, Hope spoke in a low voice. "There was nothing wrong with my steak, Clay." He continued to eat, head lowered. "If they charge us for my steak, I'm paying for it, okay? I can't handle one of your scenes." He made no reply.

The waitress returned with an effusive apology from the cook and their check. Clay studied it for a moment, nodded, and reached into his back pocket for his wallet, extracting a twenty-dollar bill. By the time she returned with his change, he had finished eating. Hope preceded him out of the restaurant, walking a good ten feet ahead. Perhaps she could start over, too.

When Hope arrived at attorney Benjamin Jamison's door three days later, at what she thought was attorney Benjamin Jamison's door, she was stymied by the nameplate: Dr. Reginald B. Savage. She pulled an old envelope from her purse and read the office number written on the back: 7215. She looked at the number on the door: 7215. She looked around for someone to ask, but the hallway was deserted. Nothing moved or made a sound; even the lights above the elevators failed to show any activity. Hope, already distraught, was susceptible to creepy perceptions, and the uniform lineup of doors, parched of color by unforgiving fluorescent lights, seemed suddenly a facade charged with malevolence. Spotting an exit sign at the far end of the hallway, she ignored a placard advising her that these were emergency stairs only, opened the door, and clattered down the seven flights. At the bottom, she leaned against the release bar of a metal door, stumbling out into a landscaped niche of spiky white chrysanthemums and blue plumbago.

"Can I help you, ma'am?" A security guard had just come around the corner, and Hope wondered if she had set off an alarm.

"Yes, you can." She explained the wrong name on the door.

"It's not the wrong name," he said. "You're in the wrong building. We have two buildings"—he pointed to an identical building across the parking lot—" and you're at the wrong one. This here is Twin Tower I. You want Twin Tower II. Lots of people make this mistake."

"I guess lots of people are late for their appointments then."

"Most people allow extra time."

She did not believe him but was in too much of a hurry to argue.

A few minutes later she was being ushered into Mr. Jamison's office by Mr. Jamison himself, his receptionist having gone home. He was a pudgy man of forty or so with a round face and glasses that magnified his eyes to look like those of a fish. Dark, frizzled hair frothed from his head, divided asymmetrically by a left part. The more abundant side looked like a wave about to break.

Ben Jamison had been Calhoun's divorce lawyer. "He seemed like a good enough guy," Calhoun had told her. "I had no complaints."

Hope apologized for being late. "I was in the wrong twin."

"You figured it out, though," he said.

"I didn't really. A security guard rescued me."

"Well, you're here now. Shall we?" He waved an arm toward his office.

Mostly straight lines met her eye; his office was sternly furnished. A long table extended against one wall, a square cabinet was pushed up against the other, and a polished, rectangular desk faced two Eames chairs. Two paintings hung on opposite walls, geometric abstracts in cool colors.

Jamison uncapped a fountain pen and straightened the yellow legal pad in front of him. "Shall we begin? Let's start with the assets."

"My husband is giving me everything."

Jamison raised his eyebrows. "Everything?"

"The house, the car."

He asked her for the make and model of the car and a description of their house, and then followed up with several questions Hope couldn't answer. How much did they owe on the mortgage? On the car? What secured the loans?

"I don't know," Hope repeated to each query.

"That's okay. I can find out. Any other assets? Stocks? Vacation home?"

Hope remembered the lot in Kemah. She and Clay had put a down payment on it a couple of years ago, a small waterfront property on which they had hoped to build a cabin someday. It was not a typical waterfront property—Kemah was not Clear Lake—but instead had evidently once been part of a farm. You had to travel down a dirt road to reach it.

"Is it paid for?" asked Jamison.

"I'm not sure. I don't think so."

He nodded, writing, and asked another question. "What is your husband's annual salary?"

"I don't know."

"Just roughly."

"I have no idea really."

He looked up and raised his eyebrows again. "Well, we can find that out, too," he said. "He'll be basing his child-support payments on his salary. Texas has no alimony law," he added.

"That's okay. I'm planning to get a job."

"Doing what?"

"Market research. For Triple Bar X Sausage. I have an interview on Thursday." Fern had helped Hope arrange this, saying Triple Bar X Sausage always needed new people.

"Good," he said, giving her an encouraging smile. He then asked for the name and number of Clay's lawyer, and she gave him the card Clay had left with her: William Stittson III, Esq., Attorney at Law. He glanced at it.

"Do you know him?" Hope asked.

"Oh, yes."

Hope waited for him to go on, but he stood up and, extending a hand, said he would be in touch.

"It was all kind of impersonal," Hope told Calhoun later. "He didn't seem too involved."

"You don't need William Kunstler, Hope."

"Well, no. I just thought this guy would be, I don't know, more friendly."

"They're technicians. Lawyers, doctors, they're all technicians, like auto mechanics. You don't need friendly, you just need someone who knows what he's doing."

"Does he?"

"What?"

"Know what he's doing?"

"As far as I know."

IT RAINED ON Thursday. Hope peered through her streaming windshield and prayed she would not miss the downtown exit. She was afraid to use the windshield wipers, because the wiper on the driver's side, now bandaged in a rag, had lost its rubber blade several weeks ago, and if the rag were to come loose, the bare blade might scratch the windshield. She compensated for her impaired vision by driving very slowly.

The wiper blades were not the only signs of neglect; the Cadillac also lurched and chugged occasionally, badly in need of a tune-up. Under Hope's stewardship, the Cadillac was rapidly yielding up its luxury status. Spilled juice stained the upholstery, splotches of jam had dried on the doors, and drawings cluttered the seats. Magic Markers lay scattered on the floor; books and toys crowded the shelf beneath the back window. The litter on the dashboard included torn envelopes, browned apple cores, a ragged map of Houston, a pair of sunglasses missing one lens, and a bubble pipe. Hope planned a major restoration soon, but not now. She had too much on her mind.

She parked at the Ten-Ten Garage so that she could take the tunnels to the Triple Bar X offices and avoid the rain. Built to shield the servants of commerce from the extremes of Houston weather, the tunnels did not disturb with graffiti or damp drafts; they were air-conditioned and brightly lit, even carpeted in places, according to the taste and budget of the corporate sponsor. Yet there was an uncanny atmosphere here beneath the streets. The fluorescent lights tinged faces a faint lavender; the tiled walls gleamed in a way that seemed leering.

Hope tugged at her suit jacket, which didn't quite fit, its hem meandering irresponsibly about her hips. She had purchased the suit years ago for a classmate's funeral and wore it today to establish herself as a sober employment prospect. Instead, though, she looked orphaned and ill-fated, partly because of the suit's brownish-green color, that of a prematurely unearthed potato, and partly because of the cut, which gave her the appearance of a cello. She looked institutional without that accompanying air of efficiency.

The tunnels were nearly empty this midmorning, the going-to-work crowd now at their desks, and the noon crowd not yet arrived. Hope glanced around uneasily. The last time she had been in the tunnels a midget wearing a dress figured with bright blue elephants had accosted her, demanding to be led to the Esperson Building. Commandeered by the little woman's vehemence, Hope had not only shown her to the proper corridor but accompanied her all the way to the correct entryway.

So when the small figure entered from a side corridor to nearly collide with her, Hope thought at first it was another midget. But then, startled and tottering on her high heels, she saw it was Frederick. He stood there for a moment, transfixed, his eyes locked on hers. Stunted and explosive, he looked to her all that was abandoned and powerful. Glancing down, she saw that his shoes, shiny and pointed, were several sizes too large. She watched them pivot, then raised her eyes to stare at him as he ran back the way he had come.

WHAT SHE WOULD remember afterward was the way his shoes slapped loudly against the floor as he ran. She couldn't remember what else he had worn.

"Didn't he have a sweater or a jacket or something?" asked Calhoun. She couldn't remember.

They were at Prufrock's, a popular bar in the Montrose. Calhoun had offered to teach her to play chess, and they sat at a scarred oak table with a game board between them. Furnished with antique velvet-upholstered sofas, silvery in the worn spots, and overstuffed chairs smelling of tobacco and cats, Prufrock's was clubby without an excessive air of self-satisfaction. Lamps with colored-glass shades cast just enough light over the game boards, and voices were low over the click of chess and backgammon pieces. The sweetish smell of marijuana was not uncommon.

"Are you sure it was him?" Calhoun asked again.

"I'm sure."

He tapped his fingers to "Midnight Rambler" and poured himself more wine from the carafe on the table. "I wonder what he was doing in the tunnels. Why didn't you follow him?"

"I was on my way to a job interview, remember?"

"Oh, right. How'd it go?"

"I got the job."

"Too bad."

"It could be worse."

"Handing out sausage samples at Piggly Wiggly? Are you kidding? Name something worse."

"Starving to death?" Hope tipped her head and put on a doll-like smile.

A cheerful nature was a prerequisite, the woman who had interviewed her had said, peering at Hope over a pair of dime-store half-glasses. "You will be representing Triple Bar X Sausage, and a good personal impression is essential."

"Oh yes. I understand that," Hope had assured her.

"Do you have a car? A car is the other prerequisite."

"I have a Cadillac."

The woman had glanced down at the papers in front of her. "Of course you do," she'd said sympathetically.

"You'll barely make enough to cover Patrick's day care," Calhoun told her.

"I have savings. To tide me over."

"Tide you over till when?"

"Till when things get better."

"Ever the optimist."

"I'm not going to ask Clay for money, if that's what you're going to say."

"There are other options. You could apply for welfare. Well, why not? Don't look at me like that."

"That would be worse than asking Clay for money."

"I doubt it," he muttered. He handed her a chess piece. "This is a rook." Hope traced its crenellated crown, regaining her composure. Welfare! He handed her another piece. "Bishop."

A subdued air of experiment obtained between them as they handed chess pieces back and forth. They had never been together outside the context of the school, had never conducted a conversation that had not had a child or children in general as its subject.

Calhoun explained the moves. "The king moves one square in any direction. The queen moves any number of squares in any direction, so long as it's in a straight line." He explained the knight's jogging maneuver, the bishop's diagonal; he showed her how to castle.

"It's complicated," Hope observed.

"Of course. It's the nature of games to be complicated. It's life that's simple."

"I wouldn't say that."

"You live. You die. What could be simpler? Your move."

Hope lost the game in six moves.

"I don't believe in giving beginners any breaks," Calhoun explained. "It creates false confidence."

"God forbid I should be burdened by false confidence," Hope said, after losing another three games. She contemplated the two fists he held out to her. "Is this supposed to be fun? Is this supposed to be taking my mind off my troubles?"

"We're honing your aggressive instincts." Hope tapped his right fist, and he opened it to show a white pawn. "You know, I can't figure out what Frederick was doing in the tunnels," he said, arranging the black pieces on his side of the board. "He wasn't likely to have been on his way to the Bank of the Southwest."

"Not unless he was planning to rob it."

"Not funny, Hope." He reached over to rearrange her bishop and her knight, which she had set up in the wrong order.

Hope studied the board for a moment, then moved a pawn forward, the same opening move she had made in the last four games. "I read in *Newsweek* that divorce is a growing phenomenon, but no one *I* know is getting a divorce. In fact, you're the only person I know who's divorced. Except Mindy, of course."

Calhoun did not reply. He seemed to be staring at himself in the mirror across the room. Suddenly he snapped his fingers. "Woolworth's maybe. Doesn't one of the tunnels go to Woolworth's? Maybe he was on his way to Woolworth's."

"For a little shoplifting?"

"Your bourgeois attitudes are getting on my nerves, Hope. To say nothing of your self-pity. You're *not* the only one getting a divorce. For example, there's Fern. Hermes didn't even say goodbye."

"They weren't married," Hope pointed out.

"Does that matter?"

"I think so. Didn't it to you?"

"No. Well, maybe. I don't know. I suppose when your marriage fails, certain hopes, certain *illusions*," he corrected, "go down the drain." He looked thoughtful. "A matter of different expectations, I guess. Love affairs end; they don't fail. But Suzanne and I were only married for six months, so I'm not sure we counted as a marriage."

"Didn't she like your carrot persona?"

"She loved my carrot persona. We had fun together—at the wedding and before. It was the after that threw us. Everything changed once we tried to keep a house clean together, once we tried to balance a joint checkbook. She actually started to *look* different to me. She had these bangs." He drew a hand across his brow. "Before the marriage they made her look street-cute. After the marriage, she looked like a Dutch mother." He frowned in an exaggerated show of disapproval and demand.

"Which was the real Suzanne—gamine or Dutch mother?"

"I don't know."

"Were you in love with her?" Hope asked softly.

He thought for a minute. "I guess not."

"Have you ever been in love?" Something furtive passed between them before Hope could catch hold of it.

"Of course."

She heard bravado in this and sensed confusion; she put her hand on his. In the moment it rested there, her heart inflated. But very gently, not quite looking at her, Calhoun slipped his hand from under hers and picked up his wineglass.

"This could be an era in history," he said.

Hope pretended to study the chess pieces, allowing her rapid heartbeat to subside. "Isn't it always one era or another?" she asked, not looking up.

"What I mean is, this divorce stuff might be an evolutionary phase. It could be that our kids will grow up to make better choices because of our screwups."

"If they survive."

"Amber and Patrick seem to be doing fine."

She supposed so. "Lots of people get divorced," she had overheard Amber tell Rachel. "Not just movie stars. Sometimes two people cannot live together even when they like each other. This is not the child's fault. They still love the child." Hope had recognized the tone of a book about divorce for children that Amber and Calhoun had found in the library.

Patrick never talked about the separation, but then he had scant vocabulary for it. And, too, he was more securely ensconced in childhood than Amber. Forgetfulness was his natural element, and the shadow of event did not darken his path for long. He raced his pedal fire engine up and down the sidewalk, as if the world were still flat and friendly.

Yet Hope felt their adjustment to be more apparent than real. "I'm not sure childhood can survive without the shelter of family," she said.

"Of course it can. Look at Huck Finn. Look at Frederick."

Hope was incredulous. "You call what Frederick lives a childhood?"

"Frederick's a free spirit."

It was remarkable, Hope thought, the illusions people could sustain in the face of all evidence. She probably wasn't including herself.

8

At the sound of the pummeling on the door, Hope and Ocie exchanged a look over the heads of the children working their lumps of play-dough. "I'll get it," Hope offered.

The open antagonism of the two policemen standing there stunned her. She had had occasion to think of the Houston police as protectors, back when she and Clay had lived in one of the small pastel pods built for returning World War II veterans off Telephone Road, houses most people would have considered bleak habitat, but in which Hope saw something touching and optimistic.

She hadn't realized they were moving onto one of the most actively criminal streets in Houston. A major burglary operation had been headquartered halfway down the block, and the head of a prostitution ring lived across the street. Once Hope saw a woman being dragged by her hair across the front lawn to a car parked at the curb.

The police had used Hope and Clay's garage as a stakeout to apprehend the king pimp. They sat on Hope's high kitchen stools and peered through dusty garage windows the size of place mats. Patrick had been six months old then; he rode Hope's hip as she served the men coffee and ranger cookies. *Thank you, ma'am. Don't worry, ma'am.*

So the hostility and the clenched fist resting on the gun holster of the shorter of the two surprised her, although she found the tall one more menacing, his lazy smile licking at her edges. She stared at the silver-plated badges pinned to their blue shirts.

"Who're you?" demanded the shorter one.

Hope stammered out her maiden name by mistake, then amended it to her married one, only to worry that maybe she shouldn't have corrected herself, maybe now the policeman would think she was giving a false name.

But he wasn't listening. He'd shifted his gaze to a point behind Hope's right shoulder, and she turned to see Ocie emerging from the art room on the way to the kitchen for more play-dough, an empty bowl in her hands. On seeing the policeman, she stopped, the hem of her muumuu whisking forward, then swirling back to settle into its folds as she stood stock still.

"If it isn't . . ." the short one said softly. "Lookee here, Morley. If it isn't Ocie Ballard."

"I don't believe we've met," she said in a clipped accent Hope hadn't heard before. She sounded like a British peeress.

He chuckled. "No. No, somehow Morley and me been denied that pleasure. But we're faithful readers of the *Forward Times*. Maybe its most faithful readers, wouldn't you say, Morley?" Morley laughed. "We keep abreast," continued his partner. "You look just like your picture, Ocie," he added in a tone of mock awe, as if she were a movie star. "That's not always so, is it, Morley?" Morley shook his head. "Sometimes a newspaper picture will show a person in her much younger days. Sometimes there's a weight discrepancy. But your picture was you to the life!"

"Did you wish to speak to me?"

"We are speakin' at you." Morley's voice was unexpectedly high-pitched. His height and heft led one to expect a baritone.

"I'm in charge here, Morley," said his partner mildly before turning back to Ocie and Hope. "We're always happy to talk to you, Ocie, but we didn't come here for that, no. We didn't know Ocie Ballard was going to be here! If we had, we'da come prepared to discuss the lack of police protection in Sunnyside. I believe that was your complaint to the mayor, wasn't it, Ocie?" He smiled. "The mayor didn't look all that receptive in the photograph, but maybe Morley and I could do something about it on our own. A little volunteer work. What do you think, Morley?"

Morley grinned, and a slight tremor passed beneath Ocie's skin before her expression smoothed. Hope watched, amazed, as Ocie flattened her cheeks and nose, ironing out what made Ocie Ocie. She shifted the bowl to one hip.

"Hello?" Calhoun appeared just behind the two women, having made his way down the hallway from one of the classrooms. Pin curls in crooked rows covered his skull; Ocie's daughter Rae and her friend Eva had been playing beauty shop. Calhoun was their only willing client, and he sometimes spent half a day with his hair in little knobs like this. It took that long for the curls to dry, according to Rae, who could be autocratic about procedures.

Calhoun looked quite ridiculous, but the two policemen did not smile. The shorter of the two pulled out a small notebook. "We're looking for . . ." He squinted. ". . . Abednego Smith. Ne-gro kid. Skinny. Five feet tall or so."

"I don't know anyone by that name," said Calhoun.

"Uh-huh. The people at . . ." He consulted his notebook. ". . . the Happy Buddha seemed to think you might."

Calhoun looked uncomfortable. "What was the name?"

"Abednego Smith."

"No. I really don't know anyone by that name."

"Uh-huh. We're talkin' 'bout theft here, so I hope you're clear on what you might be accessory to, but lemme jus' ask you somethin' else. Where's y'all's fence?"

"Fence?"

"Fence. Schools are supposed to have fences, I think. Ordinance 32947, I think. This is a school, isn't it?" Calhoun didn't answer. The policeman hitched up his belt. "I think you folks have a fence problem. Now that I think about it, now that I give it proper attention," he said peering past them into the hall, "I think I see some fire hazards, too. Don't you see some fire hazards, Morley?"

Morley did, and over the next two weeks, the Blossom Street Free School was visited by representatives from the fire department, the health department, the social services department, and the building code department. The parents learned that if they were cooking lunch for the children, they would need a food service license. A livestock permit would be required for the pet rabbits, too. There were also several

building code infractions. Some could be rectified by the parents themselves, like rehanging the doors to open out rather than in, but others—
the construction of fire exits and an additional bathroom—required
professionals. A parents' meeting was called to decide what to do.

"This is harassment!" exploded Chloe. "I think we should resist. We
can take them to court—"

"The cops were looking for Frederick," Calhoun interrupted. "I just
hope to God they are no more successful than we've been."

The twenty or so parents sitting on the floor in the science room
heard this with the latent judgment of agnostics. Frederick had disappeared, and most of them were relieved, although they wouldn't have
wanted to express this.

In the silence, Hope looked up to see Clay come through the door.
She was surprised to see him. She had stopped informing him of parents'
meetings some weeks ago, since he never came. Tonight he wore a suit;
he must have come directly from work. Moving aside a seed display, he
sat down on the edge of a table on the opposite side of the room from
Hope and, without looking at her, assumed an attitude of forbearance,
inclining one ear toward the group to hearken more closely to the
discussion.

Hope had stopped thinking of herself and Clay as a couple. For a
while she had filled the space where he'd been with enough memories
to give him presence. In some moments, she had even recalled him as
a traveler recalls home, all lamps and warmth. She was uncomfortable
sitting across the room from him, as if they were mere nodding acquain-
tances. But she supposed she would have been just as uncomfortable
sitting alongside him. *How's Mindy? Taken any impulsive trips to Galveston
lately?*

"We have to be realistic," a woman was saying. "No matter how *we*
see Frederick, the law sees him as a criminal, a fugitive. So long as we
harbor him here, we are accessories."

"You're overheating," said Ocie. Everyone turned to look at her.
"We're not accessories. We don't even have to worry about Frederick
unless we want to. He's just this kid who drops in on us when he has
a mind to. Uninvited. Now he's in trouble. Not our fault. Not our
business."

Hope stared at her. Where did this detachment come from? Ocie had spent all of yesterday combing the Fourth Ward for Frederick.

"It would be ironic if the school collapsed under the weight of good intentions," said Fletcher.

Ocie's face settled into contemptuous satisfaction.

"What do you mean?" asked Calhoun.

"Well . . . I think . . . I think we all want to help Frederick. I mean, obviously, here is a child in need, a child damaged by . . . by circumstance . . . and by . . . by history, of course. . . . But I'm not sure we have the . . . the resources . . . to accommodate . . . severe social problems."

Calhoun made a harsh sound that was half bark, half snort. "Typical white liberal shit. When it comes down to the nitty-gritty, it's hand-washing time."

Ocie laughed.

"Fletcher has spent time in *jail* for his beliefs!" Chloe said warningly.

"I think you've been blind to the consequences of having Frederick in our school, Calhoun," said one of the other parents. "*Our* school, I might emphasize."

"As opposed to whose?" Calhoun wanted to know.

"As opposed to yours."

"Look, we're really getting off the point here," interrupted the school's treasurer. "What to do about Frederick is a moot question, since no one knows where he is. Meanwhile, we've got a list of violations to deal with—" She raised a hand against the mutterings that broke out. "So-called violations." She tapped her ledger. "The question before us is: how the hell are we going to pay for these permits and repairs?"

There was some shifting of body weight, as the parents attempted to refocus their attention. Suggestions were made and discarded. The possibility of assessing each parent a certain sum was dismissed as a hardship on some, and the suggestion to increase tuition was voted down on the same grounds.

"We need a benefactor," said Calhoun.

"Oh sure. Shall we advertise for one?" asked the treasurer.

"We could have an open house and invite every progressive in the city," he suggested.

"All two of them," said Chloe.

"Right, we invite Bootsie Randolph and Carrie Whitehouse," he said, naming two women well known as liberal philanthropists, "and then a bunch of other people to keep them company. We'll have the kids' art and science projects and stuff on display, and maybe some live activities, like the AfterMath group or the Armadillo Rhythm Band."

Someone suggested they set a date for an open house, a committee was formed, and the meeting broke up around midnight amid complaints that the next day was a workday and baby-sitters still had to be got home.

Clay had not spoken a word throughout the meeting, but one did not have to know him as well as Hope did to see he was angry. She caught up with him outside.

"I want Amber out of here, Hope. I want her back in public school." He spoke without looking at her or slowing his pace. She had to half-trot to keep up with him.

"That's a rather hasty decision, isn't it?"

"Not really."

Not really. How she hated that tone.

They had reached the Cadillac, parked under the mercury beam of a streetlight. Its harsh flare drew the color from their faces; they blinked at one another like animals disturbed in their burrows. Across the street, Fern's van pulled out, one of her bumper stickers briefly illuminated by the streetlight: I BRAKE FOR HALLUCINATIONS.

"That's the kind of thing!" Clay burst out, shaking a finger after Fern's van. "That's the kind of thing! I won't have my daughter associating with criminals and drug addicts and a teacher with the morals of a sewer rat!" His invective took her breath away. Pivoting on his heel, he opened the Cadillac's door and got into the front seat. It took him a moment to realize he was in the wrong car.

Hope grasped the top of the open door. "You can't just *command*, Clay. We can discuss this, but you can't just *command*. You're no longer the lord of the manor."

He got out of the car and glared at her. "I never was." He spoke so bitterly, she realized he spoke the truth as he saw it.

9

T HERE WAS A PECULIAR ALIENATION IN ENTERING SAFEWAY OR
Kroger's or Weingarten's not as a customer or an employee,
but as a supplicant. That's how Hope thought of herself as she set up
her card table near the meat counter, smartly snapping out the legs in
an attempt to infect herself with purpose. After three weeks of this, she
still felt extraneous to the business of buying and selling food, she felt
herself a nuisance, and a ridiculous nuisance at that, dressed in phony
hoedown clothes and wearing this dumb straw hat.

I just want to start over, Hope.

Don't we all. Hope slapped down a sheaf of pink questionnaires on
a front corner of the card table. Try *starting over* when you have two
children. You don't slam into *reverse gear* with kids on board.

She jammed the plug of her electric frypan into a nearby socket,
filled the pan with sausage balls made the night before, and began to
shake it back and forth. She was not earning enough money. That
was clear. She would make the house payment this month, she would
be able to buy food and pay for Patrick's day care, but she would have
to use the savings account to pay bills. She didn't know what she
would do next month, when the Cadillac's insurance came due. Thank
God for Calhoun. He had made Amber a scholarship student, more
to foil Clay's attempts to enroll her in public school than from generosity, but still.

"When are you going on welfare?" Calhoun had asked, looking at her checkbook. He'd been showing her how to balance it.

"That's a joke, right?"

"You could talk to your husband, of course."

Hope hesitated. "I already have."

"And?"

"I didn't get very far."

Hope had called Clay after Ben Jamison explained to her that Clay's proposed child-support payments were unusually low. When she mentioned this to Clay on the phone, he exploded.

"Jesus Christ, Hope, I'm already giving you everything! Ten years of me working my ass off and you get the whole shebang, *including* the kids. Here I am at ground zero, in a crummy little apartment, for crissakes, eating beans on a board over two sawhorses, while you're sitting pretty at the solid-maple dining suite we bought at Ethan Allan, and you want more! What more could you possibly want? You've got every convenience, a washing machine, a dryer—"

"It's not for me, Clay, it's for Amber and Patrick."

"Uh-uh, don't give me that. It's your name that goes on the check, Hope. For all I know, you're out buying . . . who knows what . . . knick-nacks."

"I've *never* bought knickknacks! I've never had the least yen for *knick-knacks*! I *despise* knickknacks, especially if they're anything like your mother's collection of—"

"You're getting hysterical, Hope. Listen. Let's take stock here. You're getting the house, right? You're getting the car, right? You're getting the savings account—"

"It's not that much, Clay—"

"You're getting the savings account," he continued, raising his voice, "*and* the kids. Don't forget that. You're getting the kids. And I'll tell you something, Hope. It really gripes me to hand over that money, because, frankly, I think I could do a better job with it."

Suddenly, Hope wanted to end this conversation.

"Did your lawyer tell you to call me?" he asked.

"Well, as I said, he thought the payments were a little low—"

"See, that's the trouble getting lawyers involved. They're a greedy breed. They make things confrontational when they don't need to be."

He lowered his voice. "I think we can work things out ourselves, Hope, don't you? We've been working things out for ten years, right? What about a better-paying job? Have you tried that?"

"No."

"Well, for crissakes!"

"If I were you," Calhoun told Hope now, "I'd leave the negotiating to your lawyer."

"Well, that seems so . . . I don't know . . . like some kind of cop-out. I mean, this is between Clay and me, and lawyers just seem to complicate things."

"Maybe it's just that things are, in fact, complicated."

"Oh, that's interesting, coming from you, leading proponent of the 'life is simple' philosophy."

"We're talking about business, not life. Your lawyer to his lawyer; that's the way these things are supposed to work."

"Things never work the way they're supposed to work," grumbled Hope. Nevertheless, she did call Jamison the next day. He was in court, his receptionist said; would Hope like him to call back? Hope said she would, but when three days went by and he didn't, she dropped the matter. By then, she had decided to make her own damn money.

At that point, two sausage balls jumped ship—she had been shaking the frypan more violently than she realized—grazing her left hand. She rubbed away the grease, turned off the heat, and transferred the sausage balls to a paper plate. After fussing with the toothpicks and paper napkins, she forced herself to look around for prospects. Shoppers were sparse this morning. It was a Tuesday, the day before the specials came out in the newspaper.

Catching sight of a short, blond woman in denim culottes, Hope shrank back, thinking she recognized a neighbor. She dreaded facing someone she knew. *What am I doing here? Oh, just a little market research to keep me off the streets.*

The woman glanced her way, and Hope exhaled. This woman was stouter than her neighbor and had an interesting scar along one cheek. Hope mustered a smile. A cheerful nature was a prerequisite. "Excuse me, would you care to try . . ."

The woman hurried past without looking at her. People usually did. Those that stopped did so out of pity, Hope was sure. She was rarely successful in getting them to extend their goodwill long enough to fill out a questionnaire. Most days her quota remained unfilled.

When, later that morning, a familiar face did appear, Hope was glad to see that it did not belong to a neighbor but to Fern. Relief in the form of silliness prompted her to step forward and say, "Excuse me, ma'am, would you like to try a sample of the most delectable sausage ever to touch taste buds?"

"Oh my, I'd be delighted!" exclaimed Fern, grasping a toothpick with little finger extended. She chewed and swallowed. "Mmmm-mmmm!"

Hope offered the plate to Adam, who had been following his mother at a distance. He declined, extending his tongue toward his chin and gagging.

"We're playing hooky," Fern said. She gave Hope a close look. "You're shivering."

"It's always cold by the meats," Hope said. "I forgot my sweater."

"Oh, I've got one in the car! I'll get it for you."

"Oh no, that's okay, I . . ."

But Fern was already gone in a tinkle of the bells that were sewn to the hem of her patterned Indian skirt, and Hope was left with Adam, who gave her a sulky look.

Adam had reached the age of disproportion that afflicts boys with genes for height, when arms and legs grow with the rapidity of tropical vines from stubby trunks. The disparity engaged Hope's sympathy, while the cunning pooled in his eyes did not. Something about Adam made Hope think of traps, but whether he called up malevolent urchins setting them or animals caught in them she wasn't sure.

"How come you're not in school today?" she asked.

"I hate school." He raised two fists and shot out one leg in a karate kick.

Disconcerted, Hope turned back to her frying pan, and Adam wandered to the far end of the meat counter.

Fern returned clutching a black cardigan with embedded bugle beads in swirly shapes along the front. "Outa sight, isn't it? I got it at this primo secondhand shop."

Hope put it on. "My mother had a sweater something like this. She used to wear it every New Year's Eve to the Elks Club."

Fern laughed. "I know what you're saying. I'm from Port Arthur."

Hope looked puzzled. "Janis Joplin? Me and Bobby McGee?" Fern aimed her chin at a pyramid of soup cans. " *Freedom's just another word, for nothin' left to lose,* " she sang, with a frayed and urgent pathos very like Joplin's. A woman in a turquoise pantsuit replaced a can of clam chowder she'd been about to put into her cart and hurriedly moved on. Hope looked after her, nervously wondering if she was about to complain to the manager.

Catching sight of Adam, who was poking holes in the stretched plastic of the meat packages, Fern broke off to run over to him and yank his hand out of the meat bin.

"Adam! You little shithead. What are you doing?"

"Go fuck a duck," Adam suggested.

"He's sick today," Fern explained to Hope. "That's why he's not in school." Adam gave Hope a supple smile. "Here," said Fern, plunging a hand into the leather pouch hanging from her shoulder and handing Adam a dollar. "Buy yourself a snack. Something healthy!" she called after him. "Juice or something!"

Turning back to Hope, she speared another sausage ball with a toothpick and pointed it at the beaded sweater. "Fifty cents. I got it at Embers. Have you been there yet? It's new." Hope shook her head. "You should go. It's a trip. Cheap chic."

"Just cheap would be good enough right now," said Hope.

Fern looked around at the nearly empty aisles. "When do you finish here? I could take you there today."

Hope pointed to the stack of pink questionnaires. "I have another fifteen of those damned things to get filled out."

"Hey, no problem." Fern took one from the stack and wet the tip of a pencil on her tongue. "Putrid," she wrote as Hope looked over her shoulder. "Tastes like canned gangrene."

A giddiness seized Hope, a recklessness. "Noxious," she dictated, as Fern reached for another questionnaire. "Wouldn't feed it to my dog."

Fern wrote this down and took another questionnaire. She looked inquiringly at Hope, pencil poised.

"Pustulant."

"Is that a word?"

"Who cares?" Hope cried gaily.

*   *   *

THEY LEFT FERN's van in the parking lot and drove to Patrick's day-care center in the Cadillac. "This car was not my idea," Hope apologized.

Fern fingered the automatic window button. "Don't knock it. If John Lennon can drive to the revolution in a Rolls-Royce, we can pick up our secondhand clothes in a Cadillac." She beamed as the window began to buzz up and down at her touch.

"That's nothing! Watch this." Hope depressed the button that retracted the antenna.

"Far fuckin' out!"

Fern and Adam waited in the car while Hope went to fetch Patrick. From all appearances, Patrick was adjusting quite well to the day-care center. The same could not be said for Hope, although the distress she felt on leaving him ebbed a little each week. On the first morning she'd clung to the wall outside his classroom like a wet leaf, fully aware of her absurdity, as tears dripped from her eyes. Because what else but relinquishment was fated? They're born, they go. What indefensible hopes had been under cultivation to be so easily undone by this suggestion of the inevitable? That had been the embarrassing part.

Today he was reluctant to leave with her, convinced that tadpoles were about to hatch from the gelatinous ribbon of frog eggs floating in a half-filled aquarium. "You're early," he accused.

"Patrick, there's no way of knowing when those eggs will hatch. It could be tonight; it could be tomorrow morning. It's unlikely they're going to hatch in the next minute or two."

"They might."

Her voice turned conciliatory. "True, they might. What say we wait two minutes, and then if they haven't hatched, we leave."

"Five minutes," he said, and she gave in.

Five minutes later, the eggs had still not hatched, but he conceded with dignity and accompanied her to the door, the only remnant of resistance the sound of his sneakers squeaking against the floor. At the car, though, he gave her an apprehensive look on seeing Adam in the backseat, eating his way through a jumbo bar of cooking chocolate. Adam continued to chew without a glance in their direction, as Hope introduced them, and she had to give Patrick a boost into the backseat.

* * *

EMBERS WAS NOT at all what Hope had expected. She'd had in mind the shabby, makeshift atmosphere of a Goodwill store, a St. Vincent de Paul's. But Embers, housed in a small stucco bungalow, was staged; it had intent. The walls were studded with blown-up photographs of entertainers from past eras—Eddie Cantor, Mae West, Rudy Vallee—and big-band music emerged from two speakers in opposite corners of the ceiling. A soft sculpture of a fat woman, looking oddly lifelike in spite of long false eyelashes that were her only facial feature, guarded the doorway. She sat in a beanbag chair with one loopy leg crossed over the other, a shellacked armadillo in her lap, wearing plastic pop beads and a Japanese kimono artfully draped to slip off one wadded shoulder.

Mirrors lined the back wall, reflecting the racks of clothing. A glass display case held old jewelry, and there were several shelves of memorabilia: tin cracker boxes, Kewpie dolls, government pamphlets on canning and raising poultry.

"Don't neglect the men's clothing," advised Fern, going over to the racks along one wall and slipping on a green jacquard vest. "Or the children's." Still wearing the vest, she maneuvered past two more racks to grab a white angora beret from a wig stand sitting atop a stack of 78 records.

To mollify Patrick, who was murmuring fretfully about chocolate, Hope bought him a pair of scuffed cowboy boots with run-down heels. Enraptured, he shed his sneakers and pulled on the boots, which added at least four feet to his height, or so it seemed, as he swaggered beside Hope and Fern. At the back of the store, a rack of uniforms had captured Adam's attention.

"What about this?" asked Hope, holding a blouse with coppertone sequins to her chest. Fern turned thumbs down and, with a languid wave of a gray feather boa, moved on to another bin.

She returned a minute later to show Hope a fox neckpiece with tiny paws. "A touch of hideous is always in," she pronounced in an affected, modulated tone, patting her cheek with one of the paws. She dropped it and came closer to inspect the blouse Hope was fingering, creamy silk with passimenterie detailing on the yoke.

"Indeed," said Fern approvingly, and Hope draped the blouse over one arm.

In the course of the next hour, Hope also found a shot-silk dress the color of sea-foam ("Venus Emergent!" said Fern), a black illusion blouse in a leaf-flecked pattern (to which Fern added a red satin bandeau to be worn underneath, across the breasts), and a sand-colored shawl with silver threads. Hope tied the shawl over one hip and struck a pose.

"Do I look sort of gypsyish? Abandoned? In the cheerier sense of the word?"

"Oh my, yes."

For her part, Fern was buying the jacquard vest and a white sailor's hat, and for Adam, a short black mess jacket with epaulettes. The jacket quite transformed him. He smilingly fingered the epaulettes, his pleasure endowing him with an unaccustomed winsomeness. He nodded benevolently at the admiring Patrick.

Hope's purchases came to $8.40, rung up by a young woman wearing a dried lizard in the lapel of a natty pin-striped suit. Fern suggested they adjourn to I. Miller's so that Hope could buy some boots.

"I. Miller's! Are you serious? My whole savings account would barely cover a pair of boots from I. Miller's!"

"Cheap chic can only go so far on its own," Fern told her. "You need some authority. Look at it this way." She took the silk blouse from Hope's paper sack and held it up. "How much did this cost?"

"One seventy-five."

"Okay. Its original price was probably at least fifty dollars, so already you've saved forty-eight twenty-five. How about this?" She held up the shawl.

"Um, two-thirty, I think."

"A savings of thirty-seven seventy."

Fern pulled out, in turn, the shot-silk dress, the black illusion blouse, and the bandeau. By her calculations, Hope had just saved nearly two hundred dollars.

An hour later, Hope had the boots. They were a lovely pair, oxblood leather, with tapered toes and commanding heels.

"You're the boss now!" commented Rosamunda approvingly when they stopped for raspas, her earrings dancing against her neck, as she wagged her head back and forth. "Those boots, they're made for walking, eh?"

* * *

IT MIGHT HAVE been said that Fern and Hope had nothing in common but circumstance, which only attests to the power of circumstance. Most afternoons found them sitting in the Cadillac at the school, waiting for their children, their straw hats tossed into the back, talking about loneliness and money and the faults of men, as Hope kept an eye on Patrick, who liked to play in the hedges around the building. "We're in the vanguard!" said Fern. "Women without men!"

She missed Hermes, she said, but she'd been expecting his departure. "He always said he'd be moving on someday. He thinks he's Bob Dylan."

"Without the chutzpah."

Fern liked that. "The worst fate for a woman is to marry a weak man," she said, turning thoughtful. "You can't leave them because they need you. So you let things deteriorate until they're the ones who leave. But by that time, it's too late."

"Too late for what?"

"To waste your youth."

This did not strike Hope as Fern's problem. Fern had smoked dope in burned-out redwood trunks on the coast of California. Fern had made love in the Sea of Cortez. "I'm not sure, but I think Adam was conceived there," she said.

"I have trouble imagining Hermes splashing around in Edenic wantonness," said Hope.

"This was before Hermes. Actually . . . actually I don't know who Adam's father is." Fern glanced over at Hope to see how she was taking this. "That is, I'm not sure. I have an *idea*."

Hope was not shocked. She placed Fern in a different category from herself, a category defined by the values of spontaneity and freedom, however those flew in the face of convention. Hope imagined Fern's sexual history to be in line with these principles, very different from the furtive splendor of her own adolescence, very different from the localized pleasures of marriage. Nor was she without sin herself.

"I had to get married," she confessed, aware that the phrase might seem quaint to Fern. Hope had never told anyone this before, and there was little risk in telling Fern, but Hope's face grew hot, nevertheless."Clay's mother had a nervous breakdown when she found out. She had to be hospitalized."

"The only son," Fern guessed.

"No. But the favorite."

"A favorite son! Oh, a favorite son!" Fern clasped her hands under her chin and rolled her eyes. "That's the second-worst fate for a woman: to marry a favorite son. Unfortunately, they're irresistible. In the hands of a favorite son—pardon the pun!—a woman can lose all. Favorite sons make the very best lovers. They live to please. The problem is they live to please the many."

"Crowd pleasers!" cried Hope, forgetting they were talking about Clay, more or less.

"And killers! When they want to get back at Mama—look out!" She raised an imaginary machine gun, and the sound of discharged cartridges rattled from her throat.

In spite of the acknowledged dangers of consorting with men, they kept up-to-date inventories of those available. Fern had an advantage here; men drifted in and out of her ambit with tidal regularity. "Yeah, lots of loose dudes on the road. Trouble is I'm tired of playing gas station."

"At least they're single. All the men in my neighborhood are married."

Fern surprised Hope by agreeing that married men were out of bounds. "Women have to stick together. Things are tough enough. What about that guy Alex? The minister, or whatever he is, of your church. He's not married, is he?"

Hope was taken off-guard. She thought of Alex as a guide, a teacher, a healer even, but not a lover. She was more spellbound than attracted and had instinctively disqualified herself from what Chloe called his chorus line, the procession of women companions that filed through the church over the Sundays.

"I don't think he's my speed. Also, he's too . . . technical."

"What do you mean?"

Hope explained that on a recent visit to Alex's Open Relationships seminar, she had been disconcerted by his discussion of the variability of clitorises. He had discussed their somewhat different shapes and their size deviations, from a quarter of an inch to well over an inch. "I wouldn't have wanted my own, uh, you know, to be under discussion," Hope said.

"Oh, he was probably just showing off. What about Calhoun, then? He's looking good these days, don't you think? When I first met him, he looked kind of dorky. Now he could pass for a musician." (Calhoun *had* lost a slight pudginess around the middle and had also grown a beard.) I tried to make him myself but bombed out. I bet you'd have better luck."

"We're friends," Hope said cautiously. Sometimes, seeing Calhoun deep in conversation with a small child, sitting on his heels to equalize their heights, Hope experienced a rush that might have been desire, but might also have been simply a longing for that sort of attention. "He makes me laugh," she emphasized. It was a talent she did not underestimate these days.

When Hope and Fern were not talking about men, they talked about money, or rather the lack of it; they would not have thought to talk about money in the sense of how to make it in large quantities or what to do with it beyond paying bills. When Amber came down with strep throat, Hope debated and worried for days about how to pay the doctor. Three times she had dialed Clay's number and hung up before anyone could answer. Finally, she decided to sell her clothes dryer to a neighbor.

"You should have stiffed the doctor," Fern said.

"I don't think I could do that," said Hope, recalling how her stomach had clenched just asking for a payment extension. She'd given in easily to the receptionist's suggestion that perhaps Hope could pay a part of it now. Convinced the receptionist had been staring at her oxblood boots, she'd obediently handed over one of the two ten-dollar bills supposed to last until the following week's paycheck.

"Why didn't you call what's-his-face, your husband?"

"I thought of it, but I don't know . . . it's like begging or something. It's like admitting I'm not making it."

Fern nodded. "He probably wouldn't give you anything anyway. What about your parents?"

"I didn't think of them. But they don't have much to spare. My father's a shop teacher. And also . . . I've left home, more or less, you know?"

"Yeah," said Fern with a sigh. "You leave home and you think that's it. You think you're done with all that shit. But then things happen." She looked out of the window and back. "I may have to go back to Port Arthur."

"What? Why?"

Fern explained that she had not paid her rent for two months and was about to be evicted. "So it may be back to the home of the emotionally feeble and religiously fanatic for me. You know, I still dream in images from the *Children's Illustrated Bible*. One time my mother—"

"I have an idea," interrupted Hope. She'd heard most of this before. "You could live at Communitas."

Fern had never heard of Communitas.

"It's this big house Alex has rented. He's looking for people to share it with him. It's a new kind of family. People relate to one another as total persons: free, equal, completely open. There's no hierarchy. Not a single decision is made without total consensus." It could have been Alex himself talking; Hope was repeating what he'd said to her, word for word. He had gone on to suggest that one way to solve her financial problems would be to sell her house and live off the proceeds at Communitas. Chloe had advised her against this move, saying she didn't think Communitas would be a good place for children.

"Sounds cheap," said Fern. "Maybe I'll talk to him. Do you think he'd take me on credit? Just for a little bit?"

"I do," said Hope. "That's just the sort of thing he would do. Take you on credit."

10

COMMUNITAS WAS INCONGRUOUSLY HOUSED IN ONE OF THOSE monuments to propriety, a high-style, vaunting, three-story Victorian. Various remodeling efforts had shorn the exterior of most of the original ornamentation, but the turrets remained, watchtowers of respectability. Fern's room was in one of them. She said the room made her feel like Rapunzel.

A hip Rapunzel, Hope thought, glancing around. A psychedelic poster of Jimi Hendrix, his face in negative, his Afro in rainbow colors, was thumbtacked to one wall, while opposite, a nude woman, her arms outstretched, urged: "Come to your senses!" The mattress on the floor was covered with a "Tree of Life" spread, and an earthenware love lamp sat atop a stack of mint-green flyers announcing Earth Day, long passed.

Tonight was guest night at Communitas, and Fern had invited Hope and Calhoun. Hope had come early so that Fern's new friend Oily Jon could tune her Cadillac. "He's a kind of troubadour mechanic," Fern had told her over the phone. "He's traveled all around the country fixing cars. He's a genius, according to the grapevine."

"Ah, the grapevine." Hope's awe was not too far from genuine. Fern heard all sorts of things on the grapevine: the addresses of abortion clinics in New York and dentists in Mexico, Steve McQueen's telephone credit card number, warnings to stay away from Green Goddess due to its strychnine content. Long before Oily Jon had arrived at Communitas (which he had heard about through the grapevine), Fern had known a lot about him, including the information that he was the son of wealthy parents, although there was a little static on the grapevine concerning this, some people saying Coca-Cola money, others Pepsi.

Oily Jon was also a pianist. He liked to walk into a club and, while the regulars were taking a break, sit down and play a little. "He leaves grease marks on the keys," Fern said affectionately. She usually tagged along, "to educate her ear."

"This is how I do it," she'd explained to Hope. "This is how I fall in love. Through education. With Hermes I learned all about Walt Whitman. I can quote," she boasted.

The shift in Fern's love life upset Hope a little. It shed a discouraging light on her own, cast doubt on her desirability. Manlessness was all at once humiliating, a condition not helped any by a disastrous evening at Chloe's, where Hope had been invited to meet a petroleum engineer back from Saudi Arabia. Hope had drunk a good deal of wine and remembered nothing between the créme brulée and waking up in the middle of the night on Chloe's living-room sofa, the petroleum engineer sitting opposite in a rocking chair, teeth gleaming in a smile as he pitched forward and back, forward and back. "I haven't seen a white woman in two years," he'd whispered. Hope had fled.

Engrossed in their talk, Hope and Fern didn't notice Adam standing in the doorway, listing from side to side as he shifted his weight back and forth. He stood there for several moments before Fern caught sight of him. "What is it, honey?"

"He's on top the pole," he said. They both knew who. "Frederick," Adam added, just in case.

After an absence of several weeks, Frederick had shown up at the school one day and was living with Ocie now, in his fashion, routinely disappearing now and then, but always returning. He called her Big Buns and peed in her backyard and generally let her know she was not his first choice.

Ocie, in her exasperation, wondered just who his first choice could be. Evidently not his mother, whom Ocie had finally tracked down and whom, she learned, Frederick visited occasionally but not for long.

"A flea on a hot griddle, that boy," Ocie had commented to Calhoun and Hope as they sat drinking iced tea in the school's kitchen. "And guess what? Guess how old he is."

"Ten," said Calhoun.

"Fourteen."

"Fourteen! But he's smaller than Amber!" exclaimed Hope.

"Malnutrition," said Ocie. "Emotional deprivation. The usual."

If it weren't for Ocie's son Daryl, Frederick might not have stayed with Ocie at all, but thanks to Daryl, Frederick had "come boss." Daryl ran a mobile clothing outlet for his fellow students at Texas Southern, scouting the Third Ward stores for *bon ton* and buying when his mojo was working. Frederick was his walking advertisement. Although Daryl's wares were too large for him, Frederick wore them with such a spanking, lusty air they looked highly desirable, and Daryl credited Frederick with the rise in his off-campus business. Tonight he was wearing a silky black shirt with a gold stripe.

Calhoun was convinced that an all-points bulletin circulated Houston concerning Frederick's capture, and whenever Frederick showed up at the school, as he had this afternoon, Calhoun held on to him as long as was physically possible, disregarding resistance such as came from Fern, who had pointedly informed him that her invitation had not included Frederick.

"Invite me, invite my responsibilities," was Calhoun's response.

"What pole?" Hope asked now, as Fern jumped up from her pillow, her shawl slipping from her shoulders to the floor. Hope whisked it up and hurried after.

Outside, Calhoun, Oily Jon, his skinny, hairless chest streaked with grease, and a straw-hatted woman with a gardening trowel were standing at the base of a telephone pole, heads craned back. At the top of the pole, the old type, with hooked metal spikes protruding from the sides, was Frederick, the flesh of one little toe showing through a frayed tear in a black sneaker precariously balanced on a spike. He looked down on them, exalted and contemptuous.

"Frederick!" Calhoun shouted. "Get your ass down here! Now!"

Frederick laughed, a wrought-up sort of laugh, half shriek.

The woman in the straw hat suggested to Oily Jon that they call the fire department.

"Nooo," he said lazily. "Nooo, I don't think so."

"Why not?"

"We don't cotton to uniforms around here." This met with a peevish response, lost on Oily Jon, who turned to greet a dark-haired, stocky man in tan workclothes and carrying a lunch pail.

"What's happenin', mon?" asked the man.

Hope couldn't quite place his accent, foreign yet with the soft lilt of warm Southern evenings.

"Victor! Just the person." Fern pointed to Frederick. "Tell him to come down, Victor. He'll come down for you."

Victor did not look up at Frederick, however, but at Hope.

"This is my friend Hope Fairman," said Fern. "Victor Calais," she said, turning to Hope. "Victor's our new guy. He has a way with kids. He's the only one who can get Adam to halfway behave."

Hope tried not to look too surprised. Victor did not seem the type to be living at Communitas. Then again, maybe he was. No social rules or roles, that was Alex's motto. "Anyone can play," he said.

Victor gave Hope a sociable smile and turned his attention to Frederick. "Hey mon, you pretty high up, eh?"

Frederick looked from Victor to the top of the pole and back, his cocky expression clouding as he registered the distance between himself and the ground for the first time. He lifted one sneaker from the rung and seemed about to climb down, but in order to place it on the rung below, he needed to bend his opposite knee and stretch. When he realized this, his body went rigid, his foot dangling, lax and pointless.

"Frederick," whispered Calhoun.

"We need a ladder," said Victor.

"I'll get one," Hope volunteered, handing Fern her shawl and setting off down the street,conscious of herself running "like a girl," as the boys in her neighborhood used to say, wagtail, heels kicking up as if she were a wind-up toy.

There was no one home at the first two houses she tried, but at the third, a white-haired woman in pink foam hair curlers answered the door. Hope, winded, explained in between gasps why she needed a ladder. The woman examined Hope from the part of her hair, which Hope was wearing long and straight these days, to her oxblood boots. "Are you from the house with the dentist's chair?"

"Yes," Hope admitted cautiously. No one knew where the dentist's chair had come from. Alex said it was already installed on the lawn when he rented the house. Since then, it had mysteriously attracted other accouterments: two little wooden sunbonnet girls had been spiked into the lawn, later joined by a rusty Burma-Shave sign and an uninscribed cemetery stone. No one knew where these came from either.

"I don't want nothin' to do with your kind," said the woman. She started to close the door.

"A boy is stuck on top of a telephone pole! What if he were one of your grandchildren? Do you have grandchildren? What if—?"

"My grandkids would have better sense 'n to end up on top a telephone pole," interrupted the woman. She looked Hope up and down for a moment, then stepped out onto the porch and led the way to the garage.

Inside, an extension ladder leaned against one wall, and shouldering it, the two of them started down the street, Hope at the head, the woman at the tail, scuffing along in her bedroom slippers, pink curlers bobbing. They were breathing hard; the ladder was heavy, and they were trying to hurry.

"I hope he's still there," panted Hope.

"Where's he gonna go?" puffed the woman.

By the time they reached Frederick, a few more people had gathered.

"You didn't tell me," the woman whispered in Hope's ear. "You didn't tell me it was a nigger kid on top of the pole."

Hope's stomach shuddered. "There . . . there isn't," she stammered. "There isn't a . . . a . . . what-you-said on top of the pole. His name is Frederick."

"Don't matter what he calls hisself."

It could have been her mother talking. Maureen had a store of words like that. *Nigger, kike, wop.* Sometimes Maureen used them as casually as she would the word *egg.* Other times they were plump with hatred, like swollen ticks. But what nauseated Hope was her own silence. When her mother talked like that, and now this woman, Hope's mouth was a tomb. A few feeble sounds might escape. *You really shouldn't . . . There's no need to . . .* Cowardly sounds. Worse really than saying those words oneself. A person had to take a stand. A person had to.

Hope looked around for the woman and saw the pink curlers bobbling halfway down the street. "Put the ladder upside the garage door when you're done!" the woman shouted over her shoulder. Hope nodded, shame rolling down her skin like sweat.

Victor and Calhoun, meanwhile, had set up the ladder. Frederick had not moved. His arms hugged the pole, and he stared, not down at them but out at the Houston skyline.

"I'm coming, Fred!" called Calhoun, grasping the ladder and putting a foot on the bottom rung.

"I used to be a lineman for Bell," offered Victor.

"Oh, well, in that case . . ." Calhoun stepped back and, with a shallow bow, rolled a palm to indicate the field was Victor's. Victor began to climb the pole, testing each rung with a steel-toed boot, talking to Frederick with a slight accent that softened final consonants and buoyed up the vowels. "Hey, Fred-er-ick. You fish much, mon? You should see the fish in Bayou Teche, where I come from. Alligator gar ten feet long! I kid you not, mon. Bass, blue cats, mullet, shad, you name it, mon, Bayou Teche's got it. And crawfish! Let me tell you 'bout crawfish. . . ."

When Victor had climbed to a point directly opposite Frederick, he reached out. "Turn loose the pole, mon." Frederick kept both arms tightly wrapped around it. "Three, four hundred dollar a day, Romain and me could make, crawfish season . . . you ready to let go the pole yet? . . . crawfish season we near to lived in the pirogue, mon . . ." Suddenly, Frederick did let go of the pole, flinging his arms around Victor's neck with such force that Victor nearly lost his balance. "Whoa!" he said, steadying himself. He descended slowly.

"Kids!" said one of the men below, spitting a stream of tobacco juice into the gutter.

"A wonder they live to drinkin' age," agreed another.

"Shut up, please?" requested Calhoun. "Just everyone shut up, please, if you don't mind?"

On the ground, Frederick regained some swagger, fending off Calhoun's attempt to put an arm around his shoulder.

"You could've fallen and broken your head open and spilled your brains," said the woman in the straw hat. Frederick didn't even glance her way. "What brains?" she asked, appealing to the group with a shrug of her shoulders.

* * *

The food was memorable, at least for Hope. It was her first vegetarian meal, cooked by a folksinging duo that had moved in at Communitas about the same time as Fern.

"Mushroom *Victorious*," announced Finn, the male half. He set a steaming casserole on the table. "Life Savers for dessert."

O'Molly, the female half, followed with a salad. They could have been brother and sister, with their freckles and red hair, although Finn's was somewhat more carrot-colored. They were not related, however. "We're partners," O'Molly had told Hope earlier in a way that suggested the affiliation had been hard-won.

On Hope's left, Adam suspiciously surveyed the sample portions he had allowed Fern to put on his plate: a single asparagus stalk, teaspoonfuls of mushroom Stroganoff and bulgar with tarragon, a few shreds of salad, the bean sprouts and purple cabbage removed to one side.

"To our hero!" said Fern, raising her glass. Victor accepted the cheers with a dogged air. He had changed his clothes and wore a multipatterned, multicolored dashiki and a necklace of small glass beads, an ensemble that didn't suit him, yet broadcast an appealing gameness and susceptibility. His face had the variety of a relief map: a broad plain of a forehead, nose a straight ridge, fleshy hills along the bones above the shallow basins of his cheeks. He sat next to Frederick, who kicked the table leg in what appeared to be pleasure every time Victor said something to him.

Alex had not arrived yet, and there was some speculation about where he might be. Finn thought he might still be at the church, but Fern thought he had probably been held up at the Glow Worm, where he was picking up Vera, a six-foot-tall exotic dancer who had set off the current controversy at the church.

At first, Vera had attracted the usual brand of Unitarian attention toward the immoderate, a warm welcome wrapped around a cool denial of the obvious. Vera's father was a Unitarian minister. That was nice. Vera took her clothes off for a living. That was nice, too. But then came her Sharing. Sharing was a regular part of the Sunday-morning service. Usually someone read a favorite poem or played a musical instrument. Occasionally someone shared a personal experience, such as that of the woman with breast cancer who talked about her visualization therapy. Once a visitor, a Native American, created a medicine wheel on the floor of the church. That was about as exotic as the congregation was accustomed to.

So everyone had been surprised when Vera, barefoot and dressed in a costume of filmy, variegated-green fabric, materialized from the back of the church to float forward on the music of Ravel. Reaching the center of the sanctuary, she swayed in place for a moment, scarves quivering, eyes closed. The tempo increased, and she began fleet-footedly circling the perimeter. A piece of fabric floated to the floor, exposing a shoulder, and then the piece covering her left breast fluttered loose. It soon became apparent that the entire costume was composed of scarves, which Vera slowly discarded, one by one, until she was naked save for her nipples, decorated with gold-sequined stars, and pubic area, covered by a glittering patch in the shape of the map of Texas.

"Eroticism dissolves the conventional," Alex told them in the sermon that followed, "penetrating our encrusted routines, reducing social hierarchies to irrelevance." This, he said, was one of the functions of religion. He told them of the joy-maidens, the sacred prostitutes of ancient Greece who enacted fertility rituals, and he spoke of the obligations of wives to serve in Aphrodite's temple one night a year, offering their bodies to strangers as a pledge to the goddess. In this way, ordinary women were released from their ego orientation.

After the service, Chloe strode down the hall on the way to the community room, emanating a fury almost as palpable as smoke. Hope had to hurry to keep up. "But I see what he means, don't you, Chloe?" Hope argued. "Sexual liberation at the heart of liberation in general?"

"Stripping has nothing to do with sexual liberation, let alone liberation in general," fumed Chloe, increasing her pace. "The men were getting their rocks off, and the women were humiliated."

She repeated this to Alex and Vera a few minutes later, cornering them at the coffee urn. Vera wore a white cotton dress, and Hope found herself staring at its bodice to see if she was still wearing the sequined stars.

"Chloe's feeling threatened," Alex explained to Vera.

"I am not! But you should be, because I'm about to wipe that smile off your face!"

"What do you mean, 'humiliated'?" Vera asked her.

"The exploitation of one woman's body humiliates all women," Chloe said.

"Nobody's exploiting me," said Vera. "Did you feel humiliated?" she asked Hope.

"Well, I—"

"Striptease is female minstrel show," said Chloe, returning to her argument. "Striptease—"

"Exotic dance," Vera corrected frostily.

Chloe looked at her, then at Alex. She smiled. "I have an idea. Next Sunday, Alex can dance naked, and you, Vera, can deliver the sermon." They stared at her. "Eroticism dissolves the conventional," she reminded them. "Maybe Alex could borrow your G-string, Vera. I think that map of Texas just might do. He probably won't need the pasties. If you need any help with your sermon, just give me a call. I'd avoid mentioning Sodom and Gomorrah, if I were you."

Alex's shocked expression, she told Hope later, was triumph enough, and she decided against writing an editorial in the church newsletter protesting Vera's dance. "It would only draw attention to something best forgotten," she said.

That was not to be, however. On Monday *The Houston Post* printed a photo of Vera with the caption "Stripper bares soul et al. in Unitarian church." (How it happened that a *Post* photographer had been in attendance was a question much debated but never answered.)

Alex was in his element. A picture of himself and Vera appeared in a subsequent *Post* story, and he was interviewed on television and radio. He preached a sermon at Vera's place of employment, the Glow Worm, ten seconds of which made the late news, and he was attacked from the pulpit of at least three Baptist churches. It was rumored that he'd received an offer from the Johnny Carson show, and it was a fact that he and Vera had been asked to put together an act for a club in Las Vegas.

The incident split the congregation into two camps, pro- and anti-Alex. Chloe led the antis; she and Fletcher were talking of breaking away from the church and starting a fellowship. Hope was on Alex's side, but uncomfortably so, and, in fact, she had been staying away from the church in an effort to avoid the whole thing. She would not have minded if Alex failed to show up tonight. He and Vera would probably want to talk about the developing battle lines, and she wouldn't know what to say.

THE CONVERSATION TURNED to music. Oily Jon wanted to know if Finn and O'Molly had ever considered going electric. Even Dylan had gone electric, he pointed out.

"O'Molly and I have metabolisms better suited to acoustic," said Finn.

"Acoustic's okay," said Oily Jon, "so long as you stick to folk, so long as you don't try any rock."

"Oh, we'd never try anything like that," O'Molly assured him.

"Rock's synonymous with electric," Oily Jon added.

"Anonymous?" whispered Victor to Hope. He looked bewildered.

"Synonymous," Hope whispered back. Victor's expression did not change.

"Folk is where we've been," said Oily Jon. "Rock is where we're going."

"It's good to know where you've been," said Finn mildly.

"Whither *thou* goest, *I* will go," put in Fern, resting a hand on Oily Jon's arm.

"Rock's the first head music since baroque," he went on. "It's international, a no-boundary kind of thing. You can't stop it."

"Is anyone trying?" O'Molly asked.

"You better believe it."

"Who?"

"The typeheads."

"The who?" whispered Victor to Hope.

"The typeheads," she whispered back.

"Rock is beyond the typeheads because they can't label it," Oily Jon explained. "Rock is beyond labels. Rock is total."

"In other words: a gestalt." Everyone looked up to see Alex, who had just arrived with Vera. "Rock encompasses the mind *and* the body," he said, leading the way around the table to the two empty seats, "*Ergo* rock is a gestalt."

Everyone listened, but not as attentively as usual, the presence of Vera being too diverting. Masses of long, dark hair fell forward over her chest, stopping just above the dark nipples showing through her transparent blouse. It was hard not to look at her, a predicament she accommodated with a nice air of performance. She took a seat and everyone watched, fascinated, as she picked up a stalk of asparagus and dangled it in front of her mouth for a moment before feeding it to herself, an inch at a time.

AFTER DINNER EVERYONE gathered in the parlor. Although much of the downstairs gave way to warrens and high-ceilinged cubicles, legacy of boardinghouse days, the parlor was spacious. Here the remaining deputies of the grand tradition—mahogany woodwork, a marble fireplace, an old Turkish carpet worn through in places to the warp and weft—stood fast against the orange-crate bookcases, beanbag chairs and floor pillows, the porch glider in striped awning fabric. As everyone drifted in from the dining room, Fern visited the grubby windowsills carrying a taper match, lighting thick candles with clabbered sides. On the other side of the room, Finn and O'Molly tuned their guitars, closely observed by Frederick, while Adam stood somewhat apart, idly pulling rubber foam from a slit in the fabric of a cushion.

Finn slipped the guitar strap over his head and, settling the guitar into position, strummed a few chords. "Here's a song about a boy I know," he announced.

> *Oh, Frederick was a boy,*
> *Who said he didn't care*
> *How high he had to climb*
> *To get a breath of air.*

It didn't take long for everyone to catch on to the chorus.

> *Bring Frederick back to earth, oh!*
> *The place of his birth, oh!*
> *Where there's no dearth, oh!*
> *Of ice cream.*

Plumped up with attention, warmed and basted, the innocent in Frederick surfaced; he giggled and squirmed. Hope and Calhoun exchanged a look. Frederick giggling?

Finn apologized for not being more of a singer. "Fortunately, Molly can harmonize with a slammed door," he said.

They sang more songs: "On Top of Old Smoky" and "Careless Love," "Barbara Allen" and "On the Banks of the Ohio," as well as a few songs of their own.

O'Molly warbled in her crystalline soprano,

He left me for another one, Too bad for him,
He must be dumb.

"You could make a fortune with that one," commented Vera. She and Alex sat on the porch glider, which squeaked as she leaned forward. "I know this guy in L.A.—"

"Oily's been to L.A., haven't you?" interrupted Fern, turning to Oily Jon. He and Fern sat side by side on the floor, legs entwined. Was the whole world one big Noah's Ark? Hope wondered. Everybody paired? "He's been to San Francisco, too," said Fern. "The Haight."

"Oh?" said Vera. "Where in the Haight?"

"Cole Street," said Oily Jon.

"When?"

"Couple of years ago."

"Really? I lived on Waller a couple of years ago. The summer of love. A turning point in human consciousness."

No one said anything for a moment. It was hard to tell when Vera was joking.

"We were spared that here," Finn said lightly. "The sixties never made it to Houston."

"On the contrary," said Alex, putting a hand on Vera's knee. "They've just arrived."

"I wasn't there long," said Oily Jon. "I hit the road right after that."

"Movement," mused Alex, "the supreme way of being. Movement dissolves structures."

Listen, O lord of the meeting rivers
Things standing shall fall,
But the moving ever shall stay.

"Beautiful," commented Vera.

"Sthavara and Jangama," Alex went on, "the bipolar opposites of stasis and dynamis. Which are ultimately one. And none."

"Nirvana," said Finn. He strummed a chord. "Oh, Nirvana, oh don't you cry for me . . ."

"Do you know any zydeco?" Victor asked. He sat on the floor, his back against the wall, legs extended, the toes of his gray suede elf boots pointing up at the ceiling. Beside him sat Frederick in an identical posture.

"Zydeco?" Finn and O'Molly looked blank.

He sang, off-key,

You let the bon temps rouler,
You let the mulet couler,
Now don't be no foolay . . .

You let the bon temps rouler! joined in Frederick, attracting Hope and Calhoun's attention.

"I guess we don't," apologized O'Molly. "How about 'Oats, Peas, Beans, and Barley Grow'?"

Frederick and Victor exchanged a sardonic look, but everyone knew this one, and as they all joined in, Hope was reminded of summer camp, sitting around a campfire, far from the familiar, yet out of harm's way. The candles cast a binding light, the night a black slab held at bay by window glass. She wished Amber and Patrick were here.

Around ten, she eased out of the beanbag chair, saying it was about time for her to head home. Oily Jon had just fetched his stash, and she judged the party about to change character. Victor offered to see her to her car, and after Hope had said goodbye to everyone, they walked outside, picking their way cautiously across the lawn.

"Be careful," whispered Victor, as she nearly collided with the dentist's chair, so abruptly did it come forward, its arms spread wide to receive her. "Watch the cracks," he whispered again when they reached the buckled sidewalk.

Hope got into the front seat of the Cadillac and was searching her purse for keys when he leaned forward over the open car door.

"I like you," he said, draping his elbows over the frame.

Hope didn't know how to reply. She would have liked to drive off and circle the block once or twice to give herself time to think about it, maybe search her limited premarital experience for clues on how to act.

"I like you, too," she said finally, although she wasn't at all sure; she hardly knew him. But it seemed the right thing to say; it seemed in the right spirit.

11

Spring does not arrive demurely in Houston, blossom by blossom, but in a prodigal explosion of leaf and bloom. The smell of the city changes overnight from fungous to fragrant, a haze of pollen drifts like a descending dream, and the trees sing forth, or seem to, their dense foliage concealing warblers and finches. So the weather was in full collusion.

As Hope walked toward the corner of Smith and Lamar the next afternoon, armored by a phalanx of children, she looked more like a schoolteacher on a field trip than a woman keeping a tryst, and Victor's effort to adjust his expectations was conspicuous. A salutary smile battled briefly with dismay to finally wilt in uneasiness, as the company—Amber, Rachel, Ocie's daughter Rae, Rae's friend Eva, and Patrick and his friend Alexander—advanced toward him.

"Is something wrong?" Hope asked, nervously fingering the snap on her camera case. Victor's invitation to meet him today had tumbled her backward into adolescence—the very last territory she would have chosen to revisit, with its faint but persistent ambience of inferiority and limitation.

"Wrong? Well, I . . . no! Nothing's wrong. You, uh, have brought children."

"They're not all mine."

"No, I didn't think so," he said, eyeing Rae.

"I thought you liked children."

"Well, they like me, I guess." He glanced confidently around the ring of interested children until he came to Amber, who was coolly taking his measure. Victor put his hands in his pockets and began to jingle some change.

Standing on the corner, they made a substantial enough group to divide the flow of the crowd surging past them. Several thousand people milled through the streets of downtown that Saturday, cordoned off for Houston's first Happening. Although it had a more commercial flavor than the spontaneous events they'd seen on television, everyone was eager to sample the zeitgeist. Booth space for artists and food vendors had been contracted weeks before, and the Goodyear blimp hovered benevolently above. People had an excursionary air, respectfully keen. Most of them were downtown for the first time.

Hope and Victor followed the children, who claimed to know where they were going. "There's this giant trampoline," Amber explained. "You can bounce high as a tree."

Keeping the children in sight, Hope and Victor walked past booths featuring pastel scenes of the bayous, handmade jewelry, and amateur pottery, and haltingly exchanged bits of information about themselves.

Victor had grown up near Lafayette, Louisiana. "Gumbo capital of the world."

"I grew up in Indiana," Hope admitted regretfully.

He asked about her camera, and she explained that her hobby was photography.

He laughed. "Hobby. I never know anyone with a hobby before. Hobby," he repeated, shaking his head.

Affronted, she snapped his picture. After that, she raised her camera every time the conversation faltered, and by the time they reached the giant trampoline, she'd taken half a roll of film.

All six children clamored for tickets, which Hope bought, while the children heaped on Victor their shoes and assorted articles of unwanted clothing before scrambling onto a heaving surface about the size of a tennis court. Hope and Victor retreated to stand behind a rope to watch the forty or so bouncing, shrieking, honking children, Hope wearing a bleak expression and Victor clutching the shoes and shirts to his chest as if they were sole possessions. They looked like shipboard immigrants drawing close to a strange new land.

Next was the face-painting booth, where the children had their faces decorated with stars and flowers and bolts of lightning and made friends with an organ grinder's monkey. At another booth, everyone purchased computer-generated horoscopes for a quarter each. Victor learned that as a Pisces, a long apprenticeship was about to yield rewards. Hope was at a crossroads. "You're of two minds, Gem," read her printout. "Listen to your daring, quicksilver half."

"Have you ever noticed?" came a voice from behind them. "Horoscopes never warn of cancer or death by friendly fire."

Hope turned to peer into a pair of giant sunglasses with neon-pink frames. "Cal! What are you doing here?"

Calhoun stepped back and took off his sunglasses, tapping them against his palm. "What are we doing here?" he repeated ponderously. "Indeed, what *are* we doing here, on this gob of dirt, this clod, this lump, spinning through an uncaring universe at an unholy speed? That is the question, of course, that philosophers through the ages—"

"He's a little sozzled," interrupted his companion, grinning.

"Meet Caleb," said Calhoun. In spite of gym shorts and Converse high-tops, Caleb looked singularly unathletic: short and skinny, with a beard reaching his collarbone.

"How do you do," said Hope. She introduced Victor to him, and Caleb shook his hand, declaring himself charmed.

"Have you seen the alligator gar cruising Allen's Landing yet?" Calhoun asked them. "Not an official attraction, probably hasn't paid his booth fee, but the alligator gar is definitely the best thing happening here."

Patrick and Alexander were for setting off right away, but Calhoun had more news. "Did Chloe call you? Bootsie Randolph came through! She's giving the school two thousand dollars."

"She is? You mean we're saved?" She and Calhoun exchanged high fives and fell into a discussion about whether or not two thousand dollars would cover all the repairs, and Caleb engaged Victor in a conversation about alligator gars and their fabulous snouts. The adult discussions might have grown lengthy had not Amber nudged Calhoun in the ribs and asked if they were going to stand there and yak all day, prompting Calhoun to capture her skull in a headlock. Feigning indifference to her struggle, he chatted a few more minutes, while she stomped on his toes until he finally released her.

"You should watch more wrestling and less *Dark Shadows*," he told her, before strolling off with Caleb, whose bald spot was growing pink in the bright sun.

"Mutt and Jeff," commented Victor, who clearly found their height difference entertaining.

At Allen's Landing, the alligator gar did indeed prove impressive, a dark submarine in the caramel-colored water. Hope and Victor sat on one of the benches to watch the children, who quickly became involved in a game that called for ships and captains and hands.

Victor, it turned out, had a store of admiration for Alex. He had first seen him on TV, on the news spot featuring Alex's sermon at the Glow Worm. A couple of weeks later he started attending church. "Haven't you seen me there?"

"No, I don't think so."

"I've seen you," he assured her.

He'd also attended one of Alex's weekend encounter groups. "Whoa, that was something, all right. Alex is a very smart fella, but sometimes . . . do you? . . . sometimes it is not so easy to be in the now, do you agree? The now can be some hot seat!"

He had been honored when Alex invited him to live at Communitas. It was a chance to improve himself.

"Do you really need improving?" Hope asked.

"Oh yes. I have small education, you see, although it is also true that I was the only one in our family to graduate from high school, thanks to my grandmère. 'These boys they stay in school,' that's how she say when our pap died."

"Your father died? How old were you?"

"Fourteen. Romain, he wanted to go work on Oncle Claude's shrimp boat, but she say no."

"Your mother."

"*No*, my grandmère. My mother died when I and Romain are born."

"Then you're an orphan!" said Hope, exhaling a tenderness that settled on him, fine as flour.

"*No*, we had our grandmère. But Romain, he run away when she say he stay in school. Uh-uh, no school for him. He's too smart! And, you know, it's true. Romain, he's very much smarter than me, but people don't understand. So he has to live in the woods, you see. You have to be smart to live in the woods, I guarantee."

At that point the children gathered around them again, complaining of thirst, and they all headed back toward the booths. A white-faced mime walked alongside them for half a block, catching precisely the way Victor walked with his hands in his pockets, elbows out, something Hope hadn't noticed.

By the end of the afternoon, they had seen a magician, two puppet shows, and a juggler and had eaten empanadas, corn on the cob, and cotton candy. Hope was out of film. Victor accepted her offer of a ride home, which was over in minutes, since Communitas was only blocks away. She dropped him off at the curb, and they exchanged stilted goodbyes.

"Parting is such sweet sorrow," whispered Amber to Rachel, as the Cadillac pulled away.

"Oh, darling," breathed Rachel.

"That's enough," warned Hope from the front seat.

HOPE HAD NEVER been courted before. With Clay, the pleasures of pursuit had been eclipsed by a precipitate domesticity. So when, over the next week, Victor called daily and brought chocolates (most of which Patrick devoured, without apparent effect, in one sitting) and wildflowers (Mexican hats and Indian paintbrush and black-eyed Susans) and dedicated a song to her on the radio ("Pretty Woman"), Hope felt resurrected by the attention.

"But what do you see in him?" Chloe wanted to know.

Hope didn't know what to say. "He likes me," she said finally.

She felt equally at a loss during her counseling session that week, when Alex asked if she had slept with Victor yet.

Taken aback by his question, she nevertheless answered it. "No."

His black eyes augered more deeply into her uncertainty. "You're still married," he accused.

She shifted her position on the gray sofa. "Well, technically I am, you know. Our six-month waiting period is not up yet."

"Technically is neither here nor there. What matters is where your head is. And your head is still in a dead marriage."

"I hardly know Victor," Hope pointed out.

"Hope, Hope, you're so *cautious*."

"Well—"

"Caution is a social disease inherited from the nineteenth century. Don't think. Feel."

"But I don't know how I feel."

"Then find out! Seize the day!" He went on to praise Victor's naive and instinctive character. Victor was a natural man who would return her to a state of natural womanhood.

Hope wasn't sure about this, but she did wonder: *was* she still married? The idea of sleeping with Victor unsettled her. Not that she wasn't lonely, not that she hadn't regarded complete strangers on the street with a humbling hunger. But Victor was out of her ken; she felt off the beat with him.

THE FOLLOWING WEEKEND, he invited her to dinner at Communitas. Patrick and Amber were with Clay, so she went alone, and when she arrived, she discovered that Victor was the only one home. Fern and Oily Jon had gone to Austin for the weekend, dropping off Adam at her parents in Port Arthur, Finn and O'Molly were performing, and Alex was leading a workshop.

Hope had never seen a man cook before and was unprepared for the appeal of it. The sight of Victor chopping celery delighted her all the way to her backbone. He was making Waldorf salad. The first time he'd ever eaten Waldorf salad, he explained, was also the first time he'd been in love. The occasion was a church potluck supper, and he was in love with a girl with blond braids. He'd been twelve.

"Do you think this is enough celery?" he broke off to ask. Hope said yes, she thought so, and he dumped the celery into a bowl and began to cut up apples. He asked Hope if she remembered the first time she'd been in love.

She did. "With a boy shorter than me. *He* sat on *my* lap."

They talked about their childhoods. Both remembered the exact place and circumstances of the first time they had tied their shoes. The Ferris wheel had been Hope's favorite carnival ride; Victor preferred the cater-pillar.

They told family stories. Victor told her about the time he and Romain had set off firecrackers in the sheriff's mailbox. "Nobody ever found out who done it. We got away with a lot of stuff when we were kids!"

Hope confessed to stealing rhubarb with her brother William. "We didn't even like rhubarb. Too sour. We just wanted to be outlaws." The desire to be an outlaw was actually more Hope's than William's at the time, he being only four, but he had followed Hope wherever she'd allowed him, which turned out to be most places, because of Maureen's headaches. There must have been a special loneliness in that for William, Hope thought now, with a flash of sympathy that caused her to miss Victor's question.

"What?" she said. "What did you say?"

"Do you think this is enough apples?" Victor repeated.

Hope eyed the huge mound heaped along the counter. "More than enough." It turned out that there was too much, actually, to fit into the bowl, and Victor had to get out a roasting pan. Then he decided he should chop more celery to match the quantity of apples.

As he chopped, he told her about the time he and Romain had been out fishing and a water moccasin had jumped into the pirogue. "He jumped in and we jumped out. Then he jumped out and we jumped in. Then he jumped in again and we jumped out again. Those buggers are full of fight, I guarantee."

He went on to chop the walnuts. He told her that he could remember being with Romain in the womb. "A lot of people don't believe that, but it's true." He and Romain were like this, Victor said, stopping to hold up entwined fingers. He had not seen Romain in five years now.

"I haven't seen my brother in two years," said Hope. "I don't know when I'll see him again. He's . . . underground." It felt odd to say this. Unreal. More real was William's small face drawn tight against the sourness of rhubarb. She felt vaguely guilty that he'd had to go underground, as if she had failed to provide him with the right world.

By this time, the quantity of chopped ingredients surpassed even the roasting pan, and they had to hunt for something larger, settling on a blue enameled canner. After dumping in the apples and celery and walnuts, Victor began to stir in mayonnaise. Hope thought he might have to add the entire jar. It looked to her as if they had a good ten quarts of Waldorf salad here.

Next Victor fashioned a pizza crust from a defrosted loaf of bread dough, stretching and pushing it to match the pan's dimensions. Over this he poured a can of tomato sauce, topping it with a sausage unfamiliar to Hope—boudain, he said—and cheese. While they waited for it to cook, he apologized for not making gumbo. The truth was, the only gumbo worth eating was his grandmère's. "You will see when you come back with me," he said. Hope, dizzied by her rapid propulsion into his future, didn't comment.

The pizza, when it emerged from the oven, had shrunk drastically from the edges of the pan and was little larger than a Frisbee. It was also thick and pasty, Hope discovered, taking a bite. She watched as, wonderfully immune to failure, Victor ate all of his and, when she offered it, hers, too. Meanwhile she filled up on Waldorf salad.

When they'd finished eating, they washed the dishes. Victor confessed that he would never have had the courage to invite her to the Happening if it hadn't been for Alex. "He goes, 'Call her, why don't you? Call her, what do you have to lose?'" Alex had also inspired the chocolates and flowers. Dedicating a song to her on the radio, however, had been Victor's own idea.

Victor's confession provoked a faint disappointment in her, a disappointment that shaded into balkiness when he planted his hands on her shoulders to kiss her. His kiss was hesitant, and he touched her breasts carefully with his fingertips, as if they were eggs about to hatch. It was delicately arousing, though, and when he kissed her again, she was more hospitable. A few moments later, she allowed him to lead her upstairs to his room.

His body surprised her. Not that, except for the novelty of his uncircumcised penis, it held any rarities, peculiarities, or taints. It was more that she had assumed all male bodies to look like Clay's, more or less. She had not expected Victor's legs to be so much more generous than Clay's; she had not expected the luxury of his carpeted chest, which she longed to bury her nose in and soon did, discovering its fragrance to be woody, like bark. She didn't think she was still married. Nervous, yes, too nervous, probably, to have an orgasm, but her head was not buried in a dead marriage, it was buried in Victor's chest hair, an experience potent enough to cause her own body to stir and reach. She rolled to her back, and he moved above her, his expression grave. She felt his body tense into climax, which he marked with a groan and a sigh. Then he lowered himself to lay his head on her breasts. "Thank you," he said, once he had regained his breath.

Thank you? Hope was enchanted. Thank you? She kissed him.

Victor insisted that she have an orgasm, too, and he addressed her body with a studious, experimental air, an approach that filled her with a sense of responsibility that, nevertheless, did not prevent her patient, abandoned body from bursting into tiny, glittering, floating bits of pleasure, so delicious she was glad when he fell asleep, and she could devote herself to reliving the sensations. Engulfed in well-being, she felt homed in, at ease. Grateful, she placed a hand on his sleeping head—his stranger's head, she thought with a jolt, the curly hair against her fingers coarse in contrast to the soft bristles she was accustomed to. She had just slept with a stranger. Perhaps one always does. A solitariness came over her, not unpleasant, having more to do with simplicity than loneliness. She felt alone in the prosperous sense, all one.

HOPE USED TO say "It's Clay's weekend" to describe his turn at having Amber and Patrick. Now she said "It's my weekend," meaning her turn to be free of them.

These were the weekends Victor spent at her house. At first, they left only to go to the supermarket, where they pushed a shopping cart with jointly clasped hands, Hope raptly sensible of her naked body beneath her clothes. Her body had always been naked beneath her clothes, of course, but to feel this as a condition while standing in the baked goods aisle as Victor tried to persuade her to give up white bread was singular.

Gradually, they began to venture forth. They sat on meditation mats at the new Rothko chapel, numb with mystery. Hope took him to the Glenwood Cemetery, site of the only real hills in Houston, where the dead dated back to Houston's founding. They slurped raspas under the approving gaze of Rosamunda, who told Hope later she'd found a good man.

A place they returned to often was the small waterfront property in Kemah. Underneath the Virginia creeper and pepper vine, Victor discovered a fallen windmill, its rusty ribs barely visible. They collected shells from the narrow beach and made love in the moonlight on a rickety pier that extended thirty feet or so out into the bay, falling asleep on air mattresses to the lap of water.

One Saturday Victor took his turn as tour guide to show her where he worked. They drove out along Navigation Avenue, past the Mexican neighborhoods to the industrial expanse of the ship channel. There they climbed the observation tower at the turning basin and waved to the sailors on the decks of the nearby ships. Most waved back, shouting faint greetings in foreign languages.

Hope was moved to return with her camera the next week to hang about the loading docks noisy with the clanks and screeches of yearning machinery—winches, cranes, forklifts—where profane, purposeful men eddied about, as ponderous freighters and barges plowed the channel's waters. She ignored wolf whistles and shouted invitations as she ranged the docks. Behind a camera, she felt invisible.

"GREED," SAID CHLOE, peering through the magnifying glass at the contact sheet.

Hope took the glass and looked again at the line of workers exiting the shipyard, a giant slipway in the background. She saw compliance and stoicism in the faces, resentment even, but not greed.

Chloe, however, meant the industries along the ship channel. "Did you know there's not a molecule of oxygen between the turning basin and the San Jacinto Monument? It's all toxins—arsenic and mercury, stuff like that." She pointed to another frame. "Isn't that where the fire was?"

"What fire?"

"A couple of years ago, remember? The chemicals floating on the water caught fire. A man burned to death."

Hope was frightened for a moment, thinking of Victor.

"You should print this one and enter it in the *Post* contest," said Chloe.

Hope examined the contact sheet again, trying to distinguish Victor from the long line of men all dressed in like work clothes and carrying metal lunch pails. There was something in the photo that she hadn't noticed when she had taken it, something beyond the weariness of the men, some sort of humiliation. "Victor didn't know I was taking this picture. He might not like it."

Nevertheless, she did enter the photograph in the contest. She was relieved when it didn't win, though, and she never did show it to Victor.

12

Even Hope had to admit that Houston summers were oppressive. Houston heat was city heat: rank, thick, intense. Ninety-ninety weather, people said, and most days the humidity did indeed match the temperature. Clothes adhered to moist skin, asphalt softened beneath tires, and plastic upholstery smelled as if it were decomposing. Children were warned not to touch anything metal.

The evenings cooled to warm, though, and sometimes Hope would sit out on the patio late at night in her shorts and halter top, enjoying the solitude and the dark and the shrill vibrato of cicadas. Everything seemed larger, cleaner, stranger at night. Sometimes, when the cicadas ceased around ten or eleven, she thought she heard the secret weaving of life itself. And she part of it.

Hope had quit her job with Triple Bar X Sausage and was now an "entrepreneur," in the phrase of the classified she'd answered. The ad, promising "an opportunity to make money in your own home," had appealed to her, because with Amber out of school for the summer, she couldn't afford increased day-care costs. The opportunity turned out to be poorly paid piecework for a doll manufacturer, but Hope thought she'd come out ahead in the long run. Besides the money saved on day care, she figured her hourly earnings were bound to increase once she'd established her mass production method, which involved attaching the bias binding to the necklines of fifty little pinafores in one continuous operation, a procedure she then repeated for armholes and hems. These days a festoon of tiny, brightly colored pinafores always lay draped from her sewing machine onto a nearby chair, looping from there to the television set and over a floor lamp to terminate at a small table near the door in the family room.

She often sewed at night, so that her days were free. She was seeing more of Chloe, who had graduated from law school in June and was taking some time off before looking for a job. When she called Hope one day and suggested they enroll Amber and Rachel and Patrick in swimming lessons at her neighborhood pool, Hope suddenly realized how much she had missed Chloe. Their friendship had foundered when Chloe and Fletcher followed through on their threat to form a fellowship. Half the congregation had joined, Hope not among them. At Chloe's request, she had attended a service and a potluck, but the company—intelligent, earnest, tedious—had not moved her to leave the church, and after that, she and Chloe had seemed set by different currents.

Now, however, it was like old times. Two days a week, she and Chloe took the children to swimming lessons, bringing their own bathing suits so they could sit in the wading pool for the duration of the lesson. Settling themselves under the transparent skin of water that stretched across the shallow concrete bowl, with noodles of light rippling on their extended legs, their brown bodies glistening like wet clay from the water they splashed on themselves to stay cool, they talked.

It seemed to Hope that Houston was about to boil over that summer. Every summer saw an escalation of evildoing in Houston, and this summer saw the usual increase. But some new ingredients bubbled through this summer's stew, as Houston's somnolent streets increasingly became the site of protests and pickets. Chloe thought it had started in May with Kent State.

It was like the Kennedy assassination, everyone asking: where were you when? Hope had been driving on the Southwest Freeway, listening to the radio. She'd had to pull over, too shaken to drive. *They're killing the children*! She couldn't get the thought out of her head.

Chloe pointed out that after Kent State, the Pacifica radio station was bombed, bullets regularly strafed the storefront where *Space City!* had set up offices, and crosses were set ablaze on lawns. She talked of emigrating. She was afraid that, as war protesters, she and Fletcher might end up on some sort of liquidation list.

Even the children seemed to be feeling the unrest. Hope would gaze out her kitchen window to see a squadron of them emerge from the bomb shelter, usually led by Amber, weapons at the ready (old curtain rods, kitchen utensils—Hope forbade toy guns), murmuring quiet commands if the enemy was in hiding, hurling wild insults if faced with a frontal assault. Crouching and running for cover in the case of air attack (the smaller children tagging along, ignored by the older ones) or bellying along the slick grass against ground forces, they would maneuver for advantage under severe odds, shouting warnings, promises of protection, and rapid changes in strategy. There was no leisure for planning—the dangers were too immediate. One had to stay exquisitely tuned to snipers in the foliage, torpedoes shooting up from treacherous waters, fighters streaking the sky with bright fire. Occasionally, a cry of pain would be followed by a grotesquely twisting body and a fall, to be swiftly attended by a sound comrade. After a telescoped healing period—ten seconds, fifteen—the downed soldier would be once more whole and back in the heat of battle.

Hope was moved by these rehearsals of courage and resourcefulness. She loved the sudden victories. In the midst of the fighting, a marvelous fate would take charge. The reinforcements would arrive, the secret weapon uncork, the bridge would blow, and in moments, all would be over, and the combatants would troop into the kitchen to stir excessive amounts of sugar into a tall pitcher of Kool-Aid.

At the beginning of the summer, Frederick occasionally participated in the games. Ocie would drop him off at Hope's if Calhoun was busy. At these times, Frederick was entirely unconvincing as a fourteen-year-old; he threw himself against the barricades and triumphed over the enemy with squirmy enthusiasm. But then he got a job at Buck's Ice House, and stopped coming by.

Ocie had thought it a good idea at first and had even helped him obtain a social security number. She thought sweeping floors and stocking shelves might instill him with a bit of work ethic. But when she discovered he was working for a pint of ice cream a day, she showed some temper. "That white sonofabitch can't get away with that! Not these days. Wake up, Mr. Buck! It's the twentieth century!"

When Frederick relayed this information to Mr. Buck, Mr. Buck threw Frederick up against the wall and broke his arm. Ocie had an NAACP lawyer on the line before Frederick's cast was dry, and the very next day Mr. Buck had the good sense to close his icehouse. "That's not the end of it!" said Ocie. "That's not the end of it! We've got college education money coming, you better believe." The case was docketed for September.

Frederick was rather pleased with his broken arm, which he rested in a black arm sling.

"That's a lesson, not a trophy," Ocie warned him, pointing to his arm. "Worse things can happen, you know. Worse things do happen. So heads up, okay?"

Very soon after that, a worse thing did happen, not to Frederick or anyone Hope knew but to two black teenagers picked up by the police out near the ship channel. One boy was delivered to Ben Taub Hospital dead on arrival, the other in a coma.

Although the story was buried on page twelve in the *Post*, the news spread quickly in some quarters. It wasn't only the young bloods eager to take to the streets. The black business leaders and ministers ("the gatekeepers," Ocie called them) were also ready to confront City Hall. *Fry them motherfuckers* is what you were likely to hear on the corner of Dowling and Elgin, while around polished desks, cigar-smoking men discussed their chances of forcing a resignation of the police chief, who had located the crime in the fact that his officers had performed their duties outside their jurisdiction.

Past crimes were reviewed. *Remember Sweet?* people in the Fifth Ward asked. *Beat brainless and then thrown into White Oak Bayou to see if he could swim?* Third Ward folks, ordinarily more circumspect, recalled Minnie Lipscomb's son. *There he was, sitting on the porch minding his own business one minute and next tumbling out the chair head into heels, shot dead from a patrol car on a drive-by.*

A march was called. Ocie insisted Hope go. "The way I see it, you have two choices. You can say no and be ashamed for the rest of your life. Or you can say yes, and have it not make any difference."

"Oh. Well, then. Since you put it that way, I guess I'll be there."

* * *

HOPE COULDN'T STOP staring at skin. Tawny skin, chestnut skin, skin the color of polished onyx and acorns and maple sugar. She envisioned a photograph of this multitude of hues, along with the red and purple and green and yellow shirts and dresses, the hairdos sporting a variety of curl and sheen. She would title it *Black*. But although her camera hung about her neck, she made no attempt to use it. She was ill at ease, as she followed Ocie and Frederick through the crowd at Emancipation Park, Frederick dressed in Daryl's latest, a rainbow-striped buccaneer shirt. A lethal-looking comb poked up from his back pocket. Victor walked at Hope's side, while Chloe and Fletcher, Calhoun and his friend Caleb, marched behind.

A Keystone Cop routine ensued when they reached Ocie's friends. Everyone quickly extended hands in overstrung eagerness, only to have them collide awkwardly without connecting and be quickly withdrawn. A new try yielded the same result. Hope's mouth felt unhinged as she added her nervous smile to the group's wry acknowledgment of intentions gone absurd through an excess of sincerity. Finally, she managed to grasp the plump hand of a grandmotherly woman, who did not cease fanning herself with a bamboo-leaf fan. It was exceedingly hot.

Word floated through the crowd that the march was about to begin, and the marchers attempted a more or less linear formation. Soon parade marshals passed by, firming up the ranks and advising everyone to stay on the sidewalk.

"Why the sidewalk?" Fletcher wanted to know.

"No permit."

"No permit?"

"Insurance costs eight hundred dollars," Ocie reminded him.

"Do you think we're likely to get arrested?" asked Hope. She had in mind not the uniformed men she saw on television wielding billy clubs, but the two policemen who had come to the school that day: one short, one tall. Suddenly she didn't want to be here where she didn't belong, where she had neither business nor cause, where she was very far from what she knew.

"Arrested? Could be," said Ocie cheerfully. "Could be we'll get our heads bashed in."

"The latest look," said Chloe.

Ocie ran her fingers through her close-cropped fleece. "Stick with me, ladies, I'll keep you strictly á la mode."

Swept into the forward roll of the crowd, Hope's feet shuffled ahead. Behind her some young men in Afros shouted slogans—"Black's on track!" "Gig them pigs!"—to scattered applause. Hope looked to Ocie for reassurance.

"Bunch of no-account dudes aiming to get quoted on the corner of Dowling and Elgin tonight," grumbled Ocie.

Gradually, the strains of "We Shall Overcome" muscled up through the din, and one by one, voices began to adhere to the melody. A few effulgent voices harmonized, while others provided the amen cadence, the sound flaring out in a curve that eventually encompassed everyone. A rudimentary, unnamed sadness welled up in Hope; her throat constricted; she couldn't sing.

The line of marchers stretched for several blocks, and the scuff of feet sounded like a giant broom scouring the pavement, as about a thousand people headed toward City Hall, three miles away. There were few spectators along the way, and the only heckling occurred near Sears, when a man with a new lawn mower shouted a suggestion they all go back to Africa.

Caleb, wearing shorts and a fishnet tank top, shamelessly displaying scrawny white flesh, smiled sweetly and gave the man the finger.

"A bowler, no doubt," said Calhoun. Bowlers were at the very bottom of his chain of being.

Fletcher found the absence of police eerie. "Where's the riot gear? Where's the tear gas?" he mused, eyes sweeping the storefronts as they passed. Ocie declared their absence insulting.

On reaching City Hall, the marchers poured down the shallow concrete stairways and into Martha Hermann Square, crowding the northwest end of the reflection pool first, then surrounding its other three sides. Loudspeakers had been set up on the terrace fronting the building, where men in sober suits mingled with booted youths in camouflage.

The crowd remained restive throughout the first two speeches— by a Baptist minister and an NAACP lawyer, the same one who was representing Frederick.

"Nobody's goddam listening," Ocie complained, glaring all around her. "Nobody listening and him *summa cum laude*. You!" she said, turning on Frederick. "Listen up!" Frederick moved to the other side of Hope.

The crowd did not really quiet down until the mother of the dead boy was introduced. A small woman in a black suit and veil, her straightened hair parted and waved, she stepped up to the microphone and waited composedly as a rotund man in fatigues and combat boots came forward to lower the microphone for her.

"He was going to play him some baseball at the flats," she began, her manner conversational, as if she and the crowd were sitting in her kitchen, fondly discussing children. "Billy Lee a very fine baseball player, you know. He do love baseball, tha's a fact, and he had jus' bought him a new glove, on 'count of it bein' payday, you know, he don't play him no numbers. 'Mama,' he say. 'I'm goin' go break in this new glove, give it a little what-for.'"

She paused to reproduce her son's gesture of punching a fist into the pocket of a glove, raising her hands in front of her and making a fist with the right. But when she attempted to connect the two, a kind of muscular stutter took over. Her right hand convulsed inches from her left in a sustained spasm, jerking back and forth uncontrollably. Her hands seemed disconnected from the rest of her still, sturdy body— rogue parts. After a moment or two, she simply watched them, enchanted, as if they were talented birds, apparently forgetting where she was or that she faced an audience. Finally, one of the sober-suited men stepped forward to grasp her elbow. She looked up at him, dazed and trusting, and he led her away.

The crowd was so quiet, the pigeons could be heard cooing.

Hope was trembling. To lose a child—it was beyond bearing. A child, by definition, was immune from death. Victor put an arm around her shoulders, and she leaned into him.

The speakers began to mill about uneasily on the stage, until finally Leroy Champion, leader of the Black Battalion, stepped forward from beneath a banner held by two color guards that read BE ARMED OR BE HARMED. The crowd began to murmur, and Frederick climbed up onto a nearby bench to get a better view. Champion tapped the microphone and the crowd quieted.

They were here today, he said, to mourn a tragedy and protest a travesty. And they were here today to get something straight. "The fascist po-lice stopped Billy Lee Sams and George Bird because of a defective headlight," he reminded them, pausing. "And a defective headlight is not a crime." He stared into the crowd long enough for them to grow restive before he resumed. "Billy Lee Sams and George Bird were seven miles from home." He paused again. "And *that* is not a crime." A jet rumbled overhead, and he waited for it to pass. "Billy Lee Sams and George Bird had a baseball bat and two gloves in the backseat . . . "

" . . . and *that* is not a crime!" shouted the crowd, catching on.

"Billy Lee Sams and George Bird were black . . . "

" . . . and *that* is not a *crime!*"

The crowd was his at that point; he could have taken them anywhere. But in an attempt to educate, he went on to discuss, at disastrous length, the history of black oppression, and by the time he launched into the doomed future of the white race, the crowd had lost steam and did not respond as they might have. He concluded by echoing the previous speakers' demand for the police chief's dismissal and announcing the Black Battalion's intention to set up a free medical clinic in Billy Lee's name. Billy Lee Sams would not be forgotten, he promised, adding, in a more ominous tone, that justice would not be forgotten either. He left the microphone with fist raised and head lowered to vigorous, but not overzealous, applause.

Ocie let out an exaggerated sigh of relief. "Thank the Lord. You never know when these young bucks going to stir up the multitudes. And we don't need that right now."

A man named Pliny Dunavant was next, an unlikely speaker. Although his wobbly rhetoric was quoted now and then in the *Forward Times*, Pliny was not taken seriously as an activist. After being evicted from his apartment, he'd organized a rent strike that hadn't gone anywhere but had given him a sense of importance. He'd held a variety of jobs and was currently selling used cars—for fair prices, everyone gave him credit for that—in a temporary lot over on Studemont. He stood onstage looking as disheveled as ever in a wrinkled polo shirt hanging outside his plaid pants. Ocie looked at her watch. "Make it short, Pliny."

Predictably, his initial remarks were hard to follow as he rambled on for some minutes, rummaging around for a connection between Billy Lee Sams's death and the slave trade. "Fifty million black people slaughtered, just like Billy Lee!" he cried. He called on the government to provide each and every black person in this country with forty acres and a mule in restitution. People stirred and nodded, but the applause was scattered.

Then he hit on something. "Speeches aren't going to do it!" he shouted, in a rhetorical swerve that snagged everyone's attention. "Passive resistance aren't going to do it! Marches aren't going to do it! The Reverend Martin Luther King is *dead*! Medgar Evars is *dead*! Malcolm X is *dead*! And Billy Lee Sams is *dead*!"

"Free at last!" called out a woman from the crowd.

"Free at last!" Dunavant repeated. "Free at last!"

The crowd began to sing it out with him. "Free at last! Free at last!"

"Freedom, that's right!" he shouted hoarsely. Sweat bathed his face and stained the front of his shirt. "That's right! And we got to be ready to die for our freedom jus' like the Reverend Martin Luther King! jus' like Malcolm! jus' like Medgar Evars! jus' like Billy Lee! Each and every one of us got to be ready to die for our *freedom*!"

Next Dunavant tore a page from the history of the Alamo. He drew an imaginary line in the imaginary dust and urged those ready to die for their freedom to step over it and follow him. Then he leaped from the terrace, the crowd parting as he strode past them toward the north end of the square. Seconds later, a swarm of marchers followed him, and soon, to the dismay of everyone banked behind the microphones, from the men in sober suits to those in paramilitary gear, more surged forward to do the same, and then more. Within ten minutes, half the crowd had left the square, to go where or to do what, no one knew. They were long out of sight when Ocie took stock of their surroundings and asked, "Where's Frederick?"

13

FREDERICK DID NOT RETURN TO OCIE'S THAT NIGHT, OR THAT
week, or the next. Ocie got in touch with Pliny Dunavant, who
said he knew nothing of Frederick. His group, he said, had disbanded
after marching to Buffalo Bayou and holding an impromptu war council,
the proceedings of which he was not at liberty to divulge. He didn't
remember seeing any kid in an Afro and a rainbow-striped buccaneer
shirt. Ocie did not take this as the last word. Pliny, she said, was too
wrapped up in himself to notice much beyond his own nose.

Meanwhile, Calhoun patrolled the Montrose every evening, riding
his bicycle up and down the streets in the heat, hoping to catch a
glimpse of him. He checked in periodically at the convenience stores,
at Rosamunda's, at the Happy Buddha. No luck.

Reading the *Post*'s account of the march, a phlegmatic ten paragraphs
on page three, Hope was struck by how little it corresponded to her
experience. The reporter estimated the crowd at four to five hundred
"dissidents" (at least a thousand, Hope thought), led by "outside agita-
tors" (Pliny Dunavant? Leroy Champion? the Reverend Roland Nel-
son?). The mayor was quoted as describing the march as "a bid for
media attention." The real reason for the march was not mentioned
until the last paragraph, where the arrested boys were described as "car
theft suspects." One was apt to miss the point that Billy Lee Sams was
dead.

As the summer drew to a close, the mesh of event cowling everyday life in Houston grew tighter. The Black Battalion had been issuing increasingly bellicose warnings to white Houston, which, in turn, increased police surveillance, which, in turn, escalated the rhetoric. Each tug on the mesh was met by a corresponding one. The Pacifica radio tower was blown up for the second time, and *Space City!* began running a column—"Shoot Back!"—on the care and use of firearms. The Glad Hand Restaurant, six blocks from the school, was torched in the middle of the night, and Montrose residents formed a vigilante committee. The police openly harassed the patrons of a gay bar in the Montrose known for witty window art, and the ACLU held legal rights forums and offered attendees a free booklet, *What to Do If You're Arrested.*

Hope began to talk about moving to the property in Kemah. Maybe she could build a dome or an A-frame there. Victor recommended East Texas, where he was going the following week to visit his brother Romain. He wanted Hope to come with him, but she had not made up her mind. "There's parts of the Big Thicket even bloodhounds can't track," he told her. "If you come with me, you can see for yourself."

Hurricane season came as a relief. The threat was impersonal; there was no one to blame and nothing anyone could do to prevent it. People watched the tropical storms traverse the Caribbean on TV weather maps and checked their supplies of masking tape, feeling useful and beyond reproach. Finally, as if in response to expectations, one of the tropical storms did gather enough force to become a full-fledged hurricane. By Friday it had moved into the Gulf with winds up to 115 miles an hour.

Hope filled the bathtub with water and bought candles, masking tape, and enough food for three days. Amber suggested they provision the bomb shelter, too, pointing out that if the wind blew off the roof, they might have to sleep there. That evening after work, Victor came over to help Hope tape windows. By this time, black clouds raced overhead, and the charged air was viscous on the skin. Amber and Patrick vibrated with a holiday-like anticipation, flitting about Hope and Victor, helping to cut the tape and misplace the scissors.

It was perhaps inevitable that Clay would run into Victor at one time or another, but Hope thought she might have managed it better. She had left a message for him with his receptionist not to pick up the children that night because of the hurricane. "I should have talked to

him myself," she told Chloe later. "I didn't think." In a more stringent
mood, she wondered if she hadn't secretly coveted the encounter. She
wondered if revenge hadn't been involved.

He arrived while she and Victor were watching the weather report
on television. He hadn't knocked—it hadn't occurred to either himself
or Hope that he should—so they didn't see him at first. He leaned up
against the doorframe for a few moments and watched the weatherman
push a magnetized hurricane icon across a map of the Gulf and explain
that the hurricane was moving north-northwest at ten to twelve miles
an hour, extending two hundred miles to the north and one hundred
miles to the south and west of the center. Clay slapped his key case
against his hand.

Startled, Hope and Victor turned. Hope noted that Clay wore his
old IU sweatshirt and khaki pants that signified the weekend. She had
washed them countless times. The sponginess of the thick cotton
sweatshirt and the slick feel of the chino cloth were stored in her fingertips.

"Didn't . . . didn't you get my message?" stammered Hope.

"No."

"I called your secretary and told her to tell you not to pick up the
kids tonight because of the hurricane." As usual, Clay's impassive face
excited her to exaggeration. "I would worry myself to death, not having
them here! Sometimes the phone lines go down, you know, and—"

"Could I speak to you in private?" Clay cocked his key case toward
the kitchen, as dart players do to focus their aim. He advanced along
this invisible line, and Hope got up to follow him through the kitchen
and toward the glass patio door, now protected by a giant asterisk of
masking tape. The door proved recalcitrant (it needed new runner
wheels), and Clay cursed as he struggled with it, finally giving it a
tremendous yank. The door shrieked open, and they stepped out onto
the patio.

The wind was tearing at the mimosa tree, flinging bits of blossom
and leaf about the yard, moaning through the neighbor's pines, stirring
up dust. Along the patio, bridal wreath waved wildly in the wind.

"Who's your friend?" Clay asked.

"I would have introduced you if you'd given me a chance. His name—"

"What's he doing here?"

"He came to help me tape windows."

"Why didn't you call me?"

"Actually, I didn't call *him*. He just showed up when he heard about the hurricane watch."

"I see. He knows you well enough to just *show up*?" Clay grabbed a branch of the waving bridal wreath and broke it off. She didn't answer, and he began stripping the branch of its leaves. "He's drinking out of my mug, Hope."

She laughed. "Clay—"

"It may seem laughable to you, but that mug was a Christmas gift from my secretary two years ago. I happen to know that a good deal of thought went into its selection." Hope tried to remember which mug he was talking about. "I don't want him drinking from it. And I don't want him anywhere near Amber or Patrick either."

"Victor is very good with kids. He and Amber speak French. A version of French."

"I don't want him anywhere near my children." Shoulders hunched forward, tension articulating his neck muscles, Clay looked harnessed, invisibly strapped and girdled. Hope had often admired the way he was capable of holding himself in check indefinitely.

"In the first place, that's not really possible," she said, "and in the second place, you have no right—"

"That's where you're wrong, Hope. I do have a right. I most certainly do have a right." He began snapping the branch into small pieces, his elbows pressed into his sides.

He's trying not to hit me! she thought. Alert now to his smell, the flare of his nostrils, the sound of the breaking twigs, she took a cautious step backward. His hand flew up to strike her, and she raised her own to break its force. They froze for a split second; then Clay flung the twigs at her. A few of them hit her, pinpricks. They stared at one another, exhilarated by this brush with violence, this sudden onrush of thrilling clarity.

"Don't misunderstand, Hope." Clay's voice was new and low. "I don't care who screws you. I haven't cared about that for years. It's been a long time since you were the only duck in the barrel." Hope didn't quite register this as he went on. "But I do not want any of your gigolos drinking from *my* coffee mug." *Gigolos?* "And I do not want him around my children. Round them up. I'm taking them with me."

Her heart started to racket around in her chest. "What do you mean?"

"What I said. I'm taking them with me. It's my weekend."

"But the hurricane—"

"Round them up. I'll be waiting in the car." He turned, vaulted the bridal wreath, and crossed the yard to let himself out through the gate to the driveway. He would sit there until the children came out. He would sit there all night, if necessary. And maybe she should just let him. Maybe she should go inside and fix dinner and watch *Gunsmoke* with Amber and Patrick and then put them to bed and just let Clay sit there in the driveway, while she and Victor played cribbage or something, and the hurricane roared all around them. Let him just sit there shipwrecked.

The image of Clay shipwrecked, however, led to another one: Amber's and Patrick's faces pressed up against the window glass. *What's Daddy doing out there? Why is he out in the hurricane? Why can't he come in?*

The patio door shrieked its alarm as she opened it. Without speaking to Victor, who looked at her inquiringly, she walked past him to Amber's room and began to pack Amber's nightgown, extra T-shirts, and shorts. Amber came in, assessed the situation in silence, and collected the books from beside her bed. Next Hope gathered Patrick's clothes from his bedroom, and then carried the packed overnight bag into the family room, where he and Victor were watching television. "Daddy's waiting for you in the car," she told him. He looked at her for a moment, then jumped up and ran to his room, returning with his stuffed alligator.

She walked out with them and leaned down to speak softly to Clay so the children wouldn't hear. "You're bringing them back, right?"

"Of course."

"Sunday evening? About six?" He nodded. "And if the hurricane hits—"

"They'll be perfectly safe, Hope, for crissakes, I'm their father!"

Amber leaned forward from the backseat of Clay's new Corolla to ask could they please get going, because they were going to miss *Gunsmoke* if they didn't.

* * *

THAT NIGHT THE hurricane veered inland at Aransas Pass, about 180 miles south of Houston. Thirteen people died and the damage was extensive. Houston suffered no more than high winds and rain, however, and by Saturday evening even the winds had died down and the weather was hot and muggy again. But Hope's apprehension had failed to dissipate with the hurricane's spent force. She began tasks and abandoned them, started to phone Chloe and hung up before the connection was completed, wandered in and out of Amber's and Patrick's rooms, forgetting what she'd had in mind there.

Victor offered to take her to the Frenchtown Bar. He had been wanting to take her there ever since he'd met her. "If the zydeco don't get you, the gumbo will," he promised.

"Doesn't. If the zydeco doesn't." Hope had taken to correcting his grammar.

He waved a hand scarred by a recent welding burn. "But *m'amie*! The zydeco *will*! Loosen up, *m'amie*!"

HOPE HADN'T REALIZED that the Frenchtown Bar was in the Fifth Ward. "I hope we don't have a flat tire," she said nervously, imagining herself in a disabled car, surrounded by angry, unappeasable black faces, as she piloted the Cadillac down Collingsworth, already congested with a Saturday-night crowd. On either side of the street, crosscurrents of promenaders intersected and divided, met and folded back. Here and there, clusters of men stood smoking and talking, interrupting themselves occasionally in a lightening-quick shift of attention. "Hey, baby! You lookin' ovah-plus good!" At one point Hope had to slam on her brakes, heart racing, when one of them dashed in front of her in pursuit.

Following Victor's directions, she turned into a parking lot full of chug holes, and the Cadillac bucked its way to a space on the perimeter. Leaving the car, they skirted puddles of muddy water and walked toward the entrance, where a man sitting on a long-legged bar stool informed them that admission was six bits.

"No discounts for whiteys?" asked Victor with a grin.

The man slapped his knee and laughed as if this were a rare, fine joke, at the same time deftly taking their money without letting his skin touch theirs. He rubber-stamped the back of their hands with the same fastidiousness and gestured with an extravagant sweep of his hand for them to enter.

The building was small, low-ceilinged, and crowded. On the dance floor a dazzling confusion of patterns in bold combinations—plaids and dots and stripes and geometrics—melded and twined. One woman wearing a rhinestone beret atop a glossy red wig danced alone in passionate self-communion, oblivious to a tall man in a purple satin blouse edging up on her, his billowing sleeves a show of sheen and shadows.

Hope and Victor made their way through the crowd, searching for a table. Hope sensed people watching without watching. After they had circuited the room once, Victor waylaid a miniskirted waitress to ask about the availability of a table.

"One be up real soon!" she called over her shoulder. "Lots o' folks jus' here to eat."

This did not appear to be the case, however. Those who couldn't fit onto the dance floor were dancing between the tables, and even the seated were shaking their shoulders and snapping their fingers, feet flickering beneath the tables. An accordion, drums, and a washboard provided the music, a raspy whonk-whonk with a beat Hope couldn't follow because it kept changing, although the dancers had no trouble, the fleet stepping spicy circles around it, the heftier stomping it with lumbering enthusiasm. One stout woman with glistening straight hair laughingly pulled a man with a flamboyant, multijointed step across the floor like a string toy.

"He doin' de duck walk, missy," said an old man inches from her elbow. A nimbus of white hair framed a face as wrinkled as a walnut shell. He nearly toppled as he leaned toward her. "Tha' boy got six knees on one leg!" He cackled long and loudly at this, flashing bright pink gums.

The music stopped, and the accordion surrendered a ragged wheeze as the bandleader set it down on a chrome-legged chair. "Break time, folks! Don' go way!"

A few minutes later, the miniskirted waitress surprised them by returning and leading the way to a table the size of a chessboard. Victor ordered gumbo, boudain, and beer.

"Push and pull and rub and scrub!" sang out the accordionist, introducing the next set.

Looking out over the dance floor, Hope watched feet: a worn pair of white loafers with black piping, stack-heeled boots, clear-plastic heels in which floated tiny silver stars. Bell-bottomed cuffs swept the plank floor.

When their food arrived, Victor addressed it with mute respect, while Hope tasted cautiously.

"You like that sausage, missy?" The old man who had spoken to Hope earlier was threatening to tumble onto their plates as he swayed over them.

"Mmmmm," she said.

"Gator meat!" he hooted, subsiding into cackles as he two-stepped off.

"Rice, liver, and hog's blood," Victor corrected.

Hope preferred the gumbo, which was savory and intense, foreign in a pleasant way.

"It's good," agreed Victor, "but wait till you taste my grandmére's. You're coming, aren't you?" Victor was still trying to persuade Hope to accompany him to East Texas to visit his brother. "You can take lots of pictures, *m'amie*. Like in *National Geographic*."

Hope wanted to go, and Fern had offered to stay with Amber and Patrick. But Amber didn't want her to leave, and Hope was hesitating. "I'm not sure yet, Victor. I'm thinking about it."

When they had finished eating, Victor asked her to dance. Hope eyed the dancers, noting again that she was the only white woman. "Maybe we should let our food digest first."

"We're not going swimming, *m'amie*." He stood up, held out his arms, snapped his fingers, and ground his hips.

A dancing man is a delight to women. Hope smiled and joined him, shedding reluctance from her shoulders as she took his hand. Victor swiveled his knees down low, and she followed; they rose touching fingertips, and she spun off, pivoting in place, twitching one hip like a flamenco dancer. Opposite her, Victor moved an arm, a hip, unfurling bolts of himself, and Hope's own hips unlocked, as the beat became suddenly accessible.

"Not bad for a white girl!" It was the old man again. He grabbed Hope, and they danced in mutual alarm for a moment until he stumbled, was caught by Victor, and gently redirected. Hope laughed and shimmied her shoulders, and, careless and free, they danced in a nebula of tune and beat, as if they'd forgotten how to walk or talk and dancing were the only thing they knew.

When the song ended, Hope felt a tug on her sleeve. "I think ol' Lonnie done called in de debil on dat one!" the old man shouted in her ear. Before she could say anything in return, he had relaunched himself into the crowd, cackling loudly as he disappeared into its depths.

That's when Hope saw Frederick. Half the height of everyone around him, he stood just inside the row of tables near the bar, the only stock-still point in a sea of bodies, his arm in its black sling. Hope started toward him.

Victor grabbed her arm. "Where're you goin', *m'amie*?"

"I just saw Frederick. Over there." She turned and pointed, but Frederick was gone. The crowd had at least doubled since their arrival, and the smoke was now as thick as soft cheese. There was little point in searching for him.

"Don't worry about him, *m'amie*. Somebody watchin' over that boy." This had been Victor's firm conviction since the day he'd rescued him from the telephone pole.

The music had started again, and Victor cocked an ear. "Listen at that, *m'amie*. Those boys slicin' a secon' to make that music last forever. We don't have to *never* quit. Come on, *m'amie*."

THEY LEFT AROUND two. Victor protested that Lonnie was just warming up, but Hope wanted to go. She had not been able to relax since glimpsing Frederick. "I should have yelled. I don't think he saw me," she said, forgetting she was the only white woman in the bar.

Victor reluctantly agreed to go. "Comin' through!" he shouted, reaching out to part the bodies to let them pass. No one paid any attention to them now. Most people were passionately immersed in either the music or their own jive.

At the door, they met the man who had taken their money. "Drawbridge goin' up?" he asked with a grin, holding out a hand. Victor slapped it, and they executed an elaborate handshake involving rotating palms and fanned fingers. "See you next week, man. If she rains . . ."

". . . she only rains on the roof!" finished Victor. "Zydeco! *C'est ça je vis pour!*"

Outside, Victor bent to kiss her. Putting an arm around her, he began to sing as they crossed the cratered parking lot.

> *Moi et la belle, on avait été-z-au bal,*
> *On a passé dans tous les honky tonks,*
> *S'em a revenu—*

"Hey, mon!" he said, breaking off. They'd reached the Cadillac, where Frederick perched on the fender.

Relief akin to ecstasy flooded over Hope. "Don't tell me, let me guess. You need a ride, right?"

Grinning, Frederick slid from the fender, landing just west of a puddle.

"A ride? You bet, mon. Get in!" said Victor, making a move to throw open a door, which, however, was locked. As she searched for her keys, Victor complained that where he came from there was no need to lock anything.

"I'll drive, *m'amie*," he said, when Hope finally got the door open, taking the keys from her hand. Frederick climbed into the backseat to sit, erect and poised, arms folded across his chest, grinning, while Victor got into the front. Hope sighed and got in on the passenger side, leaning back and closing her eyes. It seemed she was required to surrender her fate to a dancing man.

They drove north on Highway 59. A deep passivity stilled Hope's nerves, and she let the splendid power of the engine carry her forward, allowed the warm, dark air to swallow her down the narrow throat of the road. She felt cradled, safe somehow, swaddled in speed.

Exiting at Old Humble Road, they passed under the North Belt to head east on Atascocita. Passing the prison farm, Victor began to sing again.

> *Goodbye, chére vieille mam',*
> *Goodbye, pauvre vieux pap',*
> *Goodbye á mes fréres,*
> *Et mes chéres petites soeurs.*
> *Moi, j'ai été condamné*
> *Pour la balance de ma vie*
> *Dans les barres de la prison.*

When they reached Lake Houston, Victor slowed down. "Want to drive across the dam?" he asked. Hope and Frederick said yes, and he drove up and out along the two-lane strip of asphalt that ran along the top of the dam. It was completely dark, except for a light on a small building at the far end.

Midway across, Victor stopped the car, and they got out. Enveloped in the roar of water, Hope had the sensation of great height. She was reminded of dreams she'd had of clambering across precarious catwalks. There was the same feeling of isolation, a shiver of the same fear even, although the roadway beneath their feet could scarcely have been more solid. She strained to hear cries of nighthawks through the sound of the falling water, but it was impossible. She could not even hear her own footsteps.

They reached the concrete roadguard. Hope could just make out the lake, which appeared shoreless in the dark, a limitless body of black. She wondered if the next time she drew a glass of water from the tap she would remember standing on the crest of a dam overlooking Houston's water supply in the dead of night with a black boy and a dancing man. She was at a loss as to how to annex this night into the familiar territory she called her life.

ON SUNDAY EVENING, when Clay returned with Amber and Patrick, Clay did not mention the previous Friday at all. He did not mention Victor. He did not mention the hurricane. He did not talk about Amber and Patrick, or what they had done that weekend. He was concerned about the lawn.

"You see those brown spots?" He pointed to several brown, amoebic shapes marring the green expanse of lawn. "You'd better take care of them right away before you lose the entire lawn."

"What spots?"

"Right there. Fungus. It attacks the roots."

She looked, seeing the spots for the first time.

"It could be chinch bugs, but I don't think so. It looks like fungus to me. I'll bet you didn't aerate this spring, did you?"

"No, I—"

"You have to aerate, Hope. On the wall of the garage, next to the rake, there's a long-handled dibble. Use that to aerate. You just punch it into the ground to make holes. After you aerate, get some fungicide. Try the garden supply on West Alabama. They usually have it. I forget the brand name. Comes in a green-and-white bag."

"I'll get some," she said.

"That fungus can spread like wildfire once it gets started," he said, slipping into the front seat. "It thrives on alkaline soil like this. Don't put it off."

"I said I'd take care of it, Clay."

14

F REDERICK DIDN'T WANT TO LIVE WITH OCIE ANYMORE. HE
wanted to live at Black Battalion Headquarters, where he had
ended up the night after the march, enlisting the next day. Although
his active participation had been disallowed because of his age, his loyalty
had not been underestimated, and the influence of the Battalion was
evident in Frederick's new disciplined air. The slouch he'd learned from
Daryl disappeared; he walked erect now with hands at his sides. He
wore his shirt tucked in. He polished the new combat boots the brothers
had purchased for him.

Everyone applauded these developments and, at the same time, worried about Frederick's association with the Black Battalion. Calhoun
tried to persuade him to return to Ocie's, but Frederick remained adamant, and Calhoun's efforts were halfhearted, in any case. "At least he's
learning to read," he explained. Frederick was making his way through
We, the People, Leroy Champion's mimeographed manifesto, under the
tutelage of the author himself.

Hope was only vaguely aware of all this; she was busy that week
preparing for her trip with Victor to the Big Thicket. She had stocked
the pantry and planned to clean the house, if she had time. A memoran-
dum for Fern had been lengthening all week long, detailing the household routine (bedtimes, garbage pickup on Tuesdays and Fridays,
double-coupon day on Wednesdays at Kroger's), various telephone num-

bers and appointments (dental checkups, Patrick's immunizations), instructions (don't let Amber eat apples, remember to turn on ventilator fan in bomb shelter). She had been sewing nearly around the clock to avoid the loss of a week's wages, and the night before she was to leave was working on the last batch of pinafores.

"What if there's another hurricane?" Amber asked.

The click and hum of the sewing machine came to a halt. "Fern will be here."

"Why can't I stay with Rachel?"

"I told you. Rachel's grandparents are visiting."

"Why can't my grandparents visit?"

"Your grandmother hates Houston," Hope reminded her. "And Grandma Lydia is not feeling well, last I heard."

"Why can't I stay with Dad?"

"He's working." Hope pressed her knee against the lever to start her machine and resumed sewing. She feared Amber's next suggestion might be Mindy.

"Why can't I come?"

Hope stopped sewing. "I'm taking a vacation, Amber."

"I don't want you to go."

Guilt: another word for resentment, Alex said. Hope started her machine again. The needle arm raced, its vertical motion blurred.

"Besides," Amber went on, "Adam is a barf-face. I hate him."

HOPE AND VICTOR's departure the next morning went smoothly, contrary to Hope's fears. Fern and Adam arrived on time, and there were no recriminations from Amber or pleas from Patrick, no series of small mishaps to accumulate in foreboding. Still, Hope felt a little flimsy and loose, not quite steady enough to drive, and she handed the keys over to Victor.

The yellowed weeds and grasses alongside the Eastex Freeway blurred into butter as the city receded, and gradually the dry fields gave way to brilliant green rice fields extending to the horizon. The landscape was stillness itself, the essence of waiting, while above, the clouds too were motionless, arrested in an upward surge. Hope's internal rhythms slowed, and they drove in silence for a long time, her enthusiasm for the trip dormant until she thought to pull out the map from the glove compartment. As a child, she'd collected road maps, filling shoe boxes with them, and as she stretched this one across her knees, a keen nomadic urge that had never lain far beneath the domestic topsoil revived.

"Fred! Fred, Texas! Can you believe that, Victor? We should visit Fred someday. And look! Winnie! We could visit Fred and Winnie in one day. Or wait, here's a better one: Sourlake. I'd like to be able to say I'd been to Sourlake. Or how about China? We could be in China in two hours. Hey. Nome and China are only five miles apart on this map. Isn't that wild?"

By the time they stopped for a picnic lunch at a roadside park outside of Beaumont, Hope had repossessed her high spirits. They ate the corned beef sandwiches she'd made and drank the two cans of beer they'd bought at a 7-Eleven, which were just icy enough to give them a brief shiver in the noonday heat.

"Tell me about Romain," she said.

Romain was good-hearted underneath it all, Victor told her. She would like his wife, Alma.

"'Alma' doesn't sound very French."

"No. Nor Catholic either. That's why they had to run away to get married. Also, Alma was only fourteen."

"Fourteen!" Frederick was fourteen. She couldn't imagine him married. She herself had only been eighteen, but between eighteen and fourteen was terrain of significant experience.

"Romain, he was only sixteen. Sixteen and Catholic. So they head for the woods. Romain's the black sheep of the family. He's the only one lives on the Texas side of the Sabine."

"Besides you."

"I mean for good."

From Beaumont they headed north, losing the high sky and horizon to a canopy of loblolly and sweet gum and ponderosa pine. The Cadillac purred past grocery shacks with rusty Nehi signs nailed to the sides, their patched porches looking like worn aprons, roadside honky-tonks, and numerous No Trespassing signs hanging from barbed-wire fences. At one point, they passed a barren tract of land that had been clear-cut, the stumps bulldozed into windrows, waiting to be burned.

It was late afternoon when they turned from the main highway onto

a narrow road with ragged asphalt shoulders, surrounded by trees and
brush. Half an hour later, they swung onto a red, rutted dirt road, where
the Cadillac pitched and tossed, branches screaking against its sides, as
it plunged into the wet, leafy maw of the Big Thicket. Towering, scaly-
barked pine, hundred-foot magnolias, beeches, yaupon, and leath-
erwood—many heavily bearded in Spanish moss, others swagged in
meandering loops of greenbrier—rose from a woodland floor profuse
with waist-high fern.

The road was little more than tire tracks when it expired at the barely
moving waters of a low creek, its nearest bank occupied by half a dozen
auto carcasses. Victor pulled up next to a 1949 Ford pickup beneath
a hand-lettered sign nailed to a ponderosa: FISHERMEN AND HUNTER'S
WELCOME. OTHER LIERS, TOO.

They got out and Victor sat down on the bumper to pull off his
boots. Hope looked from him to the creek and back again. "You mean
we're going to . . .?"

He grinned and nodded, handing her a stick that had been lying by
his feet. "Let the snakes know you're coming," he advised.

The water was surprisingly cool, given the late-afternoon heat and
the shallowness of the creek, which at its deepest point never reached
their knees. Victor had not bothered to roll up his jeans, and he sloshed
happily through the dark-tinted but clear waters, Hope's suitcase on his
head, balancing it with his fingertips. She carried his rucksack, which
was lighter, and her sandals, advancing more slowly, cautiously probing
the creek bottom with her stick.

From the creek they followed a path bordered by wildflowers, limp
in the afternoon heat.

"It's so quiet," whispered Hope.

"Nap time for the birds. Tomorrow morning you'll hear them all
right You'll think you died and went to heaven."

They came to a green clearing, where an L-shaped cabin with the
silvery patina of old unpainted wood rested on concrete blocks, its
corrugated-tin roof dappled with leaf shadows. To Hope, it was exotic
in its dereliction; she felt as if she'd stepped back into a former century.
A shaded verandah ran along the inner sides of the L, where chairs and
stools—missing an arm here, a leg there—were scattered about. Pans
and plastic jugs and a lantern hung from different posts; a white enamel

teakettle gleamed from beneath the verandah floor. As they approached, a raucous yelping and howling went up, and five narrow-chested, slinky dogs appeared, stirring a flock of auburn chickens to a desperate chorus of clucks and squawks.

"Romain's hog dogs," Victor told her.

"Hog dogs?"

"For boar hunts."

Beneath the din, Hope heard laughter from the shadows of the verandah—a gravelly, fluid laugh—and a man in a camouflage jumpsuit emerged from its far corner.

At first, Hope could not have guessed that this man and Victor were twins. Romain was taller than Victor, his hair blondish where Victor's was dark, his eyes blue not hazel. But as they embraced and broke into fast Cajun French, they became one, their voices exactly alike, identical in pitch and pace, in timbre, in certain idiosyncrasies of rhythm.

Three barefoot girls burst through the half-hinged door and leaped from the porch to throw themselves at Victor. Two attached limpetlike to his sides, while the third, the smallest, wearing round glasses that magnified her eyes, anchored herself in front by tucking two small hands inside his belt. As they chattered in French, Romain gave Hope a wink by way of including her.

The screen door banged again to announce the emergence of a diminutive woman with auburn hair. Her white nurse's shoes were scuffed and run-down at the heels, and the apron over her cutoff jeans was dirty, but these seemed marks of defiance more than slovenliness. There was an assertion of superiority in her neglect of person. I can afford to be careless, said her demeanor. What I've got is not store-bought.

"Alma!" cried Victor, jumping up onto the porch to enfold her in a hug. She nearly disappeared in his arms, being so tiny.

"Marie!" she shouted to one of the girls, breaking away. "Put them chickens up, I can't hear myself think!" She turned to her husband. "And if them dogs of yourns, Rome, don't cut their yappin', I'll give 'em somethin' to yap about. Mangy curs." Stepping to the edge of the verandah, she called, "Georges! Philippe! Come see what the cat's dragged in!" Two boys, about ten and twelve or so, slipped from behind a shed at the verge of the clearing and edged toward the house, hands stuffed into pockets. They hauled themselves up onto the veranda without looking at Hope.

Victor shook their hands and pulled their ears. They stared at Victor's elf boots. Where did he get them? How much did they cost?

"He'd better not wear them in town," Romain put in. "He might get mistook."

There was one more person to meet—Victor's grandmère, who now made her way through the screen door, leaning on a polished wood cane and wearing a crocheted cloche despite the heat. Victor hugged her and kissed her cheeks. She stepped back and whacked him on the shoulder with her cane.

"Five years and you aren't come to see me, Veek-torr," she chastised him. "You are busy making a fortune, eh?" She glanced at Hope, who realized the old woman's English was a form of hospitality.

"No, Nana, I've been busy seeing the world."

"The world?! Pssshoo." She waved a hand, batting the world to one side.

"I've been across the ocean, Nana. I've been to France."

She frowned. "Not Parrr-ee, I hope. Bordeaux maybe? Not Parrree, I hope. The people there have a . . . a . . ." She paused, searching for the English word. ". . . modern accent, very . . . modern and not *joli*."

Victor introduced Hope. The old woman examined her carefully but well within the bounds of courtesy, inquiring after her journey and asking if she would like a cool drink of water.

They were ten for dinner that night, more people than Hope was used to facing at one sitting, and she said little, feeling under pointed scrutiny, especially from Nana and the girls. Although no one directed any questions or conversation directly to her, she had the sense that a good deal of what was said was for her benefit.

They told stories—about the time Victor had given artificial respiration to a hog ("valuable livestock," Victor explained), about the time Romain had been so drunk he ended up at his own back door asking to use the phone to call his wife. They gossiped about relatives, bringing Victor up to date on the doings of Oncle Alcide and Tante Célestin and Cousin Armande and others, and they recalled several occasions when Nana's gumbo had been cause for celebration. Nana told of netting shad using Spanish moss for bait.

Dinner was a pandemonium of tongues: sometimes French, some-times English, sometimes a mixture of both, usually with two or three people talking at once. The girls giggled and whispered, and the two boys amused themselves by passing pepper when salt was requested, butter when someone asked for bread, potatoes instead of carrots. No one seemed to notice save Alma, who threatened to hang them by their thumbs from the porch beam.

To Hope, Romain and his family were spirits out of Pandora's box, fiery with ego and unpredictable energy. After dinner, they played cards, games unfamiliar to Hope that involved slapping them and tossing them into piles and stirring them around. Everyone but Nana, who had gone to bed, had gathered in a gallery-type room that ran the longer leg of the cabin's L, its floor covered by linoleum worn down in spots to the black, fibrous backing. The furnishings were a mix of rough pieces—a chair made of tree branches with the bark still on, a plank bench—and antiques—a carved oak sideboard and tables. Romain offered Hope and Victor a clear, strong liquid that burned her mouth and made her dizzy after two swallows.

As the night wore on, the children fell asleep one by one, the older ones carrying the younger ones to bed until they, too, succumbed. Around midnight Alma invited Hope to accompany her on an errand of mercy, leading her down a narrow, inclined path toward the woods. The night air was heavy with floral scents underscored by rot.

"Careful," Alma warned. "Them boys done set a trap here." She shined her flashlight on a patch of small, sharp stakes embedded in the path. It descended sharply at this point and had been slicked with wet mud. "Boys," Alma said derisively.

Entering a clearing, she wandered about for a few minutes, searching, until she found a large aluminum kettle beneath some cut branches of loblolly pine. Handing Hope the flashlight, she bent down and tipped it over, spilling out a score or more frogs creaking in alarm. "I won't have reptiles at my table," she said. "I draw the line."

"Amphibians," Hope corrected without thinking.

Alma shrugged. "Anything slimy, I won't skin, won't gut, won't fry."

Back in the cabin, Romain and Victor were deep in conversation. Alma shook a marmalade cat from the seat of a straight-backed chair and indicated that Hope was to sit there, pulling up a stool for herself.

She removed a pack of cigarettes from her pocket, offering one to Hope, who took it, feeling reckless and new.

"My only vice," said Alma, lighting up.

'Ha!" said Victor. Alma grinned.

Romain and Victor had made noticeable inroads on the liquor supply by this time, and Romain had turned serious. He advised Victor to quit his "drag-ass" job at the shipyard and return to the backcountry for the good of his manhood. "Wages are the death of a man," he said, placing a hand on Victor's shoulder and looking him in the eye. "Wages beggar the soul." He boasted to Hope that he'd never earned a dime in his life.

"I have," put in Alma sourly.

"But how do you live without money?" Hope asked. "How do you eat?"

"Like kings!" said Romain. "Deer, boar, trout—"

"Squirrel," broke in Alma. "One time we ate squirrel stew six days in a row."

"And pheasant that Sunday!" roared Romain, relishing the last word. "Isn't that right?" Bagged a half-*dozen* that Sunday. Isn't that right?" Alma admitted that this was true.

They talked for a while longer before Alma declared it was time to retire. She handed out blankets, assigning Victor to the boys' sleeping quarters, Hope to the girls'. Hope glanced at Victor, but his expression was blandly obliging.

Later, though, he appeared at the side of her cot and led her out to the verandah, where they made quiet love on an old quilt to the belling of owls, their skin damp with desire and the night air. The marmalade cat hovered over them, curious, studying them first from one angle, then another. Hope laughed softly, feeling her own body fur over and grow warm from lovemaking that had all the generosity and expansiveness of outdoors.

THE NEXT DAY Romain took Victor and Hope into the swamp. For this they needed the cooperation of the '49 pickup.

"Meet A.K.," said Romain, slapping the hood. "Almost Kaput."

A.K. had no doors, no fenders, and a wooden platform instead of a flatbed. The three of them crowded into the front seat to look out through a windshield innocent of glass. When Romain fired up the engine, the noise was deafening: A.K. lacked a muffler. The oversized tires, webbed with chain, gouged up a spume of red dirt, and the truck lurched forward. The gas gauge needle lay inert on the E.

"Does A.K. have brakes?" Hope shouted over the roar, noting that the brake pedal lay flat against the floorboard.

"Hell, no!" yelled Romain. "I want her to go, not stop!"

They bucked and backfired over what Romain insisted was a road, past ponderosa and palmetto. The dogs ranged ahead, exuberant, their noses pushing against the air.

"Hang in there, A.K.," crooned Romain. "Show us your stuff," he begged, stomping on the gas.

When Hope saw the fallen tree lying across the road just in front of them, held fast by a tangle of vine and brier, she covered her face with her hands. But Romain had done this before, had calculated the ratio of momentum to distance down to the last fraction, and the impact was surprisingly gentle, a bump, not a crash. He grinned as A.K. shuddered to a halt.

The sudden silence struck Hope simultaneously with the sight of the swamp before them, its still waters a mirror for the stately sweet bays growing in them, so perfectly reflected that the individual ridges of the bark were replicated. They looked like the columns of a palace, stretching endlessly back toward a vanishing point. Mats of sphagnum moss floated on the surface, green inkblots contrasting with the silvery pans of sunlight. Hope reached for her camera.

With Romain leading the way, the three of them slogged through the trees, their footsteps softly sucking in the marshy ground. At one point, hearing the squeal of a wood duck, he ordered them behind the cover of ferns and pointed to Hope's camera, indicating she was to prepare for a good shot. Crouching behind the green screen, Hope's thighs soon began to ache. Victor, hungover from the night before, lay down and went to sleep.

The wait turned out to be worth it. A bright-eyed wood duck and her three small ducklings paddled serenely into Hope's viewfinder, and she snapped, startling them into a fluster of wings that flung water in all directions before they settled down again and paddled away.

Romain whispered that they should move on and come back for

Victor later. Hope was worried that they might not find him again in this pathless world.

"I know every tree," he assured her.

Romain was proprietary in his role of scout, proudly pointing out this stalk of wild orchids (ladies' tresses, he called them), that clump of speckled Carolina lilies. He knew where to look. Without him, she would never have seen a lizard skeleton, bones like threads, inside the red-veined throat of a pitcher plant. He generated a slipstream of concentration and energy, pulling Hope alongside. Verbena, spiderwort, self-heal, he whispered in her ear, as she aimed and shot, her head humming with the excitement of decisions—this angle, that lens opening. Several times when she was about to shoot too soon, he laid a hand on her arm, staying her until the right moment, the moment when the wren opened wide its beak to sing or the moment when barely perceptible ripples of water became the peevish head of a snapping turtle.

They moved with a stealth that seemed a part of herself she'd forgotten, as if she had just sloughed off the encrusted movements of two decades, mere scurf. Even her camera was more an extension of herself than the apparatus she was usually adjusting and juggling. Focusing on a resurrection fern, a pale green pelt overspreading a barked oak arm, her mind and body condensed into purpose.

"She's a born hunter," Romain said to Victor when they returned to find him eating a mustard sandwich.

It was true, Hope marveled. Or if it was not, she'd been reincarnated as one that day.

"NANA LIKES YOU," Alma told Hope several nights later, as they set out on their nightly mission to free the frogs.

Hope felt like an impostor. It had become clear that not only Nana but Alma and Romain, too, assumed that Victor had brought her with him for appraisal, an assumption Hope sensed also in the excitement of the girls and the shy assessment of the boys. It was an assumption Victor had done nothing to contradict, and Hope didn't know how to go about doing so herself. Hold on, I'm not divorced yet, she might say, but what would Alma, married at fourteen, mother of five, a woman who knew how to cook squirrel and wild boar, think of that? Did people who lived in the Big Thicket get divorced? It seemed to Hope they were more likely to shoot one another or simply walk off into the swamp.

Nor had she any idea of Victor's true intentions. He had not mentioned marriage to her, ever. Perhaps here with his family, he was simply going along with their expectations, which would dissolve when they returned to Houston.

Houston. How had she got here from there, in the company of a man so foreign to her experience? Her life had changed substance somehow, had turned, as milk turns, but not sour, no, she wouldn't have missed this for anything, no, her life had not turned sour but strange. Or perhaps it was the Big Thicket that was strange. An aura of knotty enchantment issued from the dim, dense tangle, its tonic power mysteriously making itself felt.

She would like to stay an extra week. Romain had asked them to. Victor was eager, and Hope was tempted. The mental reveille she experienced over and over as she prowled the swamps with Romain struck her as portentous and vital. Having thought she had relinquished curiosity to her children a long time ago, the heightened sense of regard she was feeling here in the Big Thicket had taken her by surprise.

She decided to call Fern tomorrow, when she and Victor drove to Moscow, a small logging town where they were to ride the train Victor used to take when he worked for the lumber company. If Fern was agreeable, and Amber and Patrick, too, Hope didn't see why she couldn't stay another week. Damn the pinafores.

THE NEXT DAY, they located a phone booth outside a gas station, and Hope leaned up against the cracked Plexiglas as she dropped in her quarters. Outside, Victor paced. He was afraid they would miss the train. She chewed on a thumbnail and listened to the phone's insistent burr, letting it ring ten times before hanging up. "No answer," she told Victor, returning to the car.

"Maybe they've gone swimming or something."

"Probably. I'll call again when we get back."

The town was little more than a lumberyard, a set of railroad tracks, and a gray, two-story, barrackslike building with uniformly spaced windows.

"I lived there once," Victor said.

"You did?" Hope stared at the building, seeming to see through the narrow windows to the unpainted plasterboard walls of the austere rooms and the bare lightbulb fixture with the frayed wire. To hide her dismay, she took some pictures.

As they approached the tracks, they heard some hissing and screeching and grinding coming from a large shed, and the train emerged, sounding a sportive whistle and venting a roiling plume of steam from a cone-shaped smokestack.

"*M'amie*, let's go! Hurry!"

They climbed on board along with a half-dozen others. The sole passenger car was authentically antique, with oily wooden floorboards and broken cane seats and gaslight fixtures encrusted with dark deposits. "This way," said Victor as Hope started to sit down, guiding her instead into the adjoining car, a boxcar, where gray canvas bags and cardboard boxes lined both walls. A man sitting at a desk sorting through a stack of pastel forms did not look up. "I always rode the mail car!" Victor explained, raising his voice over the noisy contact of wheel and rail. He bounced around the mail car, touching its four corners, taking possession. He leaned out the open door, his body at a dangerous tilt, and, stepping gingerly against the swaying motion, Hope joined him there, the roadbed rushing at her feet.

"Patrick and Amber would love this!" she shouted over the clacking of wheels. She felt Patrick's small hand tugging on hers, saw Amber's mouth shaped for a question. Hope missed them then, for the first time.

When she and Victor returned later that afternoon, Hope headed straight for the phone booth. As the phone rang and rang, a truck rumbled by, then an old Ford full of teenagers.

Hope used to have dreams of opening a bureau drawer or a trunk or, once, a small handbag to find a child she'd forgotten, dead. Or she would leave an infant gurgling in a playpen and return to find it shrunken and curled into a dry leaf. Alex said these were dreams of her abandoned child self, but Hope was convinced they represented the wages of neglect. The terror and guilt of these dreams returned to her now, as she hung up the unanswered phone. She stood there for a moment gazing out through the cracked Plexiglas and then dialed the number at Communitas.

Alex answered. No, he hadn't seen Fern or Oily Jon, but since they hadn't returned to Communitas, he was sure everything was all right. "You're a catastrophic, Hope."

"What?"

"A catastrophic. As opposed to an anastrophic. A catastrophic projects all the bad things that could happen. An anastrophic projects all the wonderful things that could happen. Both are neurotic and irrelevant. What's happening is happening. Now."

"That's what I'm worried about! I'm worried about what's happening now!"

Before leaving the phone booth, she called home once more, but there was still no answer, and she shouldered her purse without collecting the quarters that tumbled back into the return box.

"I want to go home," she told Victor, who had been waiting for her in the Cadillac.

"Okay," he said, starting the engine as she got in. He shifted into drive.

"I mean home to Houston."

Victor shifted back into park. "Now?"

"Yes."

"Oh, *m'amie*, I can't think that's so good an idea. We can come into town tomorrow and call again."

"It's a feeling I have, Victor. I want to go home. I'm scared."

"It's very silly, *m'amie*, to be scared because they do not answer the phone. They've probably gone swimming or something. It would be nice to stay another week."

"I know. But I really want to go home."

"Is this the way you love them? By worrying about them?"

"I guess so."

Victor argued that he had not seen his brother or his grandmère in five years and pointed out that this might be the last time he would ever see his grandmère. "She's over ninety, *m'amie*. And besides, what about your snap, snap, snap?" He mimicked taking pictures.

"I don't care. I want to go home."

Alma and Romain did not question Hope's decision, and Nana's hug was warm. Hope was grateful to them for not pressing her to stay. Even Victor, who was clearly disappointed, had accepted her panic. It was necessary to go, yes. They drove all night, Hope at the wheel, straight through to Houston, stopping only to buy gas and Kentucky fried chicken.

15

THE SUN WAS JUST RISING AS THEY PULLED INTO THE DRIVEWAY, burnishing the blank windows and the aluminum gutters. A breeze lifted a few big, flat magnolia leaves from the tree in the front yard.

The dead lawn registered first. Instead of green grass, a brown thatch fronted the house like an oversized welcome mat. "The fungicide!" cried Hope, getting out of the car. "I forgot the fungicide!" The drawn blinds were next, giving the house that definitive air of lost luck, yet Hope did not start to run until she saw Patrick's alligator, sodden and mildewed, lying in the planter that paralleled the front of the house. The warm pavement scratched the soles of her bare feet; she'd left her sandals in the car.

Inside, everything was immaculate. The kitchen counters were uncluttered for the first time in their history—not so much as a spare spoon interrupted the expanse. Hope checked the dishwasher—empty. "There must be a note here somewhere," she said, going to the kitchen table and moving aside the salt and pepper shakers, disturbing their alignment with the sugar bowl and creamer and the paper napkin holder.

Victor found a scrap of paper stuck to the bottom of the garbage pail, but it was only a grocery receipt. Hope stared at it briefly before dropping the rucksack she'd been carrying. She ran down the hallway, stopping on the threshold of Patrick's bedroom. His stuffed animals were gone, and the floor was clean of Tonka trucks. Crossing the room, she opened a drawer: nothing. Likewise the closet.

In Amber's room the bookshelves were empty. Missing from the top of her chest of drawers were the jewel-like bath oil beads, the framed snapshot of herself and Rachel, the clamshell of potpourri, the pot of Swedish ivy. Four tiny holes marked the four corners of the Beatles poster that had hung above the bed.

Hope stood at Amber's empty closet for a long time, hand on the doorknob, staring. A wind blew through her chest; she heard its howl, felt its chill. Victor, coming up behind her, grasped her shoulders and turned her toward him, as if shielding her from the sight of a hanged body or a dusty skeleton instead of a row of empty wire hangers.

They found the note taped to the bathroom mirror. *Sorry!!!!!! Your Nazi husband has the kids. Oily and I are at his sister's. She has a piano, and Oily has a paying gig on Tuesday! Call me and I'll fill you in on the gory details. 472–3516. Love and Peace, Fern.*

Hope went to the hall phone, picked up the receiver, and, pressing it to her chest, spun the dial. Clay answered on the third ring.

"What have you done with them?" she demanded, her voice cracked and thin, the voice she could expect, probably, in her old age.

"You're back."

"What have you done with them?"

"It's not what *I've* done, Hope. It's what you've done. Let's get that straight right now."

"Where are they?"

"Look, they're okay, okay? They're safe. But I can't talk to you about it."

"Why not? What's going on? Where are they?"

"Where was your *head*, for crissakes? Wait, don't tell me, let me guess. You wanted to see Lucy in the Sky with Diamonds, right? You wanted to see the piney woods turn into peppermint sticks, you wanted to see a polka-dot rainbow. Jesus. Tramping around the country like a fucking teenager! Like some kind of Boxcar Bertha! Running off with an ignorant swamp rat and leaving the kids with a hippie half-wit. What kind of mother *are* you?" His voice broke.

"Let me talk to—"

"You should have seen them when I came to pick them up! Patrick looked like some kid out of . . . out of the Dust Bowl or something. He hadn't washed his face all week. Amber wasn't even there, and your friend and some greasy prick were watching TV *without the sound.* Stoned out of their minds."

"You don't know they were st—"

"I do. I could smell it, for one thing. Plus, they moved like jellyfish. You can tell. What the hell were you thinking of?

"I—"

"What did you expect me to do? Patrick looking like a retard, and Amber who knows where—"

"Where was she?"

"At the U-Totem."

"Amber's allowed to go the U-Totem by herself, Clay."

"The *point,* the *point,* Hope, is that your friend didn't *know* where she was, so zonked out she didn't know what day it was, and I'm supposed to stand by and say, oh, wow, far out, man, everybody's doing their own thing, that's cool—"

"Clay, you're hysterical. Calm down, and—"

"I am *not* hysterical! Hysterical is one thing I most certainly am not! Never have been and never will be! Hysterical is your department, Hope. No. I am not hysterical. What I am, though, is completely within my rights. I have a court order."

HOPE WAS SERVED with papers the next day, delivered by a young man affecting the aggrandized severity that goes with the premature assumption of authority. He looked no more than eighteen, which struck Hope as humiliating somehow.

Halfway through the first paragraph, she stopped, devastated by the faceless authority of the legal jargon. Slipping the papers back into their envelope, she rose from the table and wrapped her arms tight across her breasts, as if to keep them there. Move or disintegrate: this seemed to be the choice.

She began to prowl, passing from kitchen to family room to hallway to living room and back, feeling acutely detached, noting the furnishings and arrangements as if she were an inspector of some kind, or a thief, although she found nothing to steal, nothing to covet. There was nothing here she wanted, had ever wanted, it seemed to her now. How then had that dining-room suite and sideboard and tea caddy come to be here? Hadn't she chosen them? She didn't think so. She remembered buying them, but she didn't remember choosing them. Had Clay then? She didn't think so. The whole arrangement seemed to have been transported directly from a magazine advertisement.

The family room, the *family* room, she repeated, further unnerving herself, was more of the same. The silence was beginning to unhinge her; she put a Simon and Garfunkel record on the turntable before wandering into Amber's room. She pulled back the bedspread and lifted the sheets to her nose. Amber. The smell of dreaming flesh and book ink coalesced with memory to summon the crescent body, arms crossed in front of the chest, hands grasping shoulder sockets, her fine profile against the pillow spread with a scrollwork of hair. Hope began to sob.

"Anybody home?"

She let the sheets drop back to the bed. Calhoun.

She entered the family room as Calhoun was shutting off the turntable. He wore shorts and Mexican sandals with soles made of tires. *B. F. Goodrich* could just be made out along one edge. He'd spent most of his summer at Caleb's beach house.

He slipped the Simon and Garfunkel record into its jacket and threw his considerable weight onto the couch, the springs braying objection. He took off his battered hat and hung it on his knee. "Stop blubbering. All you need is a .38, a rowboat, and a map for Saõ Tomé."

"Saõ Tomé." She sank into the wing chair opposite him and looked around for a Kleenex.

"An island in the Gulf of Guinea. It has the purest water in the world. Perfect for raising kids."

"Oh, Cal."

"That fucker. I'm serious about the .38."

"No, you're not."

"Some people do not deserve to live."

She wiped at her cheeks with the back of her hand. "This isn't helping me, Cal, if that's your objective."

"I notice you've stopped blubbering. Do you have anything to drink? Besides hemlock? Jack Daniel's maybe?" He looked around the room, as if a bottle might be secreted somewhere among the sewing paraphernalia, which had been rearranged and straightened so that the family room had the same air of orderly depletion as the rest of the house. Spindles of colored bindings queued up behind a tidy stack of cut-out pinafores on a side table, and although a garland of pinafores still streamed from the sewing machine, it was precisely coiled on the fold-out arm rather than wreathing the room.

"I think Oily Jon left a couple of beers in the refrigerator."

"It's this ownership business," Calhoun said, following her into the kitchen. "He can't stand for you to have *his* kids."

Hope opened the refrigerator and handed him a Pearl. "It's more than that, I think. I think Victor figures in, and maybe Fern." She opened a beer for herself.

"What happened, anyway?"

"Clay told Fern he wanted to take Amber and Patrick fishing, and she let them go. Why wouldn't she? He's their father, after all. I don't blame Fern." She paused and took a sip of beer. "When he didn't return with them, though, she called him. He told her to get out of the house. That if she and her boyfriend were not out of the house in an hour, he would call the police and have her arrested for breaking and entering."

"You're kidding."

"No. Fern wouldn't lie. She doesn't know enough about what's going on to lie. And . . . I don't know . . . it sounds like Clay somehow, doesn't it?"

"In some intangible, low-down, scurvy way—yes."

Hope let this go. "So she and Oily Jon left. They couldn't reach me, of course. Victor's brother doesn't have a phone."

"Have you called your lawyer?"

"No."

"Let's call him now."

"It's Sunday."

"Call him at home."

"I don't have his home number."

"Then get it. Call information. Call his answering service. Hope. This is an emergency."

"I don't want to talk to him!" Hope burst out, feeling a sudden impulse to defend herself against scrutiny. The thought of telling Ben Jamison what had happened repelled her. The breaking wave of his hair came suddenly to mind, his fishy, spectacled eyes. "He wouldn't understand."

"*Understand?* Who cares?"

"I do. How can he take my part if he doesn't understand?"

"It's not his job to *understand*. His job is to fight. And that's what you need right now, a fighter."

"Well, I don't think Ben Jamison is a fighter either."

Calhoun thought this over. "Maybe not. But I still think you should call him. You need a lawyer, Hope, and he's the only one you've got right now. If you don't want him to represent you, get another one, Chloe could probably recommend someone, but right now Jamison is the only lawyer you've got, and you need to talk to one today."

"I could talk to Chloe."

Calhoun looked at her, as if calculating her weight or her age. He set his empty beer bottle on the counter. "Okay. Let's go."

CHLOE AND FLETCHER lived in a two-story colonial home, slate blue with white trim, a professor's house, one that respectfully harked back to the past, yet resided in the present with enviable ease. Inside, most rooms were lined with bookshelves. Good reading lamps accompanied comfortable chairs; braided oval rugs of subtle colors floated on polished wood; and the windows had valances as well as drapery. Baskets of potpourri and dried grasses contributed to an atmosphere of perpetual autumn. Hope always felt subdued in this house, inhibited by its good taste, yet she also basked in it, grateful for its genteel enclosure. This was especially true today, as she and Calhoun sat in Chloe's living room.

"I can't," Chloe told them. "I can't properly repesent you, Hope. I majored in civil rights law. Housing discrimination. That's my field. Plus, I just *graduated* three months ago. I can recommend someone, though. I know a very good—"

"But I want you!" Hope begged. "I want you sitting next to me in the courtroom. I need a *friend*."

"You need a good lawyer," Chloe corrected.

"You *are* a good lawyer, Chloe. I know you are."

"That remains to be seen, Hope, and in any case, family law—"

"*Please*, Chloe." Hope extended the envelope holding the papers she had received earlier.

"No, Hope, really," said Chloe, taking the papers out of the envelope. "I'll look at these, but I can't represent you. In good conscience, I really can't."

As Chloe read over the papers, Hope leaned back in her chair and closed her eyes. She had not slept at all last night. Calhoun took her hand. Hope didn't move or even open her eyes.

"I'll be right back," Chloe said. "I'm going to call Clay's lawyer."

While she was gone, Hope dozed off, still belayed to Calhoun. A moment later he was tugging at her hand.

"Amber and Patrick are at Clay's," Chloe said when she sat up. "You can call them if you want and talk to them. Visiting them will take a little negotiation, but you'll get to see them soon." Chloe hesitated, then sat down on an ottoman opposite Hope. "The grounds are abandonment."

Hope lowered her head and pressed her palms against her eyelids. "Oh, God."

"They have to say something."

"But it sounds so . . . it makes me sound . . ." Hope couldn't go on. Calhoun's jaw tightened.

"Hope, I think . . . I think you'd feel better if you talked to Amber and Patrick," said Chloe. "Don't cry. Don't cry, you're making *me* cry. Listen, you shouldn't have any problems with Clay. His lawyer assured me. He said he'd call him. Stop. Hope. Please. Do you want to call Amber and Patrick from here? There's a phone in my bedroom."

CLAY SAID HE'D been expecting her call. "Who do you want to talk to first? Patrick? He's right here." He sounded tolerant and helpful.

"Wait. Wait a minute. Do they know? Have you talked this over with them?

"Not exactly."

Hope put a hand to her forehead and closed her eyes. "Clay, you have to stop saying things like 'not exactly.'"

"Why?"

"Because it makes me crazy. It makes me want to rip out your tongue by its roots and mince it into tiny pieces to serve on crackers or little triangles of toast—"

"I could hang up, Hope. I don't have to listen to your ravings."

Hope made an effort. When she spoke again, her voice was low and quavering. "Just tell me yes or no. Do Amber and Patrick know you're suing for custody?"

"Not ex—No, I . . . I just told them I would be taking care of them for a while." Clay sounded nervous now, unsure.

"Are you? Taking care of them? Or is Mindy?"

"I am."

Hope sat down on the floor, her back against the bed. "Put Patrick on."

After a brief pause, she heard Patrick's small pipe. "Mommy?"

She swallowed. "How are you, pumpkin?"

"When are you coming home?"

"I am home, honey. I'll see you soon."

"Mommy, you know what?"

"What?"

"You know what?"

"What?"

"I found a ci-ca-da." He pronounced the word carefully. "An alive one. Daddy helped me."

Hope reached for enthusiasm. "You did? Good for you! What does it look like?" Her cheery tone amounted to self-ridicule, but what was the alternative?

"It's green and has big wings. You know what else?"

"What?"

"Daddy bought me a new book. A inseck book."

"A bug book! That will be handy. When you find a bug, you can look it up."

"A inseck book," he corrected.

"Right. An insect book. You're an entomologist now, I guess."

"Maybe," he said doubtfully. "When are you coming home?"

"I am home, honey. I had a nice vacation, and now I'm home."

"Oh." Hope recognized the voice of disbelief. In the background, she heard Amber demanding to talk. Patrick raised his voice. "Mommy? You know what?"

"What?"

There was a pause while he thought of something. "Jason's afraid of bees."

"I know he is."

"I'm not afraid of bees."

"That's because you're a very brave boy. A *very* brave boy." Hope could hear Amber's voice grow shrill. "The bravest boy I know. And Patrick? Maybe it's Amber's turn now. You can talk again after she's had a chance, okay? Then you can have another turn. You can have as many turns as you want."

Patrick abandoned the phone, and Amber came on the line. "Mom? Are you okay?"

"I'm fine, honey. Victor and I had a nice trip. I took lots of pictures I can show you. What have you been up to?"

"Nothing. Mom?"

"What?"

"I know."

"You know what?"

"*You* know."

Hope's tongue was momentarily paralyzed.

"Can I write to you?" Amber asked.

"Write to me! Of course you can, but—what do you know, Amber? What has Daddy said to you?"

"Nothing. I heard him on the phone." Amber was whispering now. "What's going to happen? Will I have to choose?"

"Oh, honey, no . . ."

"He needs me."

"Who does?"

"He says he needs me for now."

"Dear God," Hope breathed. A prayer did seem in order, or a curse, something supernatural to stave off what she sensed as inexorable. "Let me speak to Daddy again, Amber."

"Amber knows," she said when he came on the line. "You can't do this, Clay. For *their* sake, you can't do this."

"It's for their sake I am."

"This is going to tear them apart."

"That's already been done, hasn't it? Now it's a matter of salvage. They can only live with one of us. We can't go back."

"Can't we? Oh, Clay, can't we? I wouldn't ask anything of you. I wouldn't even ask you to give up Mindy. We'd work it all out somehow. You can't do this to the kids, Clay. Listen to me on this. I *know*. Please believe me. I'm their mother."

"Not much of one."

"Oh, Clay—"

"You're late for the train, Hope. I'm gone."

"Clay—"

"I don't want to be rude. But I am now going to hang up the telephone."

"No, I—"

He hung up. Stunned, Hope returned to the living room. "What did he say?" asked Calhoun.

"I don't know," said Hope. "I don't remember. Patrick has a new insect book." She started to cry.

Chloe stumbled against the coffee table as she crossed the room and took Hope in her arms. "Don't worry, Hope. We'll get you a good lawyer, and . . ."

Hope, her head on Chloe's shoulder, went dry and blank. Legalities. They seemed to her grotesquely beside the point.

HOPE HAD NEVER been to Clay's apartment before, and when she arrived at the address he'd given her several months ago, she didn't know which of the four mock-Colonial brick buildings, each labeled *The Washington Arms* in black script, was his. She gripped the steering wheel and considered. Maybe she could find his name on a mailbox. There must be mailboxes. She had forwarded his mail, and it must have been deposited here somewhere. She would look for the mailboxes.

She got out of the car and crossed the lush green lawn, spiked at regular intervals by very young evergreen trees. She had dressed carefully, but if one was not a connoisseur of vintage clothing, as few here at the Washington Arms were likely to be, she might have been mistaken for something of a derelict in the sea-foam-colored dress she'd bought at Embers, with its noticeable perspiration stain on the back between the shoulders, its uneven hem, and some missing buttons. She had pinned up her hair with less skill than usual, her nervousness producing some dishevelment. She did not wear makeup either, having recently come to the conclusion that she did not need an artificial face, that her own was quite good enough. So in some eyes, perhaps in those of the person on the second floor who was holding down one slat of a venetian blind with an index finger, Hope could have looked disreputable.

Thirty-eight mailboxes lined up inside the small lobby of the first building, in two rows of nineteen. Clay's name was not on any of them, however, and Hope moved on to the second building. She was met at the door by a mustachioed security guard, who wanted to know her business.

"It's very complicated, my business," she said, feeling the fatigue of misfortune and sleepless nights. The guard gave her a hard, distrustful look that persuaded her to simplify. "I'm looking for my husband. Mr. Clay Fairman. Do you know where he lives?"

The guard didn't say anything for a moment, perhaps considering the credibility of a wife who did not know where her husband lived. He said he would inquire if she would care to wait, and Hope said she would, sitting down on the edge of a planter, where the spiny tentacles of moss roses entwined a row of periwinkles.

The guard returned after a few minutes. "I'm sorry," he said, although "vindicated" might have better described his expression. "Mr. Fairman requests that you leave the premises."

"Well, he has no right," Hope said. "Mr. Fairman has no right. My children are in one of these buildings. Do you understand? My children are in one of these buildings."

"I'm sorry, lady."

In the face of his implacability, Hope grew frenzied. She beat her fist on the palm of her hand and tried to brush past him, and when he reached to restrain her, she slapped away his arm. "I'm warning you!" he called, but he did not start after her. His eye had been caught by a patrol car that had just driven up to park several yards behind the Cadillac. A policeman emerged and put on his cap. The security guard frantically motioned him forward, as Hope disappeared into the building, and the policeman picked up his pace, entering seconds afterward.

He found Hope just inside the door, investigating another row of mailboxes. He cleared his throat. "Mrs. Fairman?"

She jumped, startled, and stared into the pale blue of his summer shirt. He asked if she would mind very much answering a few questions.

"Are you taking me into custody?"

"I don't think so, ma'am. Have you been drinking, ma'am?" Hope shook her head. "Have you taken any pills?" She shook her head again. "We see a lot of this," he said, gently maneuvering her out the door. "You'd be surprised. The thing is: we need to get you home now." They passed the security guard, nearly obscured by one of the young yew trees flanking the building. He lit a cigarette as Hope and the policeman reached the curb.

"You don't want to cause a lot of trouble for yourself, do you, ma'am?" said the policeman. "I'll tell you what. Why don't I follow you home? Make sure you get there all right." He opened the door for her. "Nice car," he added.

Hope's fingers sliced through her hair, which tumbled to her shoulders, hairpins springing out, one after the other, landing on the sidewalk with soft pings.

"You don't understand," she said. "I hate this car. No one understands how much I hate this car."

16

THE FAMILY LAW CENTER WAS A NEW BUILDING, ONLY ONE YEAR old, its surfaces clean of tradition and not yet scarred by use. A glass cube formed the ground floor, overhung by a six-story block of courtrooms and offices, the whole upheld by rectangular stone pillars tapering to a point at the top, or what looked like stone pillars. Actually, the stonework was a facade, and the building rested on the points of embedded steel rods, a triumph of engineering perhaps, but up close, they seemed to Hope perilously inadequate, a sort of tragic flaw. If the building were to shift even a quarter inch, wouldn't it slide off these points and crash to the ground? This seemed to her more than possible; subsidence was a real problem here in Houston. The ground beneath the San Jacinto Monument was sinking at a rate of a foot a year. Her own house had numerous cracks in the foundation because of it. The family room sloped. Patrick liked to set his ball on the floor and watch it roll.

Taking a few steps toward the sidewalk, Hope looked for Chloe, who had gone to park the car. Thank God, Chloe was representing her. Getting her to agree had proved an uphill undertaking. Hope had had to badger. She had had to beg. But she didn't think she could have made it this morning without Chloe. As it was, she had vomited her breakfast. Her eyes were swollen and her skin sallow from sleeplessness. Last night had been like trying to sleep on the edge of a cliff. Chloe had told her what to expect today, and they had rehearsed what she would say, but Hope had the feeling she was about to disappear somehow, become thin air, events passing through her, as if she didn't exist.

When Chloe appeared at her side, she was flushed and sweaty. "Sorry to be so long! I had to park eight blocks away! We'd better hurry," she said, striding toward the entrance.

In fact, they were half an hour early. Chloe was nervous. Hope had never seen Chloe nervous before, and in spite of her own agitation, she listened, fascinated, to Chloe's chatter as they went inside. Chloe never chattered.

"There are probably worse judges than Rankin, but we could have been luckier, not only is he new, he's just been through a nasty divorce himself, and unfortunately for us, his wife really took him to the cleaners, so he's smarting, and rumor has it he was cheating on her, which would be double bad luck for us, given our case, that's the problem with the law, it's the luck of the draw, lots of people think judges are dignified and wise, but they're just people, lawyers, in fact, lawyers with political connections and family problems and egos, and oh! Hold that elevator, please." she called, breaking into a run across the lobby.

Hope didn't follow right away, stunned by the light. Plate-glass windows on all sides admitted a deluge of brightness that splattered over yellow and orange leatherette chairs, bounced up from the polished stone floor, and flashed from a black marble sculpture in the middle of the lobby. Titled *Family*, a continuous, assuring curve of rock incorporated the abstractly rendered figures of father, mother, and child.

"Hope! Come on!" Chloe called from the elevator. She was holding the door open, to the annoyance of the other passengers. "You can waste a lifetime waiting for these elevators," Chloe explained, as Hope stepped inside.

They emerged into a crowded corridor on the third floor. Twists of cigarette smoke twined and splayed above the dense talk, and occasionally a run of laughter darted into the thicket of voices. A child's falsetto piped through the din, tunneling into Hope's fortifications. Small flakes of herself detached and began to float. Amber and Patrick would not be here today. The judge would speak to them in private tomorrow.

Chloe touched her arm, indicating a double door to their left, and they entered the courtroom. It was smaller than Hope had anticipated, and dark, or maybe that was just her impression after the brilliance of the lobby. There were no windows, but recessed bulbs cast fans of soft light on the pink walls. Pictures—of a sailing scene, a sunset, a water-fall—hung on the walls, and the floor was tactfully carpeted in tweed.

She followed Chloe down the aisle separating the six rows of benches that faced a railed area with a long, polished table and chairs. At the far end of the room was a dais that included the judge's bench and, slightly below, the witness box on one side and clerk's desk on the other. Hope stood for a moment arranging these details in her mind, like furnishings in a dollhouse, before she realized that a case was in progress. She quickly sat down next to Chloe and tried to focus on what was being said. Something about gambling in Las Vegas. The judge, whose pallor indi-cated either illness or recent exile from the Texas sun, gazed down on the proceedings with an air of annoyance. He was young, in his thirties. Hope had been expecting a more paternal figure, with white hair and a well-creased face.

The man in the witness box was explaining that he could not pay half of his winnings to his wife, because he had already promised them to his girlfriend. She had brought him luck, he said.

Hope glanced at the woman sitting at the long table, presumably his wife, a petite woman who reminded her a little bit of Alma. Hope felt embarrassed for her. This was private business. She glanced around at the twenty or so other people seated on the benches. Were they, like herself, waiting for their case to be called? Or were they here out of curiosity? Would they stay for her trial?

Don't think of it as a trial, Chloe had told her over and over. Call it a suit.

Clay entered just as the lawyer for the man's wife stood up to make a point, and Hope's attention shifted. Speaking of suits. It always amazed her how different Clay looked in a suit, weighty and removed, joined up with remote forces. Perhaps she looked equally enlisted in her white Lady Manhattan blouse and navy-blue skirt, purchased new for the occasion on Chloe's orders. A white margin of skin along his hairline indicated that he had just had a haircut. A short, stocky man accompanied him, evidently his lawyer, who walked with a sharp, toes-up stride.

*   *   *

THEIR CASE WAS called about half an hour later. With the blind trust
of a gosling, Hope followed Chloe to the long table, drawing closer to
her when Clay's lawyer tossed his briefcase onto the table, where it
skittered downtable a bit before coming to rest. He introduced himself
to Chloe, and she reciprocated. They shook hands, leaving Hope and
Clay in a quandary. Should they shake hands, too? Was that the proper
protocol? They stood gazing uneasily at one another until Stittson
hitched up a pants leg and sat down, and everyone followed suit, Chloe
and Hope on one side of the table, Clay and Stittson on the other.

After some businesslike preliminaries between the lawyers and the
judge, Clay took the stand. He sat down, unbuttoned his suit coat, then
buttoned it up again before swearing his oath.

Stittson's manner was casual and encouraging as he led Clay over
familiar ground: his job and income, the length of his marriage to Hope,
his separation from her. Their matching monotones struck Hope as
rehearsed, yet at the same time soothing—nothing real could be happening.

"When you and Mrs. Fairman separated, you agreed that she would
retain custody of the children, is that correct?"

"Yes."

"Can you tell us what changed your mind?"

"I was never sure. I always had doubts."

Stittson nodded judiciously. "I understand. I was thinking, though,
a little more specifically of what happened on Saturday, August 22."

"Yes." Clay cleared his throat. "I had gone to the house to pick up
Amber and Patrick to take them fishing. The week before, my wife had
taken off with her boyfriend—"

Chloe interrupted to point out that Hope was Clay's *estranged* wife.
The judge nodded. Clay's cheeks pulsed as he clenched and unclenched
his teeth. Stittson gestured with an upturned palm for him to continue.

"When I arrived, my daughter was nowhere to be found, and this
hippie that my wife, my *estranged* wife, had gotten to take care of the
kids had no idea where she was! Her own son was in plain view, using
some pretty nasty language, in fact, and my son was there, looking like
he hadn't washed his face in weeks, but my daughter had disappeared,

and this hippie and her boyfriend were watching TV, stoned out of their—"

Chloe interrupted to suggest that Mr. Fairman's inference was unjustified and that, in the absence of any evidence, should not be allowed. The judge agreed.

"Could you describe for us the condition of the house, Mr. Fairman?"

Clay described a swinish state of affairs. A slow blush seeped up along Hope's throat in a demonstration of capillary action, as Stittson took from his briefcase a half-dozen photographs, entering them with the clerk. They did indeed reveal littered surfaces and cluttered corners, dishes piled in the sink, a shower stall freckled with mold; however, Hope, looking over Chloe's shoulder, saw not the photographs themselves, but the image of Clay, going from room to room, gathering evidence against her.

Next Clay described taking Amber and Patrick fishing. They had gone to Lake Livingston, he said; Patrick had caught a fish. The day had been fine, the children excited and happy. Clay himself had been happy. "I realized how much I missed not seeing them every day. I realized they needed me, and I needed them. And at the end of the day, I just couldn't . . . I just couldn't take them back to . . . to that . . ." Clay struggled for control.

"And why not, Mr. Fairman?" Stittson asked gently.

"For one thing, they didn't want to go back themselves. I felt . . . sorry for them. Amber didn't like the boy; she said he was always pinching her. But I guess . . . I guess mainly I was worried about their safety. I didn't like the feel of things. At that point, I just wanted them home with me."

"Permanently?"

Clay cleared his throat and took a minute to reply. "I had come to that conclusion, yes. I came to question, to seriously question, my wife's, my estranged wife's, competence."

Hope's senses sharpened, as they had that day on the patio when Clay had thrown the twigs at her.

Stittson proceeded to ask a series of questions eliciting Clay's misgivings about Hope's capacity to make sound judgments and about the dubious company she kept. Although he didn't mention Victor by name, Clay said that he didn't approve of Hope's choice of "male influence."

Hope flushed again, acutely aware of the spectators in the courtroom.

Clay also cited lax concern on her part for the children's physical welfare. On this point, Stittson produced evidence. A young woman stepped forward with a box, and Stittson pulled from it Amber's polka-dotted nightgown. Under his questioning, Clay pointed out its threadbare condition and added that it was also several sizes too small.

Hope wanted to jump up and explain. But she won't give it up! I've tried! She insists on wearing it every night! I'm lucky to talk her into letting me wash it!

Now Stittson held up the pair of cowboy boots that Hope had bought for Patrick at Embers. Clay pointed out the hole in one sole, the run-down heels, disintegrated linings, and leather scuffed to the thickness of lunch meat in places.

Patrick loves those boots! Hope silently explained. Please!

Clay went on to express objections to the school, the Unitarian church, and the people at Communitas. As his voice rose, so did his color. Eyeing him, Stittson changed tack.

"Mr. Fairman, I'd like to go back to the period of your separation from Mrs. Fairman last February. Could you relate for us the events of February 13th?"

Hope's mind raced. February 13th?

Clay answered that he had been in several meetings that day, and when he returned to his office, about two in the afternoon, there was a message for him from Chloe Whitney. The judge glanced at Chloe, frowned, and returned his attention to Clay. "She was very upset. She said that Hope had been distraught that morning and had asked her to keep Patrick. Later that day she said Calhoun had called to say Hope had not picked up Amber and Rachel from school. But when she drove over to the house to check, no one answered her knock, although the car was in the garage. The doors were locked, she said."

Stittson pressed his fingertips together, resting his chin on the nearest apex. "Did Mrs. Whitney express to you a specific fear?"

Clay hesitated. "No. She sounded frightened, though."

"I shouldn't have called him," Chloe was muttering under her breath. "I never should have called him."

"What were your thoughts, Mr. Fairman?"

"I was afraid Hope had tried to commit suicide."

"Had she threatened suicide?"

"Yes.

"In response to your leaving?"

"Yes."

"And did you find your wife, Mr. Fairman?"

"Not at first. Mrs. Whitney and I searched the entire house without finding her. We finally found her in the bomb shelter, rolled up in a quilt. I thought the worst."

"And?"

"She attacked me! She jumped up and attacked me! Totally out of control, flailing at me and shrieking."

Chloe rose to question the relevancy of this testimony, and Stittson explained they were simply trying to establish Mrs. Fairman's mental stability. Or lack thereof. Which, he said, looking at the judge, he thought had been sufficiently established. He went on to introduce the subject of Clay's fiancée.

Fiancée? Hope sat up a little straighter.

In response to Stittson's question, Clay said he and Mindy Eck planned to marry in April. Folding her hands in front of her, Hope stared at a landscape painting on the opposite wall. Clay described his relationship to Mindy with a formality that suggested a nineteenth-century courtship, a quest for a suitable mate marked by sensible ardor. He held her in the highest esteem; she was a person of warmth and discernment. Her values were of the worthiest sort.

This did not sound like Clay. Beneath the pall of her nervousness, Hope's curiosity stirred.

"Your fiancée is the mother of a young son, is she not?" asked Stittson.

"A full-time mother," Clay emphasized.

"And how would you describe the relationship between your fiancée and your children, Mr. Fairman?"

"As a very affectionate one."

Hope's folded hands tightened. Beside her, Chloe was taking notes, scribbling much faster than Clay was talking. The judge listened without adjusting his frown of annoyance, apparently a professional appurtenance rather than any expression of personal distaste.

"You have recently purchased a new house, is that correct, Mr. Fairman?" Stittson went on. This was news to Hope.

"Yes," Clay answered. "In Spring Branch."

"Can you describe your new house for us, Mr. Fairman?"

"Yes. It's a two-story, four-bedroom house with a family room and a living room and a separate dining room. It has a large backyard with trees."

What? A four-bedroom house? Hope leaned forward, dropping her hands to her lap.

"And the neighborhood, Mr. Fairman?"

"It's a very nice neighborhood. There are several other children who live there. It isn't far from the Dads' Club Y, which sponsors several good recreation programs. The elementary school, which is excellent, lies within walking distance."

Stittson yielded for cross-examination. Chloe rose, glanced at her yellow legal pad, and approached the witness stand, where she and Clay looked at each other with suppressed startlement for a moment, as if neither had quite absorbed the improbability of their facing each other like this.

"I believe you said, Mr. Fairman, that you met Mrs. Eck about a year ago September?" Chloe began. Ordinarily soft, her voice sounded pushed, Hope thought, the way film is pushed to compensate for poor light. There was the same loss of quality, the same graininess, the contrasts too intense.

"Yes."

"And when did you move out of the house you shared with Mrs. Fairman and into your own apartment?"

"At the beginning of February."

"Were you seeing Mrs. Eck during those four or five months?"

"I'm not sure what you mean by 'seeing.' I saw her at a couple of parents' meetings before she withdrew Jason from the school. Once, I remember, she called me for some advice on the purchase of a heat pump."

"A heat pump."

"Yes. I had mentioned to her that I was at work on an energy efficiency study. Heat pumps are an extremely efficient source of heat in this mild climate, and she was interested—"

"We're digressing here . . . Mr. Fairman. What I'd like to know is: was it during that period of time, between September and sometime in February, you became sexually involved with Mrs. Eck?"

"I was not . . . I am not . . . sexually involved with Mrs. Eck."

Chloe gave Clay a long look. He returned it, sitting at attention, elbows firmly anchored to the armrests. She stepped closer to the witness stand. "Is it not true, Mr. Fairman, is it not true that you were seeing Mrs. Eck, in fact spending nights at her home, as early as February?"

"No."

Chloe walked back to the table and looked at her notes. Hadn't Mr. Fairman been at the home of Mrs. Eck on the night of February 12? Hadn't he, in fact, accepted a phone call there from Mrs. Fairman?"

No and no.

Hope sat very still and very straight. To an observer who didn't know her, one of the people sitting in the courtroom, say, her expression could have been as easily taken for courtesy as fear.

HOPE AND CHLOE sat side by side in paddle-armed chairs that faced the steam table at Coney Island West, a few blocks from the courthouse. Hope's chili dog sat untouched on her paper plate; Chloe toyed with her dill pickle. "Two burgers and a bowl of fahre!" bawled the counterman.

"I didn't know you could lie in a courtroom. I didn't know they let you," said Hope, her voice slack.

"Well, of course, they don't let you. But it happens, of course, it happens."

"He swore on a Bible."

"Some people lie. He's lied before, right? I mean, it's not totally out of character, is it?"

"No." *You're not the only duck in the barrel, Hope. You haven't been for a long time.*

Chloe nibbled on a dill pickle. "There's a lot at stake here. He might consider what's at stake more important than swearing falsely on a Bible. In Clay's mind, lying might be a justifiable means to an end." She hesitated, scrutinizing Hope. "Is there any chance he's telling the truth? Is there any chance they're not sleeping together?"

"No, how could there be? I mean, I've never seen them in bed together, but—"

"We should have gotten a deposition from him. We should have hired a detective. I never thought. I never expected . . ." Chloe shook her head and took the last bite of her chili dog. "Mindy's up this afternoon. I'll try with her."

MINDY HAD CHANGED. Hope couldn't quite put her finger on it. Maybe it wasn't so much her appearance as the way she stepped forward with no attention to her feet, maybe it was the solid shelf of shoulders beneath the mint-green suit, her posture of prim militancy. Hope wasn't sure.

Stittson asked her several questions that established her as a member of St. John's Episcopal Church, the holder of a baccalaureate degree and an elementary teaching certificate, and the mother of a six-year-old son. Stittson paused to address her with a polite smile before remarking, "Mrs. Eck, Mr. Fairman has told us that you and he plan to marry."

"Yes. In April."

"Have you given any thought . . . do you think you would be willing, depending on the outcome of this trial, to take on a stepmother's responsibilities?"

"Well, of course, it wasn't an issue when Mr. Fairman first asked me to marry him. I didn't expect . . . this." As Mindy shuttered and unshuttered green eyes, eyes green as new grass, Hope realized what was changed about Mindy. Her horn-rimmed glasses were gone, and she was wearing contact lenses, bright green contact lenses. "But I've thought about it very carefully since, and I do feel that Mr. Fairman and I can provide a more stable atmosphere than . . . a more stable atmosphere. We believe in love and discipline in equal measure." She and Clay exchanged a look.

They're a team, Hope thought, with a simultaneous recognition that she and Clay had not been. For the first time, it occurred to her that Clay's affair might not have been the wild and passionate one she'd imagined but a more predictable union of like to like.

WHEN HER TURN came, Chloe came straight to the point. "Were you and Mr. Fairman conducting an adulterous affair prior to Mr. Fairman's separation from his wife, Mrs. Eck?"

Mindy touched the bridge of her nose, as if to push up invisible glasses.

"Were you?"

"No."

"Wasn't Mr. Fairman in your home on the night of February 17th?"

"No."

"Are you sure, Mrs. Eck?"

Stittson rose, but Mindy was already answering. "Mr. Fairman has never spent a night at my house. Not a whole night. Not on February 12th or any other night."

They lied! Hope told Calhoun later, with an amazement that proved quite durable. They lied! she would say a year from now, three years, ten, incredulity intact.

STITTSON CALLED VICTOR next. Victor had borrowed a suit from Alex, which did not fit him very well, and wore a tie so peculiarly short Chloe had described it as a training tie.

"Whose side are you on?" Hope had asked, startling Chloe into an apology.

Stittson began by inquiring about Victor's work history. His efforts to probe Victor's memory resulted in some confused answers, and if Hope hadn't known better, she would have thought Victor was drugged. As he stumbled through his answers, Stittson took to repeating them for the record.

"Oklahoma City, Tucson, San Luis Obispo," Stittson intoned. "Handyman, security guard, welder. Do I have it right, so far, Mr. Calais?"

"Yessir."

"Albuquerque, Beaumont, Midland," Stittson went on. "Framer, fisherman, roughneck."

Hope found herself wishing it were Romain up there, Romain, who believed, maybe not so unwisely, wages to be the death of a man.

". . . a total of six residences and that many jobs over the past two years, Mr. Calais. Can you tell us why you have felt compelled to move from place to place, job to job?"

"I wanted to see the world."

Stittson smiled. "Ah, the world. Yes. And how long, Mr. Calais, have you known Mrs. Fairman?"

"Something under a year, I guess."

"Something under a year. Would that be ten months? Five months?"

"Something like that."

"Something like that." Stittson sighed. "What month did you meet Mrs. Fairman, Mr. Calais?"

Victor thought. "April, I think."

"We are now in the month of September, Mr. Calais." Stittson held up a hand and counted off the months. "April, May, June, July, August. I suggest that you have known Mrs. Fairman for five months. Are you in agreement with my calculations?"

Victor nodded.

"Could you affirm that for us vocally, Mr. Calais? Could you speak up, please?"

"Yessir."

"And do you ever spend the night at Mrs. Fairman's home?"

"Sometimes."

"Frequently?"

Victor hesitated.

"Nightly?" Stittson pressed.

"No."

"Weekly?"

"Maybe."

"On these occasions, Mr. Calais, do you and Mrs. Fairman engage in sexual intercourse?"

Hope stared at her folded hands as Chloe stood up to question the relevance of this line of questioning.

"The point here," Stittson said, "is that Mr. Calais and Mrs. Fairman are conducting a liaison under the eyes of two young children. We are trying to gauge the temperature of the moral climate, so to speak, of Mrs. Fairman's home."

The judge leaned forward to suggest Mr. Calais answer the question.

"Yessir."

Victor was no more responsive to Chloe's questioning than he'd been to Stittson's. His anesthetized air did not change, as he spoke into the knot of his short tie, his lowered head revealing beads of perspiration through thinning hair. His answers were stunted even when Chloe asked him about his rescue of Frederick, and she was not able to portray the way he had saved the day with graceful competence, earning in an instant the trust of a hostile child. She did manage to establish that Victor only spent the night with Hope when Amber and Patrick were with Clay.

"Moral climate," she muttered under her breath as she sat down again.

"Shirley Higgins!" the sergeant-at-arms called out into the corridor, and Fern entered the courtroom. Shirley Higgins. Hope still hadn't got used to Fern's real name.

There had been some question whether Fern would be here. She had threatened to leave town rather than appear. Since a subpoena had about as much authority as a shopping list to Fern, and, thanks to the grapevine, she knew all about the mechanics of disappearance—how to forge a new driver's license, how to fake college diplomas and passports, where to get your hair dyed or a nose job—Hope had feared she would do just that. But here she was, Shirley Higgins, small hands clenched at her sides, wearing a cotton circle-skirt circa 1958 figured with musical notes, her bare feet stuffed into once-white high-heeled shoes. She's trying to look normal, Hope thought, touched. For my sake.

Fern glanced at her as she took the stand, and Hope smiled, a reassuring mother's smile, unsecured promise of protection.

Stittson asked where she was employed. Fern hesitated before answering, "The Grass Hut."

"And what are your responsibilities there?"

"I sell things."

"What things?"

"Well, for example, this week we have a special on eight-hour incense for seventy-nine cents."

Stittson gave her a look that indicated her answer had outstripped his patience. He strode back to the table and pulled from his briefcase a neon-pink sheet of paper that turned out to be a flyer from the Grass Hut. "Roach clips, water pipes, carburetors," he read. "Ten brands of rolling papers." He looked up. "Some of these are flavored," he said with what appeared to be genuine surprise. Then he held the flyer up to show a brand of paper imprinted with the American flag.

Stittson asked Fern if she had ever purchased for herself any of the wares she sold.

"We sell black lights and posters, too," she said, gesturing toward the flyer. "You forgot to read that."

"I think we established what you sell, Miss Higgins. My question is whether or not you have ever purchased any of the items sold at the Grass Hut."

"No."

"Are you sure, Miss Higgins? For example, have you ever bought a . . ." Stittson referred to the flyer. ". . . a roach clip, Miss Higgins?"

"No."

"Have you ever bought a package of . . ." He referred again to the flyer. ". . . ZigZags?"

"No."

Fern was likely telling the truth. Overall, Fern purchased very little of anything. She bartered, exchanged, borrowed, and may have even engaged in petit pilfering, but she rarely paid cash. Very thrifty in her way, she used a paper clip for her roaches.

Frustrated, Stittson asked about her marital status. She answered that she was not married.

"You have a boyfriend, though."

"Yes."

"And his name is . . .?"

"Oily Jon."

"Oily Jon. Oily Jon what?"

"I don't know."

"You don't know your boyfriend's last name?"

"I don't need to write him any letters. Not so far anyway."

"I see," said Stittson, glancing at the judge before going on to question her about the week she'd spent as Amber and Patrick's baby-sitter. He did not uncover any new information, beyond the fact that Fern's dinners had mostly consisted of SpaghettiOs and Kraft's macaroni and cheese. Under Chloe's questioning, Fern had the chance to point out that she had taken Patrick to the doctor for his immunizations, as Hope had instructed, and had not let Amber eat any apples, to which she was allergic.

* * *

ALEX WORE HIS yellow sports coat and sat in the witness chair with one leg crossed casually over the other. Yes, he said, in answer to Stittson's question, Hope had been a member of his church for nearly two years and was currently a member of the board.

"Would you say, Reverend, that Mrs. Fairman attends church regularly?"

"I believe she has a record of nearly perfect attendance."

"Can I assume then that Mrs. Fairman was present on the morning of March 1?"

"It's likely. I can't say for sure."

Stittson pulled a manila folder from his briefcase and extracted a newspaper clipping. Showing the clipping to Alex, he asked if the Reverend recognized the photo.

"Of course."

"Yes, it's a newspaper photo of Miss Vera Kay, is it not? During a performance at your church on March 1?"

"It is."

"And does it accurately represent Miss Kay's performance?"

"Well, a portion of it."

"Exactly. A portion of it. Because in this photo, Miss Kay still wears a scrap of clothing, whereas eventually, I believe, she removed every stitch, isn't that right?"

"That's not what I meant, but yes, she did."

"In church."

"Yes." The two men beamed, each confident he'd made a telling point.

Stittson next wanted to know how Reverend Sanford, as Mrs. Fairman's spiritual shepherd, reconciled the performance of a woman who displayed her naked body for money with the word of God.

From his position in the raised witness chair, Alex looked down on Stittson, seemed to be making a point of looking down on him, and said, "I doubt God sees much sin in skin. If he did, he would have given us more fur." There were a few titters, and the judge held up a deterrent hand. "I believe in the resurrection of the body on earth," Alex went on happily. "The body is the revelation and instrument of the soul.

And that is how I reconcile, to use your word, counselor, Vera's erotic exuberance and the word of God. The Word made Flesh, so to speak."

Stittson put his hands in his pockets and began to flap the panels of his suit coat to and fro."Were there any children present, Reverend?"

"There may have been. I don't know."

"Or care?"

"I do care. If any were present, I suspect they appreciated Vera's dance in a way you and I can only aspire to. 'Except ye become as little children, ye can in no wise enter the kingdom of heaven."

Stittson turned on his heel and asked his next question with his back to Alex. "You mystify me, Reverend. Are you referring to innocence?" He pivoted back to face Alex.

Alex was all patience. "No. I am referring to play. You and I have lost the ability to play, you see. We are purposeful, oh so admirably full of purpose." He paused and stared at Stittson, as if to invite the reflection that some were more admirably full of purpose than others. "And since play has no purpose," he went on, "we have no use for it. But play expresses the intrinsic value of life itself. As a very great philosopher has put it, God is Love playing with itself."

"God is Love playing with himself?" Stittson exclaimed, misquoting slightly. "Is that your doctrine, Reverend?"

"More an article of faith."

Both men smiled triumphantly, and Chloe, who had risen to raise an objection, sat down without doing so. When her turn came to ask questions, she said she had none and did not return Alex's smile.

CALHOUN HAD SAID all along that the school was on trial, and it was perhaps this conviction that made him the best prepared of any of the witnesses. In the year of the school's existence, Calhoun had become a celebrity of sorts, Houston's resident radical educator, giving talks at free school conferences around the state and doing interviews on radio and television. He answered Stittson's questions with professional ease, sometimes pausing until the right word came to mind, sometimes considering a question for several seconds or so before answering. Unable to control the pace, Stittson grew fussy. He fiddled with the buttons on his jacket, and when it came time for him, once more, to open his briefcase, he pounced on it, snapping open the clasps with a flourish, to produce more photographs, this time photographs Hope herself had taken. Clay must have found them when he'd cleaned the house. One photograph showed a naked child, liberally streaked with finger paint, taking a bath in the sink. Another showed a group of children gathered around a fort they'd built, posing defiantly with raised fists, protruding tongues, erect third fingers, and forked peace signs.

After making a show of entering the photos with the clerk, Stittson asked Calhoun if it was true that he allowed the children to remove all of their clothing during school hours.

Calhoun explained that the school was self-governing and that he lacked the power to allow, except in cases of safety. Occasionally, yes, a child might remove his or her clothes. In that picture, for example, Vicki had wanted to take a bath. It probably had made sense to her to remove her clothes first. Obscenity, he pointed out, had to be learned, and obscenity was not part of the curriculum at the Blossom Street Free School. He spoke with a self-possession, a complete confidence in his convictions, that made Stittson's efforts seem overwrought, at least to Hope.

STITTSON DEVOTED THE rest of the afternoon to character witnesses. The Episcopal priest of Mindy's church and a neighbor testified to Mindy's virtues and qualifications. Clay's witnesses spoke along the same lines.

"Fairman's a good head," testified his Reserve commander. "A man you can count on."

Hope leaned over to whisper in Chloe's ear. "Ask him about his 'pussy fund.'" It was known throughout the squadron that Colonel MacIntyre kept a separate bank account to finance his amorous adventures. Chloe shook her head.

The only smile of the day from the judge came when Clay's superior at Houston Power and Light called Clay one of the utility's "brightest lights." The man went on to say that Clay's well-defined career path had been a steady ascent and would, no doubt, continue in that direction.

A neighbor affirmed Clay as a good father. "He and I did a stint of

Indian Princess together," he said. "Dads and daughters. Smoke Ring and Spark, those were their tribe names."

Hope couldn't deny any of this.

DRIVING HOPE HOME, Chloe indulged in a monologue of self-criticism. "I shouldn't have let Alex go on like that. He's such a freaking egoist. He's so oblivious, he doesn't even know when he's digging his own grave, too in love with his own voice to hear the sound of the shovel. Should I have drawn Victor out a little more, do you think? He gets along well with Amber and Patrick, doesn't he? I should have found a way to make that point. I didn't expect Stittson to call character witnesses for Mindy. But a lawyer should *never* be surprised on the courtroom floor. That's what Dr. Friedman always said. I wrote that down, *positive* it would never happen to me. And look. I should have studied electrical engineering. Something cut and dried. Something with *no people*."

Hope silently watched storefront after storefront whisk by. She saw no reason to speak; everything had been said, hadn't it? She already saw herself, drifting this way and that, without her children. That would be her punishment—to drift. Forever.

17

SITTING IN THE WITNESS CHAIR, HOPE HAD THE SAME SENSE OF terrific height that came to her occasionally in dreams. She would wake clutching her pillow, her stomach tumbling as it bailed out of her body in a petrifying plunge. The witness stand, of course, was no more than four feet above the floor, but it might as well have been four thousand feet. Panicked by a sudden downrush of flesh, she gripped the armrests, her hands showing rays of whitened flesh along the tendons.

Chloe stepped closer and raised inquiring eyebrows. Was she all right? Did Hope want her to ask for a few minutes' recess?

Hope shook her head. To delay would be worse.

Chloe nodded, returned to the table to consult her notes, and after rearranging a couple of pages, approached the witness stand again. Setting a deliberate pace, she asked a long series of detailed questions related to Hope's care of Amber and Patrick.

How many times a day did Ms. Fairman prepare meals for her children? How many days a week? How often did she shop for food? What were her children's favorite foods? How often did she prepare them? What was her position on soft drinks and candy?

How many times a week did her children bathe? When was the last time she had cut their fingernails? Did either child require help in dressing? How often? In what ways? How often did her children require new clothing? Did she take them shopping and allow them to help choose? How many times a week did she wash their clothing? Did she fold and put away the washed clothing?

What time was each child expected to be in bed? Did Ms. Fairman read them stories? Did she sing them songs? Did she wake them up in the morning? At what time?

Who were Amber's and Patrick's friends? What were their telephone numbers? Did Ms. Fairman provide transportation when they went to a friend's house at some distance from their own? Did she provide supervision when her children's friends came to her house? What outside activities were her children involved in? Did she provide transportation, supplies, and help when appropriate?

Who was the children's doctor? Who had chosen him, Mr. or Ms. Fairman? What had been her criteria? How many times a year did her children go to the doctor on a routine visit? How many times a year did the children visit the doctor when ill? What had been her children's illnesses this past year? How were they treated? What were the details of her home nursing care?

Chloe asked all these questions and many more. It was an extraordinarily tedious and lengthy line of questioning. The spectators began to stir and rustle, and even Stittson and Clay had trouble paying attention. The judge maintained the dour expression that had marked his demeanor so far. He could have been concentrating on Chloe's argument; he could have been mourning his golf scores.

Chloe's questions had relaxed Hope, however. She knew the answers. Although her voice had located itself in an unaccustomed register, it was steady, and she was remembering to breathe.

Chloe asked how long she had been married to Mr. Fairman.

"Ten years."

"And were you employed outside the home during any of those years?"

"No."

"You remained at home to care for your and Mr. Fairman's children?"

"Yes."

"Sacrificing your future earning power and security."

Stittson interrupted to ask if this was a *bona fide* question or if Mrs. Whitney was advancing a political argument.

"*Ms.* Whitney," Chloe corrected, going on to say that she was trying to establish the fact that Ms. Fairman had sacrificed her future earning power and security in order to stay home and care for her and Mr. Fairman's children. The judge ruled against her, however, and advised her not to stray too far afield.

Throwing Stittson a murderous look, Chloe asked her next question. "Could you tell us, Ms. Fairman, how much money Mr. Fairman has contributed to his children's support since your separation?"

Chloe had promised Hope that her answer to this question would demolish Clay's "sham concern for his children's welfare." But Hope didn't think Clay's concern was so sham. He did love his children and he cared about their welfare. It's just that he had always been funny about money. He was not altogether rational on that score.

"Did you understand the question, Ms. Fairman?"

Hope nodded and opened her mouth, but her vocal cords balked at the task of exposing Clay to censure, of betraying him.

"How much money has Mr. Fairman contributed to his children's support since your separation?" Chloe repeated.

Hope looked at Clay. Forgive me, she pleaded silently, although Clay looked neither worried nor friendly. "Three hundred dollars," she said finally. Chloe stared hard at her, willing her to continue. "He paid for two months and then . . . quit."

Chloe's tight, almost angry expression relaxed. She asked about Hope's job with the sausage company and the sewing she was now doing for the doll manufacturer. She was particularly interested in Hope's income. "And out of this amount of money you must buy food, meet the house payment, pay bills, obtain health care, and so on?"

"Yes."

"Is it enough?"

"No."

"Have you thought about seeking higher-paying employment?"

Hope explained about day-care expenses and the transportation and clothing costs of working outside the home and said that overall, she thought sewing doll clothes was the best sort of job she could have right now.

Chloe moved on to Clay's leaving. What had been his stated reasons? What had he told the children? What were their reactions? She asked about the day Hope had retreated to the bomb shelter.

Hope had not wanted to talk about this, but Chloe had insisted, saying that Stittson had raised the issue and they had better kill it before it grew more heads.

Hope made an effort to marshal her wits. "I . . . I wanted to get some sleep. I thought . . . away from everything . . . the bomb shelter . . . We didn't build it, you know, it came with the house, and we never used it as a bomb shelter . . . that is, I guess no one does, really, there's been no opportunity, not opportunity, that's the wrong word, what I mean to say is that the bomb shelter is not this drastic space. The children play in it . . . it's not a locale for suicide or anything. I just wouldn't . . . not there, and not anywhere really. It's true that I was depressed when Clay . . . But I didn't consider suicide. That is, I *considered* it, but not seriously. I wasn't thinking of it at all that day."

"You were simply distraught that your husband had left you for another woman."

Stittson objected to this and was sustained.

Thin-lipped and righteous, Chloe asked about the night Hope had called Mindy's.

Hope glanced at the spectators. This was none of their business. This was not television; this was not soap opera. Or maybe, she thought despairingly, maybe it was.

"On the night of February 12, you placed a phone call to Ms. Eck's home, correct?" Chloe pressed.

"Yes."

"And did you speak to your husband there?"

"Yes."

"And can you tell us the nature of the conversation?"

"He said he was going to tell me."

"Going to tell you what?"

Hope looked at her hands, still gripping the armrests. She did not like being characterized as an abandoned woman, as a domestic leftover. "He didn't say exactly."

Chloe's gray eyes went wide. "Well, what did he mean?" she asked, recovering.

Stittson interrupted to point out that unless Mrs. Fairman was a mind reader, she could not be expected to answer that question, and the judge concurred.

Frustrated, Chloe consulted her notes. "Had you ever left your children in the care of a temporary guardian before, Ms. Fairman?"

"No."

"So your trip to the Big Thicket was your first vacation without your children, the first time you had ever left them under the care of another person for any length of time."

"Yes."

"Did you inform Mr. Fairman of your plans?"

"I did."

"Did he object to your proposed trip?"

"No."

"Did you tell him you had arranged with Ms. Higgins to care for your children?"

"Yes."

"He concurred with your plans?"

"I assumed so. He didn't say otherwise."

"And what happened when you returned?"

The workings of Hope's throat muscles were visible beneath her skin, and her mind faltered, bobbling backward, confusing the contents. The judge had to lean forward to hear; her voice was a scrap of itself. "My children were gone."

She was supposed to say more. She was supposed to describe her return, the empty house, the shock. But Chloe had warned her: Do not weep. No matter what. Judges hate it. So Hope sat there immobile, not stirring so much as an eyelash for fear of toppling her self-control, sat there wearing something like a smile, a swath of curved lip she felt wrapping around and around her head like the linen strips of an Egyptian mummy.

Chloe sat down, and it was Stittson's turn. He did not approach the witness stand right away but took a moment to open his briefcase. Hope watched him, apprehensive, wondering what record of forgotten misdeeds he might extract. It seemed, however, he had only wanted to stow some papers. This accomplished, he snapped his briefcase shut again and came toward her empty-handed. Nevertheless, her sense of culpability persisted.

But Stittson questioned her gently, so gently his interrogation bordered on parody, telling her to take her time with her answers, asking if she needed a glass of water. Most of his questions had to do with the day Hope had withdrawn to the bomb shelter. What time had she entered the bomb shelter? Hope didn't know. How long had she stayed there? Hope didn't know this either. Why the bomb shelter? Had she been afraid in her own house? No, she didn't think so. Had she realized that her daughter and her daughter's friend were waiting for her to pick them up? That they had no way of knowing where she was?

"I wasn't thinking of them," Hope admitted. "I lost track of time."

Did she think she might have frightened her daughter?

"I hope not."

Had she threatened suicide?

"No."

"No? Mr. Fairman has testified that you did. Are you denying it?"

"I remember talking to Clay . . . in that vein . . . at one time or another, but not that day."

"At one time or another." Stittson stared at her for a moment before asking her what time she had made her putative phone call to Mrs. Eck's home on the night of February 12.

Hope wasn't sure. "Probably sometime after midnight."

"You're not sure. Probably. Are you sure you made this phone call, Mrs. Fairman?"

"Yes."

Stittson had no further questions.

"I DIDN'T DO very well, did I?" said Hope, as for the second day in a row, she and Chloe sat facing the steam table at Coney Island West.

Chloe stared at the sign behind the cooks: SERVICE IS OUR MOTTO. "You did fine."

Hope shielded her eyes with one hand. "All I want is for this to be over."

"No, you don't," said Chloe sharply. "All you want is *to get your children back*." She reminded Hope of the witnesses she would be calling that afternoon: the director of Patrick's day-care center, two neighbors, Calhoun again. "They'll be testifying to your good character and your eminently obvious desire and ability to provide for your children's well-being."

"I know."

"You don't sound as if you believe it."

She didn't. This whole trial seemed to her trumped-up, grotesque. The narrow funnel of interrogation had shrunk her life to humiliating, and somehow false, proportions.

"The thing is," Chloe mused, "the thing is: *I'm* your best witness. *I'm* the one who has seen you with your kids nearly every day for the past two years. I was there, remember, the time Patrick swallowed the open safety pin, and you grabbed him and held him by his ankles and shook him, and the safety pin just slid out, and he was okay. I'd like the judge to have that information somehow. That's evidence. You saved your son's life. As a matter of course. You weren't being a heroine. You were just there. That's what I'd like to get across somehow."

HOPE'S CHARACTER WITNESSES were as predictable as Clay's had been. Hope was a good mother and a reliable person. No one had ever seen her physically abuse her children. Quite the contrary. She was consistently kind and loving. Calhoun testified to Hope's involvement in the school. She donated her time and took a lively interest in Amber's education. Clay, on the other hand, had never visited the school, had not attended any of the programs his daughter had participated in.

In his closing remarks, Stittson emphasized Hope's mental instability, her poor choice of associates, her untrustworthy judgments, her bad housekeeping. He held up Mindy as a person of superior character who, together with the children's natural father, would compose a stable household better suited to fill the emotional, spiritual, and economic needs of the children. It was *in the best interests of the children*, he stressed, for them to be in their father's care, and he hoped the court did not subscribe to a prevailing prejudice in favor of the natural mother. The natural mother, in this case, was neither qualified nor competent.

Chloe argued that plaintiff's case was undue and indefensible. Raising children required the ability to recognize not only when a child needed new clothes but also when *not* to throw old clothes *out*, she said, alluding to Amber's nightgown. Raising children required a parent willing to stay up all night and provide competent nursing care, which their natural mother had done time and time again, someone to arrange for a child to visit and receive friends, which the natural mother had done time and time again, someone to be there when a child swallowed an open safety pin and to turn him upside down and shake the safety pin loose, which Ms. Fairman had, in fact, done, thus saving her son's life. Mr. Fairman had never been involved in these ways with his children, no more than most men had. In this society, men rarely performed the strenuous daily acts of care that created vital physical and emotional bonds. Moreover, Mr. Fairman had reneged on his payments for his children's support, which had not been sufficient to begin with. What did that say about his concern for them, his regard for their *best interest*? That failure alone spoke volumes. Whereas the natural mother had not only provided the day-to-day care critical to her children's well-being, she was also doing her best to support them financially.

As SHE AND Clay took their places in the courtroom the next day, Hope noted that Clay did not look as if he had slept any better than she had. His sooty eye sockets contrasted exaggeratedly with a very pale face, as if he'd been made up for a stage role.

Stittson, on the other hand, was evidently feeling chipper, flinging his briefcase down on the table with the same vim he'd demonstrated the first day. A man who loves his work, was Hope's impression.

They rose as the judge entered, sat when he sat. With a truculent thrust to his lower jaw and an adjustment to his horn-rimmed glasses, he began to read from his decision. Chloe's fingers twittered on the polished surface. Hope sat with her hands in her lap.

The judge rejected plaintiff's argument of abandonment. "The defendant showed poor judgment, perhaps, but not intent to abandon, in leaving her children." He went on to explain that under Texas law, he was enjoined to make a decision based on the best interests of the children. There were several needs to consider. The most obvious was material.

"The father's capacity to fulfill the children's material needs is well established. The father, better educated than the mother, occupies a position of responsibility in the community for which he is well recompensed and from which he holds a reasonable expectation of advancement. Currently, the mother earns money sewing at home, but not in sufficient amount to cover household expenses. Should she find better-paid work outside the home, her ability to care for her children would be impaired. In any case, she lacks the skills that would qualify her as a major breadwinner.

"The court could, of course, order child-support payments if there were evidence that the mother could provide a household that meets her children's emotional and social needs *better* than that which the natural father could provide. This is not the case, however. The father's remarriage will provide the children with a stable family unit and a full-time caretaker. The father's fiancée is a well-qualified woman of good character who already enjoys an affectionate relationship with the children. The father has purchased a new home with ample space in a neighborhood where the children will have friends, a nearby school, and extracurricular activities. Thus the children's emotional and social needs would have a high probability of being met under the father's care.

"The importance of these advantages would be less significant were it not for other factors affecting the mother's ability to care for her children. Episodes of mental instability make questionable her capacity to provide emotional sustenance for her children and may account for several instances of poor judgment. The mother's choice of a caretaker during her absence is one example, and her enrollment of her daughter in a school under the guidance of a well-known radical is another. Furthermore, the mother's male companion could be fairly characterized as a dubious influence on children of impressionable years.

"Accordingly, for these reasons, which are set forth more fully in a written decision available to both parties, the court awards custody of both Fairman children, Amber Lee and Patrick Wallace, to their natural father, Clay Stewart Fairman." The judge went on to summarize other conditions of the divorce. When he had finished, he stood up and, after gazing quickly around the courtroom, exited, his robe swinging.

Hope did not rise as he left. She sat still as a monument. Children could have climbed up her thighs and onto her shoulders, sat on her head and dangled their feet. Pigeons could have flapped their wings around her ears or tucked their heads under feathers to take a nap in the stony crook of her arm.

She would have no memory of leaving the courtroom. She had undoubtedly done so, of course, had undoubtedly left the table (had her knees buckled? Had she looked at Clay?) and walked through the double doors. No doubt Chloe had been at her side. She had probably taken the elevator to the lobby, where there would have been so much glass, so much light, an excess of light. Perhaps she had put on her sunglasses. She'd reached her home somehow, but who had driven her? Chloe? Victor? She wouldn't recall.

What she would recall were the unmistakable spasms of a contracting uterus as she lay on her bed later, that almost forgotten tightening so close as to obliterate all else. She could not cry out, as she had done with helpful savagery at the births of Amber and Patrick; her throat was concrete. So it was in silence that she encouraged the clenching of her womb to reach the desired, voluptuous peak of intensity, and release. The contractions came within a few minutes of one another, by degrees expanding her body outward into unseen reaches, as a reed of afternoon light from between the drapes struck first the mirror, then the bureau top, then its drawers, one after another, to finally disappear in the dust that was first dusk, and then advancing darkness, which became total at a point specified in her mind, whether accurately or not didn't matter, as midnight.

At midnight, then, she heard the front door open. She registered no fear. If it had been the rapist of Braeburn Terrace, it wouldn't have mattered to her.

"It's me, Hope. It's Calhoun."

These were the first and last words of a very long night in which he would hold her, the buttons of his shirt making impressions on her cheek, his leather belt creaking whenever he stirred. He would tuck the soggy strands of her hair behind her ears and stroke her back and breathe lightly on her, his body long and solid beside hers, companion bones.

18

THEIR ABSENCE WAS A PRESENCE. SHE WOULD STAND AT THE stove and not feel a head graze her hip or a hand tug on her sleeve. She would sit down at the dinner table and not see them in their chairs. The backyard was empty of their voices. They were nonexistent everywhere.

Some days she set off in the Cadillac in pure pursuit, without motive or object, driving for hours around a city overexposed by the sun, whitened and lifeless, a world blanched and grown dumb. Gradually, the thrumming of the wheels against the pavement loosened her grip on chronology, and as her sense of beginnings, middles, and ends grew elusive, she would slip into another realm, a realm where a small black cat might turn to reveal a bloody jaw before disappearing into a pittosporum bush, a realm where crosses beckoned her to follow.

She saw the cross in an empty field north of the city. Pulling over, she got out of the car and ran across the field after it, feeling light, light, light as the bones of a thistle seed. From a distance, she could have passed for a girl out on a coltish run. Behind her the cough and hum of traffic from the freeway mingled with the squawk of grackles as her bare legs rolled out from denim shorts in regular rhythm, her feet scrubbing the hissing weeds.

It wasn't a cross at all. What had looked like a cross from the road turned out to be a fence post juxtaposed onto a leafless bush with two lone horizontal branches. Hope placed a hand on the fence post to assure herself of its materiality, but even the feel of the rough, splintering wood against her palm failed to erase the apparition. She wondered if seeing the cross was related to her dreams of dead babies.

Could be, Alex said, when she consulted him. But her dreams of dead babies were not about her children but about herself. "It's the death of your old self you're dreaming," he told her as she sat on the old sofa in his cluttered office, worrying a scrap of paper into a pellet. The coming attraction was to be rebirth. "You are acquiring new consciousness," he assured her. He flinched as the paper pellet hit him, just above his left earlobe.

She talked about the nesting instinct of grief. "Limbs are unlikely residences," she told Chloe, "as is the head. Grief is more liable to settle somewhere in the trunk." Her own grief, after scurrying fruitlessly through her body for days, nosing into nooks and crannies in furtive search of a likely residence, finally burrowed into the left corner of her pelvic cavity, where it gnawed gently at her soft parts.

Rosamunda had a solution. Hope should make a pilgrimage to Our Lady of the Remedies in the church of San Bartolo. "That's what I do, every year. Ai, the sorrows of the *madres*," she said, her tawny dunes heaving beneath her jersey. She pointed to the photograph thumbtacked to the wall. Her son. Missing.

"How is Our Lady of the Remedies on pains right here?" Hope asked, patting her left side.

"No problem."

Hope wasn't necessarily contradicting herself when on another occasion she told Chloe that grief intensified life. Enveloped in a new, raw skin of preternatural awareness, she registered a three-degree drop in temperature as if it were the onset of a bitter winter. A subtle shift in the light had the force of a planetary perturbation. Her vision amplified, and she saw photographs everywhere—in the torn patch of a fiberglass fence, in the chalk marks on a sidewalk, in the straight edges of a gelded box hedge—but since she never carried her camera with her these days, the images slipped back into the uncelebrated.

Sometimes she haunted parks where children played, hesitantly approaching the swings or the sand ring to hover there for a brief instant before the watchful mothers leaped up from chatting or reading or repacking a diaper bag and hurried over, talking to their children in loud voices and eyeing Hope suspiciously, Hope the pariah, Hope the unfit mother.

Awash in remembrances of unfitness, she spent hours picking over the past, extracting instances of negligence and lapses of self-control: the time she had shut herself up in the bathroom to escape an indefatigable Amber, the time Patrick had fallen with a handsaw she had forgotten to put away, marring his innocent white neck forever with a faint, pink dotted line. Hope could brood over these crimes—that's how she thought of them—for hours.

And that was the past. There was also the present to absorb. She dreaded the daytime ringing of the telephone.

"Mommy." She knew from the hiccups that Patrick had been crying. "Mommy, come and get me."

The pain in her throat made it hard to talk. "I . . . I . . . I can't, honey."

"You *can*," he insisted, his belief in her power immutable.

At some point, Mrs. Clarke, Clay's housekeeper, would come on the line to apologize. She was at her wit's end. Patrick refused to accept her care. He would not let her touch him or his clothes. "If I so much as take a T-shirt out of the dryer, he won't wear it," she told Hope.

"He's having a few adjustment problems," Clay agreed. "It's to be expected. He'll be all right. Children are very resilient."

"Are they?" Hope asked Calhoun one night at Prufrock's, gazing at him across their unplayed game of chess. He looked away, avoiding her eyes, full of need and claim, eyes that might daunt sturdier loyalties than his. Calhoun was proving to be an unwilling light at the end of her tunnel. She called him often, sometimes in the middle of the night, and he usually answered, but more guardedly lately; he'd grown thrifty with his responses. Hope was convinced he was abandoning her. And who could blame him? She would abandon herself if it were physically possible.

"People are always saying children are resilient," she said. "But what sort of proof do we have of it? It's more a justification than anything proven, isn't it?"

"I don't know," he said warily.

"The loss of a child is the loss of hope."

"Amber and Patrick are not dead," he reminded her.

This was true. Hope saw them every other weekend, enough for her to witness the direction their lives were taking, cross-current to her own. Amber, in fifth grade at Spring Branch Elementary, complained about having to wear a dress to school. She was earning Girl Scout badges at a desperate clip, Mindy having signed her up for a neighborhood troop.

Patrick attended nursery school at Mindy's Episcopal church, where he had already attracted disapproval for drawing a picture of Adam and Eve expelling God from the garden. Hope was heartsick at the thought of him subject to playtime, naptime, storytime, juicetime. She didn't like to think of his life submitted to schedules; she didn't think he was ready to be smoothed and shaped into citizenry just yet, not Patrick, not her godling.

The days they visited her were almost as unbearable as the days of their absence. She felt small and momentary, translucent, made of tissue, a condition that might have been cured, or at least ameliorated, had she simply clasped their compact flesh to her own more loosely packed substance, but she hung back from them now, constrained and unsure. She was sometimes glad when her weekends with them were over, a realization that iced her from the inside out.

She had always believed that to release a child from one's own body was to embark on an irreversible path in life, and a sentient part of her continued on that path. The physicality of maternity alone meant that a mother was always a mother. One Saturday, feeling a great need of height—a hill, a bluff, something more than the knuckles of land around Houston—she drove the four hours to Austin, where she parked in a spot west of the city and climbed a chaparralled slope to its scrubby top. Here she released a long, ululating cry of the flesh that would have harrowed souls had anyone been listening.

Another day she thought she saw her brother William at the just-built Galleria, a new shopping center with an ice rink. Hope had gone there intending to soothe herself with long sweeps across the ice. Swimming and skating had always come naturally to her, as if she had been born to water in all its forms.

She recalled the Thanksgiving Day she and William had escaped the relatives, thanks to a freak cold spell, the coldest November Indiana had seen in fifty years, to go skating at the frog pond on the outskirts of town, which was not round but long and narrow, so that one could skim its length with a sense of travel and release. They'd been the only skaters that day, gliding up and down, up and down, and the more they'd skated, the more Hope felt they were fairy-tale children, like Hansel and Gretel.

Hope still had a pair of skates. Houston had offered no opportunities to use them until now with the new ice rink opened in the Galleria. In a bizarre sort of way, the Galleria had something of a fairy-tale quality itself, a three-tiered shopping center inspired by the Galleria Vittorio Emmanuele in Milan. A huge Plexiglas skylight illuminated the ice rink at its heart on the first floor.

On ice again, Hope's body was once more virgin and unsmudged by stretch marks, insensible of the crowded rink and ice severely scarred with blade cuts. She was skating the frog pond again. She could still recall the precise rhythm of William's quick-stepped gathering of velocity, followed by his long glide.

She did not register the commotion on the Galleria's second tier until she noticed skaters clinging to the railing around the rink, heads craned back. Above them a crew of people wearing domino masks, identically dressed in black turtlenecks and pants, were creeping past storefronts, hugging big sacks to their chests. Their leader wore a tailcoat, a sparkling wig of silver plastic streamers, and, instead of a mask, glasses with a fake nose. He held something in one outstretched hand: a wallet, a handgun, a bird's nest—it could have been any of these; Hope couldn't quite see. What she did see, though, and quite clearly, beneath the wig and false nose, was her brother William. She tipped forward and fell.

A man in an unnecessary muffler helped her up, and, trembling, she leaned against the railing. "Are you all right?"

"Oh, yes."

"You look pale. Can I call someone for you?"

"No. I just need to catch my breath."

Around them people discussed what they'd just seen. Only one woman thought it had been a real robbery. Most thought it was some sort of sales promotion.

"It was guerrilla theater," Hope explained. They stared at her. "My brother William described it to me. Surprise theatrics conducted behind enemy lines, he said." The man who had helped her to her feet started to withdraw. "Harassment of the status quo," she added. The man skated off.

The incident made Hope melancholy for days. Spinning herself a cocoon of nostalgia, she became suspended in former, if not necessarily happier, times. She looked everywhere for William, obsessively driving the Loop. Sometimes the city played tricks. One day, she found herself in a pocket of streets named for operas, where Hansel turned into Gretel and finally became Bohème. Another time, in the northeast part of the city, she found herself cruising three parallel streets named Little, Boy, and Blue. What a city, she thought, what a clumsy, audacious city, a child of a city really, with a child's sense of play and omnipotence.

As the weeks passed and William failed to appear, she wondered if she had really seen him at the Galleria. More likely, she had created a mirage out of memories. When you thought about it, how could she possibly have determined his identity, given his get-up? She had projected her thoughts of him onto a random event.

Rosamunda rejected this explanation. "Your brother he misses you," she said. "That's why he appeared to you." The thought haunted Hope for weeks.

On days when the dense weight of loneliness pressed on her with enough force to compact her into a tiny speck, she would drop by Communitas, banking on the presence of other humans to restore her proper size. It usually worked. Her own impulse to engage would worm its way up through the packed soil of her resistance to bloom into a fairly creditable passage of hours. She especially enjoyed Finn and O'Molly. Never having known her as Amber and Patrick's mother, they never inquired about them. Instead they asked her to listen to a tape they'd made for a Pacifica program, or they sought her opinion of a song they were writing about the new no-knock law. They seemed willing to discuss these things with her in spite of the fact she no longer had opinions. "Oh, I don't know" was her inevitable answer, as she rocked back and forth on the squeaking porch glider. But they showed no impatience, unlike Chloe, who accused Hope of drifting into a social coma.

"The tide is turning, Hope," she reported, exhilarated and exhausted from meetings and letter-writing campaigns and candlelight vigils. "This moratorium thing is going to work. It's got to."

Hope didn't care. Vietnam was beyond her powers of imagination.

Her concern did not extend beyond the envelope of her own skin, and even in regard to her own skin, Hope was lackadaisical.

"Oh, I don't know," she replied to Chloe's repeated requests that Hope let her file an appeal.

"You have grounds, Hope. I've gone over that decision with a fine-tooth comb. Rankin made some mistakes."

"Rankin?"

"The judge, Hope. The man who took away your children."

"Oh."

Hope began to avoid Chloe. Fellowship, with its lesser demands, its looser weave, suited her better than friendship just now, and she began to spend more and more time at Communitas, where she often spent the night with Victor.

Victor was solicitous beyond what anyone had a right to expect, and Hope was becoming accustomed to toying with her dinner in his company. He ate with apologetic enterprise, baffled by her lack of appetite. Rescuing a boy from the top of a telephone pole was one thing; hanging on to a woman drowning in regret and self-doubt and foreboding was another. Sometimes Hope understood this and would smile reassuringly across her plate of uneaten food. Other times she raged. "Get out of my way!" she burst out one night when their hands collided while reaching for the salt.

Hope would have liked to blame him for what had happened. When he regarded her in that deferential way, his eyes begging her to let him be of help, the desire to make him her whipping boy became almost irresistible. What stayed her hand was the two-inch pile of photographs of the Big Thicket: proof of her culpability. There was a part of Hope that did not regret that trip.

He tried to rehabilitate her through sex, but desire had left her, the memory of it so much debris after the floodwaters had receded, a sodden shoe, a rusted hubcap, an empty blue jar. She went through the motions, though, as a way of establishing existence, and Victor affected not to notice her blanched ardor. What she liked best about him just now was his dreaming shape in the dark. She sometimes fell asleep with a finger resting on his backbone.

*   *   *

FERN THOUGHT SHE should meet new people. She herself was now working as a cocktail waitress, and she encouraged Hope to do the same. "I'm making three times what I made at the Grass Hut."

Hope stifled a nasty remark. If Fern had quit her job at the Grass Hut a week before rather than after the custody suit, it might have made a difference. Fern's winsome disarray, her buoyant belittlement of the world's ways, were beginning to grate. Nevertheless, one night as Hope was guiding the sewing machine needle around the three hundredth or so pinafore armhole, she decided to take Fern's advice.

The next day she discovered that jobs were easily had in the dimly lit world of cocktail lounges. Offered three, she accepted one close to Communitas, a place on Montrose Boulevard called the Trap Door. She returned home to pack up the pinafores and spools of colored bindings to send back to the doll manufacturer, and after that, between the hours of five and midnight, Saturday through Thursday, Hope could be found wearing a black taffeta short-skirted costume and black net stockings (the cost of which was deducted from her first paycheck), shuttling distractedly between the bar and the tables, oblivious to her incompetence, bringing gimlets when gin slings had been ordered, scooping up insulting tips of pennies and foreign coins and, once, Monopoly money. She dropped things. Swizzle sticks slid through her fingers, glass tumblers detonated at her feet, paper napkins drifted lazily to the floor. "I can't hang on to *anything*," she cried.

Nick, the bartender and owner, a balding man with shirtsleeves pushed up past his elbows, assured her she was just nervous and would catch on soon. He showed her how to slant her head when she smiled, how to bend at the knees when setting down drinks. He urged her to make eye contact. Hope was grateful for his help but failed to master any of the moves and gave up the false eyelashes Fern had recommended, after repeatedly getting glue in her eye.

THE DAYS PASSED; Hope was not quite sure how.

"Halloween?" she said one day. "When?"

"Next *week*," Amber told her impatiently. She and Patrick had brought their costumes to show her. Amber would be dressing as a zombie queen. Patrick was to be a skeleton. Later, Hope asked Clay if she might accompany them on their rounds of trick or treating, but he said no, not this time, because Jason had to be included, and he thought it would be better all around if he did the chaperoning. This seemed reasonable enough, but his denial of her request threw Hope into another numbing depression, prompting Fern to throw a Halloween party to cheer her up. Hope smoked marijuana for the first time that night but experienced no effects beyond thirst and a woolliness in her head. "I'm not cut out for this era," she sobbed, and the party broke up early.

In November, Hope sold the house and moved to Communitas. There was hardly anything to move, because she had been selling off pieces of furniture for months. She decided not to sell the property in Kemah. She needed a refuge.

Emptying the bomb shelter turned out to be the big job. All her photographic equipment—trays and tongs and the developer tank, bottles and paper and safelight—had to be readied for storage. Hope took great care with all this, cleaning everything thoroughly, wrapping the utensils neatly. Had Clay seen her, he would have been impressed.

Alex persuaded her to get rid of her boxes of mementos. Out with the old, in with the new, he said. A cleansing, a purification, was necessary. So she piled the dance programs and yearbooks and diaries and dried autumn leaves from Brown County into the brick barbecue in the backyard and held a solitary memorial bonfire. But as the satin ribbons curled into charred shadows of themselves and pages of her young handwriting crisped and blackened, she sickened at what she had done. It occurred to her for the first time that Alex was not always right, and she was glad she had kept the portfolio of Amber's and Patrick's drawings, their Thanksgiving turkeys made of pinecones and their bread-dough Christmas ornaments, their painted bricks.

All in all, leaving the house was not as wrenching as it might have been. She wept on confronting the penciled marks on the hall-closet door recording Amber's and Patrick's heights, and she regretted the loss of a darkroom, but the house had never been hers, and she was not sorry to leave it, especially now.

After a delicate discussion with Victor, she decided on her own bedroom at Communitas. Their schedules were not compatible, she pointed out: she worked until after midnight, while his alarm went off at 5:30

a.m. This was not the only reason Hope wanted her own room, but it was the easiest to articulate.

She chose a second-floor room that looked down on the backyard with its venerable pyracantha and crape myrtle. A tall, slender yew tree pressed against the furthermost window. Influenced by photographs of Georgia O'Keeffe's adobe home in Abiquiu, its rooms swept clean by the purgative desert wind, Hope envisioned the second-floor bedroom in the same spirit—bare, stark, ungarnished. The high, white walls would be unadorned all the way to the ceiling's grooved molding. A Navajo rug might be allowed to lie diagonally on the dark wood floor, a pallet along one wall. The three side-by-side windows would remain uncurtained, open to the world.

But the second-floor bedroom did not end up that way, maybe because there were no purgative desert winds in Houston, or maybe because a Victorian edifice as commanding as this was unwilling to relinquish tone, or maybe because Hope could not resist a garage sale. In any case, a troop of secondhand furnishings began to populate the room: two large willow baskets, rectangular with hinged tops, for her clothes; a chest-high oriental vase, in which she arranged dried eucalyptus leaves and peacock feathers; two basket chairs with pillows. She bought an old tin trunk for storage, and its top was soon colonized by green plants—small brass pots of ivy and wandering Jew, a sweet potato vine Patrick had cultivated for her. From her old house she brought only a mirror and her bed, which she covered with a brightly colored Peruvian bedspread. Carrying the mirror upstairs, she had been briefly disoriented by the sense that she was walking into herself. Later, she re-created the perception in an eerie self-portrait, the first photograph she had taken in a long time. She didn't show it to anyone.

Chloe was unable to hide her dismay on seeing Hope's shrunken surround, but Amber loved the room, saying she had read about it in books. Patrick liked to open and shut the door, which made a pleasing two-part sound—*ka-tuck*—as the latch bolt engaged, and was otherwise noncommittal. For her part, Hope felt the room suited her, and she spent a good deal of time there, lying alone on her bed, listening to the yew tree scrape against the window, swaddled in her grandmother's quilt, rolled up into herself, into the pit of herself, the bitter almond of a peach stone.

19

HOPE FOUND COMMUNAL LIVING BOTH QUEER AND CONSOLING. Take the bathroom. Four different tubes of toothpaste plus a yellow box of baking soda sat on the bathroom countertop; two competing brands of tampons and a box of sanitary napkins shared a shelf below the towels. A Mickey Mouse soap hanging from a rope and a loofah sponge, labeled "Finn" and "O'Molly" respectively, hung from hooks, and in the medicine cabinet next to Hope's aspirin was Alex's grimy bottle of Old Spice shaving lotion. It was strange to be living intimately with people to whom you were not joined.

Yet lying in bed alone, Hope was often comforted by the sound of the tub being filled or the smell of morning coffee being brewed. She was grateful for Oily Jon's ubiquitous odor and O'Molly's recurrent soprano. She was even comforted at times by the murmurings coming from Alex's room next to hers. She pondered the ease with which women slipped in and out of Alex's life, women who seemed to lack the angles, the protuberances, on which anything might snag.

She was not sorry to surrender the command of a house. The democratic meetings held weekly to administer what O'Molly called the nitty-gritties might be an unwieldy approach to housekeeping, but they intrigued Hope. The smallest detail demanded debate. Were they spending too much on carob bars? Should they all chip in for jug wine, or should each person be responsible for his or her own

213

high? Who was leaving dirty socks in the living room? Why? Was this a sex-linked trait?

Except for the dirty socks, Hope found the housekeeping standards congenial. Dust tended to accumulate, and the grime in the grout looked permanent, but every once in a while a convivial housekeeping spirit seized a majority, and a respectable cleansing would take place, usually to the full-volume pulse of rock music.

Everyone took turns cooking, with the exception of Alex, who proved so unreliable he was finally dropped from the schedule and charged an extra five dollars a week. Oily Jon was the kitchen's guiding spirit. He insisted on mindful preparation and forbade processed food—it was unresponsive to vibrations. Food had to be live, he told them, in order to receive the karma of the cooks. Processed food was not spiritually absorbent and was, therefore, to be avoided, especially potato chips. "Potato chips are among the deadliest substances known to man!" he exhorted them. "My mother used to crush them and sprinkle them on casseroles. What do you think of a mother like that?" The household went along with his dietary rules, sensing that something more than nutrition was at stake. "There's tolerance here," Hope told Chloe.

She occasionally thought of Communitas as a raft.

This interested Alex. "A raft! You mean a life raft?"

"Sort of. A safe place on the move. Where a few souls have banded together for the journey."

Alex liked that; it was exactly the way he wanted to hear Communitas described: on the move, headed toward change, growth, against the tide, although that wasn't quite what Hope had meant. She was thinking more literally. It seemed to her that half the country was on the move these days. She often came home from the Trap Door to find two or three people in sleeping bags on the threadbare Turkish carpet. Pilgrims.

Calhoun (who regularly dropped by with Frederick now that Frederick had apprenticed himself to Oily Jon, a move both Calhoun and Ocie applauded as an alternative to the Black Battalion) accused her of romanticizing this nomadism. Certainly it was at the opposite pole of Hope's domestic experience. The pilgrims seemed to her much younger than herself (although most of them were in their late twenties, like Hope), and she marveled at how lightly they traveled, bedrolls and packs on their backs, their relationships fluid and transformable. A couple might arrive, separate, often without argument, and find new partners—all within the space of a week. She found their adaptability as amazing as their immunity to regret. She loved their variety, or as Alex would have put it, their different orders of energy. There was much talk of energy around Communitas.

"Energy," Chloe said contemptuously. "Not one of them donates fifteen minutes' worth of precious energy to the Peace Center."

True, yet the vitality was nevertheless real enough, made up of a renewable enthusiasm generated by perpetual shifts in the dynamics, a contagious eroticism, and the bond of alienage. In this house bright with strangers, there were times when Hope felt she'd been transported to Oz, the movie Oz. Sometimes there was that same sudden opening up into Technicolor.

She adapted easily to the change in aesthetic, which valued the interesting over the pleasing. The rules seemed to be: nothing should match, nothing should be new, everything should be colorful, and as much as possible should be handmade. Texture reigned; the variety of weave and pattern, the odds and ends of furniture, and the interspersal of the natural—sticks, stones, feathers—gave the house an air of movement.

Hope worried about Amber's and Patrick's reactions to Communitas. It was bound to seem irregular to them, maybe even lunatic. They said nothing about it when they visited, although they were markedly reserved. They held the other members of the household in some suspicion, but Chloe thought this might possibly be a form of sibling rivalry—someone else was living with their mother, had taken their place. Then, too, no one made any special effort to make Amber and Patrick feel at home. To the household they were just two more pilgrims. No one was rude, but no one paid any particular attention to them either. Chloe said this was because the people at Communitas were all children themselves. "You've got half a dozen centers of the universe there," she said.

"I think it's more a matter of style," Hope said.

"An infantile style."

Maybe, but they all took care of one another, in their fashion. When Janis Joplin died and Fern did not go to work for a week, broke into sobs at the dinner table, and refused to comb her hair or make her bed, the household coalesced into one big lap for her to curl up in. Hope

did her part, although she questioned whether or not Fern was entitled
to grief. How could Fern mourn someone she'd never met?

"She's mourning the death of her alter ego," said Alex, who spent a
lot of time with Fern, comforting and counseling her. He suggested she
write down her feelings, which she did. It was a short list.

> *gone into darkness*
> *beautiful hurt*
> *lost*
> *the trouble with death is*
> *there's no repeat*

O'Molly turned it into a song. "It's physically impossible to sing and
be depressed at the same time," she told Hope. "If you sing a sad song,
you might feel sad, but you won't feel depressed. Depression can't survive
exhaling in the form of musical notes."

Hope had to admit this seemed to be the case with Fern. Perhaps
one's spirits *were* a matter of ventilation. Fern sang O'Molly's song often
and even began to talk about a singing career. "I was meant to sing,"
she said one night at dinner. "Wasn't I born in Port Arthur? It's just
that God forgot to give me a voice."

"One of those oversight things," murmured Finn.

"Do you want to sing or be a rock star? Most people just want to be
rock stars," said O'Molly.

"I want to sing. I want to drink Southern Comfort and really belt it
out."

The household took care of Hope, too. Alex's cure was to take her
flying. Part owner of a Piper Cub, he rose early every Monday morning
to spend the day buzzing the beaches of Galveston or skimming the hill
country around Austin. He sometimes took Hope with him, in spite of
her lack of enthusiasm. To her everything looked too orderly, the confusion of life on the ground smoothed and muted by altitude. From the
air, the earth showed none of its scars. There was no scraggly growth,
no odd accretions. The landscape was at once miniature and immense.
Nothing was to human scale, and Hope felt less human herself, thinned
and vast.

Alex, on the other hand, seemed to inhale substance with every breath.

"Born to fly-eye-eye-eye!" he sang over the drumfire of the motor. "Isn't this grr-reat?" he would shout. "Aren't you just happeeeee? Aren't you just glad to be aliiiiive?"

She preferred her darkroom. Finn, who was a carpenter by day for a group of renegade architects known as the Prairie Dogs, had made for her a darkroom in one corner of the house's old summer kitchen, throwing up two walls around the sink to make a space about the size of the bomb shelter for her to work in.

"There's generosity here," Hope told Chloe.

Hope liked her surroundings, too, a heavily wooded section of the Montrose with the wide avenues of a formerly well-to-do neighborhood. Directly opposite Communitas, the street split and met again at the north end to enclose an undeveloped three acres, creating an oval-shaped green. Numerous peace seekers wandered there: the elderly and the young, the hip and the dazed, the poor and the working poor.

The sounds of guitars and hammers were ubiquitous. Nearly everyone seemed to be a musician, a carpenter, or a musician/carpenter. Sometimes the spacious arpeggios of a Bach partita could be heard nearby. Hope often fell asleep to its strains, wondering who was playing. Finn and O'Molly didn't know either. They referred to a "phantom violinist." Hope liked the idea. It gave the neighborhood a fairy-tale quality; it hinted at happy endings.

FREDERICK REFUSED TO go to the ophthalmologist's. Ocie was convinced he needed glasses, and she had convinced Calhoun as well. But neither of them could convince Frederick. "I think he's scared," Calhoun told Hope. "Ophthalmologist. Try saying that as if you never heard it before. Ophthalmologist. Doesn't it sound scary?"

Hope agreed that it did.

"Maybe he'd go in the Cadillac," Calhoun suggested.

"Oh. I see. You want *me* to take him."

"I think he'd go in the Cadillac."

Calhoun was right on both counts. Frederick did agree to go with Hope, and he was scared. Driving to the ophthalmologist's, he sat ruler-straight in the passenger seat and did not even lean forward to turn on the radio. When they arrived, he insisted Hope stay with him.

The ophthalmologist, a friend of Ocie's, showed them into the narrow, darkened examination room. Frederick took a seat in the big, padded chair, eyeing the equipment suspiciously, and Hope sat on a small stool. As the doctor examined Frederick's eyes, he chatted with Hope as he would have with any mother, the kind of light chat meant to reassure and project competency, but it washed into Hope's ears on a wave of sadness. What if Amber and Patrick needed glasses someday? They might be as uneasy in an ophthalmologist's office as Frederick, and she wouldn't be there. Partly to deflect the doctor's patter and partly to reassure Frederick, she began to ask questions. Could the doctor really see inside the eye with that thing? What did it look like?

In spite of his fears, Frederick survived the examination without serious loss of self-regard and was rewarded a week later with a pair of horn-rimmed glasses. They changed his world.

"Hey! They's *lines* 'tween them poles!" Frederick exulted, as he and Hope came out of the ophthalmologist's office. "Hey! Look! Them leaves is movin'!"

Hope was astonished as he. In her case, though, what amazed her was what he had *not* been seeing. For the next hour, she drove him around the streets of Houston; Frederick couldn't get enough of looking. "Turn here," he'd say, "turn there," and she did.

Eventually, they found themselves in the Fourth Ward on a street off West Dallas. She figured, belatedly, that Frederick had known all along where they were going.

"Stop," he said, and she pulled over to park. The street was lined on both sides with shotgun houses: narrow, weathered two-story buildings with peaked roofs and slender, lancelike columns that argued for a turn-of-the-century construction date. Each house sat no more than the length of a broomstick back from the curb. Two and a half concrete steps led up to porches the width of a double window. Pink geraniums in coffee cans decorated some steps, a clump of cannas blazed along a foundation here and there, an occasional curtain or dishtowel covered a window.

Frederick reached over to honk the horn.

"Hey!" Hope protested, and he honked the horn again.

A girl of fourteen or so came out of the house next door and stood there, scratching the top of one bare foot with the toes of the other. A heavyset woman emerged from behind her.

"Ben!" called the woman. "Is tha' you?"

In a flash, Hope knew why they were here. "Is she your mother?"

Frederick screwed up his face. "Nah. Tha's Edna. My mama Cluny."

They got out of the car, Hope so self-conscious under the gaze of the two next door that she stumbled. Self-consciousness: the mildest form of paranoia, according to Alex.

Frederick cleared the two and a half concrete steps in one jump to land on the porch, where he moved to one side a splintered, hingeless door propped up against the doorframe. He signaled for her to follow.

Inside, they found Cluny, a slender woman the color of strong tea, sitting at a table listening to the radio, an evangelical station from the sound of it, her hands folded in front of her. Her hair was severe: parted in the middle and plaited in two braids pinned on top of her head. She had a stalk for a neck, long and straight.

"Mama, it's me, Frederick."

Cluny looked up blankly for a moment, then smiled to reveal a brilliant front tooth with a gold star inlay. Something like happiness or maybe hope or maybe just relief tinctured her expression for a second before it was censured and replaced by something more plaintive. She lowered her chin into her throat. "Ohhhh. Ohhhh," she moaned, raising eyes glistening like hot tar to Hope. "He in trouble again, ain't he? I tries. I tries, missus, to put the fear o' God intuh that boy, but the debil got dibs."

Hope, confused and uncertain, managed to stammer, "Fr . . . Frederick's not in any trouble that I know . . . know of."

"His name not Frederick," said the woman, suddenly adamant. She got up and turned off the radio.

"Yes, it is," said Frederick.

"No, iss not. His name Abendigo," she told Hope. "Abendigo. He say Abendigo a nigger name. Huh! S'a Bible name's what it is." Dark lids closed over her great eyes. "Shadrach, Meshach, and Abendigo come out o' the mist o' the fiery furnace," she intoned. "'And the princes, guvnurs, and captains, and the king's consluhs, been gathered t'gether, saw these men 'pon whose bodies fihre had no power, nor was the hair o' they heads singed, neither was they coats changed, nor the smell o' fihre had passed on 'em."

Hope didn't know what to say. It didn't matter; the woman had opened her eyes and shifted her attention to Frederick.

"Wha's on yo' face?"

"Glasses."

She studied him. He looked diligent in glasses, even a bit mandarin. "Lessee," she said.

Frederick took off his glasses and handed them to her. She put them on and looked around the room. "Hmmm. Hmmm." She took them off. "They don' work for me," she said. "Do you like 'em?"

Frederick said he did.

"Hmmmm. People been here lookin' for you," she said. "Po-lice." She turned back to Hope. "People could call you Ben, I tell him. But no, he stick on that Frederick business. I don' care, I call 'im Abendigo, jus' the same. You know why? For pro-tec-shun. Shadrach, Meshach, and Abendigo come out of the fiery furnace. Yes, indeed."

"Children . . . children need protection," said Hope.

"Yes'm. They do." The woman gazed at her. She seemed to expect something more.

"It's not always easy to protect them," said Hope.

"No'm, it's not. World's too wicked for chilrun. Next world be differen'. Next world we all be like chilrun. Jesus take care of us, yes, he will. 'Suffer the little chilrun,' he say, and don't they, though? Don't they jus' suffer? Do you have chilrun?" she asked.

Hope's insides loosened, threatening to disarrange. "Yes."

Frederick's mother stared at her. It may have been, and probably was, a simple invitation to continue, but Hope felt compelled to be more exact.

"That is, I don't *have* them exactly. I have children, I have had them, borne them, of course, and for a time . . . but now . . . but now . . ." Hope's tongue could not overcome the rising chaos inside.

"Where are they?"

"They're . . . they're not with me."

"I can see that, o' course. Don' need glasses to see that."

"Well, at this moment . . . as we speak . . . they're . . . they're in school."

Frederick's mother looked angry for a moment, then shifted her gaze to Frederick. "Uh-huh. School. Uh-huh. Where *he* been?" she asked Hope. "He work for you?"

"Oh, no! We're taking care of . . . that is, he's living with . . . with Ocie," she said, wondering where to start, not wanting to start. There were complications here she was not up to, unlocated land mines she didn't know how to avoid, and besides all that, in the middle of all that, she shouldn't even be here, above all, shouldn't be here with Frederick, *this woman's child*, she thought, the thought knocking her sideways into the perception that everything was all wrong somehow.

"I come here in a Cadillac," said Frederick. Hope blinked and the room came back into focus.

His mother looked at him, speculative and wary. "You did?"

"Yeah. Wanna see?"

The three of them went out onto the porch.

"There she is," said Frederick, pointing.

"Hmmmm. Hmmmm." His mother didn't sound altogether approving, nor disapproving either. Hope thought her opinion of the Cadillac was probably about the same as her opinion of Frederick's glasses. Neither would work for her.

20

A WINTERY DISCONTENT SET IN AT COMMUNITAS IN JANUARY
and, as the days wore on, seemed to be gaining a permanent
foothold. Hope, who had spent Christmas Eve but not Christmas Day
with Amber and Patrick, was despondent, feeling less and less a part of
their lives. Finn and O'Molly had grown quarrelsome and talked of
breaking up their act. Adam started to dabble in crime—a security man
from the nearby University of St. Thomas caught him using a screwdriver
to pry open the coin box of the soft drink machine in the basement of
the Student Union—and Fern, shaken by this, tried to lean on Oily
Jon, who skillfully evaded her weight, increasing the intensity of her
anxiety. Even Alex was out of sorts, as the fellowship formed by Chloe
and the disaffected half of his congregation gained recruits. So when
the Ultimate Vehicle drove up to their doorstep, the household greeted
it with rash enthusiasm.

The Ultimate Vehicle was an experiment. Although scaled-down
versions would begin to appear over the next few years and eventually
become an ubiquitous type of recreational vehicle, none would ever
match the Ultimate Vehicle for ingenuity. A dining table unfolded
from the van's side panel, and four collapsible chairs were stored in
a space between the floorboard and the road. Framed reproductions
turned into hinged shelves when needed to hold something, and from
the ceiling a narrow set of stairs could be pulled down, leading to a

sleeping loft, where the top opened out on each side to reveal four beds.

The Ultimate Vehicle was piloted by a California friend of Alex's named Tad, with the help of three women—Tina, Lesley, and Crista— known collectively as TLC. A disconcerting air of portrayal pervaded the women's presence. Tina played the seductive one; Lesley, the bold and boyish; Crista, goddess of the hearth.

"Me and TLC, we're driving around the country spreading the good news," said Tad, leaning against the parlor doorframe, one hand on a canted hip, the other holding a Pearl beer. Prematurely silver hair fell in sculpted waves to his shoulder, and a tanned face gave his blue eyes the startling quality of woodland flowers.

Everyone had gathered in the parlor. Hope and Victor sat on the porch glider, Alex sat in a beanbag chairs, and Oily Jon sprawled on the floor. They were the only other members of the household present. O'Molly had flown home to Wisconsin, Finn was camping on Hope's property in Kemah, thinking things over, and Fern was in Port Arthur, picking up Adam, who had been visiting her parents.

"What good news?" Hope asked.

"Tad shows people how to live off their investments," said Tina, whose beauty lay in her perfect proportions and crimped blond hair that rippled luxuriously from a center part.

"He's kind of a consultant," said Lesley. Lesley had impressed everyone at dinner by eating with her fingers, the dirt under her nails seeming not so much slovenly as a comment on an overfastidious civilization.

"He used to be a Wall Street broker," added Crista from across the room, where she sat next to Oily Jon.

"I separate people from their dependence on the work ethic," Tad explained.

"Here's someone who needs your help right now," said Alex, pointing to Hope. "She just sold a house."

"If you don't put your money to work, you'll have to work for your money," Tad warned, smiling. His chest, revealed by the deep V of his Mexican wedding shirt, was the color of maple syrup. Seized with lightheadedness, Hope smiled back. The porch glider creaked as she rearranged her legs.

Victor cleared his throat. "I'm, uh, interested in your, what you call it, mon, Ultimate Vehicle."

"Are you? Maybe I'll show it to you later." Tad crushed his beer can and went into the kitchen for another.

That night Tad pulled off a feat Hope had never seen before: he retained center stage in the presence of Alex. He did this without insisting on himself, borne aloft, so to speak, by the three women. He was like a tuning fork. He had only to say something and they would chime in on different pitches.

"Actually, my financial acumen is not my chief talent," he began at one point.

"He's an alchemist of the emotions," interrupted Tina.

"The result is not so much gold as dynamite," said Lesley.

"His specialty is desire and fear," added Crista.

Their chorus hung in the silence for a moment, and the mood changed pitch to accommodate it. Hope was suddenly aware of everyone's spatial relationships. She had not noticed, but she did now, that Lesley had seated herself on the floor at Victor's feet and that Crista's and Oily Jon's boundaries had become contiguous. The distance between Alex's and Tina's beanbag chairs, while remaining constant, now unaccountably amused them. Only Tad was standing .

"So Vic," he said when the conversation faltered, "how about a tour of the Ultimate Vehicle?"

Victor leaped to his feet. "You bet, mon. Let's go!"

Their progress out into the chilly night was unsteady; by this time, everyone had drunk quantities of red wine. Victor, walking slightly behind Hope, kept stepping on her heels, annoying her. Beside him, Lesley provided sports commentary. She was a football fan, an exotic interest in this company.

Reaching the curb, Tina did a quick shuffle-ball-change. "Ta-da! Allow me to present . . . the future!" The future was high and long and sleek and blue, a vehicle clean of the whimsy Hope had seen on vans belonging to the pilgrims. "Tad talked Detroit into financing it as an experiment," Tina explained.

"Tad can get anyone to do anything," Lesley said.

When Crista failed to chime in, Hope realized that she and Oily Jon had not come with them. She thought fleetingly of Fern, but her head

was buzzing too pleasantly for anything disagreeable to gain a foothold.

They went inside, where Tad demonstrated the clever properties of
his brainchild. Victor, especially, was impressed, and expressed a fervent
desire to have an Ultimate Vehicle of his own. They filled their wine-
glasses and settled down again. Alex produced a small pouch of marijuana.

"We've been everywhere in the UV," Tina said. "Florida. Washington state. Maine."

"Indiana?" Hope asked.

"Indiana even."

"Don't you get tired of traveling?"

"Roots are for trees," said Tad, lightly tracing her backbone. Somehow he had ended up sitting next to her, while Victor sat propped up
against the opposite wall, eyes closed, elf boots neatly aligned to one
side. Lesley was massaging his feet. Commotion ran rampant in Hope's
chest.

"The only problem with traveling," Tad said, "is finding good hair-
dressers."

"Tad can't stand to have a hair out of place," Tina confided to the
group.

"It has to be cut just so," added Lesley, looking up from her task.

"I respect my hair," said Tad lightly. "At one time, long hair was a
symbol of sovereignty. Only the nobility could wear their hair long.
Needless to say, the clergy was pretty ticked off." He grinned at Alex.

" 'Doth not even nature itself teach ye, that if a man have long hair,
it is a shame unto him?' " declaimed Alex, throwing wide an arm. He
passed a joint to Tad and got up to refill everyone's wineglass.

Tad took a deep drag and paused, offering the joint to Hope. She
shook her head, and he passed it on to Tina. "Yeah," he said, without
exhaling, "the pulpit pounders had a field day calling up the hellish
terrors awaiting the disobedient longhairs. It was a question of power,
of course."

"It always is," said Tina, inhaling.

"Invariably," said Lesley.

Tad breathed out with a light smile. "Even the pope got into it.
Longhairs were excommunicated while living and not prayed for when
dead."

" 'But if a woman have long hair, it is a glory unto her,' " said Alex under his breath, as he bent to pour wine into Tina's plastic tumbler and take the joint from her limp fingers.

VICTOR HAD FALLEN asleep and Alex had coaxed Tina onto his lap on the pretext of testing the sturdiness of the collapsible chair when Tad leaned over to whisper in Hope's ear, "I want to show you something." He led her up the narrow stairs to the loft, where light from below stretched their outlines into lean shadows. With cunning motions that reminded Hope of Vera's dance, he unzipped his jeans to reveal an erection. He struck a playful, proud attitude, and she laughed, noting at the same time how slim were his hips and legs, how dark his pubic hair in contrast to his silver, satin crown, how fraudulent his "trust me" smile.

"Your turn," he said.

She unbuttoned her work shirt.

"Gorgeous," he said, coming close. He squeezed up her breasts, one in each hand, like ice cream cones, and began to lick her nipples, which quickly came to attention.

"Gorgeous, gorgeous," he crooned into the tiny hollow behind her earlobe, his hands moving beneath her miniskirt, catching her panties with his thumbs and peeling them down her legs. He knelt to kiss her pubes.

Hope's skin went thin, leaking warmth. She fingered his lovely silver hair, incredibly fine, baby's hair, as silky as it looked.

They finished helping one another undress, and he guided her to one of the four narrow beds. "Lie still," he whispered. "If you move so much as an eyelash, I'll have to stop."

So of course it was excruciating, the flossy drift of his hair over her throat and breasts and ribs, the breeze of it on her thighs and knees and ankles, toes. And then his hands. They might have been her own hands, so sure were they where to go, and out of nowhere it suddenly came to her—a *ménage à quatre*!—an idea that dismayed her less and excited her more than she would have thought. She wondered briefly if Lesley had succeeded in seducing Victor.

They were quiet as ice skaters, and when their surfaces finally merged in a seamless glide toward pleasure, his fuzzy belly a dear animal against hers, she whispered, "I love you," which was not true, but she loved *something*, with every tactile cell, and as her body multiplied to encompass it all, she spoke the only words she knew to say in that situation.

She should be ashamed. That's what Maureen might have said, but Hope reminded herself that she didn't have to listen to that voice anymore. As she stood on the front lawn with Alex and prepared to say goodbye to Tad and TLC the next morning—they were on to New Orleans—her only regret had to do with Oily Jon, who was leaving with them. Victor was still asleep. Tad had been unable to rouse him when he'd gone to Victor's room to fetch Lesley. Across the street, a neighbor was busy fertilizing her azaleas; the sound of a lawn mower came from down the street.

"Thanks for the loaner," whispered Lesley, as she gave Hope a quick hug. Her flippancy hit a wrong, thrilling note with Hope. This was what it was like to be a pilgrim, to whom sex was a need and a pleasure, on a par with good food.

Tad enclosed Hope in a chaste embrace, for which she was grateful. Anything amorous would have been embarrassing. She was not sorry to see him go. Well, not too sorry. Well, sorry but not devastated. She would have given more to keep him in her bed for a while longer if her desire for him were not matched by distrust.

"You really ought to let me help you with that house money," he told her. "Nothing chancy. A couple of mutual funds would do it for now."

"I'll think about it." She sat down in the dentist's chair.

"Good girl." Tad moved on to embrace Alex, giving him a slap on the back and looking past him one more time to Hope. With the back of his hand, he gave a toss to his hair. She laughed—how could she not?—and was still smiling as the Ultimate Vehicle drove off.

"You look like the cat that swallowed the canary," said Alex, coming over to her. "Remember that sermon I preached a couple of Sundays ago? 'Emancipation Through Appetite'? You look like a newly emancipated woman to me."

"Let's don't talk, Alex."

"The very image of the emancipated woman, I'd say. I'm proud of you." Hope slipped out of the dentist's chair and started toward the house. "Sex without love is self-love!" he called after her.

She entered the house shaking her head, not disbelieving his words—she would have to think about them—but wondering that he felt free to shout them in the middle of a Saturday morning in a quiet neighborhood where people fertilized azaleas and mowed lawns.

She went upstairs and stretched out on her bed. Home free. She had enjoyed herself with nothing due. Last night had been last night. A beginning, an end. It occurred to her that a person could leapfrog through life this way! Simplicity. That was the key to happiness.

THE NEXT DAY Fern sat at the kitchen table, a pile of used Kleenexes in front of her, eyes red from crying. "What did she look like?"

"Pale. Nondescript. She wore a flowered dress that merged with the wallpaper," Hope said, staring miserably into her coffee cup. It was easy to empathize, easy to recall how she had felt when Clay left. Pranks. Is that what they had been up to? Pranks? It seemed so. Which discredited the suffering somehow, made something childish of it.

"What did he see in her?" Fern wanted to know, as Alex entered the kitchen, poured himself a cup of coffee, and sat down with them.

"A dietitian, I think," she said recalling the conversation she'd over-heard from the kitchen, as Oily Jon and Crista were preparing dinner together. *Nearly every man, woman, and child in this country suffers from a vitamin B deficiency*, she'd heard Crista rant, exciting Oily Jon, who had responded in kind. *I know! Depression is only one of the symptoms! Stagnant tongues, shrinking lips, dandruff*—Hope had wondered: *Shrinking lips?*

"I don't think this is about another woman," Fern said. "I think this is about the Road. I think it's that damned Road again."

"You and Oily Jon were getting stale anyway," said Alex. "That's what happens in exclusive relationships."

Hope expected a protest from Fern, some sort of defense of herself and Oily Jon, but Fern seemed to accept what Alex had said. "It's not just Oily Jon. It's Adam, too."

Fern had returned from Port Arthur without Adam. Her parents had offered to keep him, and Fern had agreed. She was worried that Adam would get into worse and worse trouble here. His breaking into the Coke machine at St. Thomas had frightened her.

"It was my mother's idea," Fern had told them, funneling her voice into the audio equivalent of postnasal drip: "'Adam needs a sty-a-ble envrynment. He's at a dy-in-gerous ay-age.'" She slammed her coffee mug on the table. "Fuck. Adam's been at a dangerous age since he was born."

Her parents had paid for Fern's bus ticket back to Houston. "But I got off at the first stop and hitchhiked the rest of the way. I wanted to feel free, you know? I wanted to feel *myself* again." She paused. "The truth is: I'm not equipped for a kid."

"Who is?" said Hope, although privately she thought Fern's self-assessment correct. A fractional nature lay beneath Fern's uninhibitedness. Chloe said Fern was less than the sum of her parts. Hope thought it was more that her parts didn't quite add up. Still, where Adam was concerned, who *was* equipped? She wondered about Fern's parents.

So did Fern. "Look what a mess they made of me," she mused, threading a skein of her long hair over and under the fingers of one hand.

"I wouldn't say you were a mess," she told Fern.

"No?" Fern brightened. "I guess we never see ourselves as clearly as others do."

Fern missed Adam more than anyone thought she would. Packing his clothes into cardboard boxes to send to Port Arthur, she broke down, and the sounds of lament could be heard for a long time behind her closed door in between changes of Janis Joplin recordings.

IN HER DISTRESS, Fern kept the subject of the Ultimate Vehicle uppermost in everyone's mind, to Hope's growing uneasiness. She and Victor had not discussed the Ultimate Vehicle or its occupants or what had happened. What *had* happened? Hope wondered, and no doubt Victor wondered the same, yet neither asked the other for an accounting. A tolerant reticence obtained between them. When they talked, they made observations on the blandness of the late-January skies, or exchanged anecdotes from work. They maintained a demeanor peculiar in its orthodoxy. Victor would come home from the shipyard, shower, and change into a clean blue work shirt before going into the parlor to sit on the porch glider and read the newspaper. If she wasn't working, Hope would be in the kitchen, not only because Oily Jon was gone, but also because the domestic tasks of cooking and washing dishes provided camouflage of sorts. (Perhaps it always had.) Victor usually went to bed before ten, while Hope lingered for another hour or two in the parlor.

Beneath the unspoken, however, Hope thought she heard the sound of something unraveling. She noticed, too, that the photograph of the two of them on Romain's sagging porch had disappeared from Victor's bureau. He quit wearing his dashiki and beads. He did not suggest dancing at the Frenchtown Bar.

One night she went to her bed to find him already in it. She undressed in the dark and lay down beside him slowly, body segment by body segment, so as not to set the mattress in motion, although she suspected he was not asleep. They lay like this for a long time, side by side but strictly partitioned, the bed ticking lightly in response to their heartbeats. Birds fussed in the yew tree outside her window, and an insistent wind herded clouds past their uncurtained expanse. Had Hope and Victor been less scrupulous, talking might have been easier. But the moment demanded truth, and overwhelmed by this obligation, they faltered.

It was Victor who finally mustered a voice, not quite his own but recognizable. "Did we lose it, *m'amie*? Or did we use it up?"

Hope had no answer.

"Tomorrow," he went on after a pause, "tomorrow, *m'amie*, I can go to Tucumcari, where I've never seen."

He could have simply been putting forward the idea for consideration, but in Hope's ears, it was a decision already made. Her eyes filled to the edges, in spite of her relief. "I will miss you, Victor."

"Oh, *m'amie*," he whispered, turning to her.

They made love for the first time in two weeks. Hope kissed his hair and ears and his tightening thighs, waiting for a moment as his sex lifted before bending to it, while he drew his fingers through her hair and wound it around his wrists, anchoring himself. When he finally reeled her in and up, he looked at her as if she were someone new, frightening her a little before his familiar mouth framed her name. *Hope.* She returned his own in a whisper—*Victor*, an acknowledgment, a title—and he stroked her body until it began to stutter and her sounds scrambled.

And then, side by side again, they were two mere, bare bodies with sticky spots.

The next morning Victor packed his few belongings and called a taxi, refusing to let her drive him to the bus station. Whether through tactful design or chance, no one else in the household was about. When he started out the door, Hope grasped his elbows from behind and pressed her face between his shoulder blades, bringing him to a halt. He stood in the doorway for a moment, then, without turning, patted her hip and proceeded out the door. As he descended the stairs, she stared fixedly at a cardinal preening itself in the branches of the live oak at the curb, so that, strictly speaking, she never saw him leave.

21

FREDERICK THOUGHT HOPE SHOULD BUY SOME COME-BACK-BOY Powder. The two of them stood inside the Vudu Curio Shop examining the wares—rattlesnake rattles and black cat skulls, Stop Gossip Candles and Lucky Scrub Floor Wash—while they waited to photograph Frederick's friend Reba, the owner of the shop, who was changing her clothes. The shop was dark and small, the sparse spiritual supplies arranged neatly on beaverboard shelves. Hope was intrigued by the merchandise. A photograph was forming in her head: a still life of wolves' teeth, dried monkey testicles, and a packet of Come-Back-Boy Powder.

"You could get that dude back easy," Frederick said. If you *wanted* to—that was the unspoken qualifier, half blame, half lament.

Hope had not anticipated the impact of Oily Jon's and Victor's departures on Frederick. She hadn't even thought to tell him. He had come over one afternoon, expecting to work with Oily Jon as usual. The two of them had been spending long hours together, their heads nearly touching under the canopy of a raised hood. Guildsmen, they spoke only to the matter at hand: a broken fan belt, a faulty solenoid, a damaged distributor cap.

"Oily's gone," she told him. The subtle movements of his face muscles had reminded her of the slow-motion crumbling of a demolished building. Then, within seconds, the film ran backward, and they reconstituted. Hope wasn't sure which process made her feel worse.

These days, instead of heading for the garage, Frederick would seat himself in the dentist's chair on the lawn and call Hope's name until she came out. "That Caddy girl need a spin," he would remind her. "If you don't take her out, her heart rust."

Frederick was not so much interested in cars as in her Cadillac. Tending the Cadillac's engine, Frederick wielded a flare nut wrench with a coolness his friends on Downing Street would have admired, but he was not much interested in improving the health of Fern's Volkswagen van or Finn's Rambler. It wasn't the four-stroke cycle that inspired him but the Cadillac's long nose and heavy front overhang. Working under the Cadillac's hood was simply dues, willingly paid so that you could ride through Sunnyside looking potentate-proud and going places.

> *I'm a maniac for the fast track,*
> *For the fast track in mah Cadillac.*

Hope was a willing chauffeur. Working nights, her days were free, and as the Cadillac bumped along the dirt streets of Riceville or Kashmere Gardens, acquiring a light shroud of dust, she was temporarily delivered from loneliness. She usually brought her camera along, stopping to photograph a fig tree spread with drying laundry, a group of children playing underneath the freeway. Residents were more amiable than she would have expected, maybe because Frederick was at her side or maybe because of the camera. They often thought she was from the newspaper, and even after learning she wasn't, they led her to rotting floorboards and potholed streets that needed documenting . Others regarded her camera as an opportunity for play, teasing one another and putting on the style. *Take Bizbo's picture, missus! He a sight!*

A chief ingredient of Come-Back-Boy Powder, Hope learned from the typewritten description, was crocodile bone marrow. Applied to the face, it produced a lovable complexion. Sprinkled lightly on the ground, it created an irresistible love trail to your door.

"I think Victor is out of range," she told Frederick. "He's probably in New Mexico by now. And who knows where Oily Jon is?"

A gust of air escaped Frederick's teeth. In his view, Hope and Fern had played a careless game. He implied they had thwarted the community at large by failing to keep their men securely anchored. He turned on his heel, heading toward the back of the store, where Reba had reap-peared and was winding a colorful turban around her head. Picking up her light and camera bag, Hope followed.

"It don't cost much, Come-Back-Boy Powder," Reba said, seating herself on a high stool, as Hope set up her equipment. "For a dollar fifty you get yourself a real bargain, 'specially if your man was carryin' cash on a steady basis."

"Does it work long-distance?" Hope asked, turning on a small flood-light and aiming it toward Reba. What fascinated Hope was Reba's glabrous skin. Front-lighted like this, it resembled polished metal, a fitting emblem of Reba's armored personality. "What if you don't believe in this voodoo stuff?" Hope asked, bending to look through her lens. "Can it still do any good?"

"Can't do no harm."

Reba's face, a series of glinting planes, filled the viewfinder, and Hope was swept up in a moment of piercing lucidity. She had it! Struggling to keep her voice low-key, she said, "Well, if it can't do any harm, can it do any good?"

The spirit of commerce glinted from Reba's eyes, and her speech spread out, an alluvial fan of irony. "You gettin' ovahclevah on me, missus. A dollah? Special fuh you."

"Done," said Hope, snapping the picture. She felt like a thief.

THE DAY WAS sunny and mild enough for Hope and Frederick to roll down the windows as they headed for Cluny's. They often ended these excursions there, and today Hope had used Cluny as an excuse to refuse Frederick's request to drive him to Downing Street. "I have a new photo for your mother," she told him. "Besides, Ocie says Downing Street's going to get you in trouble sooner or later," she reminded him.

Downing Street, or more precisely Black Battalion Headquarters, had a lot to offer Frederick: brothers, a future, even a past, thanks to Leroy Champion's passion for history, but Ocie tended to think in terms of Downing Street's reputation as the bloody back door to the Fifth Ward. Fights and drug dealing were part of the habitat; sometimes a murder sobered the scene. "Frederick could go either way," she said. "He could end up a dentist or dead on the street."

Hope glanced at Frederick, slumped deep into the seat with both feet braced against the dashboard. "What do Big Buns know?" he muttered.

"She knew enough to keep you out of Boysville."

They arrived to find Cluny sitting on the front steps with two of the neighborhood elders, Edna, the heavyset woman next door whom Hope had glimpsed on her first visit, and an old man everyone called the Professor. The Professor rose with difficulty and remained standing until Hope had seated herself. Edna inquired whether Hope might like some light refreshment. Their patinaed politeness never failed to move Hope. Simply being human established a person as worthy of courtesy in their eyes. "No, thank you, Edna," she answered. "No thank you *kindly*," she added in an effort to match Edna's impeccable manners.

"Did you bring pictures?" Cluny wanted to know.

"Yes." Hope handed her a manila envelope, and Cluny took out a photograph of Frederick reflected in the mirrored wall of an office building. Hope took many photos of Frederick, and even when he was not the subject, he often managed to insert himself into her pictures, popping his head into a lower corner or jutting a black fist up through the center of her composition. Hope usually printed a copy for Cluny, who attached them to her bare wood walls with shiny brass thumbtacks. By now she had a substantial gallery of eight-by-tens—of Frederick climbing the Calder crab at the Contemporary Arts Museum, Frederick racing through the downtown tunnels, Frederick riding the escalator at the new Galleria. Hope had kept the most memorable photo, though, one of Cluny herself, sitting on her bed, gazing at a wall of multiple images of her son.

"Today we were taking pictures of Reba," Hope said.

Edna moved her head back and forth in a narrow arc to indicate disapproval.

"That woman no Christian," said Cluny.

"We were just taking her picture," said Hope.

"She agent o' de debil."

"No such thing as devil," Frederick said disgustedly.

Cluny threw him a glance. "You jus' a foolish boy."

"No such thing as God either." Frederick muttered this into his chest, but Cluny heard him and leaped up, arm raised.

"Cluny, Cluny, Cluny," murmured the Professor, slowly rising and putting an arm around her. She sat down again, but the Professor remained standing, perhaps checked by the prospect of having to refold his arthritic bones. "We were speaking of DeGale when you came up," he said to Hope, silently entreating her to help him change the subject.

"Oh. Do I know DeGale?"

"I don't believe so," said Edna. "I don't believe you had the good fortune. DeGale was one fine man."

"He's gone now," said the Professor.

"They's some question," said Cluny.

"What happened?" Hope asked.

"DeGale in a car accident two nights ago," Cluny explained. "Died in the 'mergency room. Although they's some question. The doctors, they translated his heart to a white man."

"Transplanted," the Professor corrected.

"DeGale's wife prob'ly tricked," said Cluny. "Tha's the only thing I can think of. Othe'wise, I don' believe she'd hand ovah his heart that way."

"Wouldn't do any good," said the Professor. "White man wouldn't know what to do with it. Hearts shrivel up from lack o' use in a white man's chest." He glanced apologetically at Hope.

"Maybe a white man with a black man's heart feel things a little differently," said Edna. "Maybe tha's the s'lution to all this integration thing. Maybe we should all change hearts."

Cluny shook her head. "God don't want peoples runnin' 'round with the wrong hearts bangin' up against they ribs."

"I don't mean *literally*," said Edna.

"Black or white don't make no difference!" Frederick said contemptuously. "Heart's not some simple-ass valentine. Hearts beat. Tha's all. Tha's all they do. They send blood all over you body—feet, nose, brain. In *most* cases, brain," he added, glaring again at Cluny. "Isn't that right?" He appealed to Hope.

"It's complicated," Hope sidestepped, disappointing him. But to agree with him would have been to endorse his scorn for Cluny, and besides, Hope's sentiments tended to gravitate unauthorized toward Edna's idea of everyone exchanging hearts.

"You don't got no *conversation*," Frederick complained to Hope afterward. "You don't got no man and you don't got no conversation."

Hope had no man; that was a fact. And she did miss Victor, more than she'd anticipated. Late at night, as she passed by his empty bedroom on the way to her own, she found herself listening for his softly accented speech—*m'amie*! She missed the way his smile burrowed into the corners of his cheeks; she missed the way he tugged on her little finger to get her attention. Then too, his leaving had cast her, once more, among the unchosen, the unattended, the unseconded.

Chloe had little patience with this interpretation of events. "A woman without a man is like a fish without a bicycle," she quoted—without much authority, in Hope's view. As far as she knew, Fletcher had never left Chloe's side for more than his annual week at the Modern Language Association Convention. What did Chloe know about Ladies' Night at the Stampede Ballroom, where Hope and Fern had tried to keep up their spirits one night recently, dancing in the arms of men with sour beer breath? She doubted Chloe had ever set foot in the subterranean hive of bars and boutiques beneath Old Market Square, where men and women eyed one another hungrily in dim light. After a few of these dismal excursions, Hope had decided she felt less lonely alone in her room, listening to the sounds of the household—doors closing and opening, the ring of the telephone, the steam heat puffing into unaccustomed action.

Sometimes she drove out to Kemah, where Finn was building an A-frame cabin. "Communitas South," he said. "A getaway." He and O'Molly were singing harmonies again, their artistic and emotional differences resolved. They often spent the night in the so far roofless cabin. "This is a healing spot," he told Hope. "A bringing-together spot."

She wandered the property now, often to the enterprising sound of Finn's hammer, and recalled the times she'd spent here with Victor, making love on the rickety pier, collecting shells on the strand. Fighting back the undergrowth, she found the fallen windmill Victor had discovered and remembered the way he had grasped its rusty struts, testing their strength, evaluating their usefulness.

Hope found herself thinking a lot about Calhoun—his surprising length on her bed that night after the custody trial, how different he looked with his eyes closed. She had not seen him in a while. He hadn't been in church lately, and, of course, she no longer had much to do with the school. They hadn't played chess in a long time either, and he wasn't dropping by the Trap Door the way he used to when she was first working there.

Maybe he found the Trap Door depressing. Hope did. She hadn't at first, but now she did. The cheap captain's chairs clustered around the little toadstool-like tables, the plastic-mesh-covered globes holding candles, the red-black-and-gold carpet—it all added up to a room you might drink to forget.

One slow night she looked out on her three tables of customers—a quarreling couple by the cigarette machine, a table of blustering businessmen away from home, a solitary man slowly relinquishing consciousness—and experienced a wisp of panic. Failure: all three tables spoke to her of failure, the failure to connect, the failure to be alone, and without thinking, she hurried to the pay phone in an alcove near the rest rooms and dialed Calhoun's number. Just to hear his voice. Just to steady her nerves.

"Have you given up on me as a worthy opponent or what?" she blurted out when he answered.

"Hope? Is this you? What time is it?"

"I don't know. Yes. Did I wake you up?"

"Sort of."

"I'm sorry. Working these hours, I lose track. I just ate supper an hour ago."

"It's almost midnight."

She was struck by the thought that he might have someone with him. "Oh. Should I hang up?"

"I don't know. What did you want?"

"Uh, well, I was just wondering. If you would like to play some chess. We haven't played. In a long time."

"Hope, are you okay?"

The receiver was slippery from the sweat on her palms. "Pretty much, I think. Tomorrow night?"

"I think so. What is tomorrow night, anyway?"

"Friday. My night off."

"Okay." She heard him yawn. "Prufrock's? Eight or so?"

"That's exactly what I was thinking! Prufrock's! Eight or so! Do you want me to pick you up?"

"And ruin my reputation? I haven't caused a drop of fossil fuel to be consumed for over a year now. Are you trying to tempt me?"

The question undid her.

22

Hope arrived at Prufrock's, cheeks pink and eyelashes damp from the light rain falling outside. She stood in the double doorway leading to the central room, embarrassed by the bright and silky red rain cape she'd bought at Embers. It was too dramatic for her, she realized that now; she couldn't carry it off. It made her look like a person trying to attract attention. And indeed, a few people did look up from their game boards as she stood there. She wanted to explain to them that she hadn't bought the raincoat so much as something to wear as for the idea of bright red in gray rain, a flare in the mist.

Seeing no available tables, she flagged down a waitress, who explained that Fridays were always crowded because Friday night was poetry night. Calhoun arrived about five minutes later, his crumpled felt hat rainsplattered and his alpaca poncho dusted with tiny drops. With his beard and long hair, he looked as if he'd just stepped out of a log cabin. He surveyed the crammed room.

"It's poetry night," Hope told him.

"Bad poetry I'm not in the mood for. How about a walk?"

"In the rain?"

"We're dressed for it."

"Okay."

The rain had let up some, although moisture still hung in the air, creating faint haloes around the lights and neon signs. Turning from the brightly lit street, they headed toward the residential streets. Calhoun asked how Amber and Patrick were doing.

"Fine. We've started swimming Friday nights at the Y. The Friday nights I have them, I mean. Patrick's a natural. Did I tell you that Clay and Mindy are getting married? In April?"

"I guess we expected that."

"I guess."

"Do you mind?"

"Yes. They *lied*. That's what keeps me from forgiving them." She sighed. "Although I probably wouldn't forgive them even if they hadn't."

"I hope not."

"Well, I wouldn't. Still, the lying sticks. Alex says there are two ways to control people. You can beat them up or you can lie to them."

"They deserve each other," said Calhoun.

"No, they don't! They deserve to be all alone and working at a place called the Trap Door!"

They skirted a puddle that had collected in a broken piece of sidewalk. They had reached the neighborhood near the Rothko chapel, and they walked for a while in silence, passing a few early-blooming azaleas and a flowering quince. A smell of damp oak was strong in the air. As they crossed the courtyard in front of the chapel, something black and tall loomed up in their path. Putting out a hand, Hope touched metal. "What's this?"

"Looks like some kind of sculpture." They circled what appeared to be a column sitting on top of a pyramid, inspecting it as well as they could in the dark.

"This wasn't here last summer. Victor and I used to stop by the chapel sometimes. It wasn't here then."

"Have you heard from him?"

Hope regretted bringing up Victor. "No. But then, I wouldn't, I don't think. It's hard to imagine Victor writing much."

"What happened, anyway?"

"It's a long story."

"Is it?"

She thought for a moment. "No. A very short story, actually."

"Two worlds colliding?" Calhoun maintained that all relationships boiled down to this.

"In our case, it really wasn't. More like two worlds drifting into the wrong galaxy."

"That happened to me once. I never found my way back."

"So who is this?" she asked softly, touching his sleeve.

"That's what I've been wondering."

Hope didn't know how to proceed. She wanted to draw him out in a way that put herself on a new footing with him.

They walked without speaking for a while. They were approaching Hope's neighborhood; the phantom violinist was at work on the Bach partita. Hope wished Calhoun would take her hand.

"Cal, are you . . . this is probably none of my business, but are you . . . you don't have to answer this . . . but are you . . . are you seeing anyone these days?"

Taking her suggestion, he *didn't* answer, at least not right away, and they walked another block in silence. That means yes, she thought, disappointment drawing tight her innards. She shouldn't have asked. Why be so obvious? There were ways to find out things without actually asking; there were ways to gauge and manipulate situations like this. Unfortunately, she didn't know any. Unfortunately, those were just the sorts of things other women knew and she didn't.

"I'm seeing Caleb," he said finally.

It didn't sink in at first. In fact, his answer set trembling a twig of joy. I'm seeing Caleb, he said, and next he would say, and nineteen children and my landlady and the old couple on the corner and the people in the Montrose Neighborhood Association and Ocie and Chloe and Fletcher—and that's only a few of who I'm seeing. Then he would look at her. Right now, I'm seeing you. And he would be. He'd be seeing her, really seeing her. But Calhoun didn't say any of these things.

"Caleb?" she repeated.

"Are you shocked?"

Oh. Oh. *Caleb*. Oh! Hope's face grew hot, and she was grateful for the dark.

Hope had never known a homosexual. Not personally. Not that she knew of. When she was in high school there had been rumors about the music teacher. Queer. That was the word then. That's how she had thought of it, too, as something peculiar and not very specific, something off, something erroneous, having to do in some unimaginable way with sex. And the truth was, even now Hope could not bring to mind, not graphically, an act of love between two people of the same sex.

"Are you?" he persisted.

"What?"

"Shocked?"

"No. No, I'm not shocked." It wasn't shock. Something was jammed.

"You're not saying much."

"It's just . . . it's just that I don't want to *lose* you!" she burst out, turning to face him, clutching his elbow with one hand and grasping his waist with the other. Standing there, he in his alpaca poncho and slouched hat, she in her red cape, they looked as if they were about to demonstrate an authentic folk dance from some mountainous region unvisited by tourists.

PERVERT ALERT. THAT's what Clay used to say on rounding the corner of Westheimer and Montrose. Passing this corner on the way to and from work five nights a week, Hope had become used to the flamboyant male couples promenading arm in arm. She enjoyed their high spirits, their enthusiasm for costume, their eager flaunting. She had often wished she were audacious enough to join them.

Now she tried to imagine Calhoun and Caleb among them. She couldn't, not Calhoun anyway. Hope was having trouble picturing Calhoun anywhere, even in familiar places like the church or the school. Instead she was seeing Mr. DeLisle. She was recalling the nasty stories that circulated about him. Stories about little boys in rest rooms. Stories taking place within the damp cement confines of the school basement, where the band instruments were kept.

"I grew up with the same stories about the Catholic priest in our town," said Alex. He and Hope sat at the kitchen table, eating a late breakfast. Hope had made Sumatran coffee left by one of the pilgrims, and its aroma filled the kitchen as she munched on a piece of toast. Alex ate cornflakes, about which he was rather finicky. Soggy flakes were anathema to him, and he carefully sprinkled only a few at a time into his bowl of milk. "Fantasies of the weak."

"What do you mean?"

"We're all born bisexual; it's just that only a few survive. Society hammers the weak into conventional reproductive roles. Breed: that's the message. So in boredom and envy, the breeders foist their repressed fantasies on the rest of us."

Calhoun as survivor. This was a new perspective.

Alex lit a joint, and the smell of marijuana mingled with that of the Sumatran coffee. "Do you want to go up with me today?"

"I thought I'd do some developing."

"You spend a lot of time in your *dark room*," Alex said, smiling.

"Yes," said Hope, getting up to carry her coffee mug to the sink. Alex smoked too much. Soon his speech would begin to slow and all would be well with the world.

"I keep forgetting. You're the girl who likes to keep her feet on the ground," Alex said.

"I try."

"Well, it's safer. I'll say that." His dismissive tone, his implication that she was unadventurous, annoyed her, especially since she feared he might be right. The recklessness she'd felt the night of the Ultimate Vehicle, the wantonness, the sheer *confidence*, had dwindled. Yet she felt that, given another opportunity for adventure, sexual or otherwise, she could rise to the occasion. She considered herself capable of sexual abandon, even if she lacked the conquistadorial temperament for perpetual seduction.

"The ground's not all that safe," she said, defending herself by challenging his premise. "Think of the obstacles. High in the sky, you don't have to deal with many obstacles."

"That's what I love about being high. In the sky."

Hope studied him for a moment, alert. "You should be more careful, Alex. It would be a long way to fall."

"A lovely distance," Alex drawled. "A perfectly loverly distance."

"YOU HAVEN'T LOST me," Calhoun had said, almost peevishly, as if she were missing some essential point.

But I have! she had wanted to cry out. She had been counting on him. She had been in love with him. She thought so. A little bit, anyway. He had always been a . . . possibility. Or maybe not. Maybe she had not been in love with him. Maybe he was just the most honest and interesting and kind person in her life. Lost!

"Nothing has changed," he had said. "We're still friends. Aren't we?"

"OH. IT'S YOU," Calhoun said when she phoned. Hope waited for him to say *How are you?* or *What's happening?* but he didn't.

"I was, um, calling to invite you and Caleb to dinner," she ventured.

"Don't do us any favors."

She sighed. "All *right*. It *was* a shock. I admit it. Now I'm inviting you to dinner. You and Caleb. On Friday. My night off."

"Who will be there?"

"I'm not sure. Finn and O'Molly probably. Fern. Maybe Alex."

"We'll probably have to leave early."

"I guess that means you'll come?"

"I'll have to check with Caleb. He's very choosy, you know. He doesn't suffer the ordinary, the *conventional*, with much grace."

Hope put up with this. She owed him.

In any case, it turned out that Caleb was delighted. He called Hope to say so. "We'll bring dessert," he said. "I insist."

THEY BROUGHT DUTCH apple pie, and by the time it was served, everyone had been well fed, and Fern was trying to induct Calhoun and Caleb into the Red Coyote Tribe.

"Can a person really join a tribe?" Calhoun wanted to know. "Isn't a tribe more something you get born into?"

"No! Look at Woodstock," O'Molly pointed out.

"Woodstack . . . wasn't that a rock concert? Somewhere in Maine?" inquired Caleb. Snaggle-toothed and diminutive, Caleb's look of thwarted satanism was misleading; Hope found him sunny and puckish. Opposites attract, she thought, sensible of Calhoun's gloomy bulk on her other side.

"Wood*stock*," Fern corrected sternly. "*New York*."

Caleb formed a silent O and nodded.

Calhoun wanted to know what, or who, the Red Coyote Tribe was.

Fern stared at him. "Didn't you read about it in *Space City!*? Over five hundred people showed up."

"Showed up where?"

"On Hippie Hill!"

"Were you entertaining the troops?" Caleb asked Finn and O'Molly.

"They were, but that wasn't the main thing." Fern said, cutting off Finn's response.

"Oh. What was the main thing?" Caleb asked, turning back to her.

"The main thing was the manifesto."

"Ah, the manifesto." Caleb nodded. "And what was . . . manifested?"

"That we want a free planet!" said Fern. "Free food, free music, free media, free health care, free bodies, free people, free time and space, everything free for everybody."

"I see. A modest proposal," said Caleb.

"Yeah, well, in a tug of war, you don't start out in the middle," Fern said.

"I'll second *that* strategy," Caleb said. "Sign me up. And my friend here, too."

"Speak for yourself," said Calhoun.

"It's not something you sign up for," said Fern. "The Red Coyote Tribe is a state of mind. You're there or you're not."

"I'm not," said Calhoun.

"I'm not always," admitted Finn.

"There's thunder on the hill, man," Fern advised him. "Be there or be square."

"I *was* there, remember?" said Finn, exasperated.

By this time, everyone had finished dessert, and Hope suggested they go into the parlor. "Your pie was extraordinary," she said to Caleb, as they left the table. "Really special. Was it the apples? Some special kind?"

Caleb put a hand on her arm. "God made the apples, dear heart. *I* made the pie."

Caleb took a seat next to Hope on the porch swing. Calhoun sat nearby, talking to Finn.

"This is our first foray into society as a couple," Caleb whispered, his grin demolishing any notion she might have had that he might be anxious about this.

"I hope you're having a good time."

"Swimming"

Hope like talking to Caleb, because she didn't have to contribute much. In the space of thirty minutes he quoted George Bernard Shaw, Cornelia Otis Skinner, and *Architectural Digest*. Caleb was a very sophisticated person, Hope decided. A little out of her ken. A little out of Calhoun's ken, too, she would have thought.

Caleb told her that he and Calhoun had gone to the Houston Grand Opera the week before to see *La Bohème*. "He cried," Caleb said, tipping his head in Calhoun's direction.

"I did not," said Calhoun, turning around.

"You almost did."

"I didn't even come close."

"You cried inside. I saw you. He keeps it all inside," Caleb confided to Hope. "He's afraid of emotion."

"Overblown bunch of nonsense," muttered Calhoun.

"The opera? Or our emotions?" demanded Caleb.

"The opera."

"Opera—the voice of the id!" Caleb declaimed, chin high. "It *will* be heard!!"

"That's for sure. The next time I'm interested in hearing from the id, I'll read the tabloids and save my eardrums."

"Oh words," said Caleb dismissively, waving a hand made interesting by the serpent ring on his thumb. "Words inevitably fail when we most need them. Speech is quite vanquished by strong emotion. Only music, *operatic* music, can do justice to love and hate."

"Oh, right," Calhoun said sarcastically. He spoke to Hope. "You haven't heard anything until you've heard an upper-register account of a tight shoe."

"Insensitive brute," Caleb said, pouting.

Hope blushed, embarrassed. Seeing this, Caleb patted her arm. "*Joke*, dear heart. We're not in *Kansas* anymore."

"Or Indiana, for that matter," Calhoun added.

"Which is okay with me!" Hope said, glad that Calhoun and Caleb had come to dinner, happy she had invited them. If nothing else, Communitas afforded her hospitality more latitude.

Still, a loneliness stole up on her as the evening wore on, in the midst of expansive spirits and fellowship, a loneliness of the body. She sang along with O'Molly and Finn and she laughed at Caleb's wit all the while yearning for . . . opera.

23

THAT MARCH IT SNOWED IN HOUSTON. THE FLAKES BEGAN FALL-ing in the early morning, cartwheeling down, gaining shape and mass, to lie light and loose on the tropical foliage. White cauls settled on the redbud buds and chinaberry berries, and thimble-sized portions of crystals collected in the trumpets of the blooming azaleas. Bewildered birds watched from the shelter of sugared trees, as dreamers turned in their beds, and the world outside their windows tumbled in soundless commotion. People emerged from their front doors, toting lunch pails and briefcases, to stand, struck shy, in driveways all over the city, flexing bare fingers in the unaccustomed cold.

When Hope looked out, her first impression was one of plenitude. All the spaces in the world appeared to be filled. So much whiteness had an eerie intimacy. This is what the heart of peace looks like, she thought. And at its center, a black child-king.

So dreamlike was this vision, it took Hope a moment to recognize Frederick in the dentist's chair on the front lawn. She rubbed a fresh porthole in the moisture-clouded pane and looked again. Yes, there he was, looking out on the quilted world with royal gaze and little raiment.

Snatching up Alex's flight jacket and a corduroy cap of Finn's, she ran out to him, the cold striking her full in the face. "You'll catch your death," she scolded.

He gave her the skeptical look the maternal always provoked in him, slipped from the dentist's chair, and stuffed first one spindly arm, then the other into leather sleeves that still held the shape of Alex's musculature. He looked up at her, white flakes disappearing into the darkness of his face. Droplets speckled the lenses of his glasses. "You ready?"

"For what?"

"The zoo."

"The zoo! Today?"

"You said."

He was right. She had promised to take him to the zoo this weekend to see the crocodiles. "But it's snowing!"

He canted a hip. "No jive."

"How about breakfast first?" she asked. His lids dropped a half-centimeter, sign of resistance. "The zoo doesn't open until ten anyway," she told him. "*If* it opens at all today."

"Ten *sharp*," he emphasized, starting for the house, which was how she knew he must be very hungry. Food was rarely incentive enough for him to enter the house.

THEY PUT PLASTIC bags secured with rubber bands over their shoes, and their feet thus protected, they set out, Hope with her camera around her neck and a rucksack on her back (another bequest from a departed pilgrim) holding sandwiches and a thermos of hot chocolate. They walked in silence for a while absorbing the sights.

"There's something different," Hope said finally.

"No jive."

"I mean besides the snow. There's something else."

The sounds, she decided on reflection, the sounds were different. It wasn't only the absence of traffic noises, it was the way voices meshed in a chattery, tuneful score, a descent of children's voices piping above the neighborly palaver and the greetings of strangers. Yes, it was true: strangers were greeting one another. They greeted Hope and Frederick, too. Usually, people, white people, either avoided looking at them or glared belligerently. But today a number of people smiled and said hello. Hope glanced at Frederick to see how he was taking this. He kicked through the snow with composed unconcern. Little was allowed to penetrate his cool.

At the Mecom Fountain they paused to watch the waters fan into their prescribed arcs. Screened by the falling snow, and without the usual ring of snarling traffic, the fountains had taken on a mythical aspect. Hope half expected water nymphs to jet up out of the flow.

They followed the pointing finger of a horsed Sam Houston to the zoo entrance, crossing a deserted street and a miniature railroad bridge to come to the duck pond, where orange-billed ducks paddled on the shirred, gray water. Frederick took the stale bread they'd brought from the rucksack and ran to the pond's edge, as the entire fleet bore to starboard and steamed toward him, quacking loudly. Hope lifted her camera. Happiness spiraled up in her: Black Boy in White Snow: Beauty.

Reaching the zoo entrance, they hesitated. The gates stood open, but the zoo was deserted. Not a footprint disturbed the whiteness. The low buildings, water fountains, and booths were like the furnishings of some grand estate, sheeted against their owners' return. Close by, sea lions barked. "*There* the party," said Frederick, stepping inside the gate to make the first footprints for Hope to record for posterity.

The sea lions did seem especially sportive. At Hope and Frederick's approach, a half-dozen of them slid from the artificial rocks into the aqua-tinted water, some corkscrewing their way down to the bottom of the pool, others shooting forward with show-off acceleration. Hope envied their bodies' minimal resistance. One nonparticipant, an elder judging from his silvery head, remained perched on a fake peak in the center of the pool, whiskers bejeweled with frozen droplets.

Frederick was impatient to find the crocodiles, and they checked the map at the kiosk. The crocodiles could be found by taking the path to their left. "Slow down!" she called as he took off, but of course he didn't.

When she caught up with him, he was already leaning over a low fence, holding out a sandwich to the dozen or so crocodiles lying motionless, eyes closed, on a band of white spiked by a few thin green blades. "Here Lyle," he called softly. "Here Lyle. Lyle, Lyle, crocodile. Come on, boy. Come on."

Lyle, Lyle, Crocodile. Over a year had passed since the two of them had shared a beanbag chair, tears slipping down his dusty cheeks. *Madam. We do not permit crocodiles in this store, you know.* How Frederick had changed. And how he had not! An upwelling of love rocked Hope. One could love more than one's own children. This simple insight should not have surprised her, but it did, and, overtaken by a sudden urge to keep him safe, she started toward him, anxiously calculating the odds of a crocodile springing into action and snapping up his offering, hand and all. Not great, she decided on reaching him. The crocodiles might have been taxidermied for all the life they showed. Maybe their blood had frozen. Nevertheless, she put an arm around him, a gesture to which he submitted gracefully, under the influence perhaps of the soft snow all around them.

They visited the big cats, the bears, the gorilla. By noon, they were still the only people in the zoo, just two more animals, Hope thought, two-legged, free-roaming ones. A photograph began to form in her mind: snow, footprints, black, white, boy, woman, rhinoceros. Rhinoceros?

"Reba'd pay some money for that horn," Frederick said, pointing.

She read to him from the plaque: "'A rhinoceros's horn is not a horn but a compacted mass of hairs attached to a roughened patch of bone.'"

"It's a horn. Don't matter what it's made of."

Convinced, Hope didn't argue.

Sitting down on a nearby bench, she offered him half of her sandwich, which he accepted. The snow had stopped falling by this time. It was still overcast, but there were signs of warming. The roofs of the buildings dripped at their corners, and the birds had thawed out enough to declare territories. Frederick said he was ready to go home.

"We haven't seen the giraffes yet," Hope said. "The giraffes are my favorites. They're the tallest animals in the world, you know." Frederick chewed his sandwich, unimpressed.

They found the two resident giraffes behind their barn, towering graciously over the snow-dappled ginkgo trees surrounding their yard, daintily nibbling on the leaves. Such sweet dignity, Hope thought. Enchanted, she almost missed the delicate rise and fall of reticulated hide at their feet in the snow.

"Frederick! Look! A baby!" she exclaimed.

At this the baby began to struggle to its feet, gingerly placing its small hooves a considered distance apart and then shakily straightening its legs as the parents swiveled their ears forward and back and blinked luxuriously lashed eyes. One of them lowered a long, sloping neck to nibble on the baby's bristly mane, and Hope snapped the picture.

"LUCK." HOPE SAID the word aloud, feeling the hard *k* bounce off the back of her throat. Hope had never felt lucky before. Good things had happened to her, of course, but that unexpected fitting-together of events with resulting good fortune was another order of experience. If she hadn't let Frederick talk her into going to the zoo that day and if she hadn't insisted on seeing the giraffes and if Calhoun and Caleb hadn't dropped by and if their relationship weren't a kind of photosynthesis in reverse, with Caleb's enthusiasm blooming in proportion to Calhoun's skepticism, Caleb would never have been provoked to lunge about the Communitas kitchen under Calhoun's gloomy gaze, waving his arms and saying, "This is probably the only photo *in existence* of an African giraffe in the snow! Let me run it over to the *Post*. An ex of mine runs the features desk. After the *Post* buys it, we'll sell it again all over the country. Sunday supplements! *International Wildlife!*"

Whether it was due to Caleb's influence or his enterprise or the simple worth of Hope's photo, the baby giraffe did end up on the front page of the *Houston Post* the next morning, alongside a story about the freak snowfall. Both ran under the headline MIRACLES OF NATURE. And was Hope ashamed to contribute to this deplorable trend of treacle? Calhoun called to ask.

"No!" she exclaimed exuberantly. "I'm getting *paid*."

"How much?"

"Twenty-five dollars. Would you believe? Would you believe such *luck*? I can't. I'm heading out now to buy extra papers."

"Won't that narrow your profit margin?"

"Oh, Cal. Be happy. For me."

A few days after the photo appeared, Hope received a note, forwarded by the *Post*, from her old photography teacher. "Good work," he wrote.

Good work! Mr. Freytag thought she'd done *good work!*

Gil Freytag was no longer teaching the photography class at the Rec Center, she learned when she called, too much work for too little money, but he'd had a one-man show and won some awards since then. He'd been written up in *Contact* as one of the best nature photographers in the Southwest. He spoke easily of his success, neither boastful nor self-deprecating. As he talked, Hope recalled some of his photos—backlit thistle heads, spectacular vistas.

"And what about yourself?" he asked. "What are you stalking these days besides baby giraffes?"

"Oh, nothing much, I'm not very, you know . . . well, actually . . ." Hope closed her eyes briefly as ambition warred with lack of confidence. "Actually," she went on, "I've been shooting quite a bit, mostly around here, mostly city stuff, you probably wouldn't . . . but I've also got these photos of the Big Thicket, which I took months ago, and maybe you'd like to . . . they may not be worth . . . I mean, I would just be *thrilled* if you would . . . the truth is I'm not sure . . ."

"Bring 'em on by," he interrupted, giving her his address.

"I WOULDN'T HAVE recognized you!" he said on opening the door to her, taking in the oxblood boots, tie-dyed T-shirt, denim miniskirt, and vest covered with scatter pins she'd found at Embers: a tiny rhinestoned American flag, an enameled alligator, Superman. Whether he disapproved of the change or was just surprised was unclear.

He, on the other hand, had not altered in the least. He wore the same scuffed Tony Lama boots, faded jeans, and plaid shirt with fake pearl buttons she remembered him wearing to class.

After introducing Hope to his wife, Coylene, a large woman in her forties who said hello without turning off her vacuum cleaner, he led the way downstairs to a pine-paneled basement. Hope spread out her photos on his pool table. She'd brought a few of her shipyard photos, including the long line of lunch pails emerging from the slipway, and some of the Montrose—the hanging oak with the banner DOO DADDY DONE IT—as well as some of the school. The bleached and wary faces from parents' meetings struck her as portentous now. Most of the photos, however, were more recent: from Sunnyside and the Fourth Ward, some eerie shots of the downtown tunnels, two quirkily optimistic ones of Rosamunda's raspa stand, the interior of the Vudu Curio Shop, Reba the warrior queen. There was an immediacy to all of them; they were glimpses, not views. Some were not fully in focus, some had awkward obstructions—a telephone pole butting in from one side, a horizon tipped askew. There was a feeling that something just outside the frame had disturbed the balance, had knocked time slightly sideways.

Freytag studied and restudied the photos, picking up one, then setting it down and picking up another. Overhead the vacuum cleaner whined. "I don't know. I've never seen anything quite like these," he said, a little doubtfully. "They're . . . they're kind of odd. Animated in the wrong places. Not wrong," he said quickly. "Unexpected. Have you thought of going back to school? A friend of mine teaches at U of H. Maybe you should apply."

"I've never thought about that."

"Well, think about it. You've got an eye. But you need some technique." Seeing her face, he added, "I'm just saying you've got some things to learn."

"I'm tired of learning things!"

"Oh? Sorry to hear that." Something crashed over their heads. "A woman possessed," he confided. "I know better than to offer to help her. Once she tried to throw a coffee table at me."

Hope tried but could not quite visualize the woman she'd met hefting a coffee table over her head. "I didn't really mean I didn't want to learn anything," Hope said. "It's just that I don't want to go back to school. I want to *do* something."

"Well, you *do* things in school. You work hard."

"I know, but . . . but I'm tired of living . . . I don't know . . . in the margins. Let me show you these." She drew her Big Thicket photos— the wood ducks and ducklings, the wild orchids and baygall trees—from her portfolio and laid them out.

"This was your first time in the field?" he asked, rubbing a deeply dimpled chin.

She cleared her throat. "Yes."

"So we could say you're bound to improve." Her heart plunged. Straightening up, he pointed to a pine sapling growing in the middle of a rock-strewn stream. "Like that one. If you'd used a quarter-second shutter speed, you could've made that water *move*. And this orchid here. You should have stopped the aperture way down and used a flash."

The noise of the vacuum cleaner ceased, and the thuds and scrapes of moving furniture began. "Her period," he said, jabbing a finger toward the ceiling. "She always moves the furniture when that time of the month comes 'round. Would you like a beer?"

Hope nodded, and he went over to a copper-toned dispenser standing in one corner of the room. From it he drew two beers, tipping each pilsner against the stream for a neat, half-inch band of foam. "With some background, you might could do something," he told her, handing her a glass. "If you went back to school, you'd get some guidance."

Hope sipped her beer. Overhead something rumbled: heavy furniture on rollers, a sofa maybe. "Why not you? Why can't you give me some guidance?"

He studied the collection of scatter pins that studded her denim vest. "Yeah . . . uh-huh. Yeah . . . well . . ."

The ceiling rattled as something upstairs crashed to the floor. Hope raised her eyebrows. "The coffee table?"

"Might could be. Her strength triples under the influence of raging hormones." He extended a collegial smile. Exempted from the ranks of those who clean and suffer raging hormones, Hope smiled back, ignoring the kink of guilt in her chest and the suspicion that it was more rewarding to be Mr. Freytag's student than his wife. She turned to study one of the framed photos that hung on the walls, a rocky creek descending a mountainside dense with ash, willow, and spruce.

"I took that one up around Santa Fe," he said. "The water from that little stream eventually ends up in the Rio Grande."

Hope was intrigued. The Rio Grande she'd known when Clay was stationed at Harlingen Air Force Base was a trickle along the Mexican border, its arid banks littered with the cardboard homes of the destitute. She'd done a lot of wandering in the Rio Grande Valley, with a three-year-old Amber in tow. Clay was routinely absent on training missions, and she had not found congenial company at the Officers' Wives Club. *The military is not a job, it's a way of life*, a colonel's wife had informed her at an orientation meeting for newcomers that Hope had attended, her first and last meeting. So she knew the Rio Grande quite well at its southern extremity.

"I've had this bug for a long time now to photograph the Rio Grande from its headwaters to the Gulf. Paradise Lost." Hope saw what he had in mind: from mountain stream to cardboard litter.

Hope looked again at his photo. "It's a big project."

"Big! We're talking tonnage! We're talking hundreds and hundreds of miles! Getting all that on film could take a lifetime," he said happily. He paused, studied his beer, and grew gloomy. "Meanwhile, you gotta put the beans on the table. I do quite a bit of commercial work," he apologized. "Tenneco, Bank of the Southwest, Rice, Braniff. It's rotten work. You have to deal with a bunch of jerks who haven't a clue about photography, which is okay, I don't expect them to, it's better, in fact, that they don't. But wouldn't you think they'd have a notion as to what they want on the cover of their asinine brochures? You show them this and this and this, and they're saying no and no and no and not quite. Except for the money, it's a total waste of time. You probably wouldn't want to get involved."

"What?"

"We could both think about it."

"Think about what?"

"I *might* could use an assistant. For the commercial stuff."

"Me? A job? I don't have to think about it. If you have a job, I want it."

"'Course, we'll have to check with the wife first. She's the accountant in the family." They listened. The noises above them had stopped. He reached into his shirt pocket and pulled out a package of chlorophyll gum, shaking out a couple of small green squares. "To discombobulate Mama's nose," he explained. She took one. He winked.

A WEEK LATER, Hope was lugging around tripods and lenses and flash equipment for a shoot in the Astrodome. She'd already learned some lingo. Pix, she said now. Negs. She was a professional photographer's assistant. She was earning money without having to bend at the knees or furnish a perpetual smile.

This is life, she often said to herself these days, as she raced around scouting sites and finding props for Gil. This is life. What she'd lived before was life, too, but invisible life, full of effort and sacrifice and triumphs and failures no one noticed or cared about. The time she'd flipped Patrick upside down to dislodge the open safety pin he'd swallowed? No one had pinned a medal on her. The time Amber had run to her, comic page in hand, suddenly and radiantly literate? No one else had witnessed. Her life connected to the real world now. Sitting at a conference table with Gil, she did not share his disdain for his clients. They made her feel important.

After a while, he let her help in the developing room. Working in the glow of the safelight, she grew adept at molding images and even tried a few experiments. "Good work," Gil said, from time to time.

She still missed Amber and Patrick, but she no longer missed them every minute, every day. Their absence was a crater she had learned to detour. The eye adjusts, learns not to see, or at least not to see all the time.

24

Hope was meeting new people. More accurately, she'd been meeting new people for a while now, and the evidence had begun to accumulate. Stopping by the Richwood Food Market or the Baby Giant, Hope was very likely to run into someone she knew, Raymond maybe, a Coushatta Indian whose lustrous black hair swayed gently over his shoulders on weekends and was stuffed up inside a wig during the week so that he could keep his job at the Department of Public Safety. They talked about the Big Thicket, where Raymond had grown up. "Nothing a stick of dynamite wouldn't cure," he said of the lumber companies there.

Or she might come across Martha, a librarian by necessity, a groupie by inclination, who kept Hope current on the rising stars in the redneck rock world. It was Martha who tipped Hope off to Bobby Bridger's fifty-five-minute song assessing American history from the point of view of a nineteenth-century beaver trapper, which Finn and O'Molly added to their repertoire.

Running into people like this, knowing some of their particulars, Hope felt, maybe for the first time, at home in the world. She got the jokes painted on the windows at Mary's. She knew what to order at Los Troncos. And she was not surprised, walking down Albany on her way home from the Baby Giant one afternoon, to see a small group of people gathered outside the old De Pelchin Faith Home. She knew that the three-story brick building had been recently purchased by the twelve-year-old Mahara-ji and his entourage, arousing nearly everyone's curiosity. He had recently ushered in the new Golden Age at the Astrodome, and the lure of the millennium attracted numerous sightseers. It was not at all uncommon to see people hanging about the building, hoping for a glimpse of him.

"Here he comes," said a woman in a beaded headband to Hope, who had stopped to see what was going on. In the next moment, a limousine appeared in the drive, turned left, and headed toward Westheimer. Hope thought she saw him, a small figure behind the smoked glass.

"You know, I feel sorry for him," she said to the woman. "He's a little young to be worshiped."

"Better he should learn a hook shot." The voice came from behind her, and when Hope turned, a slow, blissful feeling uncoiled from between the spurs of her hips. To say the man standing there was tall and dark-haired, rakishly disheveled, was not to the point. His attractiveness for her was beyond words; his appeal could not be pinned to characteristics. It was a matter of recognition. Their mutual gaze, a kind of eyeclasp in lieu of touch, precluded speech.

Around them, conversation continued. "Did you see him? Chubby little guy." "Yeah. Is he Buddhist, or what?" "Dunno. *Something* eastern."

Gradually, the group dispersed, one by one, until only two were left standing on the sidewalk, and without benefit of invitation or decision, they were soon drifting down Albany together, exuding the serene grace of the trustful.

His name was Gideon. They were neighbors; he lived only a block away.

Astonished, Hope asked, "How could it be we have never run into each other?"

"I'm a recluse," he said. "Usually."

Not only was Gideon her neighbor, it turned out he had also attended the Unitarian church once. "The church with the stripper, right? I read about it in the paper. I stopped by, but I can't stomach that humpot stuff."

"Humpot?"

"Human potential."

"Oh."

He even knew Calhoun slightly. "We were both extras in *Brewster McCloud*."

"I almost was," Hope said. They might have met two years ago!

"I signed up just so I could talk to Altman," Gideon went on. "I wanted to interest him in this idea for a movie that I've had for years. A movie without dialogue, just music and images. A man and a woman. They meet and are attracted to one another. They become lovers. They don't know anything about one another. Body language is the only language they speak. Years go by, and they're still lovers. More years go by, they grow old, and they're still lovers. They know nothing about one another beyond their aging bodies. Then they die."

Hope thought this a very beautiful idea. "What did Altman think?"

"I never got to talk to him."

"Oh."

"I know. Anticlimax. The story of my life."

"I'm sure it isn't," Hope said, gazing at him.

Gideon was a native Houstonian; his paternal side boasted city founders.

"I'm from Indiana," Hope said apologetically. "But I *love* Houston. I see quite a bit of it in my work." She paused.

He tipped his head, smiling. "Which is?"

"I'm a photographer's assistant." She felt she had impressed him.

They must have walked the entire Montrose that day, just their force fields touching, the tension between them delicious. At dusk they stopped at a Chinese restaurant, improbably named the Texas Star Café. The food was excellent, although Hope and Gideon could not have reported this. They sat staring at each other across the artful food in stomach-tumbling silence. Hope dropped her chopsticks twice. She didn't know how to use them, for one thing, but the real problem was fingers acting like strings.

GIDEON'S ROOM OCCUPIED nearly the whole second floor of a capacious two-story bungalow. The walls were painted the soft buff-gray of nuthatch plumage, and the woodwork, mantel, and window casements a clean white. On the street side, flanking the fireplace were two alcoves, fitted with purple-cushioned window seats below the arched, multiple-paned windows. Purple was the only color in the room; in addition to the cushions, an iris-hued rug lay on the gleaming, dark hardwood floor and an eggplant-colored vase held a bare branch on the mantel. Books, a music stand, a straight-backed chair, and a futon were the only furnishings.

"It's exquisite," Hope marveled. "So simple, so . . . pure."

"My ex-wife got all the furniture," Gideon explained. A violin case sat on the floor. He opened it to show her a violin varnished the color of honey, the grain of the wood wavy, like hair. He had had it made in Salt Lake City, its maker a perfectionist who had labored over it for more than two years. "But it was worth the wait," Gideon said, running his hand along the instrument's waist.

Placing a blue bandanna on his shoulder, he rested the violin there and drew his bow across the A-string. He adjusted a peg, and Hope sat down on the futon. He hadn't played more than four measures when she recognized the music she had been hearing for months through her bedroom window, its minor key and single line drawing her, time after time, to a place within herself.

"You!" she exclaimed. "It's you! The phantom violinist!"

He lowered his bow.

She felt like a child, all want and expectation.

THE WORLD BECAME a place to make love in. Existence had no other rationale. If Gideon called her in the morning, Hope canceled whatever plans she'd made and arrived at his doorstep within the hour. If he called in the night to say he was thinking about her, she said come on over. Now.

They researched arousal—how little could they get by on? Gideon touched the tip of his tongue to the back of her knees. She kissed his instep. Erogenous zones.

They experimented with surfeit, sending out for Mexican food when they got hungry, getting out of bed occasionally to shower, to look out the window. They had dragged the futon to the center of the room, and lying there, naked and happy, surrounded by so much empty space,

Hope felt set loose. "This is what we are made to do," she said one day. "We evolved from the slime for this."

Gideon objected. "What about spiritual impulse? What about art? Chartres? *Hamlet*? *Guernica*?"

"Frills."

He leaped up and took out his violin, tuning it with a stern concentration at odds with the naked wantonness of his body. As he began to play the Bach partita, Hope thought the fluid beauty of his wrist so acute, it seemed the source of the music.

When he finished, she rose and walked over to place a fingertip on his neck, where the violin had worn a reddish splash in the shape of a small butterfly. "You win."

They looked up words in the dictionary to see what they might inspire. "'Heartstrings,'" Hope read aloud, "'tendons or nerves formerly believed to brace and sustain the heart.' Isn't that wonderful, Gideon? 'To brace and sustain the heart'?"

Taking a straw from a glass of orange juice by the bed, Gideon drew a heart on her chest, not a valentine heart but an organ, lopsided and saclike, slightly to the left of center, the candy-striped straw traveling up, over, and down the swell of her breast, leaving a wet, pale orange outline. "Zing!" he said, drawing a line to radiate from his design, and then another and another. "Zing! Zing!'"

Sometimes desire would bloom in her again hours after lovemaking. His kisses would drift softly through her skin to float in her blood; his nibbles would work their way through to her vital organs. "I'm in love," Hope told everyone.

Not everyone approved. Chloe advised her to concentrate on her work, and Fern reminded her that men weren't worth the tumble. Alex informed her that falling in love was nothing more than infantile desire plus hormones. "Not that there's anything wrong with infantile desire, but you've got to know it for what it is. Hormones are not that reliable either." Deaf in the mysterious grip of sexual attraction or infantile desire or hormones, Hope didn't really hear any of this.

Calhoun and Caleb were her only allies. Just being around them made her lonely for the special rapport of lovers. "One feels incomplete without it," she said, and they agreed.

* * *

ON THE DAY Clay and Mindy got married, Hope bought a bottle of champagne. "To celebrate," she told Gideon, arriving unannounced at his door.

"To celebrate what?" he asked, but she wouldn't tell him.

The champagne was cool and peppery in the mouth. Gideon kept it cold in a terra-cotta flower pot filled with ice. They made love, and afterward, leaning back against the pillows, Hope proposed a toast. "To Clay and Mindy," she said.

"And who are Clay and Mindy?"

She set her champagne glass on her naked stomach, centering the stem on her navel. She took a deep breath; the glass rose and sank but stayed steady. "You tell me."

Gideon put his eye to the glass, looking through her navel to revelation. "Hmmmm . . . Clay and Mindy . . . Clay and Mindy . . . yes, it's coming to me . . . Clay and Mindy . . . furry little puppets, aren't they? Kukla, Clay, and Mindy? Furry little guys with white felt triangles for teeth?"

"Exactly," Hope said, kissing him to validate their balmy rapport, full of reckless surrender and the conviction that nothing else mattered.

IF SHE COULD only narrow her life to Gideon's long, planed body, she could be happy. For the first time since that day in September when she had walked out of the courtroom, insensate with loss, she had a chance. It seemed to her now that she had never been happy before. She had not been happy as a child, she had not been happy as a wife, she had not been happy as a mother. Emptiness and misery, emptiness and fakery, emptiness and responsibility.

Gideon did not grant misery or fakery or even responsibility a place in his universe. One sidestepped misery with pleasure: drink, music, and sex were always available. There was no point to fakery: how could it matter what people thought of you? Responsibility, well, one could choose to assume it or not, just as one could choose to wear an overcoat or not.

When Gideon talked like this, Hope felt so free. She avoided mentioning Amber and Patrick, intuiting that he would not be interested in a woman so encumbered. Encumbered. This was a new way of thinking about herself. She wasn't sure if it was new with Gideon or a previously unacknowledged attitude.

In any event, it was not hard to avoid talking about Amber and Patrick, because the subject of children did not come up much, although childhood was frequently touched upon. "My childhood was perfect," he said, with an odd air of finality, as if all that was worthwhile had ended there. He told charming stories about how he'd taught his parrot to insult the cat, how he'd built a magic world in miniature within the tangle of his mother's shrubbery. He showed Hope his clipping collection. At age eight, he'd played "Flight of the Bumblebee" for the Rotary Club, and at twelve had been the youngest person to ever win a statewide competition. Hope sifted through the clutch of yellowing newsprint, trying to understand the immediacy the clippings had for him.

She tuned herself wholeheartedly to his wavelength. This required industry, since she knew next to nothing about music. "Take thirds," he suggested to her one night. "A major third is the perfect expression of male sexual contentment. A minor third, on the other hand . . . "He paused, looking at her. Hope mentally scurried in search of a response. ". . . female receptivity," he finished for her. "Don't you think?"

Hope said she wasn't sure. Later, she looked up the terms in the dictionary: thirds, minor, major. Not much enlightened, she filed away his observation in case it might become clear to her at some point. She wouldn't ask what he meant. It was important not to say the wrong thing, sound the wrong note, miss the beat. Gideon lived in a world of nuance, and she feared disturbing its delicate symmetry. Loving him was a game of cat's cradle. The joy lay in the surprising new patterns. The tension was in not tangling the string.

25

Hope was asleep when the phone rang. Expecting Gideon, she leaped out of bed.

It was not Gideon, however, but Calhoun. He didn't bother to escort her gently into shock. "Frederick's been shot."

Hope leaned against the wall to steady herself as doorframes tilted and the flowers on the wallpaper left their neat rows to swim about in confusion.

"It's only a flesh wound, luckily," he said. "The bullet went right through his arm. Didn't shatter any bones."

Only a flesh wound. Only? she wondered, as she drove to Ben Taub Hospital. The innocent weakness of flesh—what could be worse to wound? She tried to recall what else Calhoun had said. Some kind of police assault on Black Battalion Headquarters. Three dead, including Leroy Champion. Nine wounded, including one policeman and Frederick. The Fannin Street lights flashed by like the roving spotlight of a prison yard, and a siren went off in her mind. She grasped the wheel tightly and concentrated on Fannin Street. *Get hold of yourself. Calm down. Frederick is alive.*

The emergency room was still chaotic when she arrived. Nurses and orderlies, their gowns stained and streaked, dodged the gurneys and wheeled metal tables and sidestepped the turquoise plastic chairs and canvas bins stuffed with bloody towels and sheets. A half-dozen or so uniformed police formed a tight group in one corner, their voices low. As Hope stood for a moment trying to get her bearings, someone pushed her aside to make room for a shirtless man, his brown chest lit up with a burst of wet vermilion in its lower right corner. Hope's stomach billowed.

"I hate white people."

Hope looked to the speaker. It was Ocie, her dark face rigidly composed in a mask of hostility, glazed with faint purple from the fluorescent lights. "I . . . hate . . . white . . . people," she repeated, more loudly this time.

"We can hear you, Ocie," said Calhoun in a low voice.

"You, too," she said, glaring at him.

"You've been wanting to say that." Hope's voice shook.

"Yes."

Hope felt as if she had slammed full-face into a granite wall.

"I want you to *know*," Ocie said. "I want you to feel it in your *skin*."

Ocie's gaze skimmed Hope's surface, a flame held close, and Hope imagined her skin melting inward, absorbed into her flesh. "What . . . what about Frederick? Have you seen him yet?"

Ocie's eyes filled. She nodded and turned away.

"What happened?" Hope asked, wrapping her arms around herself to stop the chattering in her chest.

The occasion was obscure. The police maintained they'd had a call reporting a sniper on top of Black Battalion Headquarters, Calhoun explained.

"If you believe that, you'd probably like to hear about the time Sweet Baby Jesus called me collect from Paradise," suggested Ocie. She glared defiantly at the policemen in the corner.

"Shhhh," Calhoun warned. "Cluny might hear you."

Ocie glanced down the hall. "She can't; she's with Frederick."

"Abednego," Hope whispered, more a reminder to herself than a correction. Survivor of the fiery furnace. "Can I see him?" she asked.

Calhoun pointed out a curtained cubicle about halfway down the corridor. "Walk right in," he said. "Nobody's paying any attention."

Frederick was sitting upright in his hospital bed, Cluny in a chair by his side. He looked as if he'd been dusted with ash. His left arm was in a sling, the same arm Mr. Buck had broken. "I been shot," he said, looking up at Hope, his eyes enormous with disbelief.

"Does it hurt?" Hope asked him.

"Uh-uh."

"He full o' happy juice," Cluny said.

Frederick, not that much bigger than Amber to begin with, looked even smaller swathed in the white sheets of a hospital bed. "Oh Frederick," Hope whispered, putting a hand on his ankle beneath the covers.

"Leroy dead."

"I know."

"He my brother."

"White mens got no heart," said Cluny.

"They don't need heart. They got guns," Frederick said. "That's what the people need, too. That's what Leroy say."

Hope's own heart thrashed in protest. But she didn't argue.

"I been shot," Frederick repeated. He looked down at his arm as if it had just flown in the window to land at his side.

"And he jus' a chile!" cried Cluny.

Frederick started to say something, but his eyelids fluttered down over his eyes, and he drifted off. Hope stood silently by the side of the bed, looking at Cluny now and then but not for long, shaken by the depths of acceptance in Cluny's eyes.

For the next hour, they watched Frederick sleep and listened to the voices coming and going in the hall. *"That cop gonna make it?" "Yeah. God, I'm hungry. Haven't had anything to eat but a Mars bar. You want to go in on a pizza?"*

Around midnight, Hope decided to go home. "I'll come back in the morning," she whispered to Cluny. "Can I give you a ride home, or are you going to—"

"How my Caddy girl?" Frederick asked, eyes fluttering open.

"Lonely. Waiting for you to get better," Hope said.

"When I get out, I take her for a little spin."

"Okay."

"Me driving."

"Well, I don't know about that, Frederick. I—"

"I could have *died.*" His look was not unfamiliar to Hope: *You owe me.*

*   *   *

THE SHOOT-OUT at Black Battalion Headquarters made the front page of the *Post*. That in itself was history, Calhoun pointed out. The *Post* even reported the rumor that the police had planted the gun on the alleged sniper. (Another rumor, not printed, held that Pliny Dunavant had "turned Leroy in.") That there were more rumors than facts was indicative of the confusion over the event. The shoot-out was not like the violence surrounding the demonstrations in Montgomery or Atlanta or Birmingham that everyone had seen on TV but an explosion along the continuum of hostilities between the police and the minority citizenry. A good part of the city saw in the event a dangerous uprising of the black community. Another part, which included Hope and her friends, saw the event as "a police attack on some kids playing soldier," as Calhoun put it. Their view was accompanied by a new note of futility, a loss of confidence in the idea that racism was something they could combat with goodwill and common sense. There was even a feeling they should not combat racism at all, that they "had no right." "We're all responsible," people were saying, which while true in the large, abstract sense, led to paralysis in the small, personal sense. The couple at the church who had adopted a black daughter grew defensive. The interracial backyard barbecues now seemed beside the point. It was no longer possible to believe that integration was simply a matter of everyone doing the right thing and minding his manners. It was probably not even possible to rid oneself of one's own unconscious racism, went the thinking.

Hope dreaded talking to Ocie. *I hate white people* still occupied her ears.

They ran into each other one day at Cluny's, where they had both gone to visit Frederick. Ocie came straight to the point. "You know what I said that night at Ben Taub? I meant it . . . and I didn't mean it." She spoke thoughtfully, but seeing Hope's dutiful nod, she exploded. "You didn't have to take it as if it were coming from Mount Sinai, you know! You could have talked back—" Hope opened her mouth to protest, but Ocie went on. "Maybe not that night, okay, but you could have called me later, you could have said, Girl, we need to talk. But you didn't. No, everything is always left up to me! As if I *knew* everything! As if I were the official interpreter! I'm not in charge of racial affairs, you know."

"Did I say you were?"

"Yes."

"That's ridic—" Hope broke off. Maybe she had, sort of. Or at least made an assumption. "You're the only black friend I have, Ocie."

"I know. And it's damned burdensome."

"Well, I'll try to make it less so," Hope said stiffly.

"Good." They had left it at that, trusting time to smooth out the edges.

Over the next weeks, however, Hope and Calhoun saw less and less of Ocie, and when school ended, she told Calhoun that Rae would not be attending the Blossom Street Free School in September. Rae would be better served by a new private school sponsored by a group of black parents, she said.

"I couldn't argue with her," Calhoun told Hope dispiritedly. "She's probably right."

FREDERICK DECIDED TO stay with Cluny on his release from the hospital, which caused her to look on the shoot-out as a blessing. "The Lord he move in mystr'ous ways," she said happily. Although Frederick did not really need much care, she bustled about him, following the doctor's instructions to the letter, insisting on helping him dress, praying at regular intervals. She acted as if events had come about just as prophesied, as if she had known all along Frederick would be restored to her, and that he would finally see the light.

"I don' see no light," Frederick muttered when she said this. "You don' even have electricity." On another occasion, when Cluny was urging on him a freshly ironed shirt, he threatened to run away again. "I'm goin' to hop in that Caddy girl out front and take off," he threatened, glancing at Hope.

"No, you won'," Cluny assured him, her complacency intact. "For this my son uz dead and is 'live agin; he uz lost and is found,'" she intoned.

"Cluny, Cluny, the boy's tired of that talk," chided the Professor.

"He don' hear enough of it," Cluny retorted.

The Professor and Edna treated Hope with the same courtesy they always had. They talked freely about the shoot-out. The Professor expressed a profound lack of surprise. He said it was just like the Texas Southern "riot" of '67. "Which was not a riot," he told her. "They called it a riot, but it was a 'serious disturbance.' That's what the Kerner Commission said, a 'serious disturbance.' The students had hot tempers and rocks and bottles. The police had guns. The police said the students had guns, too, but I don't know. Maybe one or two. There's always one or two. But the policeman who was killed that day was killed by a ricocheting bullet. One of their own, I'd say. They had their excuse, though. Nearly destroyed the dormitory, 'looking for weapons.' This here Downing Street business is the same thing. Snipers, they say. Uh-huh."

At the same time, the Professor had serious doubts about the Black Battalion. "They're young. They think they're going to live forever," he said. "It distorts their judgment."

"Guns," Edna spoke up. "I never do like guns. I don't care whose finger's on the trigger." The shoot-out did alter her view of black-and-white relations, however. She no longer advocated an exchange of hearts. "It's best to just stay away from white people," she said. "Just stay out of their business. Give us equal and let us be, I say."

Hope wondered whether Edna was politely ignoring her white skin or had just gotten used to it.

IN THE WEEKS that followed the shoot-out, Frederick underwent a change. He had survived the fiery furnace to emerge, his poses burned off, with an air about him that said: *This is it. It's narrow but it's mine and I claim it.* Given what he had said about guns the night he was shot, Hope had expected a radicalized Frederick, but this didn't seem to be the case. Instead his astonishment at what had happened solidified into ambition. He surprised everyone by saying he intended to become a doctor. No one had ever heard him express any plans before, let alone any that entailed formal education.

"He's got the money," Ocie pointed out. Frederick's case against Mr. Buck had been settled some months ago, and Ocie had persuaded him and Cluny to put most of it in the bank.

Hope kept her promise to let him drive the Cadillac. She chose the safest place that suggested itself, in the very far north of the city, beyond the airport even, on the newly paved streets of a subdivision yet to be built. Neon-pink triangles of plastic fluttered on the strings marking the boundaries of the raw-earth plots, and a lone house on the corner advertised itself with a sign out front: MODEL HOME.

Drawing up alongside it, Hope got out to exchange places with Frederick. He slid into the seat and gunned the motor, alarming Hope with his eagerness for risk.

"Wait a minute," she said. "Let's check out the basics. Turn off the ignition."

He did. "Both hands on the wheel," she said. "Ten and two o'clock." He did this, too. "Now accelerate."

"Nothing's going to happen without we start the motor," he said sarcastically.

"Nothing's going to happen unless you show me you know where the accelerator is."

He stomped on the accelerator. "Now put your foot on the brake pedal," she said.

"I know what to do," he said impatiently.

"Well, maybe you do, but I just wanted to see if you were going to use the same foot to accelerate and to brake. Beginners sometimes accelerate with their right and brake with their left."

"I *know* what to do."

She flung up her hands. "Okay. Do it then."

He started the Cadillac, slipped it into drive, and pulled away from the curb, driving to the end of the street, where he braked smoothly and turned right.

She waited until they were well down the street before speaking. "You must have driven before, Frederick."

"Sure. Getaway cars."

"I hope not, Frederick. I sincerely hope not."

He smiled.

They drove around for a long time, up and down streets named Hillsdale and Rolling Ridge and Mount Oak, in spite of the fact that there wasn't a hill or a ridge or an oak in sight. The land in every direction was as flat as a tabletop. A marble wouldn't roll on it. Not even a mesquite disturbed the horizon. Perhaps it was the absence of feature that made what Frederick did seem so deliberate.

She heard the screech of metal on metal before she quite realized they had bumped up over the curb and were heading into the front yard of the model home. "Frederick! Stop!"

He looked confused, his foot frantically tapping about for the brake pedal. Out of the corner of her eye, she saw a man emerge from the model home at a run. Go back in! she signaled, waving her hands in a shooing motion. Before we run into you, she was thinking.

By the time Frederick found the brake, they were in the middle of the front yard, and the sign, squashed and bent, now advertised a MDL HE. Hope reached over and turned off the ignition.

"What happened?" she asked him after the car shuddered to a rest.

"I don't know." He had the same look of surprise she'd seen on his face at the hospital: the world was not quite fitting the picture in his head.

Hope arranged to pay for a new sign, and Frederick continued his driving lessons without further incident. For a while, they drove the farm-to-market roads outside Houston, through the barbed-wire corridors, the straightaway asphalt pouring underneath them. Soon, though, Frederick graduated to the city streets. Exuding genteel dominion, he drove with a courteous condescension, nodding with knightly civility when relinquishing right-of-way or allowing a car to enter his lane. *Noblesse oblige.* Even surrounded by horn honkers, he maintained his chosen profile. Hope would have liked to capture it on film. "Buddha at the Wheel," she would title it, an apt description of his half-smile, his poised and concentrated expression.

As time went on, he grew somewhat proprietary toward the Cadillac. One week he showed up with an old Cadillac hood ornament, a venerable Winged Victory from the forties, which he cemented just behind the Cadillac coat of arms, and on another occasion he attached two American flags with chrome flag holders to the fenders. His most recent addition was an extra bullet-shaped light, which he fixed to the roof.

Clay observed the first two acquisitions in silence, but the bullet-shaped light inspired protest. "Are you out of your mind?" he asked Hope that Friday when she came to pick up Amber and Patrick.

"Don't you like it?"

"I don't even think it's legal."

"Well, I think it's a nice touch," she said.

Clay stared: at her, at the chrome bullet, and back at her. Then he turned and went into the house. She had the feeling he had just relinquished the Cadillac, once and for all.

26

S UMMER HAD ARRIVED SO QUICKLY, HOPE COULD NOT RECALL WHEN
the canna lilies began to bloom or when the heat thickened to
smear the outlines of trees and buildings and create waves substantial
enough to cast shadows. Her work had kept her busy, for one thing.
Hope said that now: her work. She had been invited to show at *Exposure*'s
annual exhibition of new photographers in September, and she felt
entitled. As she roamed the city, looking for new subjects, new angles,
new light, she seemed to herself a different person, more substantial
and more located in her wanderings than when she had been anchored
by a house and children.

"Maybe it's for the best," she said one day to Chloe, whose shocked
look kept her from continuing.

Her work also kept her from orbiting Gideon, and for that she was
grateful. Their affair, scarcely three months old, had begun to leak its
passion, and Hope had to resist a compulsion to run about with makeshift
vessels, catching and saving what she could. After three months, Gideon
was still outside her life. He was incurious about her friends, her job,
Amber and Patrick, Frederick, the violence at Black Battalion Headquarters that had shaken the city. Gideon wore indifference as if it were a
badge of distinction. It was part of his languor. He did not read newspapers or own a television set. He was the only person Hope knew who
had never made a single comment on the Vietnam War.

For her part, she knew scarcely more about Gideon than he knew about her. She did not know what he did for money or what his interests might be beyond the Bach partita. She had never met any of his friends. She had, however, met his mother.

"Bootsie Randolph is your *mother*?" Hope exclaimed when he mentioned it one day. They had been driving through the changing shade patterns of River Oaks that afternoon, and he had suggested they stop by his mother's so that he could pick up his mail. "Bootsie Randolph is your *mother*? But she's the one who saved the school last year! Your mother! She's the one who donated the money we needed for the repairs. Bootsie Randolph your *mother*?" Gideon, in the passenger seat, looked out the window and made no comment. "Chloe says if it weren't for Bootsie Randolph, the Peace Center would have folded a long time ago. The Free University, too. Bootsie Randolph!"

"Enough already, okay?"

Hope was able to hold her tongue only until Gideon guided her through two more streets and into a circular drive. "Is this your mother's *house*?" she asked. "House" didn't seem quite the right word. Built of stone, with high arched windows, a portico, and a second-story balcony spanning the facade, the fourteen-room mansion was opulent even by River Oaks standards.

"This is it."

Inside, they followed the sound of voices to what had been a conservatory. Elephant ears and philodendron and schefflera still thrived in the light-filled room, glassed on three sides, but tables and telephones and a mimeograph machine now confused the botanical calm. A half-dozen or so people worked at a long table, while others wandered about with sheaves of paper or clipboards and a couple more talked on telephones. The mimeograph machine clunked and wheezed.

Bootsie, silver-haired and large, with a shelflike bosom that advanced through the mill of people like a driven wedge, came toward them. "Gideon! . . . What . . . a . . . surprise!" she gasped, struggling for breath. Seeing Hope's alarmed look, she tapped her chest. "Emphysema . . . I sound . . . as if I'm about to . . . keel over . . . don't I?" She gave a strangled laugh. "It's a . . . great advantage . . . when you're . . . testifying before planning . . . commissions . . . and the like."

"Mother is a great testifier," Gideon said, looking sulky. "Mother, this is Hope."

Hope took her extended hand. "I've always wanted to meet you. You saved our school. The Blossom Street Free School?"

"Oh yes . . . yes . . . Mr. Calhoun's school . . . a most impressive fellow . . . one can't turn him down . . . has some very sound ideas . . . on how to educate troublemakers. . . . We have a gaggle . . . of troublemakers here today . . . as you can see . . ." Bootsie waved a hand. ". . . and we could always use . . . more. Are you . . . by any chance . . . a trouble-maker?"

"No," said Gideon. "She isn't."

"Perhaps . . . Gideon . . . you could allow . . . your friend to speak . . . for herself. You see, my dear . . ." she said to Hope, "we are saving . . . the Big Thicket . . ."

"Mother is always saving something," Gideon interrupted.

". . . from the lumber companies. It's the troublemakers who . . . make a difference . . . in this world, but . . . Gideon . . . does not approve . . . of troublemakers."

"Not true. It's not that I don't approve. It's that I don't—"

"Care," supplied Bootsie.

Mother and son stared at each other for a moment in a kind of flirtatious hostility that led Hope to question Gideon's avowal of his perfect childhood. Fern said you could tell a lot about a man by the way he treated his mother. Hope wondered.

"The Big Thicket is certainly worth saving," Hope said, avoiding the subject of troublemaking. "I've been there. I think it's the most . . . penetrating place I've ever been."

"Yes, well . . . it won't exist . . . in ten more years . . . yet alone . . . penetrate . . . if the lumber . . . companies have . . . their way," said Bootsie.

"Have you been there?" Hope asked Gideon. "It's this almost super-natural place."

Bootsie held up a hand. "Super . . . Natural. Josh!" she called to a spectacled young man talking on one of the phones. "What do you think of this for a slogan? 'The Big Thicket . . . It's Super Natural!'"

Josh put his hand over the receiver and half rose from his seat. "Super

. . . Natural. Hmmmm. Well, we could think about it, Bootsie. Although Candace had a good idea, too, you remember."

"Oh, yes . . . I do . . . Well, it was just . . . a thought." She turned back to Hope and Gideon. "We're trying to . . . get . . . our propaganda act . . . together today."

"Yeah, well, we have to go," said Gideon. "I just dropped by to pick up my mail."

"Those letters are . . . at least a month . . . old . . . by now, Gideon. I hope . . . there was nothing . . . of importance . . . among them."

"Probably not."

Bootsie acknowledged this with a nod. "It was very nice . . . meeting you, dear . . ." she said to Hope. "You have . . . lovely . . . teeth." Bootsie's own teeth were in noticeably deteriorated condition, striated with tobacco stains.

Hope took her hand. "I . . . I would like to help. On this Big Thicket thing. Not today," she said quickly, sensing Gideon's displeasure. "Not today, but some other time."

Bootsie gazed at Hope for a moment, her labored breathing eddying about them, a disturbing current. "I like you," she said finally. "Few of the females . . . Gideon brings around . . . are potential troublemakers."

Females? Hope had wondered later. The word struck her as oddly generic. Its pluralness registered with her, too. Female*s*.

THE PASSAGE OF TIME had regulated Hope and Clay's relations; they were experienced negotiators now and managed transactions with utilitarian efficiency. Concentrating on the reasonable and practical this way, Hope could avoid wondering if Mindy was caring for Amber and Patrick with sufficient love and attachment, could avoid seeing that Mindy, pregnant now, was exhausted and stunned. Less than a year ago, Mindy had been the mother of one well-behaved son. Now she was mother to an increasingly rebellious prepubescent girl, a withdrawn little boy who identified with insects, and a two-thirds-developed infant. Hope culti-vated cheer and sympathy and told herself that everything was probably all right. When Mindy, splotchy-faced with bluish crescents beneath her eyes, body brimming and swaybacked, greeted Hope's arrival to pick up Amber and Patrick with an irritable *"Finally,"* Hope fished up a soothing smile and apologized, because it was true that she was often late, late from a shoot or having stayed too long at Gideon's or having miscalculated the time it would take to grab a Frenchy's Po Boy with Frederick.

"*Finally*," Mindy would say, turning from the door. "Amber! Turn that music down! Patrick! She's here."

The least Amber could do was keep her own room straight, Mindy told Hope. Especially now. Patrick did, and he was a boy. She, Mindy, was not the hired help, after all. If Amber spent a little less time on the phone, maybe she'd have a few minutes to lend a hand. Or do her homework. Mindy was not speaking for herself here but for Clay. Had Hope seen Amber's last grade report? Clay was not happy with it, Hope should know. Also, Amber was starting to talk back.

"That's not exactly the end of the world, is it?" Hope spoke with the dispassion of one no longer intimately concerned with the behavior of children.

"If you don't talk to her about it, I will," Mindy threatened.

So Hope dutifully raised the issue. "You shouldn't talk back, you know," she told Amber. "Not unless your civil rights are at stake."

Amber responded by grinding a finger into the side of her nose.

Hope did not insist. Her heart just wasn't in it. She rejected her former complicity with conformity, her role of enforcer of the status quo. These days, she took a broader view of good behavior. Good behavior was not so much thank-you-ma'am as being faithful to friends and hospitable to differences.

Despite a few episodes like this, Hope felt an equilibrium of sorts had been achieved by all involved. But with the onset of Amber's menses, the precariousness of this equilibrium, if not its illusoriness, came to light. It had not been Hope, of course, but Mindy to whom Amber had brought her bloody underwear. Mindy, reasonably if not overkindly, gave her a used sanitary belt and a Kotex pad and ordered her to wash out the stains in the bathroom sink. Instead Amber stuffed her panties in the trash, ran to a neighbor's, and called Hope.

When Hope arrived, Amber, who had been sitting at the neighbor's kitchen table, untouched cookies and milk in front of her, burst into tears.

"Oh, honey, don't. Sweetheart, come here." Hope fell into a chair and pulled Amber onto her lap, cradling Amber's head against her breasts, stroking her back and neck and arms, hands shuttling across elbows and shoulder blades and vertebrae, weaving a cocoon of care. "Mmmm, mmmm, mmmm," she crooned, fingering away a serpentine strand of hair that clung to Amber's wet cheek, recalling the strawberry birthmark that used to be there, a mottled starburst on gossamer skin. The moment blurred—her baby, her sweetpea, her turtle. "Mmmm, mmmm, mmmm."

Immersed in their joint bodily presence, Hope did not at first realize that the neighbor, distressed and anxious to extricate herself from a state of affairs not in keeping with the premises, wanted Hope and Amber to leave. She explained that she was already late for an appointment, and did Hope think she could resolve her difficulties as soon as possible?

Well, of course. Hope thanked her and took Amber back to Communitas, calling Clay from there to explain what had happened. Amber was feeling better, she said, but did not want to come home just yet. Could she spend the night? Clay put up no resistance, perhaps in deference to the mysteries of womanhood. Hope promised to return Amber after school the next day.

That night, with Amber sleeping beside her and the fragrance of the jasmine O'Molly had planted last November floating in through the open windows, the resident owl softly inquiring from the yew tree, Hope lay awake, thinking. The curse. You weren't supposed to say that anymore. Chloe said calling an important part of a woman's reproductive cycle "the curse" was an example of the psychological oppression women suffer. "We'll be the last generation 'cursed' by our bodies, if I have anything to do with it," she has vowed. "Rachel is going to be *proud* of her menstrual blood."

Maybe. Pride was in vogue. Recently, one of the pilgrims had shown Hope a diary she kept of her menstrual cycle, which detailed her moods, the phases of the moon, physical changes. "Our divine mystery," she had said.

More like divine injustice was Hope's experience. She recalled her own first period. She'd howled in protest as her brother William left with a neighbor for an afternoon of swimming at the quarry. A child's mutinous resistance to anonymous sexual forces? Or simple envy of a brother's freedom?

Things were different now, of course. Tampons had been a great advance. But were they safe for eleven-year-olds? She didn't know. She, the mother, didn't know. She would have to ask Chloe. Chloe would know. Now that she thought about it, Amber probably would know. Kids knew so much these days.

Do not put these solids into your uterus, Hope had read over Amber's shoulder a few months ago, coming upon her reading an article in *Space City!* about self-induced abortions. *Coat hangers, knitting needles, slippery elm bark, telephone wire, curtain rods. They may burst your womb and bladder or cause infections and hemorrhaging. Do not put these fluids into your uterus: soap suds, Lysol, pine oil, alcohol. Do not pump air into your uterus. It will collapse from the air bubbles created in the bloodstream. Death comes suddenly and violently. Vacuum cleaners (not to be confused with vacuum aspiration) can extract the uterus from the pelvic cavity.*

Most of this had been as much news to Hope as to Amber. The experience of one generation was no longer of any use to the next. The timeline had collapsed. Hope wished, though, that she had said something to counteract knitting needles and curtain rods. She might have said something about falling in love and the transport of union with the opposite sex, although when she pictured an anonymous boy body alongside Amber's girl body—his narrow flat chest pressed against her delicate, crushable cones, lanky legs on lanky legs—she was dismayed, not glad. Who knew better than she the formidable power of sex to cut unexpected channels in one's life, diverting the flow in unanticipated directions? She considered telling Amber the cautionary tale of her own out-of-wedlock conception but decided against it. She didn't want Amber to think she had started out life as a mistake. But she would have to say something. Girls Amber's age in India were having babies. Children bearing children. Well, how many people had a proven claim to adulthood? Wasn't it always children bearing children?

Beside her, Amber murmured in her sleep, and Hope placed a hand on the narrow back. Her baby, her sweetpea, her turtle. The node of the universe, its central budding point.

THE NEXT MORNING, Hope drove Amber to school, and then spent the morning hunting down Civil War uniforms for a shoot. Finally finding some at the Harris County Heritage Society, she spent nearly an hour in finicky negotiations for the loan of them in exchange for a donation and then spent another exasperating hour making arrangements with the building superintendent of the Old Cotton Exchange Building. It wasn't until afternoon that she and Gil were able to brainstorm some shots, and she had barely managed to type up a sequence before it was time to pick up Amber at school.

Amber was uncharacteristically quiet, and after a couple of attempts, Hope did not press her for details of her day. As they rode in silence along the Katy Freeway toward Spring Branch, Hope's scattered parts began to reconnect, and she was tempted to keep on going, speeding over surfaces, free of drag, reducing life to the smoothness of the road, the future to a place on the map. At the Bingle exit, however, Hope eschewed the open road and took the off-ramp, as usual, and drove to Clay's neighborhood.

"Are you okay?" she asked Amber, as they turned onto his street. The gaslight on the smooth green lawn glowed, although it was not yet four in the afternoon.

"I guess so."

"What's wrong?"

"Why did he have to marry her, anyway?" Amber burst out. "Why did any of this have to happen? It seems like a whole big breakup for nothing. I don't think he's any happier. He sits in the garage late at night rocking."

"Rocking?"

"Yes. You know the rocker that creeps?" Of course Hope knew. His mother had given it to them when Amber was born. "He sits in it and rocks," Amber said. "I can hear it creeping across the garage floor." Hope stopped at the curb, and Amber gathered up her things.

"Try not to worry about your dad, okay?" Hope said. Amber looked at her as if she had just requested she not breathe. "*Try.*"

Amber nodded, and Hope watched her get out of the car and walk up the concrete path, back straight, bearing what had to be borne. There is no such thing as childhood, she thought. Not in the sense of bulletproof shelter. Not in the sense of halcyon days.

* * *

SHE DROVE AROUND for a while, trying to escape the shag end of the day, as her mother used to call it, that part of the day when the natural light is ground fine as dust, the hour or so before lamps are lit in windows, to signal home. Hope was familiar with pitfalls of the shag end of the day, and she understood the choices. One could wallow or one could seek distraction. Wallowing was not to be despised; little gold nuggets could sometimes be found in the wallow. The shag end of the day was perfect for wallowing, but you could go too far. You could get stuck. Hope felt in danger of getting stuck. At the moment, distraction seemed the better part of valor. The butterfly on Gideon's neck fluttered in her mind's eye. She wasn't that far away from the Montrose. She could be there in ten minutes.

Reaching Gideon's street, she stopped. His windows were lit, and she stood in front of the building for a moment, watching for a glimpse of him, wondering whether or not to go up. She had often arrived unannounced, ever since the day of Clay and Mindy's wedding when she'd rung his bell with a bottle of champagne in hand, but she felt less sure of her welcome today.

The truth was, Hope had begun to suspect Gideon of seeing someone else. He was often out when she called and evasive when in. She wouldn't have asked, of course. To do so would have been to rend the refined rapport between them, to injure what was special. And in any case, Gideon was free to see other women. Should she choose, she was free to see other men, too. She just hadn't chosen.

"It's me," she whispered when he came to the door. Upstairs, a naked woman was lying on the futon; she was sure of it.

Gideon peered at her, swaying a little. "Well, of course it's you. Come on in." He turned back to climb the stairs, leaving the door open for her to follow.

Gideon had been drinking. She could always tell when he had been drinking because his hair looked as if it had been brushed from back to front. Alcohol seemed to go straight to his hair roots, befuddling their sense of direction. There were other signs, too, but you had to know him well. You had to know his normal walk in order to see in this subtle swagger something different. He held his arms slightly away from his body, like a gunslinger, and planted an emphatic foot at each step, as if claiming territory. Hope saw this, yet she followed.

When they reached the top of the stairs, he turned, one hand on the doorknob, to see if she was behind him. "Hi," he said with a confident grin. Then, swinging back abruptly to lead the way into his flat, he slammed full force into the closed door, which he had forgotten to open.

"If you get a black eye later, you can tell people you walked into a door," Hope joked. "You'd be telling the truth." He gave her a truculent stare. "Have you been drinking?" she asked stupidly.

"No."

She couldn't think how to challenge this. She looked at her watch. "Maybe I should come back another time."

"What did you want?"

She gazed at the butterfly on his neck. "I don't know."

He invited her in, and, after quickly ascertaining the absence of a naked woman on the futon, she sat down there herself.

"I was just getting ready to practice," he said, gesturing toward the open case on the chair, which exposed the honeyed curves of his violin.

"May I listen?"

"If you want to."

He played his Bach partita, *the* Bach partita, the music she had first heard, and still heard, from her bedroom window. She wasn't sure he practiced anything else. So familiar was she with the piece, she could mentally supply the notes he missed now in the arpeggios. The phone rang, but he kept on playing, and when he had finished the partita, he flopped down on the futon, extending a hand to fumble at the buttons on her blouse. Seeing he was stymied by the relationship of button to buttonhole, Hope undid the buttons herself and then stood up to remove her jeans and underwear. Gideon undressed, too, his own openings and closings presenting less difficulty than hers, and they lay down together, his hands skittering along her body this way and that, as he searched for his place. She kissed him, tasting sour breath. "Gideon—"

He muttered something in response—she couldn't quite make it out—and grabbed her hair, pulling on her scalp. His eyes closed, he rolled over on top of her.

No. The denial came to her with force, as if someone had spoken aloud. No. She slipped out from under him and got up to dress. "I have to go."

Gideon opened his eyes and looked up at her without saying anything, perhaps without seeing anything; she wasn't sure.

She tucked her blouse into her jeans. "I just stopped by for a minute." She paused for a moment, expecting a protest. Gideon smiled. Hope walked to the door and out.

27

"THE PLANET IS FULL," CAME THE WHISPER OVER A CRACKLING telephone line. "The rent is due. Pass it on."

Hope, standing in the upstairs hallway, gripped the receiver. "William! Where are you?"

"Where are *you*? I had to call *home* to find you. Dr. Gizmo told me that they hadn't seen you since Christmas before last."

"It was about time I left home," she said, with a lightness that was a bare step away from self-betrayal, as if turning her back on her father had not left her shaken for days and forsaken for months, as if her feelings at this moment were not hammering away at her rib cage. William, oh, William. "Where *are* you?" Her words came out a keening.

"Talking to you." His voice, too, was light and high.

In the static on the line Hope heard the turbulent sea of those who leave, the anguish of distance palpable. She wanted to bring him close, but there was too much to say and it was too difficult to speak when neither of them had shape, when they existed for one another as mere electrical energy, an acoustical phenomenon inside a wire.

"Nothing has changed," he said, "as far as I could make out, except that Dad has moved the Lunatic Lab from the cellar to the garage."

"Ah, the cellar," she said, calling up the memory, smelling its sweet, damp earthiness, seeing in the dim light, more shadow than light, the shelves of home-canned peaches and pears and cherries and green beans and tomatoes and pickles.

"It was a wonder he never electrocuted himself," said William. "The cellar was always flooding, remember?"

"Yes. We used to pilot a packing pallet across it, remember? Remember poling our way past the furnace? past the coal bin? to the far shores of the rag barrels? And hiding in the rag barrels?"

"I was always afraid of that furnace, afraid it would explode."

Hope prickled with awareness of what they were *not* talking about—her divorce and loss of Amber and Patrick; his resistance and protest activities, possibly lawless but possibly not. She was trying to think of a way to ask him about these when he burst out, "What happened, anyway?"

"You mean between Clay and me? You mean . . . the kids?"

"Yes."

What *had* happened? She could provide facts. Mindy. Victor. The Big Thicket. The courtroom. If facts were what he wanted, no problem. But to explain what happened? In the sense of spontaneous combustion? In the sense of the barn burning to the ground? What could she tell him?

"Two worlds colliding," she said finally. "I guess that was it, basically. In the aftermath, we shot off into different orbits. My problem is that Clay took the kids with him."

"I never liked Clay."

"No, you never did."

"He never liked me."

"No."

"But what happened?

He did want facts. Well, people do. The first question after a suicide is: how?

So she told him about Mindy and Victor and the Big Thicket and the courtroom, not in order of events, not distinguishing between the important and the unimportant, but instead handing him a mixed ragbag of facts. He would have to sort it out as best he could. She hadn't done so herself yet. At times, the static grew loud, and he asked her to repeat, and with great effort, she did. But she would have preferred not to be talking about this at all. She would have preferred to be speeding along in the family car with him in wordless comfort.

"How are you doing now?" he asked when she ran down. "What the fuck is Communitas, anyway?"

Downstairs Finn and O'Molly were rehearsing, from Alex's room drifted the fragrance of marijuana, and in the bathroom, Fern was spraying her hair gold for the first gig of her new girl group, Brew. "A place to molt," Hope said. "A nest. Safe, more or less, but temporary. Once you have your new feathers, you fly away." She had never explained Communitas to anyone this way, not even to herself.

"Are you about to fly away?" he asked.

"No."

"Are you safe, more or less?"

"I'm a photographer."

He laughed. "Does that mean you're safe?"

"It does, kind of. Behind a camera, I do feel safe. What about you? Are you safe?"

"Depends on how you look at it. I'm married."

Now it was her turn. "I don't believe it!" To whom? To someone as dangerous as himself? "When?"

"I can't tell you," he said.

An arrow lodged, quivering, in her heart, but she persisted. "Did you have a wedding cake? Did you dance? Was it one of those City Hall things with strangers? Or one of those Universal Life Church things with wildflowers and decorative weeds? Was it sunny? Or rainy?"

"Really, Hope, I can't say anything—"

"William! William. I have to know *something*." Some fact, some piece of driftwood to hold in her hand and feel.

"It was rainy."

"A good omen," she said, genuinely relieved. "Rain is romantic."

"You saw too many Hollywood musicals at an impressionable age."

"That must be it. Corrupted at an early age by happy endings. Which, of course, we know now, in the light of modern science . . ." Her voice was light as ash. It trailed off, and William did not break the silence. Each of their lives had changed while the other wasn't looking. They were no longer Hansel and Gretel.

"I should go," he said.

"No! I mean . . . why?"

"I have a rule: Never stay in any one place for more than fifteen minutes. I've already exceeded it."

"Is that anything like the rule about not trusting anyone over thirty?"

"A lot like. If AT&T calls you, ask them about their defense contracts. And don't pay them a dime."

"Are you getting me in trouble?"

"No. As long as you're not a Goody Two-shoes about this and remember that AT&T can afford a fucking phone call better than you can, you won't get in any trouble."

"Okay."

"You don't know me is all. That's all you have to say."

"Well, I don't. Not anymore."

"Hope."

"William. I have a question."

"Don't ask it, Hope."

She gripped the phone. "Didn't I see you at the Galleria last year? Wearing a silver fright wig and a funny nose? Carrying a water pistol? November, I think?"

"Hope, I can't tell—"

"How can it matter now to tell me where you were last November?"

He was silent for a moment. "Yes."

His figure flew across the ice, clear and present, skimming the surface of a recalled childhood greater than its reality.

WILLIAM WOULD NEVER return home. Even if the war ended, he would not, Hope was convinced. She wondered how her parents felt about this. They had never talked about it. Once William went underground, his name no longer came up much, and when it did, it surfaced securely tethered to events in the past. Perhaps her own name was similarly tethered these days.

The decision to visit them came to her in pieces. One day on a shoot, she looked through a lens focused on the new Alley Theater and saw instead her parents' wedding portrait, her father in a pin-striped suit, his hair slicked like a vaudeville entertainer's, her mother also in a suit, a gardenia corsage pinned to one shoulder, her expression mischievous and knowing. It occurred to Hope she might photograph them now, thirty years later. The idea surfaced and fell away again and might have disappeared entirely if O'Molly's father hadn't died.

The event upset Hope. Not that she had known O'Molly's father, not that she grieved. But it occurred to her that no one close to her had died, that the death of a loved one, as the phrase went, was an experience still before her, and she was seized by the urge to talk to her own parents, to repair the damage before it was too late.

"My father hated the idea of me singing in public," O'Molly mused on the way to the airport. She took a Kleenex from the box on the Cadillac's dashboard. "He hated my songs."

"Did he actually say so?"

"He said they gave him the pip. You see, I was supposed to be a doctor like him."

"Not your brother?"

"No. Dad always favored me. Maybe because I was the oldest. My poor brother could have been a garbage collector, for all Dad cared. I was the one destined to disappoint."

And now you always will be, Hope thought, glancing at O'Molly's tearless profile as they sped past the refineries. The parental blessing is out of reach now.

HOPE PICTURED HERSELF drowning, as her mother's voice drowsed through her veins. They sat at the kitchen table, its peeling yellow paint revealing the grain of the wood, rough to the pads of Hope's fingers as she traced an imaginary place mat for herself. Maureen ate from a can of Vienna sausages as she talked, their fatty, garlicky smell mingling with that of coffee, infecting Hope with a mild nausea. She had abandoned all pretense of listening. It didn't matter to Maureen, who could talk and talk and talk without any encouragement, or even response. Hope imagined an engine inside her mother's chest—not unlike one of Wally's perpetual-motion machines—complicated circuitry distributing words up into her throat and out her mouth. Something demonic was at work, Hope thought. She saw her mother disgorging words into an ever-widening void.

". . . sideswiped," crowed Maureen. "Ceci never even saw the car. She probably darted out in that jumpy way of hers, hoping for the best. Her mother died instantly. Or course, it was foolish for Ceci to go to the Creamery on a Sunday in the first place, I wouldn't if you paid me, kids in their hot rods, half of them can't even parallel-park according to your Uncle Art, and then Ceci always such a nervous driver." Maureen paused to stare at Hope. "How would you like to bear that scar? Your mother dead and you without a scratch. Her mother didn't even *want* an ice cream cone."

"How do you know she didn't?" Hope always looked for flaws in her mother's stories, inconsistencies, signs of untruths. She had no clear idea of what she was trying to disprove, but whenever she caught her mother in a falsehood, however trivial, she became a ruthless crusader for accuracy. "How do you know that?"

"Her mother was a diabetic! Diabetics don't eat ice cream!" Maureen replied. "And I'll tell you this. Ceci will take her guilt to the grave. *To the grave.*" Coffee sloshed in their cups, as Hope rose from the table. "Where are you going?" Maureen demanded.

"Out."

"Well, leave your father alone. He's busy."

"SEE HOW THIS magnet rises toward the second magnet? The attracting magnet? Now look . . . see? It's moving out of range. Because of the motion of the lever. Now watch. As the attracting magnet moves out of range . . . the repelling magnet comes forward!"

Wally's newest contraption looked to Hope like a miniature gallows.

"There's no reason in the world why this shouldn't work, Hopie. Think of it this way. It takes less energy to slide two magnets apart sideways than to pull them apart, right?"

"I guess."

"And there you have the essential principle. I think I've got it this time. The sun is self-propelled, isn't it? It rises and sets daily without pulleys. All I'm doing is tapping into the mystery."

Hope sighed. "Could we take the portrait this afternoon, do you think? We keep putting it off. I'm leaving tomorrow, you know." She had been here for three days and had been ready to leave after one. William was right. Nothing had changed. Nothing ever would.

Wally reached out and stilled the magnets. "I thought you might stay an extra day."

"Why would you think so?"

"Oh, I don't know." He turned off the lights over his workbench, and they walked out together into the backyard. As they ducked under Maureen's empty clotheslines, he touched her arm. "It comes to that, you know," he said, pointing to two blackbirds, a glossy male and a dusty female, sitting on the far clothesline. "In the end, it comes to that."

Hope looked. Does it? Does it have to? Two birds on a bare clothesline?

How SMALL THEY looked! Hope nearly cried out with the surprise of it, as she bent down behind her tripod to look through the lens. They did, in fact, look like two birds on a clothesline, sitting side by side on the couch, feet aligned neatly on the floor in front of them, arms close to their sides like folded wings. Maureen looked especially tiny, swamped in a full-skirted taffeta dress with a flesh-colored panel in the bodice that made the neckline look more low-cut than it was. Yet Wally also looked small, swallowed up, not by his gray suit but by the jungle blooms of rose and gold that patterned the sofa. The shrinkage! Hope thought, the fearful shrinkage! She seemed to be seeing them from a point very far away. The standpoint of judgment, she thought, feeling slightly ashamed. From this distance, she could see the antagonism that defined their common boundary, the parts of themselves that touched. It was an antagonism mostly generated by Maureen, a necessary antagonism, Hope saw now, the friction her father refused to believe in. The worst thing that can happen to a woman, Fern liked to say, is to hook up with a weak man.

Still, they were a pair. And there was something to be said for loyalty, wasn't there? For two birds on a bare clothesline?

Maureen trained a hostile stare on the camera, defiance in the angle of her chin, while Wally looked back with melancholy apprehension. Hope placed a finger on the shutter release. "Say cheese."

"Limburger," responded Wally without smiling.

"Wllleeeeee! Eeeeee serious." Maureen spoke through her teeth without moving her lips so as not to disturb her smile.

"Cheddar," he amended, and the shutter clicked.

28

Hope returned from the humid heat of Indiana to an even more humid, hotter Houston. She and Gil were working outdoors that week, photographing the construction-in-progress of One Shell Plaza, and Hope felt in danger of liquefying. A thin film of sweat encapsulated her body; droplets ran down her nose and fell from her earlobes. Her camera slipped from her hands, saved from destruction by the strap around her neck, which stained her neck with heat rash. She took salt tablets. She considered shaving her head. "Just to feel the breeze," she said.

"Wait till we get to Big Bend," said Gil. "Triple-digit temperatures every day."

"I can hardly wait."

Actually, this was true; Hope was looking forward to the trip she and Gil and his wife, Coylene, would take in a week to the Big Bend of the Rio Grande in West Texas, where the two sources of the river merged. They would spend two weeks there, camping and photographing the river.

Hope thought of calling Gideon to let him know of her plans, but she didn't. Nor did he call her to give her the opportunity. She couldn't quite shake the notion she had walked out of his life the night she had walked out of his flat, his beatific smile imprinting on her back. She didn't say this, though; she said that things were not the same.

"Well, of course things are not the same," said Alex. He and Hope and Fern were sitting on the front porch, enjoying the warm night air and talking over the shrill grating of the cicadas. "Romantic love is an illusion; everybody knows that."

"They do?"

"Of course. Romantic love is the pursuit of one's own pleasure. Bestowing perfection on the beloved disguises the selfishness of that pursuit. 'I'm in love,' we say, the ultimate extenuating circumstance. I'm not opposed to romantic love, of course. Whatever works."

Hope wished he wouldn't say "of course."

Fern was shaking her head. "It's the drinking. That's the problem. Drinkers get in this cloud. Nothing else matters. You're not there; they don't see you. I know from my father. Does he change?"

"What do you mean?" Hope asked.

"Does he change personalities when he drinks?"

Hope recalled the sullenness, a brutishness even, that sometimes broke the surface of Gideon's charm. At these times, Hope sensed something about to crawl out and bite her from behind the lovely foliage.

"That's the key," Fern said. "When they change personalities. That's when you know you're dealing with an alcoholic."

"I think he's seeing other women," Hope said.

"I doubt it," said Fern. "He doesn't have time. He's busy drinking."

Hope stared at her knees. Gideon, her beloved, her darling man, her phantom violinist!

BIG BEND WAS the Big Thicket all over again, not in likeness of terrain or vegetation or atmosphere—it couldn't have been more different—but in Hope's exhilaration and joy. The harsh beauty of these desert mountains, continually remade by the great river cutting through them and carrying off the sediment, roused her imagination and sharpened her seeing. Canoeing down a wild canyon with Gil and Coylene, she saw in its monumental twists and turns the grandeur and seductive intricacy of hell. Sitting alone on a cobble bar at the end of the day, she watched the dying light play against the ancient limestone walls and sensed the elasticity of time. Climbing a bluff to look down on the river below, she saw not a linear band, with a beginning and an end, but one ray in the watery web sustaining the earth.

She also experienced here, just as she had in the Big Thicket, an extension of her physical senses, the flowering of a preternatural competence. One evening, on a solitary after-dinner hike, she saw—in her mind's eye it must have been, for she happened to be looking at a blooming octillo—the diamond pattern of a rattlesnake's skin. The pattern saturated her eyes—she would wonder later if this was what it was like to be blinded by a vision—and when she came to herself, at a dead stop on the path, there it was, a rattlesnake, stretched out motionless across the path a good six feet away. It stirred but did not coil, as Hope stepped backward, very, very slowly, gradually widening the gap into which her body heat flowed until she was out of range.

"I will never forget that diamond pattern," she told Gil and Coylene that night. "The way it flashed into my brain, obliterating everything else. It was the most remarkable experience."

"I had a similar thing happen once," said Coylene. "I heard a scorpion."

"A scorpion!"

"I know. You're not supposed to *hear* scorpions. But I heard it, a scratchy sound. And saved myself from a nasty sting, I warrant."

Hope was glad to be in the company of this stout, rosy-faced woman. Coylene had turned out to be an admirable wilderness companion, right up there with Romain. The woman Hope had first met angrily charging around her house with a vacuum cleaner was quite another being in the wilderness. In the wilderness, she exuded a child's delight and an animal's physical ease. She could ride a horse, paddle a canoe, and scale a rock face with more skill than Gil himself. "You're an inspiration," Hope had had more than one occasion to tell her, as she tried to keep up, panting and flushed in the heat.

The three of them worked well together. Coylene sometimes assisted Gil, so that Hope could take her own photos. Sharing camp and cooking duties, they would camp in one spot for a couple of days, then move on in the Freytags' Land Rover, the canoe lashed to the roof.

They returned from Big Bend with another chapter in Gil's saga of the Rio Grande complete. "It gets sad after this," he told Hope. "The river gets dammed up twice south of Big Bend. At that point, the river is pretty much in the hands of our clever little species. By the time it gets to the Gulf, it's pretty much lost heart," he said in a rare revelation of authorial stance.

BACK IN HOUSTON, Hope felt her contents had shifted a half inch. She was not a different person, her outlook had not undergone an overhaul, but she had altered a little, a bit, a degree or two. She had climbed a desert mountain, she had been swimming in the shadow of ancient canyon walls, she had seen a rattlesnake.

About a week after her return to Houston, Gideon appeared on the Communitas verandah, violin in hand. She had not seen him for nearly a month, having been first in Indiana, then on the Rio Grande, the space in between marked by noncommunication. The July evening was close; the still air, dense with the fragrance of legustrum and the petroleum flower, drifted in through the window screens. She was alone.

"Hello?" he called softly, chuckling, running his bow along a screen. "Hello?"

Hope let him in. Stirred in spite of herself, she gazed at the butterfly on his neck, glanced down at his lovely, slender bowing wrist, and reached out a hand to touch him. He smiled.

He had an utterly charming smile, an enthralling smile usually, but an irreversible change in direction was underway in the mesh of Hope's mental gears. She was analyzing. Gideon's smile was one she'd seen often in the yellowed clippings and photographs of him as a child. One, in particular, had lodged in her mind: a five-or six-year-old Gideon with slicked hair, small hands folded under one cheek, head tipped engagingly, smiling for the camera. It was the same smile she saw after he had made love to her, or cooked dinner, or played the Bach partita. The smile of a crowd pleaser. What was it Fern had said about crowd pleasers? She couldn't quite remember. Her hand fell to her side.

They sat down on the porch glider, its rusty springs screeching. He propped up his violin and bow in one corner and turned to her.

"Did you hear me practicing?"

"No." It occurred to her that his endless practicing of the Bach partita was more an obsession than a passion. His perpetual striving for perfection suddenly struck her as morbid.

"You didn't?" He was surprised, and so was she. All the windows were open. Had she grown so used to the Bach partita that she no longer heard it? Or was he hallucinating?

"You missed the sarabande then. I've changed the phrasing. Obedience, that's the key."

She couldn't tell whether or not he was drunk. Gideon could be entirely coherent when drunk, his words precisely enunciated. That he had been drinking was clear from the fragrance of fermentation he exuded, from the way his hair looked as if it had been brushed from back to front. "Obedience?" she repeated.

"Obedience to the urge that rises."

His languor was about to drive her to melodrama. "I don't know what you're talking about," she said grumpily. "You're not making any sense."

He looked at her, and she stared back, half hostile.

"New embraces, new combinations," he said.

Was he talking about music? Or other women? Hope stared at the hand-embroidered symbols on his work shirt. They had been finely done, lovingly done, by an ex-girlfriend.

He gestured with a wounded arm. "A movement away from the thing we are."

"Oh, Gideon," she said, as pity, that vandal of desire, overtook her.

"You don't understand, do you?" he said, smiling, as if pleased with this conclusion. When she didn't answer, he picked up his violin and bow, pulled from the latter two loose hairs, and stood up.

She did not watch him leave; she didn't need to. She knew he would saunter down the steps, swinging his bow, escorted by enough luck to make his solipsism viable, and that he would turn in the right direction and reach home safely, if home was where he wanted to be. There would be a spring in his step. He might whistle snatches of his Bach partita. She knew that he had come here with something beautiful in his head, something to which she was supposed to respond. She knew that she had just let the strings of their cat's cradle go slack.

29

FIVE MORE MILES, AND THEY COULD MAKE A WISH. HOPE KEPT AN eye on the Cadillac's odometer, which now read 59,995. Behind her Patrick also watched, elbows on the backrest of the driver's seat, while Amber sat in the passenger seat reading, feet propped up against the dashboard.

They were on their way to Kemah for the weekend. The grooves between road sections were delivering a regular beat to the tires—*ba-dump . . . ba-dump . . . ba-dump*—the two-beat rhythm of Highway 45.

Patrick's breath lifted the tendrils of hair at her neck. He pointed as a digit flipped from eight to nine.

"Get ready," she announced, and a minute later, the numbers rolled to 60,000.

"What did you wish for?" she asked Patrick.

"I can't *tell*," Patrick told her. "If I *tell* it won't come true."

"That's just a superstition," said Amber.

"What did *you* wish for?" Hope asked her.

"It's stupid to wish on miles. Dad just made that up."

Make a wish, kids, we're breaking a hundred here, You're going to be making lots of wishes. These cars last forever. How jubilant Clay had been, how proud at the wheel.

Amber flipped on the radio, tuning in to Hudson and Harrigan. Patrick burrowed into the backseat and began singing one of his songs.

Fly, Fly,
Why, why?

The cabin smelled of new wood and stain and sea breeze and wrack—the windows lacked glass, leaving the cabin open to outside smells. The cabin was one large room, with the exception of a bathroom and a sleeping loft, unfurnished except for one of Fern's stained-glass creations hanging from the ceiling in a front center window. Hope liked it this way, she liked the expectant air, the blank readiness.

They changed into swimsuits and headed for the beach and the green water, shot through with ribbons of sunlight. The waves were gentle here, lightly ruffled with foam. Diving into one of the more sizable ridges, Hope relished the sudden change in world. A resonant silence rang in her ears, and all thought dissolved as she began to swim, her body a silken stream. Underwater, immersed, everything was of a piece.

To return to the surface was to return to the demarcated and weighty. And wordy. Shaking the water out of her ears, Hope listened to Amber's corrections to her breaststroke. Her timing was off, her extension short. Meanwhile, Patrick floated and dove and glided around them, a natural fish not yet trained to perform.

When they tired of swimming, they spread out their towels on the grass and lay down to watch the clouds riding at anchor above.

"I can disintegrate them if I want to," boasted Amber.

"Oh? How?" Hope wanted to know.

"Concentration. See the one that looks like a curly wig?"

"Yes."

"Watch."

For the next minute or two, Hope gazed at the cloud. Perhaps the tight curls did relax a tiny bit, but Hope couldn't be sure. Amber, however, claimed success. "I have powers," she crowed.

Her claim didn't set well with Patrick; a bas-relief of longhorns took shape above his eyebrows. "You know what?" he said after a moment.

"What?" Hope asked.

"I can spell Mississippi."

"You can? How?"

"M-i-*ss*-i*ss*-i-*pp*-i."

"That's right! Good for you, Patrick! That's wonderful!"

The balance of power satisfactorily restored, Patrick stood up and trotted back into the water.

At noon, Hope served the picnic lunch she'd packed and afterward persuaded Amber and Patrick to go for a walk with her. Amber ran here and there through the underbrush, as if under some imperative to leave footprints on every possible square foot, while Patrick explored more soberly, tracing the veins of a leaf with an index finger, turning over rocks to watch the scurrying insects with pleased concentration. The diffused light through the trees reminded Hope a little of the Big Thicket, and she was suddenly overwhelmed by the memory of Romain and the day they'd spent together. She would always be grateful to him. Something good had started for her that day. Romain had taught her something even more valuable than the great deal she'd learned since from Gil. Romain had taught her patience. A form of hope really, its disciplined form. She was grateful to Victor, too. Going about with Victor had stitched perceptions into the fabric of her life that would always be with her. And if she hadn't gone with him to the Big Thicket, she would not be looking forward to a show at Exposure; she would still be living on Chisholm, wandering from room to room in search of herself.

And what about this outcome—how did it weigh in the scales? Hope's mind blanked under the strain of conceiving an answer.

They came upon the fallen windmill, and within minutes Amber had organized its geometries into a schooner with herself at the helm, assigning lookout duties to Patrick. He did not seem to mind his subordinate role and busied himself aft, arranging sticks and dandelions and stones into a construction he was able to coax up to an improbable height. Whispering and chuckling, he could have been playing a different game altogether, although when Amber called out to ask if he had sighted any dolphins, he looked around purposefully before saying no.

For supper, they cooked hamburgers on the hibachi Finn had left behind, and after washing the dishes, they played Go Fish and War by kerosene-lamp light, since the cabin lacked electricity. Around ten, they arranged their sleeping bags in a row on the floor of the railed loft and lay down. The moonlight streamed through the windows. "This is what it's like to sleep underwater," Amber said. They lay there listening to the night broadcast of country sounds: frog creakings and owl hootings, tree rustlings and moving water.

"You want to know a joke?" Amber asked, just as Hope was drifting off.

"No," said Patrick.

Amber ignored him. "There was this woman, and she kissed a frog."

"I think I've heard it," said Hope.

"No, you haven't. She kissed a frog, and guess what? He turned into a handsome prince."

"Are you sure I haven't heard it?" Hope asked.

"I'm sure. Then *he* kissed *her*. And guess what?"

"What?"

"She turned into a motel!"

Hope smiled into the moonlight. "You're right. I hadn't heard it."

Amber sat up on an elbow. "Patrick doesn't get it, do you, Patrick?"

"Yes, I do."

"No, you don't. You're too young. Isn't he, Mom?"

"Well, I'm not sure. He's a little older now that he can spell 'Mississippi.'"

Patrick nestled up against Hope's side. Not to be left out, Amber followed suit, and Hope slipped her arms around their shoulders. A golden shower of well-being descended on her, like pollen.

"Mom, can I tell you something?" Amber asked after a few minutes. "Something I'm not supposed to?"

Beside her, Hope felt Patrick's body tense. "What do you mean, you're not supposed to?" she asked.

"Dad said not to."

"Is it something that's bothering you?"

"Yes."

"Does it concern me?"

"Kind of."

"Okay. What is it?"

"We might move to California."

Patrick sat up. "You weren't supposed to tell!"

"I don't want to go," Amber went on. "And you know what else? This morning in the car? I really did make a wish. "You know what I wished?"

"You're not supposed to tell!" Patrick wailed.

Amber reached for Hope's hand. "I wished I could live with you."

"I WAS GOING to call you," Clay said. He and Hope sat on the stone benches surrounding the reflection pool of Hermann Square, where a man in waders was advancing slowly through the water, sweeping a net back and forth beneath the water. The torpid air was thick with exhaust from the cars passing the square on all four sides, noisy with growls, whines, and occasional screeches. As people from the nearby office buildings opened brown bags and unwrapped sandwiches, platoons of grackles and pigeons came to attention.

Hope had not been in Hermann Square since the march for Billy Lee Sams and George Bird. Looking toward the City Hall steps, she recalled the dead boy's mother, standing there so still except for hands fluttering like sparrows, and behind her, Leroy Champion, in black beret and camouflage, hovering, like a benevolent bird of prey. Dead now.

Hope was trembling. "You can't do this, Clay."

"Hell, I can't *not* do it. I have a chance to be *pivotal.*" He popped the top of his soft drink can and dropped the tab through the opening.

"You shouldn't do that. You might swallow it."

"Always the mother."

"*Not* always the mother!" she cried out. "That's why we're here!"

People turned to look. "Shhhh," Clay urged. "Sorry. You know what I meant."

Neither of them spoke for a minute.

"No one knows photovoltaics the way I know photovoltaics, Hope," he began again, quietly.

"I thought no one knew much about photovoltaics."

"What's known I know. The Institute needs me, Hope. Christ, my country needs me. You don't realize."

"I realize you're trying to take Amber and Patrick half a continent away from me."

"This is a job offer, not a kidnapping, for crissakes. California schools are the best in the country, you know. Public schools, I'm talking about. In California they're like private schools except they don't cost anything. Anyway, who's stopping you from moving there, too?"

"And leave Houston? What about my life?"

"What about it?"

Hope unwrapped her sandwich, and the grackle patiently eyeing her was quickly joined by a bevy of pigeons. She began to rip apart her sandwich and toss them bits. The birds fought over the scraps of lettuce and ham, then busied about tidying up the crumbs.

"It's the opportunity of a lifetime, Hope."

"For *who*? Do Amber and Patrick want to go? Have you asked them?"

"It's on the agenda. Mindy and I are still talking it over."

"Amber doesn't want to go."

Startled, Clay knocked over the empty can he had set on the bench. It tinked a couple of times on the bounce, then settled into a clatter, rolling away from them. "She doesn't? How do you know?"

"I just . . . I just don't think she does." Hope got up to retrieve the can, walking slowly, taking the time to collect herself. The iridescent green of the soft drink can sparkled in the sun as she reached down to pick it up. It was warm in her hand. Left here for any length of time, it might burn. She would welcome that: a single point of pain. She tossed the can into a nearby trash container and returned to the bench.

"Amber's had to cope with some difficult changes," she heard herself say. "I think this may prove too much for her."

"Are you and I talking about the same kid? Nothing's too much for Amber."

"That's a convenient way to think of it."

From Hermann Square, Hope drove straight to Chloe's. Chloe had set up an office downstairs in what used to be the dining room. Thick books sat on the shelves, and her walnut desk was large and polished. Behind her file cabinets gleamed. Hope sat down in a leather armchair and told her about Clay's plans. "Is it too late to go back to court?" she asked.

"No, but are you sure?"

"Yes."

"Then I have two pieces of advice."

"What are they?"

"One. Get yourself a good divorce lawyer." Chloe's look was dour and unforbearing. Hope hesitated. Chloe leaned forward, and the brass pendant she was wearing—the biological sign for female—clunked on the desktop. "One. Get yourself—"

"Okay," Hope agreed.

"Two," Chloe continued. "Move out of the hippie-dippie dump you're in and set yourself up in the suburbs."

Hope recalled the house on Chisholm, the bomb shelter, the St. Augustine grass. "I'm bad at lawns," she said.

"Get good. And start sleeping in your own bed. Every move you make is evidence."

"Thanks, Chloe, that should help my ulcer."

"I'm a lawyer, not a doctor. You need to establish a lifestyle that can withstand the finest grind of the wheels of justice."

"Lifestyle. Sounds like a swimming stroke."

"It wouldn't hurt to think of it that way. It's time to leave the raft, Hope."

IT SEEMED MORE like abandoning ship. The next morning at breakfast, Hope watched Finn carefully spread butter to the edges of his toast. Next he would stir vitamin-B powder into his orange juice, turning it the color of infant fecal matter. She would miss this routine; she would miss him and O'Molly. Fern. Alex.

"Like . . . it's the end of an era," said Fern, gripping her coffee mug in both hands.

"It's only been a year," Hope said. "I don't think that's long enough to qualify as an era."

"Eras don't have to be long, just significant."

"Where will you go?" Finn asked.

"I don't know yet," Hope said. "Chloe says I should go back to the suburbs."

O'Molly shook her head. "I can't see you in the suburbs."

"What about the cabin?" Finn asked.

O'Molly clapped her hands. "The cabin!"

A winged euphoria lifted Hope up, transforming her flesh into something transparent, able to pass through obstacles, and she was seized by optimism, as if everything had already been settled in her favor.

"*Pax*." Alex skated into the room just then, raising two fingers in the peace sign. A smoking joint rested in the fork. His bare feet looked old, the tendons standing out in sharp relief.

"I thought you were flying today," Hope said.

"I am. *Fugio ergo sum.*"

Hope searched his face. Last Sunday he had preached to no more than thirty people, a number that had seemed even smaller with chairs set up for a hundred.

"How's this for a sermon idea?" he asked them now. "A system of human knowledge based on eroticism, a theory of consciousness based on contact. Take the newborn child ... " He broke off to study his wrist, focusing on it with an expression of glad concern, moving it this way and that. He looked up. "What was I saying?"

"Take the newborn child ..." prompted Fern.

Alex frowned for a moment, then beamed at them once more. "It's gone," he said with a rapturous smile. "Whatever it was, it's gone. Gone, gone, gone," he sang, sweeping the air with his hand. A trail of smoke hung there briefly before dissipating.

30

O N MOVING DAY, CALHOUN, CALEB, AND FREDERICK CAME TO
help. Caleb's hair was just starting to grow back, a transparent
yarmulke on his bald skull. He had been arrested a month ago in front
of a gay bar for "failing to move on," and during the night he had spent
in jail, the gendarmes, as he referred to them, had shaved his head.

The exposure of Caleb's glabrous head had shocked and sickened
Hope. There were raw spots on his skull, and the back of his skull was
ridged like a terraced hillside.

Caleb, however, had remained sportive. "Just right for hot weather,"
he'd said, patting his head.

"I wouldn't let 'em do that, man," said Frederick, reaching a hand
to his back pocket to check on his hair pick, which he had already used
twice this morning to extend the range of his Afro.

"They tied me to a chair," Caleb said in the same reasonable tone
one might use to say: They gave me a peanut butter sandwich. "I'll bet
you didn't know that barbershop clippers were essential tools of law
enforcement, did you? Along with handcuffs and clubs."

"They cold, man," Frederick sympathized. "They got no respect."

Calhoun put an arm around Caleb. "We're plotting our revenge.
Caleb's going to run for mayor and appoint me police chief."

Caleb shook his bald head. "Not this year."

"I didn't say this year. But when you do, we're going to kick some ass."

Frederick thrust a fist in the air.

"Innocents," said Caleb to Hope, with a blighted smile.

The three of them were a more than sufficient crew for Hope's small store of belongings. Her photographic equipment and sparse furnishings fit easily into the truck she had rented, and they were ready to go by eleven o'clock. Alone in her room, Hope glanced around the spare, high-ceilinged space—her garret, her tower. She'd been desolate here, and bored. How many hours had she logged daydreaming? Tedium, loneliness, fantasy—roots of freedom.

The household gathered on the verandah to see her off. "Let go," Alex advised. "Let *go* in order to *go on*."

"Oh, Alex," Hope said, holding out her arms. "Can't you just say a simple goodbye?"

"No," he admitted, allowing himself to be enfolded in a hug.

They would grow apart, it occurred to her. She would eventually find the Unitarian church too distant for regular attendance, and he, immersed in his here-and-now, would neglect to call, to visit. She supposed she understood what was inflated in him, and mistaken. She suspected there might be a time when she would look back on these days as undercautious and overzealous. But she had known joy here and optimism, in large part thanks to Alex. "I can't either," she whispered, pulling away.

Next to Alex stood Fern, wearing the sea-foam dress from Embers Hope had given her. They embraced, their bodies lingering for a moment, storing up warmth. The unlikeliness of their friendship had not diminished its intimacy, and their parting might have gotten teary if Finn and O'Molly hadn't burst into song:

> *Adieu, adieu,*
> *We are so blue,*
> *That you,*
> *Aren't glue.*

Calhoun placed his hands on Hope's shoulders and turned her around. "March."

"Don't look back," called Alex, and she didn't, instead lifting a blind hand as she set out across the lawn, past the dentist's chair to the curb, where the Cadillac was parked.

"Can I drive the truck?" Frederick asked Calhoun.

"No. Learner's permits don't extend to rented trucks. You can ride in the cab, if you want, though."

"Nah, I'll go with her," Frederick said, indicating Hope.

"Okay. See you there," said Calhoun, as he and Caleb climbed into the truck.

Hope opened the Cadillac's door on the driver's side, then paused. "Remember that telephone pole?" she asked Frederick. She looked up, seeing a much younger and somewhat smaller Frederick at its top.

"Yeah," said Frederick cautiously.

"Remember Victor?"

"Uh-huh."

"I just wondered. If you remembered." Memories of the lady with the ladder and Victor and the Happening and the Big Thicket and the pilgrims and the Ultimate Vehicle mingled with regrets of leaving the Montrose and Rosamunda's and the Richwood Food Market and the Mahara-ji. The telephone pole blurred. "Can you drive?" Her words were half-whispered, but he heard her.

"Can I *ever*."

"I mean, do you know the way?" she amended, speaking more clearly.

He snapped his fingers and struck a pose. "*Do* I."

"Little brush talking like big wood," she commented, a phrase she'd picked up from Ocie.

THE UNLOADING WENT quickly, and by late afternoon her furnishings had been arranged in the cabin, her bed in the loft, her wicker baskets, oriental vase, and tin trunk in the large space below. Hope was pleased. What had looked cluttered and haphazard in her small bedroom at Communitas now looked artistic and intentional.

"Very nice," Caleb said. "Very nice, so far. It wants a good reading chair, however, and fortunately, I know where one is. My mother stored oodles of stuff when she moved to her apartment."

Everyone was hungry by this time, and they drove to a wharf restaurant south of the drawbridge and watched the returning sailboats as they ate. Then it was time for Calhoun and Caleb and Frederick to leave; Calhoun and Caleb had to return the rental truck before five, and Frederick had a date.

"A date?" Hope repeated.

Yes. With a certain Cicely.

"Oh."

So they left, and she was alone. At least she could turn on a light; the cabin had electricity and running water now, as well as glass in the window frames. Hope had spent the small sum she'd made on the sale of the house on Chisholm to provide what she was fairly certain a judge would consider necessities.

There were still things to unpack, and Hope started. But without the buffer of company, a score of worries trooped in to fill the vacuum in her head. First came the scurrying little ants of worry. Could Finn put up a wall or two to partition the sleeping space? Where should she set up her darkroom? Wasn't she likely to feel lost living so far out? Then came the big, tentacled cephalopods of worry. Would she win custody this time? And if she did, would Amber and Patrick be happy? Would they make friends and enjoy school? Would she have enough money?

She went to bed and tried for a while to read but finally gave up and turned out the light. Outside, the water lapped up to the beach, talking to the shore in its equable, unvaried voice, a voice utterly unconcerned with human affairs. The sea did not care. Perhaps it was not always necessary to care, not every single minute. Perhaps it was permissible to give oneself up occasionally to an endless, elemental rhythm of monumental indifference. The thought cheered her, and little by little, like an advancing tide, the sea's voice made its way through Hope's ear to lap up against her own inner shores, where the simplicity of its language spread out to envelop her, and she fell asleep.

HOPE AND CLAY'S new hearing was set for December. The family court calendar was crowded, Hope's new lawyer explained; meanwhile, she had filed an injunction to keep Clay from taking Amber and Patrick out of the state. The next night, Hope received a phone call.

"Why don't you just shoot him and have done with it?"

It took Hope a minute to recognize the voice on the telephone as Mindy's. "What do you mean?"

"Everything was settled. Now it's not. You just love to stir the pot, don't you?"

"No one is stirring the pot, Mindy. Amber wants to live with me."

"Kids are notorious for not knowing what's good for them. Unlike judges."

Hope lay awake that night, trying to convince the judges of her worthiness. She earned money now, she pointed out, not a lot but enough to support herself and her children with help from their father, which was, after all, only fair, wasn't it? She had a house, well, maybe not a house, a cabin, to be precisely truthful here, this was a court of law, after all, but a large enough cabin to shelter herself and her children. She was a woman of good character, maybe not spotless but good enough, and who could say more? She was suspicious of those who claimed more, herself. She loved her children. True, her ex-husband loved them, too, in his way. That was the problem. He loved them in his way, and she loved them in her way, and neither of them approved of the other's way. Two worlds colliding.

THE NEXT FRIDAY evening, Hope drove out to Clay's to pick up Patrick and Amber. It was her weekend to have them, but she hadn't spoken to Clay since that day in Hermann Square, and she wasn't sure they would be there when she rang the bell.

Clay answered the door. "I want to talk to you," he said, the command of his tone at odds with an unprosperous appearance: eyes sunk deep into charcoal sockets, skin the color of yellowed ash. Beltless, wrinkled khakis hung irregularly about his hips, and a brown stain—spilled coffee?—blemished his IU sweatshirt.

"Where are Amber and Patrick?"

"Mindy took all three kids out for hamburgers. They'll be back in an hour or so. That will give us enough time. I want to talk to you. Do you mind if we talk in the garage?"

"I guess not."

"We won't be disturbed there."

Not unexpectedly, the garage was a marvel of organization. Clay had built shelves and labeled each section: Electrical, Lawn & Garden, Auto. Frequently used items––a claw hammer, pliers, an extension cord, a graduated set of wrenches—hung from a pegboard. Hope admired this display of orderliness. The systematic way Clay made things fit still impressed her. The Toyota occupied one of the garage bays; the platform rocker from Lydia occupied the other.

"Mindy won't let me bring the rocker into the house," Clay explained, turning on a fan, which cranked up noisily before settling into a hum. "She says it will ruin the carpet. The way it creeps." Hope, careful not to sympathize, took up a perch on a nearby sawhorse. "Mindy's quite the little housekeeper," he added, sitting down in the rocker. Hope wasn't sure whether this was an oblique comment on her own failings or an ironic allusion to Mindy's limitations. The rasp of the rocking chair was the only sound for several minutes.

"So Amber wants to live with you," he said finally, sounding somewhat dumbfounded, even a little confused, as if he were reporting on something both ordinary and strange, a creature, say, that looked like a cat, meowed like a cat, but breathed underwater. "California has the best schools in the nation," he said after a pause.

"The merits of California are not at issue."

"She's not fourteen, you know. Until she's fourteen she doesn't have the right to decide."

"Oh, rights. What are they anyway? Where do they come from? Who invented them? It seems to me Amber has as much right to decide where she lives as we have a right to decide for her."

"We're the grown-ups."

"Are we? And if we are, so what? It seems to me grown-ups are very good at disguising what *they* want as what's good for the children. I don't care what you say about California schools, Clay. This is a career move, not an educational opportunity."

Clay began to nod. There was something strange in the movement, not a strictly up-and-down action but more a swaying, like the crown of a tree in a high wind. Gradually the nodding became more pronounced; he seemed to have been overtaken by an involuntary tic. With each movement, an element of his expression collapsed: the mouth wobbled and fell aslant, the chin dimpled in distress, and the flesh of his cheeks constricted. Hiding his eyes behind a hand, he began to sob.

"Oh, Clay," she whispered, her composure giving way. "Oh, Clay. Oh, don't." He dropped his hand to look at her, his swollen face mottled and damp. "It's hard on Amber, too," she reminded him. "She loves you. She loves me. Put yourself in her place."

The rocker had been creeping slowly toward her all this time, and he now sat within an arm's length. "I'd undo it all if I could, Hope." He placed a hand on her knee and slid it slowly up her thigh. The familiarity of the gesture rooted through to her heart, and she reached out to brush his earlobe with the tips of her fingers. He buried his head in her lap.

From the house came the bang of a door. He lifted his head, coyote-like, as if catching a scent. There was a fleeting craftiness in his expression, the faint glee of the outlaw. Hope saw it and jumped up from the sawhorse, propelled by relief, as if she'd just missed being struck by a bus, as if she'd just stepped up onto the safety of the curb, hot exhaust belching about her ankles.

He looked up at her. "It's okay. They won't come out here."

"I don't care if they do."

The rocker cawed briefly as he stood up. "Hope. I can't face another custody battle."

"So what were you trying? To settle out of court?"

"You're hard, Hope. You've turned hard."

She didn't say anything.

"You won't win, Hope."

"I might."

"You won't. You haven't talked to Patrick yet."

PATRICK'S ROOM WAS in keeping with the rest of the house and its Early American furnishings, but whereas the downstairs theme was the cozy hearthside, here it was life at sea. A captain's chair sat opposite a compact lift-top desk appropriate to tight cabin quarters. Everything was ship-shape. No toys or books cluttered the floor. There were no signs of insects, dead or alive. Even Patrick's desk was clear of papers and Magic Markers and rubber bands and glue and scissors. A modular storage unit with brass drawer pulls in the shape of anchors occupied an entire wall. Hope imagined all the materials of childhood stowed there, in drawers.

This was the first time Hope had ever been in his room, and no doubt would be the last. No one else was home. Clay, Amber, and Mindy had gone to Jason's Pop Warner game, where Hope would pick Amber up after she had talked to Patrick. I could steal something if I wanted to, Hope reflected. I could set the house on fire.

Patrick sat on his bed beneath a print of a four-masted clipper ship under full sail, legs looking like stovepipes,extending straight out in stiff new jeans. Hope sat beside him, one hand on the ship's wheel that formed the headboard of his bed.

"You can drive through trees there," Patrick said. "Daddy said so."

Hope's heart cleft in two, its parts falling away to leave a windy space. *Daddy said so.* She heard in Patrick's voice an unquestioning belief that the ability to drive through trees was not only true but desirable. He would have displayed the same confidence had she been the one to say so. Patrick still had faith in grown-ups. Amber, maybe not, but Patrick still believed that grown-ups knew what was true and desirable. Grown-ups knew a lot of things; not much surprised them. They might say, *At the end of this road is a lake*, and, miraculously, there it was. Which proved, didn't it, that while you, the child, lived in a moment-to-moment world of whim and chance, grown-ups had this uncanny knowledge of what was going to happen. In California, there would be trees you could drive through, as well as prosperity and happiness. Patrick trusted this would all be so. What other choice did he have?

Do children ever forgive their parents? Once they've grown up and seen and judged? Had she? "They . . . they do have very large trees in California. Very old," she managed to say.

"Older than dinosaurs," said Patrick.

"I don't think they're older than dinosaurs."

"They are."

Hope studied the print above his bed before speaking. "Patrick, I want to talk to you about . . . about Daddy's going to California. I want to . . . we need to . . . what do you think, I mean, feel . . . about it? Do you want to go with Daddy to California? Or stay here with me?"

She hadn't meant to put the question so baldly. She searched his face apologetically.

He didn't answer. He left the bed and went to his desk, raising the lid and rummaging around until he came up with a half-eaten pack of

Life Savers. Removing three—pineapple, orange, and lemon—he set them aside and put the next one—cherry—in his mouth. Then he fit the other three back into the pack, buried it, and closed the desktop. By this time, he wore a tidy expression that left no part of himself exposed. He seemed to have disappeared down a rabbit hole to his own interior, and she had lost the ability to track him. Cut off from the dailiness of his life, she was no longer able to intuit the feelings behind his reticence, could no longer extrapolate meaning from a gesture.

"Do you want to stay with me?" He didn't answer. "Or go with Daddy in California?" He nodded. She thought he nodded; it was a very slender nod. *Say it,* she silently pleaded. *Say it so I will know for sure.* "Are you sure?" she asked aloud. He nodded again.

Hope returned her attention to the print above the bed, not to the clipper ship with its eighteen sails, plus jib, gaff, and staysails, but to the sea, the sad, sad sea enveloping the world, cradling all seven continents in its melancholy, salty embrace. More than two-thirds of the earth's surface was sadness. Our own bodies were ninety-eight percent sadness. Life was unsustainable without sadness. She had learned all this somewhere.

31

CLAY DID NOT WANT TO RETURN TO COURT. "I CAN'T TAKE IT, you can't take it, the kids can't take it." As usual, he was speaking for all of them, yet Hope was not prepared to say he was wrong. Shifting the receiver from one ear to the other, she looked out at the waves, to steady herself.

"Amber wants to live with you," Clay went on, "Patrick wants to live with me. Maybe we should just . . . maybe that's not such a bad arrangement."

"It's a terrible arrangement."

"It's a terrible arrangement, yes, but it might be the best we can do under the circumstances."

"You could change the circumstances, Clay. You could stay here."

"Or you could come to California."

"I don't *know* anybody in California."

"I don't know anybody in California either. What's that got to do with it?"

It was as if the two of them looked at the world through different ends of the telescope: what was large to Hope was small to Clay, and vice versa.

"If I pass up this opportunity, I'll be stuck here with all the oil-and-gas guys. I have to go, Hope. I have to have sun."

"There's plenty of sun here."

"There's no mentality for it, though! California's a sun *culture*."

"So you say."

"Look. I'm going to California. That's a fact. I'm going. Mindy's going. Patrick wants to go, too. Amber . . . doesn't. So I don't see any other way to do this."

"I don't know. I need some time to think." She started to say goodbye, then stopped. "Clay. Clay, tell me one thing. Are you any happier?"

There was a long pause. "Are you?"

A chasm of silence opened up between them, an oracular gloss on their actions, or so it seemed to Hope. Minutes went by as they failed to summon the purpose to either speak or hang up, and they remained in dumb, immobile attachment for a long time.

CHLOE WAS AT a loss. "I don't know," she said the next day from across her desk. "What does your lawyer say?"

"She says I have an excellent chance of regaining custody of Amber."

"I just don't know. If Patrick weren't sure . . . Are you sure he's sure?"

"He said he was."

"If he weren't sure, if he were on the fence . . ."

"I don't want to put the kids through anything they don't need to go through. Clay doesn't either. And I can't . . . I don't want to *force* Patrick." Hope's fingers began to fumble along the surface of Chloe's desk, blind worms in a maze. "I mean, I just don't think it would work for anybody, least of all him, and . . . Where's the goddam Kleenex? Aren't lawyers supposed to keep Kleenex handy for their clients? Like psychiatrists?"

Chloe left her desk and crossed the hall to a tiny bathroom. The spindle of the toilet paper holder could be heard spinning furiously. She returned and handed a prodigious wad of toilet paper to Hope, who stood at the window, watching the children in the schoolyard across the street. She blew her nose. "Girls on one side, boys on the other," Hope said bitterly, pointing. "That's the way it was on my school playground, too. Is it some sort of blueprint for life, or what?"

"I think things are changing."

"They aren't changing; they're coming loose."

* * *

THE DAY BEFORE they were to leave, Clay and Patrick came to say goodbye to Hope and Amber. The four of them stood outside the cabin late that afternoon in the warm but thin September sunlight. Clay had declined Hope's invitation to come inside, saying it was best to keep their farewells short and sweet. This was fine with Hope; there were no chairs to sit on anyway, and she felt more at ease outside. A breeze riffled the light leaves of the saplings; an occasional blat from a passing barge signaled the presence of ocean waters nearby.

Patrick was showing Hope his new compass. "I have maps, too," he said, reaching into his new backpack. He and Clay would be driving to California, stopping along the way to see the bats at Carlsbad Caverns. Mindy would fly.

Hope had determined not to break down. It was essential that she not. If she were to break down, Patrick might break down, too. And then Amber might break down. Probably Clay would, too, and she'd had enough of that.

She looked up at the sky and took a deep, shaky breath. "I think fall has finally arrived."

Clay tensed in an alert sort of way, as if his body were taking measurements. "There's no such thing as fall in Houston, Hope. Houston's on the same latitude as Calcutta, for crissakes."

"It's the light," she said. "There's a change in the light." She extended her hand. "Good luck."

Amber, who had not said a word and did not now, thrust a book— *Guide to California Insects*—at Patrick, who thanked her, looking a little dazed. Hope knelt to hug him, to memorize the span of his shoulders, the smell of his hair.

"Easter, right?" Clay was saying to Amber, holding her close. "We'll be seeing you for Easter, right?" Amber nodded, and Hope took her hand, as they watched Clay and Patrick walk down the drive and climb into his Toyota.

Nasty little car. Suddenly Hope hated its putative gas mileage, its stellar repair record. She glanced at the Cadillac, which had new fender skirts, thanks to Frederick. The Cadillac, at least, had presence. And then Clay and Patrick were gone.

Hope spoke of Patrick's leaving as a loss of blood. Calhoun found this a melodramatic way of putting it, but Hope said Patrick was her blood, her flesh and blood, and was it so strange to feel a draining out? A weakening of the soul at the prospect of his living a half-continent away?

THE FOLLOWING WEEK, the "New Faces" exhibition opened at Exposure. Hope entered the gallery a little unsteadily, as if she were walking a tightrope, but looking composed enough, if in a brightly painted, wooden sort of way. Beside her slouched Amber, her camouflage jacket scarcely doing the job, her vitality and emerging beauty combining to spotlight her in a way that both thrilled and affronted her. A woman in gleaming high heels tick-tacked past them into the crowd of about fifty people circulating the room. "There are a lot of strangers here," Hope murmured, eyeing the room suspiciously.

Amber touched her arm. "There's Mr. Freytag, Mom."

"Oh!" Lurching forward, Hope headed in the direction of the refreshment table.

"Hey! Rachel!" Spotting her friend, Amber ran off, too.

A woman with freckles and frizzy hair was talking to Gil, his gibbous belly hovering over the dividing line of his new elaborately tooled leather belt. "Hope!" he called when he caught sight of her still a few feet away. "Hope!" He grasped her arm, as she joined them. "Hope, you remember Judith, don't you? She was in your class at the Rec Center." Hope heard a plea for rescue in his sham enthusiasm, and she forced herself to beam an ersatz smile.

"My work is very different from yours," Judith informed her. "More subjective."

Hope's smile wavered. "Oh. More subjective. Yes, well, subjective is, um, always interesting."

Judith stared at her for a moment, made a rapid calculation, and turned back to Gil. But by this time, Gil had managed to distance himself by a few feet and was extending a hand to an admirer. "Your Rio Grande photographs are wonderful!" the woman was saying. Some of Gil's work-in-progress had appeared recently in a magazine. "I smell a book!" she trilled.

"You're supposed to mix," Gil chided Hope a few minutes later. Both Judith and his admirer had moved on.

"I don't know anybody," she said.

"Aren't those your friends over there?"

"Where?"

"Over there."

She turned to see Chloe and Fletcher on the other side of the room. They seemed to be waiting for something dreadful to happen. "Oh. Yes. Yes, those are my friends."

"Aren't you going to say hello to them?"

"Oh. Yes. Yes, I am. Going to say hello to them."

"Nice crowd," said Chloe when Hope reached her and Fletcher. "Have you sold anything yet?"

"I don't know."

"Where are your pictures?" asked Fletcher.

Hope waved a hand in the general direction of the far wall.

"Well, let's go and take a look," Chloe said.

"Do you really want to?"

"Isn't that what we're here for?"

"What about some champagne first? You haven't had any champagne yet, have you?" Hope started back toward the refreshment table, but Chloe slipped an arm in hers, altering her course. "Get with it, Hope," she said, steering her to the far corner, where an older couple were studying Hope's pictures. Hope shrank back, not wanting to hear what they were saying.

"You sold one!" Chloe whispered in Hope's ear. A red dot had been stuck in the right-hand corner of Hope's image of Cluny in rapt obedience to her wall of Fredericks.

Hope recoiled in a flash of lucidity and shame. How had she not seen this before? Photography was an ignoble business. A gross invasion of people's selves, their souls. She was in the business of selling souls!

She looked around. Every face in the room was white. She'd invited Ocie and Frederick, but she doubted they would come. Ocie was tired of being the token, and Frederick was not likely to come unless coerced. The only black face here today would be Cluny's, hung in a frame on the wall.

"I'm going home," Hope mumbled, starting off.

"What are you talking about!" Chloe hissed, grabbing her arm.

"Mom, can we have some champagne?" Amber and Rachel had come up, their faces flushed from a recent encounter with two boys they knew from the church.

"No," said Hope distractedly. "There's sparkling cider for kids."

"Just one glass?" Amber persisted.

"You're too young to drink champagne."

"In France, kids drink champagne. On special occasions," Amber pointed out. "Isn't this a special occasion?"

"Amber, please." Hope felt like a seawall about to give.

"My hair looks funny," said Rachel, pointing to a photo of herself and Amber playing dress-up. Rachel wore a bra-slip of Hope's over a T-shirt and jeans, one strap sliding from her shoulder, while Amber was draped in a filmy blouse and full skirt. Both girls were swagged in the contents of Hope's jewelry box, their feet encumbered by high-heeled shoes.

Amber studied the photograph. "Your hair doesn't look funny. It looks like Linda McCartney's."

Chloe had also been peering closely at the photo. "Indoctrination, pure and simple. You could title it *Boot Camp*."

"I didn't have any particular message in mind," Hope mumbled, although she was uncomfortably struck for the first time by the air of perverse allure.

"This is an odd one," Fletcher said thoughtfully, standing in front of a photo of one of Patrick's Lego constructions, a composition made strange by the camera's eye, which had given equal value to the inscrutable face of the thermostat on the wall, the aggressive visage of the air-conditioning grille, the serpentine electric cord snaking its way along the floor, rearing up to connect with its outlet. The familiar looked strange.

Hope twisted away, nearly running into Gil, who was bringing her another glass of champagne, and a woman in a pale linen pantsuit. "This lady wants to ask you a question, Hope." Hope downed the champagne.

"I was wondering . . ." The woman pointed to the only Big Thicket photo Hope had included, one of Romain poling his pirogue through a fog-shrouded swamp. ". . . how did you get that shadow?"

In the original print, the shadow had not existed, although Hope had seen it as clearly as if it had, a darkened image of the boat cast onto the fog-ridden water. She had made at least a dozen prints before the image had finally appeared as intact and numinous on paper as in her head. The shadow was her tribute to what Romain had taught her, meant to convey something of the wonderful stillness at the heart of shadows, a stillness pure and deep.

"Did you use a special lens?" the woman wanted to know.

People were often more interested in technique than in inspiration, in the how rather than the why, which was fortunate in Hope's case, because she found technique much easier to talk about. Even so, she didn't answer. She stood there, lipstick smeared, an escaped strand of hair looped over one ear, and stared at the woman.

The woman turned to Gil. "Is she really the photographer?"

Gil assured her that Hope was indeed the photographer. "Don't be misled by the freckles."

Hope cleared her throat. "The shadow, yes, well . . . it's a matter of longer exposure." She gave a fairly creditable explanation of how she had used a cardboard shield to cover all but that spot, how she had extended the printing time for the shadow alone, allowing it to deepen and deepen until she'd had the sensation of falling into it. Hope did not say this last part aloud.

"Well, you've done a very nice job," the woman said.

Hope thanked her vaguely, and the woman said something about wanting to be a photographer herself. Or had she said she wanted Hope's photograph for herself? Hope wasn't sure; she was having difficulty remaining in the conversation.

The problem persisted. Calhoun, Caleb, Finn, O'Molly, and Fern all arrived at about the same time, and as they stood talking, Hope failed to catch much of what was said. She would listen intently for a moment, and then her mind would slither off on its own. *The Glad Hand* . . . she heard and then moments later, wondered: reopened? or rebombed? *The Sunshine Collage* . . . a concert? or a new boutique?

"Have you met the other photographers yet?" asked Gil, at her side again.

"No."

"Come along then."

One by one, he introduced her. They were all as edgy as she was, with the exception of the last, a man wearing an embroidered Afghani cap at odds with the farmboy looks of one who had never crossed a

Texas boundary in any direction. Studying his photographs, black-and-white abstracts of stones, Hope stuttered something about contrasts.

"That's what photography's all about," he informed her. His tone put her in mind of Alex, and she wondered: where was Alex, anyway? He was supposed to be here. Something started to skid in her mind, and she stared intently at the man in the Afghani cap, concentrating all her available mental resources on what he was telling her.

"All matter emanates light," he offered. "Light carries all the information we need to see the world. It's the only thing we really see." He held up a hand. "What you're seeing here is not my hand, but light. Photography is the art of light."

"Negatron," she said, dipping into Amber's vocabulary. She grabbed his hand. "You don't understand. Photography is the art of loss. Because the moment, the moment you're looking at, has passed. It's *gone!*" she said, now shaking his hand back and forth, as if to dislodge his mistaken notions. "Don't you feel that, looking at photos? You're looking at something that has *passed*. That is *no more.*"

She registered the alarm on the man's face at the same moment she became aware of her heaving chest and wet cheeks, and she would be forever obliged to Gil, who put an arm around her shoulders and smilingly produced a one-word explanation—"champagne"—to the small group that had gathered around them before leading her away, forever in Gil's debt, because she knew she was going to cry in bulk, and she would not be able to stop, and it was best to run into the ladies room, where Chloe eventually found her clutching a postcard from Patrick picturing a giant sequoia tree, which you could not drive through anymore, although you used to be able to, as you could see in this postcard, the passageway cut out right there through the heart of the tree, big enough to drive through, but you couldn't now because you might damage the tree's shallow root system, and it would fall down.

32

ALEX HAD NOT RETURNED FROM HIS FLIGHT IN TIME TO ATTEND Hope's show at exposure. The flight was supposed to be a quick trip to the Austin hill country and back, but Alex altered his plans on the wing to extend another three hundred miles into the Bofecillos Mountains near the Mexican border, raw slopes supporting an occasional mesquite, acacia, or ocotillo, armed vegetation at the ready with hooks, claws, and spines. Calhoun said it was a reconnaissance trip. Eight months later, in May, Alex crashed his Apache there.

By this time, Hope and Amber were settled in the cabin in Kemah. At times Hope felt as close to Amber as when they'd lived in one body. Stem to fruit, that's how Hope described it to Chloe. Other times Amber seemed to Hope a thoroughly unforeseen creature unconnected to herself. A wittingness would flash in Amber's blue eyes, she would chop the air with a decisive hand or deliver a definitive thrust of the hip, and suddenly Hope would be in the presence of a stranger pushing at Amber's permeable, twelve-year-old boundaries. A rush of maternal feeling overcame Hope at these times. This stranger, this nascent worldling, needed protection until claimed.

Meanwhile, they dickered back and forth on various matters of propriety. Their exchanges were timeless in their unoriginality. No, Hope said, Amber could not wear lipstick to school. "You're too young."

"Other girls are wearing lipstick."

"We're not talking about other girls, we're talking about you. Wait till next year, when you're in junior high."

Amber continued to lobby; Hope maintained her position. She confided to Chloe that Amber was spending too much time in front of the bathroom mirror as it was. Amber's incipient beauty was like an unlit match. Any moment now it could flare up into something dangerous.

"I know what you're talking about. Rachel is asking for a training bra. A *training* bra! Can you believe it? As a concept?"

The two friends sometimes discussed their daughters as they sat folding brochures or licking envelopes at Farenthold Campaign Headquarters. They had caught the political fever that spring. Hope had never attended political rallies and fund-raisers or joined volunteer work crews before, and she never would again. But in Texas, 1972 was a year when blacks, Chicanos, and women ran for everything from city council to governor, and Hope got swept up in the tide of rising expectations. Even Calhoun got involved. Caleb induced him to campaign for Gore Vidal for president. Calhoun said it was a doomed enough endeavor to interest him.

Hope and Chloe's candidate was Sissy Farenthold, "the first woman to run for governor who wasn't the wife of one," Chloe explained to suspicious voters. She and Hope were ebullient supporters, two of the ten thousand people crowded into the Convention Center on the Saturday after the primary to celebrate Farenthold's second-place finish, which had put her into a run-off. Chloe said she'd never seen such a crowd at a Houston political rally, and Fletcher noted morosely that the crowd outnumbered his antiwar rallies by an order of magnitude. The crowd listened, enthralled, to a tall, thin blues singer bent over a battered guitar, his face the color of a dark plum.

> *I wanna be your iceman*
> *Coal man ain't no good.*

"Oh, Lightnin'," murmured Ocie at Hope's side. Ocie was working on Barbara Jordan's campaign, and she and Hope always showed up for each other's rallies. Frederick was here, too, marking the beat with his whole body, turning it this way and that, sinuous shoulders signifying ease and pleasure, elbows jutting outward to make way.

I wanna be your iceman
Coal man ain't no good,

sang Ocie. She knew all of Lightnin's tunes.

When he finished, Farenthold came out on the stage, and the embrace of the middle-aged white woman and the black, elderly blues singer touched off the rocketing hopes of the crowd. The Convention Center quaked with applause; even Calhoun managed to slap his palms together, as the ovation segued into the Viva! handclap. They *could* overcome. They *would* overcome.

The ten-thousand-hands-clapping was still in Hope's ears as she pulled up to the cabin and saw Finn sitting on the ground with his back against the wall. He stood up, and she smiled and waved, cutting the engine and tossing her keys into her leather pouch. She was glad to see him. She wanted to talk to him about building a deck, right where he'd been sitting.

Amber and Rachel, who was spending the night, ran up the walk ahead of her, chanting, "We want Sissy! We want Sissy!"

Seeing Finn's face, Hope quickened her pace. "What's wrong?" she asked on reaching him.

He waited until the girls had run into the cabin. "Bad news."

Patrick! Hope thought. But Finn was not a likely messenger of bad news about Patrick.

Alex had gone down on the Mexican side of the Rio Grande, Finn told her. Two days ago. A farmer had witnessed the crash, but it had taken the authorities two days to arrive on the site.

"It's very remote country," Hope whispered.

Finn looked surprised. "Have you been there?"

"Near there. I was in Big Bend with Gil and Coylene Freytag last summer. Gil and I took pictures." They flashed through her mind now: the savage walls of the Santa Elena Canyon, the prickly pear cactus and the bull muhly grass, the black silhouettes of the Sierra Quemada—the Burned Mountains. Her mind stuck on an image Gil had captured of a storm at sunset. The photograph, with its bursting vermilion clouds and the descending red rain over a jagged profile of peaks, suggested an explosion, not an event in nature.

A cardinal sang nearby. A car passed. Hope was suspended in that long moment before impact. The accident had not quite happened. Alex was not quite dead.

LATER, WHEN THE actuality of Alex's death did strike, she sought comfort in her Big Bend photographs. She showed them to Calhoun. "At least," she said, "Alex died in a beautiful place. It's a miracle that anyone saw him go down. This is the kind of country where accidents just disappear into the landscape."

"That's probably what he counted on."

"What do you mean?"

"It wasn't an accident."

"What?"

"It wasn't an accident. He offed himself."

Hope didn't say anything for a long time. "I don't want to think that, Cal," she said finally.

"You don't have to. That's why he did it the way he did."

ALEX'S FUNERAL WAS attended by many, including his ex-wife, whose small, earnest face was doughy with grief and reminiscences of Alex as the boy she'd met in Bible college. Tad of the Ultimate Vehicle was there, too. Hope spoke to him, but he didn't remember her. Alex's family was represented by a brother in a poorly fitting black suit and string tie, who buttonholed mourners to inform them that no one, *no one*, back home called the deceased Alex. "*Sandy* we called 'im. *L'il* Sandy in the beginnin', when he jus' commenced tent preachin' and waren't but ten."

Hope heard all this and wept. Oh, the striving, she thought. Oh, the disappointment. Oh, how patchy and pointless it all was. Her camera hung by its strap in a closet for weeks. There was nothing worth looking at, nothing worth recording. How dare the sun shine. How dare the canna lilies bloom.

Rosamunda assured her that God knew what He was doing. Once in her village in Mexico, she said, there had been a great drought and no crops could grow and the people had no food and were hungry. And suddenly a great rainstorm came up, with thunder and lightning, and everyone was happy, except that lightning struck a certain Reynaldo and killed him. But after that there was more rain and the crops grew and the people had food.

"So you see, how it is with God," said Rosamunda. "He has a system. Do you ever look up in the sky at night?"

"Yes."

"And what do you see?"

"Stars."

Rosamunda nodded. "The souls of the dead. They sparkle, right?"

"Yes."

"They're happy."

Hope liked to repeat this story, even years later, not because it comforted her, which it didn't, but because she recognized in it a more compassionate accommodation to the weakness and vulnerability of the human condition than she, Hope, was used to.

ALEX'S DEATH MARKED the end of Communitas. Finn and O'Molly left soon after the funeral for Austin, where they found another communal hearth, a permanent one this time. They became fixtures of the Austin music scene, married other people, and founded a songwriting/recording/performance collective with some fellow musicians. They continue to sing folk and play acoustic, as if there were no such thing as heavy metal or hip-hop. Their fans, distinguished more by loyalty than mass, attend their concerts and buy their tapes in sufficient numbers to sustain them in a life of modest artistry, comfortable fellowship, and minimal fame. *I dreamed I saw Joe Hill last night*, they still sing. *Down in the valley, the valley so low.*

For Fern, the demise of Communitas was more disruptive. It was Ocie who rescued her from homelessness, finding an apartment for her in a small, low-rent complex where some of Ocie's welfare clients lived. Fern was to manage the complex in exchange for rent. At first, Fern was an unresponsive manager, as deaf to the complaints of leaking faucets and dysfunctional air conditioners as to the owner's requests for more assiduous pursuit of defaulting tenants. But when a threat of eviction illuminated what was expected of her, Fern roused herself to enough action to ensure her continued rent-free residence.

The real change in Fern's life, however, came when she became a grandmother (a bit prematurely; she was not quite forty). She gained weight physically and emotionally, overnight it seemed, her child-woman profile crescendoing into plump matronage, as she acquired a store of advice and a drive to meddle. Her parents' raising of Adam had worked out badly, she told Hope, and she was replenishing her karma with his daughter, Annabel. "She finally took hold," admitted Ocie, in whose stern eyes Fern had not previously measured up.

Ocie may have been softened a little by Daryl's bad-boy phase. It only lasted a year or so, but twice she had to compromise her pride by pulling strings to keep her son out of jail, and although his crimes were petty—a joyride, defacement of public property—they iced her ordinarily resilient sinews. "Think of Lee Otis," she said. "Thirty-three years for possession."

"But the verdict was overturned," Chloe reminded her. "The judge ordered a new trial. Times are changing."

Ocie politely declined the proffered optimism, saying she preferred it not be Daryl who tested Chloe's premise. After some hair-raising months, Daryl corrected, borrowed some money, and started a pipe supply company that eventually made the Top 100 list in *Black Enterprise*. Her daughter, Rae, went east, became a fashion model, and married a New York Jet, a tight end.

Calhoun and Caleb have endured. Calhoun travels a good deal, having quit teaching a few years ago in order to devote himself to the lecture circuit. He receives numerous invitations to speak and lead workshops in educational conferences around the world. The Italians, especially, are interested in his work.

Caleb owns and runs a restaurant, the Singing Chicken, where the food is slightly overpriced and slightly overpraised, minor discrepancies people overlook for the pleasure of the histrionic company. Caleb's political enthusiasm survived Gore Vidal's defeat. Their house in the Montrose, where they remained even when the Montrose became unfashionable and seedy again for a time, is familiar to at least one of Houston's former mayors and a number of legislators. He and Calhoun go to most of the important political events in Houston, where they often run into Chloe.

Chloe and Fletcher were divorced in 1982. Hope was not the only one jolted by this event. Friends pointed to their eighteen years together, their collaborative resistance to the status quo, and their matched sensibilities to justify the collective disbelief. But Chloe told Hope that it had been a mistake from the beginning. "We just didn't notice at first because we were so busy—first with getting Fletcher through graduate school, then me through law school, then the antiwar effort and the women's movement—those things took up an incredible amount of time and attention. But one day, it got quiet. Reagan was president and Rachel was in college. I was vice president of the local bar association and Fletcher was tenured. We looked up. And split up."

After her divorce, Chloe's career gained momentum, not a consequence of the divorce but because the network established during Sissy Farenthold's gubernatorial campaign had not only survived but flourished. When the Freedom of Information Act was passed, Chloe drew some notoriety by threatening a class-action suit against the Houston Police Department for promiscuous wiretapping. (She had been right in her suspicions that they had tapped her own phone.) Chloe was recently appointed to the U.S. District Court.

"Mom is in her element," Rachel says, adding, "Of course, she always has been."

Yes, Hope thinks, Chloe was always at home, even when she was challenging its foundations. Unlike herself, forever riding the waves of those who leave.

Hope and Rachel always have lunch when Rachel, a software consultant, is in Houston on business. These are emotional occasions for Hope. In the composed young woman seated opposite, Hope sees the golden child. She doesn't see the golden child in Amber or Patrick, because she has become accustomed to them as adults, but Rachel, whom she sees only once a year or so, inspires blurred vision, and Hope is recalled to scenes of two little girls, freshets of will and promise, playing in the backyard: making mud pies, disciplining dolls, jumping rope.

> *Spanish ladies, dressed in lace,*
> *Spanish ladies, small, black case,*
> *Wrap it up in tissue paper,*
> *Throw it down the elevator,*
> *Spanish ladies dressed in lace.*

"It's a rhyme about abortion, Mom," Amber said when Hope wistfully recited it to her. Disconcerted, Hope said she supposed it was. She had never thought about it.

In spite of Amber's attempts to penetrate the scrim of Hope's nostalgia, Hope continues to see the golden child in Rachel. Although she knows her vision is not a true one, she thinks it is somehow necessary, perhaps as a counterweight to the bad dreams she still has of Patrick. In a recent one, he falls from a great height to spill the contents of his head on the pavement. She wishes he *would* spill the contents of his head, not in that gruesome way, of course, but figuratively, so that people can know what he is thinking or feeling now and then. His wife wishes this, too.

Hope's violent dreams contrast absurdly with Patrick's uneventful life. Accidents do not happen in Patrick's house in Walnut Creek, California. For one thing, he works tirelessly to prevent them. Weekends are likely to find him bolting things to the wall to foil earthquakes, updating the security code of his alarm system, or checking the electrical wiring in the attic. His forehead is often contracted in the longhorns of his childhood. He worries that his job as personnel manager for an electronics firm will be eliminated in the current restructuring, he worries about crime in the streets, he worries about California's changing demographics and how his young son is ever going to compete. Hope worries about Patrick's worrying, which provides Clay with the opportunity to categorize anxiety as a genetic condition.

Clay does not worry about Patrick; he has no reason to. He points out that Patrick is usually home when you call him and has never pierced anything. Clay and Mindy live in Indianapolis now, where Clay returned after taking an early retirement. He enjoyed a heady few years during the seventies, when he administered a seven-figure budget, but then had to watch his department decline in importance, as solar power gradually became relegated to the status of a do-it-yourself technology. Offered an attractive retirement package, he accepted it. Two years later, his mother died, and he and Mindy moved into her house. Their daughter recently graduated with honors from IU. Jason, on the other hand, dropped out of college. Mindy thinks Clay should hire him if Clay follows through on his threat to start his own business. Clay has been reading about a new thin-film process that would make solar cells much cheaper, and he is debating whether or not to enter the market. Meanwhile, he watches his investments.

Amber visits them frequently, and Clay pretends to ignore the platinum crew cut, the pierced eyebrow with its tiny gold ring, the authentic World War II leather bomber jacket. Amber's mailing address is Santa Monica, but she is usually on location, where she manages logistics for a select clientele of filmmakers. It is Amber who sees that trailer trucks full of costumes arrive on time and have a place to park, that a bull scheduled to appear in a pasture at a certain time does, that locals are flattered or bribed into maintaining reasonable distance and goodwill, and that hundreds of other eccentric tasks are accomplished. The job calls for a military mind able to encompass strategy and detail and the political grid at one and the same time, and Amber is very good at it. It is an opportunity to order a large number of people around and make a large amount of money.

She and Hope argue cheerfully about money sometimes. Hope considers the amount Amber makes obscene, but Amber says money is energy. Like gas, it gets you where you want to go. Hope believes in a cutoff point. She says Amber's sense of scale has been skewed by the movie industry. She cannot *believe* a task force of one hundred people is required to strike a set. She is *horrified* at what it costs to send a stuntman through a candy-glass window. "All that money," she complains, "for an illusion."

For her part, Amber regards Hope's bohemian poverty as needless. Nothing to be ashamed of, but needless. "'To make money, all you do is to give it some quality time," she says. "You should try it, Mom."

They go back and forth like this. Since Amber has dental insurance and Hope does not, Amber has a slight edge. After a visit, they return to their separate lives refreshed and eager.

The two of them return to Indiana every year when William makes his annual trek from Calgary, begun when President Carter pardoned the Vietnam draft evaders. Hope likes his wife, a loud and serious woman, but feels a special bond with their son, who looks startlingly like herself. She gave him a camera for his eighth birthday. William enthralls her with stories of their life in the Canadian farm community where he farms and tends bees. He and Hope have long, companionable talks together, and what always meant family to her is briefly restored.

Maureen and Wally are getting old, surprising themselves, as well as their children. Somehow no one anticipated this. In precarious health, they have chosen to address old age shoulder to shoulder. When one falls ill, the other scurries about filling prescriptions and making soup. They perpetually switch roles this way in a narrowing theater of operations. Hope is less judgmental of them now.

Hope has not married, although her current *amour* has been current for a decade. We've *been* married, she explains to people who ask why they do not tie the knot.

She sometimes thinks of Gideon; apparently he will always be her phantom violinist. She received a postcard from him some years ago, postmarked New Orleans. On the back of a picture of Jack Benny playing the violin and wearing his hallmark expression of long-suffering misunderstoodness, Gideon wrote to say he was sober, finally.

She runs into Bootsie now and then, at one fund-raiser or another, but they do not discuss Gideon; they talk mostly about the Big Thicket. Bootsie and her group were successful in having the Big Thicket declared a National Preserve. Hope credits that campaign with furthering her career, because the owner of a Los Angeles gallery, which now accounts for a good portion of her sales, happened to see some posters featuring Hope's Big Thicket photographs and signed her up.

After surviving on small grants and fellowships and part-time teaching positions, Hope is finally able to live by her art, a source of pride, if not wealth. People continue to be drawn to her world of the mismatched, the inexplicable, and the haphazard, to which she remains loyal and which perhaps explains her continuing fascination with Houston. Her photographs of the city number in the thousands now. They include the empty downtown office buildings that marked the bust of the late eighties as well as the tent cities thrown up by the homeless.

Sometimes she wanders into the Fourth Ward, looking for Frederick. She watches younger kids in bright colors play kickball and teenagers in black swagger to the beat of their boom boxes, and she wonders what happened to him. Ocie says he became a social worker in Dallas, where she heard he adopted a child he found shut up in an unlit oven. But Calhoun says no, that Ocie must be mixing Frederick up with someone else, because Frederick went to Africa, where he took up with the Masai. Calhoun has a letter from Frederick postmarked Kenya, proving that Frederick did, at least, go to Kenya in 1979.

When Hope wanders the old neighborhood, she is not looking for Frederick himself, or course, but for a skinny, ragged child with shoes way too large for his feet. She never sees him. She sees many young boys, and they are sometimes skinny, and their clothes are sometimes ragged, but their unlaced sports shoes always fit their feet.

So Frederick remains a blur in one of corner of the canvas of her life, indistinct but significant. Maybe someday she will receive word of him in some form, and when she does, she will understand something of life and her own will no longer be unfinished and Frederick's will no longer be a mystery.

The last she saw him was the day she sold him the Cadillac—his sixteenth birthday. By this time, the Cadillac was already his; he had colonized it, ornament by ornament. Nearly every square inch of surface had something cemented to it—a bronze Egyptian cat, a crystal ball, a girlfriend's beads—all the knickknacks, trinkets, and souvenirs Frederick deemed worthy. Some came from the Vudu Curio Shop—a pair of antlers with aphrodisiacal properties crowned the space above the windshield, rattlesnake rattles hung from the inside rearview mirror. The car was still recognizably a Cadillac, though, and Hope's old Unitarian bumper sticker—TO QUESTION IS THE ANSWER—was still visible.

After paying Hope in cash—part of the settlement from the broken arm he'd suffered from Mr. Buck; by this time, he had abandoned his plan of becoming a doctor—Frederick had circled the Cadillac chirping and purring and sparkling, patting its hind end and kicking the tires (a joke; he had rotated them himself a few weeks previous). Wearing flagrant clothes from Daryl, he exuded impatience to get on with his life. Finally grown taller than Hope (although not much), he seemed to her especially tall that day. Perhaps it was his Afro, which gave him an additional six inches. "I'm goin' places, Mama!" he told her. "I'm goin' *places!*"

She hoped he had. She had gone places herself in the Cadillac, proving the possibility. And if she lacked certainty, if she allowed herself to consider the odds against him, perhaps doubt can claim some credit as the respectable handmaiden of hope, which otherwise would have something frivolous about it.